Bewitched, Bothered &

Be Vampyred

Bewitched, Bothered & Be Vampyred

A Collaborative Novel By

Mary Jo Putney
MaryJanice Davidson
Vicki Lewis Thompson
Patricia Rice
Susan Grant
Gena Showalter
PC Cast
Alesia Holliday
Sophia Nash
Kathryn Caskie
Jennifer St. Giles
Linda Wisdom
Judi McCoy
Shelly Laurenston
Rachel Carrington
Lynn Warren
Elizabeth Holcombe
Michelle Rowen
Fiona MacLeod
Terese Ramin

Triskelion Publishing
www.triskelionpublishing.com

**The reviewers are raving about *Bewitched, Bothered &
BeVampyred*!**

"In Brokenoggin Falls, you never know what will jump out
of the ground, the closet or from any other nook or cranny.
…   **BEWITCHED, BOTHERED & BEVAMPYRED**…
will have you laughing as each new character is brought into
the mix, a bit more information is given or an answer from a
previous episode is answered. … I laughed my way through
this anthology. Not only is this a great cumulative effort, it
has the added incentive to buyers in that all proceeds [from
the eBook] are going to the International Red Cross to aid
the victims of international disasters. I highly recommend
this anthology!!" ~ Brenda Edde, Romance Junkies; *Blue
Ribbon Rating*: **5**

"*Welcome to Brokenoggin Falls, Michigan. It is the only
little town in the world that warns travelers to remain in
their locked vehicles at all times, with the windows up, and
to NEVER pick up strangers because ALL the locals ARE
strange and NEVER harmless.* … Twenty authors got
together to create this preternatural soap opera. …   The
authors obviously did some hilarious brainstorming sessions
before any of them began writing. They had to think up the
residents and give them appropriate names…bestow
humiliating powers or curses on them, and then give each
character a surprising twist somehow. … I stress to you
again that this is like a soap opera. A lot of bed scenes,
some hot, some not. An awesome novel by some of today's
outstanding authors!" ~ Detra Fitch, Huntress Reviews; **4
Stars**

"…this anthology is a nice breezy read to provide some
chuckles for a good cause. …all in all, it's about the authors
letting their hair down and having some fun… If there are

some genuine romantic undertones and some genuine sexy moments to be found amidst the ongoing silliness, consider that a karmic bonus for your good deed in giving ... to the International Red Cross." ~ Mrs. Giggles; *Rating:* **86**

"Bewitched Bothered & BeVampyred is a different kind of story. ...the authors of this story do an incredible job... These stories are funny, spicy; some of them are spicier than others, and they are fun to read." ~ Lydia Funneman, Writers Unlimited Reviews

"This anthology was written by 20 great authors... And has it all. And when I say "all" I mean it: witches, warlocks, werewolves, love, lust, romance, flirts, pre-teenage triplets that create havoc, busty post-teenage triplets that chant naked under the moon, vampyres, naked vampyres, dragons, half-dragons, harpies, fairies, trolls, demons, half-demons, mother-in-laws, toads? ... I can't really decide which story I loved most. ... Hilariously funny, very sensual, at times very erotic but always unpredictable and absorbing. ...your pleasure guaranteed..." ~ Tanja, Cupid's Library Reviews; *Cupid-Plot-Factor:* **5,** *Cupid-Pleasure-Factor:* **5**

"How often can you have fun and benefit charity? ... The only thing that matters is that however often you can do so, now you have another opportunity, as this diverse group of well loved authors unites to create a sexy and fun cross between Passions, Dark Shadows, and Desperate Housewives all to benefit victims of disasters and incidentally, those lucky enough to read it." ~ Amanda Kilgore, Huntress Reviews

"Brokenoggin is a beautiful but strange little hamlet... On the surface, the town looks normal—paved streets, charming antique lampposts...if you discount the vampyres, witches, warlocks, and all manner of other beasties roaming the night; naked, gorgeous and well-hung men wandering the streets flaunting their assets; werewolves who put the Dog in Hound Dog; and a feral herd of Chihuahuas on a midnight run. Core to the stories, beyond fabulous primary and secondary titles—you have to get the book just to read those—is that girls just want to have fun. … Quite cleverly, the authors have blended their voices to create a smooth story that, although not necessarily required, readers should read in order to understand the overall plot. Observing characters as the protagonists in one tale and through their neighbors' eyes in another is a unique experience that is simply fascinating and refreshing. Readers will be happy to see some of their favorite authors, as well as some new names, soon to become favorites." ~ Kathy Samuels, Romance Reviews Today http://www.romrevtoday.com/

"I loved this book. I couldn't stop laughing!!" ~ Candy Bezner, Reviewer: Karen Find Out About New Books; Reviewer: Coffee Time Romance; *Rating:* **5 cups**

Triskelion Publishing
www.triskelionpublishing.com
Published by Triskelion Publishing www.triskelionpublishing.com
15508 W. Bell Rd. #101, PMB #502, Surprise, AZ 85374 U.S.A.

First e-published by Triskelion Publishing
First e-publishing April 2005
ISBN 1-933471-00-X

First printing by Triskelion Publishing
First printing July 2005
Second printing November 2005
ISBN 1-933471-29-8

eBook Cover design by Michelle Rouillard
eBook Cover design copyright © Michelle Rouillard March 2005
Print Cover design by Michelle Rouillard June 2005
Print Cover design copyright © Michelle Rouillard
Pixie Cover photo by Brian Caskie
Cover photo copyright © Brian Caskie March 2005

Edited by Terey daly Ramin & Gail Northman

Triskelion Publishing is proud to announce that the authors of this book are donating 100% of their royalties to the Red Cross disaster relief fund. A portion of publisher proceeds from the sale of the print and other editions of this work will also go to the aid of those in need.

100% of the cover price of the digital (downloadable ebook) edition of this work has been, and will continue to be, donated to the Red Cross disaster relief fund.

For anyone in need of an escape from harsh reality, a good dose of laughter and a random act of kindness anywhere, anytime

This is for you.

CONTENTS

Before-Word

Season 1 Episodes
In which we meet Janice Thinksalot, sheriff-etc. of Brokenoggin Falls; her distant cousin Remo-the-werewolf (aka Romeo aka much-prettier-than-he-is-bright); a petite Medium named Hesther; Seth, a vampyre with a Womanized 2x2 stake through his chest and no heart – and a soon to be lost memory; and Nihil (aka Annihilation aka The Big Bad) Jones, of the Seattle vampires, soon to be locked in AnnMarie Hathaway's faulty skeleton closet with the rest of the things no one in Brokenoggin Falls wants to deal with.

In which the Harpy screaming bloody murder in the Clock Tower must be dealt with and a coffee coven meeting catches Hesther and a would-be cabana boy in a compromising position with a defrocked Warlock named Gavin.

In which the well-endowed Tawdry triplets accidentally raise the dead while dealing with an overzealous peeping John.

how he dresses (or doesn't dress), and our vampyre Seth has to have a fang fixed.

In which Emma, mother of 12 and one of Brokenoggin's few truly human residents, casts a spell and everyone *except* the amnesiac vampyre Seth gets amnesia.

At a birthday party for the Disdaine Triplets, the little darlings decide they aren't pleased with the party or the guests and use magic to create their own fun. That night the town and all its residents are visited by the infamous Night Mares who wreak mayhem as only giant ponies prancing through your house can. (First episode with story & characters created by Lynn Warren.)

In which our un-frocked warlock gets his… ummm… comeuppance.

A succubus finds her true love.

Due to technical difficulties, the chapter numbering is screwed up. I'm guessing the skeletons are at fault somehow.

In which Murphy's Law comes to Brokenoggin Falls and a demonstration of "Be Careful What You Wish For" is brought to bear when a reluctant witch accidentally turns her husband into a toad when he forgets their wedding anniversary.

Harmony Faithful, pastor of Brokenoggin Falls Community Church (all faiths welcome), learns that there's more to Brokenoggin than meets the eye. (Story and new characters by Susan Grant.)

Technical difficulties abound in this non-existent episode.

(Or: *There's No Such Thing as a Dragon*)
In which Claudia Choo deals with an irate dragon-in-law and discovers her accountant husband's hidden nature.

(*Lord of the Forest Trolls – Return of the Garden Gnome*)
Wherein Sam learns what it's like to be a garden gnome in the Disdaine Triplets' front yard.

Wherein teenaged Destiny Hopewell attempts to leave Brokenoggin and comes radically unglued in the process. (Story and new characters by Michelle Rowen.)

Before-word

Bewitched, Bothered & BeVampyred was a true labor of love and real collaboration for all of the marvelous authors involved. Since I'm not only the editor / producer / creator but also one of the authors in this book, I'm probably the best one to tell you a little about how it about:

It's not your usual "anthology" with individual stand alone stories – though a couple of them *do,* in fact, stand alone. The concept is arranged like a single television season with 20 episodes (really 21, if you count the ones messed up or rearranged by the skeletons) and a series premier episode and interlinking characters. (Of course, this series would *have* to shown on cable since no network would be able to do it, what with some of the more erotic eps and all. ☺)

Not only did we have to cooperate over the chapters (or episodes) once a storyline was arrived at, but we also had to consult with one another regularly in order to make sure our characters didn't cross too far over into each others' plot lines and even character lines. As you'll see from the bonus material included at the end of this edition of the book, a number of us wanted to write about Earl and Claudia Choo, the dragon couple.

The work was not, however, written by committee the way many TV shows are.

The overall story arc involves a vampyre (the pyre part is an important pronunciation distinction locally) who's come looking for his soul mule / soul mate in the little hamlet of Brokenoggin Falls, MI (in the Upper Peninsula), but instead winds up naked with a bad case of amnesia that makes him forget he's even a vampyre. He falls (sort of) for the local sheriff, who's also the only law enforcement officer in the Brokenoggin area. She's got a BIG, beastly secret.

In real life, the majority of the authors who contributed to this anthology write romances, often with very little paranormal-fantasy elements involved. For many of us this was a not only a step into the wide world of fantasy, but an eye-opening, imagination-expanding treat.

Characters included in this work are the vampyre and his werewolf sheriff (who also has an even deeper darker secret); witches; griffins; a centaur named Rowdy; Chinese dragons; a wyvern & his half-sister; a flaming Faery Fae Queen and her-his faithful subject Joe the Fae local Veterinarian; the Disdaine triplets (I'm not sure what they are except that they're 11 and really naughty); a sexual wizard & Dorothea; Forest Trolls & a harpy; a succubus & an incubus; a couple of reformed demons and a pastor and a former demon slayer; and Annihilation Jones from Seattle's soulless vampiric The Naga police force (aka The Big Bad), who's not quite a match for the biggest local bad of them all.

Like episodes in Dark Shadows / Desperate Housewives / Bewitched / Lost – or any good television show – often a pair of episodes works closely together, and sometimes stories arc over the course of the season. Characters visit episode to episode, no matter who wrote the episode or invented the characters. And trust me: a wonderful time writing was had by all of us—and the fact that our royalties and some of the publisher's proceeds on this print edition will go to help the Red Cross' disaster relief fund?

Priceless.

Cheerfully,

Terese Ramin aka The Writing Wench

16 June 2005

THE LEGEND OF BRAUGH-NAUGHTON
Or
How Brokenoggin Got its Name
By
Jennifer St. Giles

Within the verdant forest boughs
Beneath the mists and moon
Upon the waves of sorrows dwells
The broken hearted loon

Once a man of brawn and valor
Who traveled far and wide
To vanquish and to conquer
All evils but his pride

Renown, the great Braugh Naughton
Wooed many a winsome maid
Though never loving any one
Upon their hearts he played

Until he met a maiden so fair
His calloused heart did weep
To know the silk of her silver hair
And promised pleasures to reap

But she to another was chained
Toiling her days as slave
To a wizard of blackened mien
A sordid evil knave

So hidden in the forest boughs
Beneath the mists and moon

Beside the Lake of Sorrows dwells
The lovers wrought with doom

"I'll fight to the death to save you maid,"
Braugh Naughton did declare.
He listened not to her crying nay,
Nor heeded her wrenching, "Beware."

At sunrise, they did duel
Battling with sword and mace,
The dastard wizard and love's fool,
Who fought with honor and with grace.

And when the battle turned its favor
With Naughton winning, fair and true
The wizard, with evil zeal and furor
Cursed the lovers, and himself too

To this day, and forevermore
Their fates remain entwined
And written in this tragic lore
For all to read and pine

The wizard's magic became not his own
But slave to the beck and call
Of all who are lucky to roam
The land of Braugh Naugton's fall

For The lady fair with the silver hair
Became the illusive moon's silver shine
Touching the water and the mists of the air
So fleeting and yet so fine

And the great Braugh Naughton
That warrior of valor and fame
Who heeded not his lover's caution
A crazy bird he became

Who for his lady love he cries
Beneath the mists and moon
Upon the waves of sorrows lies
The broken hearted loon

Episode 1.0 Series Premier

NAKED CAME THE VAMPYRE

By

Terese Ramin

In which we meet Janice Thinksalot, sheriff-etc. of Brokenoggin Falls; her distant cousin Remo-the-werewolf (aka Romeo aka much-prettier-than-he-is-bright); a petite Medium named Hesther; Seth, a vampyre with a Womanized 2x2 stake through his chest, no heart, and a soon to be lost memory; and Annihilation (aka The Big Bad) Jones of the Seattle vampires, soon to be locked in AnnMarie Hathaway's faulty skeleton closet with the rest of the things no one in Brokenoggin Falls wants to deal with.

Among a host of other things, Terese Ramin is the award winning author of almost 11 books for Silhouette Books, and the creator of Brokenoggin Falls. The phrase "It's all Terey's fault" follows her about constantly. Hopefully by the time you read this, she'll have updated her web page at www.thewritingwench.com or www.tereseramin.com or both. Otherwise you can find her at TereseRamin@sbcglobal.net or http://www.groups.yahoo.com/group/askmdecrankipants – where she answers writing related questions.

i: Janice

Now Entering

BROKENOGGIN FALLS NATIONAL FOREST RESERVE AREA

For Your Own Safety Please Observe The Following

- **Remain in your locked vehicle at all times; Do not leave it under any circumstances**

- **Keep windows rolled up & doors closed**

- **Keep hands, fingers, feet, heads and all appendages inside your vehicle without fail**

- **Do not — Repeat, DO NOT — pick up strangers within or near the reserve; they are always strange and NEVER harmless**

- **Encouraging the residents is strictly forbidden**

- **In case of emergency — SCREAM! Someone will be right along to investigate the commotion or remove the remains, as necessary**

- **Enjoy your stay & have a nice day!**

Janice Thinksalot swept the headlights of her rebuilt Chevrolet Caprice police cruiser across the wood-burned sign in a broad arc when she made the shoulder-to-shoulder yoo-ey back into the confines of her patrol jurisdiction. Michigan's scenic highway 28 was darker than usual, she realized, the sky starless despite the clear night.

There was also no moon.

She grimaced. Boded ill, that. No good ever came of a fine, cloudless, moonless summer night without stars in Brokenoggin. You could be sure of it.

Fine hairs on preternatural alert, Janice powered down the Caprice's front windows and sniffed the air that flowed through. Pine, spruce, cedar, fir, sand, loam, rich forest decay, moss, wild turkey...

She turned her head quickly, eagerly after the bird scent, muttered an oath and snapped her attention back where it belonged. Damn it! She was *not* out here to dog turkeys no matter how much the thought made her mouth water and her belly grumble. She was on Periwinkle Moon Patrol (the literal color of Brokenoggin's third full moon of each and every month), and there was a lot of potential mayhem left for the Falls' area's sole town cop slash police chief slash medical examiner slash sheriff-jailer-forest ranger-state Smokey to handle.

Not to mention that she was having a little trouble with her own inner beast lately.

She glowered at the black upon black non-reflection in the inside review mirror. Came of starting to look—and sometimes feel—fifty-ish, no doubt. Sag-to-the-knees boobs, cottage cheese thighs, scraggly chicken neck, jaw jowls and all.

Damn it.

Vanity, thy name be Janice, she thought dryly, rolling her eyes. Nothing like a long night and a lot of empty blacktop to send a person's thoughts down the least attractive inner roads. Speaking of which...

She made an abrupt turn onto a narrow fire road thickly

bordered by old growth forest. Gray sand grabbed the Caprice's tires, caused its butt-end to slew before the car settled into place, straddling the scrubby-growth weeds and grasses between the tire tracks.

In the darker-than-darkness, Janice switched off her high beams and gave the suddenly lighter shadows on either side of her a thorough appraisal. If she remembered correctly, the Lord of the Forest Trolls (LOF-T, as his royal annoyance was also known) had called a meeting of all the forest creatures for tonight to see if they could determine who was throwing trolls into the sunlight and turning them into stone Garden Gnomes. Maybe—

Whump!

The sound of something hitting the Caprice's roof and bouncing off the light bar startled Janice in a way she hadn't had her heart jumped in a very long time. One hand already on the door handle and the other on the shotgun ever-ready in its rack on the front seat floor hump, she stamped on the brakes and jammed the cruiser into park with a free finger even as she hauled the shotgun out of the vehicle with her.

For a few moments night bloomed, then…

"Yooooooowwwwwl, yaaaa-haaaa!"

"What the…?"

Reflexively, Janice snapped *on* the shotgun's safety, let it slide through her hands until she could use it like a fighting staff, and crouched, rising when instinct told her the timing was perfect to smash the huge, slavering male wolf hurtling down upon her across the jaw. The blow brought the beast to earth in fine smack-down mode, whimpering and howling.

The darkness shimmered slightly and the wolf-shifter's—for such he was—human face formed first. "Hot damn, Janice." The rest of his naked human body emerged quickly. "What the hell you tryin' ta do, eh? Lighten up, eh? I'm just havin' a little fun."

"At someone else's expense, Remo." Janice returned the shotgun to its meant-for position and thumbed *off* the safety. She stepped up close and prodded her—what was he, maybe seventeen times removed?—relative in the balls with the twelve gauge's business end. "I keep tellin' ya, mess with me when I'm on the job and it's your tail—bushy or human at the time, makes no difference to me."

Remo shrugged, unfazed by her threats or the shotgun barrel's location. "It's Romeo now, ya know, Janice. Romeo Bighorns. I changed it legally on my centennial. And I think the ladies around here would miss me sure 'nuff."

"Privately—" Janice gave the shotgun a little shove around the soft parts, and Remo-Romeo flinched. "I think there's something you'd miss more than they would. Eh, Remo *Nohorns*?"

"*Mmghtp gbftohs ghriop*," her not-removed-far-enough-from-here cousin muttered under his breath.

"What was that?"

"No wonder you don't have any friends, you menopausal old bitch," Romeo enunciated clearly, but very, *very* sotto voce.

Janice blinked once, then smiled her toothiest and most menacing law enforcement *I-am-so-sure-you-didn't-say-that* smile, tipped her head and viewed him sideways, eyebrows lifted. "Again?"

"Uh…" The self-named Lothario shuffled quickly in place. "I said, maybe I better pick up the garden gnome someone pitched at my head before it bounced off your whoop-whoop bar and get in the back-a your cruiser and let you drive me over to AnnMarie's—which, by the way, is where I was headed before someone tried to kill me—so I can shore up the door to her skeleton closet before they get out and all manner-more-a hell breaks loose—"

"*Janice, Janice!*" The radio inside the Caprice cruiser

squawked to panicked life. *"You've got a sixty-seven-eighty-two with a possible six-six-six in progress in the unconsecrated sector of Brokenoggin cemetery grid forty-nine. I repeat six-seven-eight-two with possible six-six-six in unconsecrated sector four-niner, Brokenoggin Falls cemetery. This is not a drill. Repeat, no drill."*

"Sixty-seven-eighty-two? What the…?"

For half a tick, Janice and Romeo stared at each other equally bewildered by the odd call numbers. Then, with maddening calm, Janice dropped the shotgun barrel dirt-ward and went to reach through the cruiser's window to retrieve her radio mike. Unhurriedly she brought it to her mouth and pressed the *on* button.

"Get a grip and say again, Hesther," she instructed Brokenoggin's volunteer dispatcher. At four-foot-three-inches, Hesther Bellhallow was a petite Medium of largely interesting-repute who felt it was only smart business on her part to know everyone else's. How else could she be expected to properly traverse the spirit world and give them accurate readings? "It sounded like you called an Apocalypse in the cemetery with Undead walking. Over."

"Vam-PY-res, Janice," Hesther gibber-shrieked. *"On unhallowed ground. Walking. Fighting. Stabbing each other with two-by-twos or four-by-fours or something big and pointy and wooden. The end is coming, I've seen it! If you don't get back here and do something about it, we'll all be undead in our beds and having wild sex by morning."* She stuttered uncertainly to a stop on the last pronouncement, sounding as though she might be rethinking the entire *this-is-bad-because?*…scenario. With a population of only five hundred and sixty-seven (sometimes), Brokenoggin Falls' singles scene often left something to be desired.

"There's no such thing as Vam-p*ý*res, Hesther," Janice said reasonably, accenting the 'Y' in *Pyres* exactly as

Hesther had, and making it sound as though the whole "undead thing" had more to do with funeral pyres than Vlad-the-Impaler or bats or Dracula legends. "We've discussed this. The dead can't be *not*. Over."

"Well," Hesther sobbed, *"something isn't dead that should be, and it's walking around with a great big long piece of lumber through its chest right where its heart should be. If that's not a Vampyre, I don't know what isss—"*

The last word broke off abruptly. There was the sound of scrambling and clattering, then clattering and scraping—as though furniture was being dragged across a wooden floor—then Hesther was back, more hysterical than ever.

"It's coming, Janice. It's coming right here. OmiGoddess, what am I going to do? You have to help me, you have to—Janice?" And then she screamed.

Resigned, Janice dropped the mike. "Oh shit." She had time to gesture a thumb at the Caprice and say, "Bring it in for me, eh, Rom—" before the elements that ruled the atmosphere surrounding Brokenoggin Falls swirled her up and whisked her to Hesther.

When the sign said, *"In case of emergency scream and someone will be right along"* it meant literally.

It also meant Janice.

***

ii: SETH

Scream re-entry was rarely precise and often painful.

Janice was never sure if she'd enter a scene of chaos and mayhem, wind up flattening the person who'd screamed, or landing head first at the source of the scream's cause. All too often she found herself only half-dressed and ill prepared to deal with the situation—which was no doubt why she felt like she'd been cursed with the position as town sheriff, lo, those many moons ago. Literally speaking, she had been cursed—and cursed but good—by her entire tribe after they'd caught her attempting to free...

The Beast of Brokenoggin Falls.

Now she was its—and the town's—guardian, jailer and ward.

It was a damned lonely and thankless job, and she... Well, she disliked it.

Strongly disliked it.

But it did have the occasional perk.

Now, for example, when she arrived out of the scream summons sprawled across the southern half of the sexiest naked torso she'd ever seen—er, *felt*—in her life. Considering that was some two hundred fifty-ish plus at least eighteen puppy years or so...

For a split second, it occurred to her to wonder why the guys who dropped into Brokenoggin Falls after midnight never seemed to be wearing any clothes. Then she saw that, sure enough, Hesther had called it spot on, there was definitely a four foot two-by-two staked through the center of Studly Gorgeous' chest and he was, by all that was holy, not dead, which left him...

Undead, in the flesh. And he appeared to be fighting to stay that way.

Something unfamiliar trickled through Janice. An emotion, perhaps, or something even more rare and therefore more frightening and exhilarating and connected to her long unused and oft-rejected libido—or possibly both. She didn't know and it didn't matter—she didn't stop to analyze it because she rarely stopped to analyze anything. In less than a heartbeat, she chose sides and acted.

Right hand wrapped around the twelve-gauge barrel that had apparently survived the jump cradled through her elbow, she put her left had down between his magnificent rock hard, tree trunk thighs to push herself erect. It landed on a long, thick, equally solid and very alive *something*. Startled, she looked down then up into bold eyes the color of the night sky, rimmed by the longest, densest black eyelashes ever created. Surprise and wry amusement sent black eyebrows fleeing upwards toward the tumble of curly, jet hair mussed over his forehead.

Embarrassed, Janice moved her hand. Teased, the cock thickened and came to greater attention.

"Not now, Janice," a voice one shade deeper and six shades sexier than Barry White's rumbled, "I'm busy."

He shoved her upright, used the momentum and a tug from her to haul himself after.

"But I promise—"

He dropped a full-of-tongue kiss on her open mouth (an awkward move, what with the stake protruding from his chest and all).

"—we get through this without dying, do something about this thing in my chest, and—"

He pulled her to the side and blocked an imprecise round of flying stakes with an upraised arm.

"—we'll go somewhere and screw for a century because that's how long I've been searching for you, my entire life and beyond. You're the only one who can make me whole. You complete me—"

A volley of rocks and arrows fell around them this time, followed by a barrage of bottles filled with… Janice tasted the droplets that fell on her. Water? The gorgeous, not dead being who'd been—according to him—searching for her forever and who'd just promised to fuck her for a century and who…

Wait! Janice stopped dead in the middle of the action and gulped. What had he said? He knew her name and she *completed him*? Was that a movie line? She didn't watch a lot of movies; with so many people screaming around Brokenoggin and whisking her wherever, she didn't have much chance.

But no. Even if it was a line of some sort, the object of her instant infatuation still hadn't let go of her hand. And just as an object of unknown origin came hurtling toward her face, he once again yanked her out of the way, reached out and snatched the missile out of the air.

It was another of the small, water-filled bottles.

Janice's Undead looked at it, snorted in disgust and flung it back from whence it came, growling, "Holy water, Nihil? As I lay dying the first time, they baptized and named me with the stuff. If it doesn't work on you when you begged the demon to make you a vampyre, what idiocy makes you think it'll work on me when I fought like hell not to?"

"Yet here you are." The voice in the darkness was oily and unholy, a poisonous thing crawling down Janice's spine. Of all the unnerving creatures that resided in Brokenoggin Falls, Janice knew there'd never been anything as evil here before as what she faced now. She retrieved her captured hand and unhinged her right elbow, slid the shotgun into place, even as the voice continued, "Still a vampyre, Seth, one of the damned, in love with a legend that doesn't exist." The voice was closer now. Night vision tuned, Janice could just make out the too-pale outline of a human-looking face above a powerful-if-beer-bellied, leather-clad, biker-built form. "Where there is no beast, there can be no beastkeeper. If she doesn't exist, you can't save her nor she, you...or anyone."

"Brave words for a bloodsucker about to be put down by the myth herself," the naked, staked hunk called Seth roared. He looked over his shoulder at Janice, bloodless face alight with faith and fervor. "Do it, love. I'll run interference. You raise the beast they've forced you to deny for centuries, and annihilate the very devil they've sent to enslave us all."

Then he flung himself forward, straight at the murderous Nihil. The Hell's Demon threw back his head, laughed and raised his deadly crossbow, and the unconsecrated earth quaked beneath their feet.   Grave markers shifted, the earth opened wide, unleashed the slavering hounds of hell.

From wherever she was, Hesther Bellhallow screamed and screamed.

Clueless as everyone but Seth and the vampyre demon he called "Niall" seemed to be about what was going on Janice nevertheless tucked the twelve-gauge tight and leveled it. The hellhounds bore down on her, but she stood her ground, concentrating on not hitting the first male person or thing to ever call her *love*, to ever come looking for her— no matter how insane he might be—or to know her name without ever being told. It was the sort of fairy tale every little girl dreamed about no matter what manner of creature she was, and no woman could quite bring herself to stop believing in no matter how many centuries she lived or how inactive her tamped down libido became.

In the middle of disaster, he acted like he full on believed in her so crazy or not, how could she not believe in him back?

She started to squeeze the shotgun's trigger at the same moment that a scream-leap jerked at her when someone elsewhere within Brokenoggin's borders shrieked in terror.

"Not now," she swore, but the jolt had already joggled her aim.

She tried to correct and fire again quickly, before she was whisked completely away from the scene, but Hesther was screaming again and the two scream-needs crossed wires somewhere in the magick ether and—

Seth cried out and fell blunt-stake-end-first across Nihil who looked simply stunned and dropped without a sound. The hounds of hell closed on the spot where Janice was last, snarling and snapping, a freak thunderstorm sprung out of nowhere, and—

Janice crashed butt first onto the light bar atop her

rebuilt Caprice cruiser, breaking it, and causing Remo-Romeo to swerve off the highway and into a ditch outside the gates of the Brokenoggin Community Church cemetery, consecrated section.

Then chaos really broke loose.

***

iii: Janice & Seth

Later, when things died down, (meaning Janice finally got back to the scene of the Vampyre Brawl and pumped a lot of spelled hemlock-and-foxglove loaded shells into things that didn't normally reside in Brokenoggin Falls and Remo changed into a werewolf and dined on what was left) Joe the town's veterinarian and general practitioner (who better to look after werewolves and other…preternatural…creatures?) arrived on the scene to minister emergency aid to the survivors and supervise the disposal of the dead.

"This is bad," Joe said, eying the cemetery full of upheaval before going down on his knees beside Seth. He gave the four foot two-by-two stake a gingerly stroke. "This is very bad." He looked up at Janice, trying hard to be stoic and unemotional and cop-like at the vampyre's side across from him. "I thought we'd decided there was no such thing as Vam-Pýres."

Janice shrugged. "Myths and legends," she said. "We harbor all the myths, guess now we're getting the legends, too, eh." She gestured at the stake. "Can you take it out? Can you save him?"

"Tricky." Joe shook his head. "Made a big hole—" he indicated the entry and exit wounds "—through and through. Took his heart clean out, 'cept fer mebbe a piece the size of my thumb. Should be dead, but if he's a vampyre, means he's already dead…" He scratched his head. "I guess.

"Anyway, lumber's treated, Womanized. Figure that's what's keepin' him from not turnin' to dust. Either that or it's because it didn't take out his whole heart. But I'm a veterinarian and a crypto-zoologist, a *mythos*-zoologist. The things I work with have working lungs and a heart that beats, blood that flows. All the people in Brokenoggin are special, but they live and breathe. This…" He shook his head. "This is out of my purview."

"So you're sayin' leavin' the lumber in would be better'n taking it out?"

Joe shrugged.

"But…" Janice hesitated, eyeing the two feet of stake that stuck out Seth's chest and back. She knew that as a law enforcement official she sometimes had the imagination of a flea, but still… "Won't it be a little, er, *awkward* for him to have all that wood sticking out of him all the time?"

Joe gave her a look that said she'd suddenly developed Medusa hair—which unfortunately in Brokenoggin Falls was entirely possible. Janice patted her long, inky black hair back up under her sheriff's hat, bit her lip and dragged an embarrassed regulation-clad toe along the bloody ground. If it was a stupid question, she didn't know. And if she didn't know, she had to ask, right?

"He said he came here for her, Joe." Hesther rose uncharacteristically to her defense. "I heard him. Said he wanted to screw her brains out for the next century cuz that's how long he's been looking for her. Kinda difficult to do with that chunk of lumber growing out of him. Might make positioning chancy—" She paused to lick her lips significantly. "If you catch my drift."

"Holy heck, Hesther." Joe grimaced. "The dead here caught your drift."

He sighed and reached across Seth to pat Janice's hand. "Look, what I meant was, I'll cut the two-by-two flush to his chest and back, make sure it's secured in there with Super Glue around the seams, slap on a coat of Goop back and front to seal the wood over, then add a Duct Tape strapping. Oughtta hold until I can find out enough about his physiology to come up with something better'n more permanent. Meantime…" He smiled slightly. "We'd probably better see if we can get the town coven to, ah, do something about those scream summonses you keep getting. This guy's going to need a lot of TLC and since you saved him you're responsible for keeping him aliv–, er, *in existence* now…"

Janice's throat muscles tightened once on a convulsive swallow. Just what she needed, more responsibility. And yet…

Seth stirred restlessly, moaning, and reached for her hand. When he found it, even in unconsciousness he brought it to his mouth, held her open palm there as though to absorb her, her scent, her presence.

"Thanks, Doc," Janice murmured. She used her chin to indicate the vampyre who'd attempted to annihilate Seth. "What about it?"

Joe raised an eyebrow.

"How do we get rid of it so it doesn't come back?" Hesther elaborated.

"You're asking me?" Joe coughed in disbelief. "Until tonight these things didn't exist. How the dickens should *I* know how to get rid of one? I *don't* know. Cut off its head, cut out its heart and bury *that* in consecrated ground, burn the carcass—no, in fact do all the other stuff, then give the carcass to The Beast to crunch up and burn. If there's any bone dust and ashes leftover, take it *out* of Brokenoggin Falls and bury it with a dozen cloves of garlic in a grove of wolfbane."

"Yes, but what do we do with the head?" Hesther asked earnestly.

Joe's jaw dropped.

Before he could form an adequate, non-sarcastic response, however, Remo loped over to nuzzle Hesther's hand and change back into a very naked, very happy-to-see-her man.

Hesther's breath caught. A hand fluttered to her breast. "Oh my, Romeo! Whereforever have thou been? Come home with me this morning, won't you? I believe I have some heaven and earth for you to move in me."

"Sure, Hesther." Remo grinned. "Let me find my clothes and finish up here and with the skeleton closet lock over at AnnMarie's. Meetcha at your car outside dispatch— you drive the Jetta, yeah? See if we can put a little hum in your squeezebox right ther—"

"Whoa, T.M.I.!" Joe coughed, interrupting. Embarrassed he busied himself tending Seth.

"Way Too Much Information," Janice agreed, grimacing. Were there no seriously committed couples in this burgh or did she just not run into them on the job? She sent her cousin a, *boy I wish I didn't know you and wasn't related to you* look. "Hound." Then to Hesther, "I don't want to *hear* it over the radio, understand? And whatever you do, *don't scream*! I'm sick of getting screamed up by kids who want to see how fast they can conjure me, frustrated adolescents, pre-menstrual and mid-life witches of all genders, and everyone in the throes of get-the-fuck-out-of-here-Janice-so-we-can."

Hesther nodded. "Gotcha, sheriff. Don't kick the broadcast button, and keep the verbalization to a minimum. Copy." For a moment, she studied Janice shrewdly. Then very woman-to-woman, she twitched a significant eyebrow at Seth. "Want me to touch any, ah, *part* of him, see if I can read him?" she stage whispered. "Find out what his real intentions are toward you?"

"No!" Janice's usually impassive face mobilized itself into disbelieving, absolutely mortified horror. She knew that's what it did because she felt it pull itself in wild directions, eyes to jaw to chin and mouth, each of them stupefyingly shocked. At the same time her insecurities

shouted, *'Fuckin' A, babe, go for it! Touch the boy's cock and tell me abso-freaking-everything.'* But her self-respect—or maybe that should read her innate stoicism—made her say, "Leave me alone, leave him alone, leave *well enough* alon—"

Woozy and unbalanced, Seth suddenly sat up and sagged against Janice's athletically supported bosom.

"Mmmm," he mumbled dreamily, "nice."

He reached up to fluff her breasts more comfortably under his head—instinctively it seemed, searching out her aureoles and nipples in the process. Janice's Ennel athletic bra, however, made her bosom regretfully immune to such shenanigans: once hooked into it, her bustline didn't move and her sensitive areas didn't feel. Useful for those highly active moments on the job when she had to kick butt, but generally a bust (pardon the pun) for moments like these when a gorgeous, partially out-of-it guy who'd seemed genuinely attracted to her when in full possession of his faculties wanted to feel her up. Nobody in real life ever did.

"Huhnnn," he sighed in what sounded like disappointment, using his left hand to smoosh her right breast under his cheek as best he could while his thumb grazed the spot where her nipple probably was. "They'd be beautiful you know if you let them go free. We'd both enjoy it so much."

"Oh…*brother*," Joe groaned disgusted. "*Et tu*, Janice? I thought we were supposed to be lonely Norwegian bachelors together."

"I'm not Norwegian," Janice mumbled, blushing as fiery red as her native coppery-bronze skin would allow. No one had ever said anything so…so…*lecherously romantic* to her before in her life. And at two hundred fifty-seven plus eighteen or so puppy years, that was a lot of unlechered-at life.

Joe rolled his eyes. "Even so, Janice *Thinks*alot."

"Thinks a lot? Who's thinking? Who wants to?" Echoing Janice's exact sentiments, Seth stirred and sat up again. "And who's Janice?"

"Ummmm…" said Hesther.

"Hoooo boy," said Joe.

Janice sat back on her heels. "Seth?" she asked tentatively.

"I don't think so," he said doubtfully, "but I don't know. Maybe I am. Do you know? And where I am?" He touched his tongue to his overlong incisors curiously. "And what? And what I'm doing here? And—" Grimacing slightly, he shoved a careful hand through the hair at his temple revealing a bloody gouge and a pair of stray hemlock-and-foxglove shotgun pellets that must have struck him when Janice shot Nihil and he was in the way. "Who that is?"

He pointed at Nihil.

"Oh, Seth." Janice, defeated, disappointed and aghast when she saw his head wound.

"We'd better get you over to my surgery," Joe said briskly, "take care of this stake *and* that wound." Out of the corner of his mouth to Janice, "I guess now we know what hemlock and foxglove does to vampýres when you shoot 'em in the head with it—gives 'em amnesia."

"Go to hell, Joe," Janice swore. She felt like crying she really did. Because just when she finally had someone—vampyre or whatever—who might be for her, he wound up not knowing who she was five minutes later because of her damn shotgun, which she hardly ever used. "Just go to hell—"

"Shhhh, sweetheart." Seth stroked her cheek with a cool finger. "Shhh. It's all right, don't worry." He caressed her lips with a rough, sensuous thumb, and his cock lifted high. "So pretty. Do we know each other—" he sent a significant glance to his lap. "Well?"

If whopping big lies were among the skeletons AnnMarie kept in her closet, Remo had better get over there and put a big damn lock on the door. Because if this one got out, or if Seth's amnesia cleared up, Janice was about to buy herself a packet more trouble than she already owned.

Janice's heart jumped. She swallowed. "Omigod." Inside the Ennel bra her nipples wanted room to tighten and bud, but didn't have any. Her breasts wanted to swell and bloom, but couldn't do that either. And her libido leapt up from between her thighs like a supertrain leashed but revving for over two centuries, tore out of the station on a squeal of hot pheromones released to the warming predawn air and a low moan. "Yes, Seth" she breathed and, leaning very close, played her fingers lightly down his chest. "Maybe you should write this down so you won't forget again because we know each other very well indeed."

"Holy crap," Joe muttered.

Then he put a stop to the flirtatious byplay right then and there before things got completely out of hand, convincing Janice the medical emergency was best served first before its, hers and her inner beast's passions were further inflamed.

Or something like that.

When Janice and Seth both agreed on the spot, they were out of there.

As to Nihil…

Left alone with the apparently lifeless spawn of Satan who'd tried to annihilate Seth for reasons now known only to him (and whoever'd sent him), Remo (who made a much better Romeo than he did a vampyre-disposer-of *or* a handyman) studied the situation for about six seconds. Unable to ascertain if anyone was actually serious about all that stuff Joe'd suggested they do with the vampyre's body and too alpha male to stop and ask for directions, he carted Nihil's remains off with him to AnnMarie's. There he shoved Nihil—whole—through a very small crack between the door and the doorjamb into the closet with the rest of Brokenoggin's skeletons before he slammed the door tight and installed six shiny new keyless locks, floor to ceiling...

Wrong way in.

Episode 1.1

THE HARPY IN THE CLOCK TOWER

By

Rachel Carrington

In which the Harpy screaming bloody murder in the Clock Tower must be dealt with and a coffee coven meeting catches Hesther and a would-be cabana boy in a compromising position with a defrocked Warlock named Gavin.

Rachel Carrington is the prolific author of fantasy, paranormal and contemporary romances for a variety of publishers. To learn more about her work, go to http://www.dawnrachel.com/.

The screeching was loud enough to wake the dead. Add to that the interminable flapping of wings and the thump of a body against the stone walls inside the clock tower and every citizen within a thirty mile radius of Brokenoggin Falls was lying awake in their beds. And not happy.

"For the love of God, will someone please do something about that damned creature!" The shout came seconds on the heels of a pop that sounded suspiciously like a small caliber pistol.

Janice climbed from her bed and reached for her uniform pants in anticipation of being whisked away by the end of a scream. Sometimes, being a police officer really sucked, especially, when she had no idea what in the hell she was supposed to do about the noise. She'd asked for volunteers, but not too many people were willing to risk their own lives to deal with a harpy.

"Welcome to Brokenoggin," she grumbled.

***

Last call came too soon for Hesther Bellhallow's tastes. She still hadn't finished scanning the room, looking for her date for the remainder of the evening. The blazing neon sign above Brokenoggin's only tavern blinked half-heartedly. The owner had never taken the time to fix it, but Hesther kind of liked it that way. It added a dirty appeal, which fit with her persona.

She slid off the barstool just as the door banged against the far wall.

"That damned harpy won't shut up!" Bare feet slapping against the plank floor, Gavin surged into the room, naked as the day he was born. He stomped past a line of fallen drunks and plopped down, three stools away from Hesther.

Her immediate departure forgotten, Hesther took notice.

Why was it she'd never really paid attention to the disgraced warlock's attributes before? She plopped back down onto the wooden stool and slid what was left of the rum and coke closer. Perhaps this night had promise, after all.

"Evening, Gavin."

He barely spared her a glance. "Go away, Hesther. I'm tired and a little bitter right now."

Hope escalated. Perfect. A man without a mission. She scooted the barstool closer and bumped her elbow against his. "Want to talk about it?" Making sure her cleavage dipped low enough to give him a birdseye view of her own abundance, she placed her hand on his wrist. "You look like you could use someone to talk to."

He raised one eyebrow. "Are you sure talking is all you had in mind?"

"I ain't serving no more drinks," the bartender interrupted with a growl in his voice.

"That's okay," Hesther said with more perk in her voice than even she'd heard in a while. "We weren't staying long."

Gavin watched Hesther pour herself off the stool once more.

"Why don't you come on home with me? You could use a friend."

He couldn't hide his interest, not that Hesther was complaining. He had more than enough 'interest' for her, as a matter of fact. She sashayed toward the door, pausing to peek over her shoulder. "Don't worry. I have plenty of things at my place to keep you warm."

"You better be careful around that one," the bartender warned. "I heard she eats her mates."

Gavin grinned. "Oh, but I can certainly hope so." He thumped his way to the door.

***

"Order, order. This meeting will come to order." Earl

Choo banged the gavel, his ruddy face even redder than ordinary.

The room fell silent while chairs scooted and feet shuffled on the floor. Expectant faces gazed upon Earl.

He cleared his throat. "That's better. Now, Mayor Dumas asked me to preside over this meeting since he can't seem to make it back to town right away. He's stuck in Flagstaff."

"Probably means Falstaff," Hesther whispered as an aside to Gavin.

Morgan Falstaff flitted down, landing on Hesther's shoulder. "I take offense to that. I'm particular about my dalliances." He folded his legs primly, resting his painted nails atop his knees. "Right now, I have my eye on that cute little Cuban."

Hesther's antenna went up. "Cute little Cuban? Who are you talking about?"

"You mean you don't know? Mavis told me that's he's been in town for only a few days, but he looks like a displaced Cabana boy. Hubba-hubba." He wiggled his eyebrows suggestively.

Hesther leaned back against the plastic chair, her mind whirling. Cabana boy and a wizard. Could life get any better than this?

"If everyone would pay attention, please, we're here to discuss the harpy situation." Earl raised his voice over the hubbub.

Janice took a step forward from her usual spot as peacekeeper at the front edge of the room. "I'd like to discuss changing the terms of my scream summonses," she said firmly. "I'm getting too many bogus scream calls and it's mighty inconvenient winding up where I'm not wanted or needed when I should be elsewhere."

"I'm sure that's all very valid, Janice," Earl placated, "and no doubt the coven can come up with something, but right now we've got to do something about the harpy—"

"Her screams call me every five minutes," Janice said—and as though to demonstrate blipped out of and back into the room when the harpy screamed shrilly twice in rapid succession. She held her head, swaying dizzily. "See?"

"Yes, but—" Earl tried.

"Shoot her!" someone yelled from the back for the room.

"She could be a mother," a woman inserted in a disgusted tone of voice.

Earl sent Janice a helpless look and banged the gavel. "Look, I don't think violence is the answer."

"Like she wouldn't rip us to shreds if she had half the chance," Gavin muttered with much disgust. "Just like a woman."

Hesther elbowed him. "I didn't hear you complaining about women last night."

The wizard shoved a hand through his hair and coughed. "Yeah, well, that was different."

Hesther checked her watch and held up her hand. "Could we move this along, please, Earl? Some of us have things to do."

"Or people to do," Morgan took his turn at cattiness, but Hesther only chuckled.

She wouldn't deny that most citizens in Brokenoggin considered her somewhat of a tramp, but she'd long given up denying her assets. And she'd been blessed with many. Of course, praying to her sister witches helped. They were more than willing to keep her body parts in the shape and position they were supposed to be in. Could have something to do with Hesther's own willingness to turn a blind eye to some of their less than favorable activities. And their newest recruits.

She leaned in closer to whisper in Gavin's ear. "Can you meet me at my house around eleven this morning?" She trailed a finger around his ear lobe. "I have an idea." Her gaze dropped to his lap. "And if you're going to stay with me a while, you should really think about putting some clothes on. I think it will be most uncomfortable to walk around with such a noticeable boner."

Gavin shifted and crossed his legs, but Hesther caught the wince on his face. Feeling naughty, she made a particularly vivid suggestion in his ear and watched his face turn beet-red. He cleared his throat loudly as Hesther slithered out of her chair.

"We'll be done shortly, Hesther, if you could just take your seat, please." Earl's voice held a note of desperation that made Janice get to her feet.

"Hesther, please." The law enforcement officer swept a hand toward the chair.

Hesther huffed out a breath. "Very well."

***

Gavin couldn't breathe and it wasn't any wonder considering Hesther had taken to stroking his leg. He'd only meant to sleep with her once, just to piss off the other wizards who couldn't bang a witch if their lives depended on it. Oh, Hesther would never admit she was a witch, but he knew. He might not have all of his sensory perceptions, but he recognized a witch when he saw one.

He smirked and moved again, an action that brought Hesther's hand dangerously closer to his male member. He gurgled and tried to brush her away. He felt eyes on the back of his skull and knew Morgan Falstaff hadn't taken his gaze off the action. "Could you please stop?" he snapped.

Hesther gave him an impish smile and continued to rub him.

Damned little vixen, he snarled silently. The door creaked open behind them and steps echoed across the tiled floor of the cafeteria where all town meetings were held. The local high school was the only place big enough to house five hundred and some odd citizens. Well, actually, Gavin's mind, they were all odd.

"Oh my," Hesther breathed beside him.

His head swiveled as a swarthy young man, wearing snug-fitting jeans and a white t-shirt, strode past the row of chairs to the front of the room.

"That must be Mr. Cabana." Her strokes intensified and Gavin wanted to complain, but what the hell? Did it really matter that her instant attraction to the Cuban had brought about a renewed increase in her ministrations? After all, he was the one reaping the benefits.

"I will take care of the harpy," the young man announced in a tone loud enough to draw every eye in the room.

Gavin's lips curled into a sneer. So he wanted attention, did he?

Hesther leaped to her feet again. "We would be so in your debt, Mr...." She paused for information.

"Just call me Juan."

Gavin saw Hesther's hips twitch and he wondered if the sex was, indeed, over. He couldn't mask his surprise when she snatched hold of his hand and practically dragged him from the cafeteria.

***

The harpy screeched. Hesther moaned and sweat broke out on Gavin's forehead. She hadn't given him time to figure out what she wanted after they'd left the town meeting before she launched herself at him.

Her lithe body curved around his, her legs going around his waist. She fisted her hands in his hair and smeared lipstick kisses across his face. It didn't matter anymore that they'd barely made it to the bottom floor of the high school and that any minute, the meeting could adjourn. Hesther assured him they were safe enough in the stairwell, but Gavin didn't really think she cared.

Sex, sex, sex. The woman had it on the brain. And she was damned good at it.

"Pardon me," came a heavily accented voice from over Gavin's left shoulder.

Hesther's head popped up and her eyes lit with delight. "Oh, this is perfect," she cooed. "Hello, Juan. Could I interest you in a small party?"

***

"Perhaps we should wait until we're invited." Claudia Choo traipsed after her sister witches as they followed the beaten path to Hesther Bellhallow's Colonial-style house. "She could be entertaining."

A snort. "She's always entertaining."

Claudia looked over her shoulder. "Earl will be expecting me home soon."

"Honey, you're not going to want to miss this spell. We've been working on this for days and if all goes well, not only will that harpy be history, but so will all of our troubles."

A chorus of cackles made Claudia more uneasy, but as Hesther's house came into view, she relaxed somewhat. Hesther always made them feel welcome. And she always had coffee and some of the best-tasting donuts in town. She could really go for a donut right now.

The quartet of witches neared the front door and as Claudia opened her mouth to speak, the head witch, a tall, spindly woman who preferred to be called Greta, didn't bother to knock.

A tangle of limbs, brown, creamy, and tanned, poured into Claudia's line of view. She clapped a hand over her mouth as other body parts became visible.

"Hello, Hesther," Greta sing-songed.

Hesther's dark head shot up, her make-up smeared and breathing heavily. "Greta?" Her head swiveled to the clock over the mantle. "Is it noon already?" One brown hand curved over her breast and she moaned, holding up two fingers. "Two minutes. That's all I need. I'm almost there."

Greta muttered her disgust and stomped past the threesome. "I'll be in the kitchen."

"I'll just wait outside," Claudia suggested hopefully. Never, in all her years as a married woman, had she ever seen anything so outrageous. Or exciting.

Hesther struggled to extricate herself from Gavin's arms and as she stood, hands on hips, her breasts sat right where they were supposed to sit. Claudia hated her for that.

"Don't run away, Claudia. There's plenty to go around for everyone. How long has it been since you've had a good romp?"

Before Claudia could answer, an explosion rocked the kitchen and Greta bounded out into the living room, face dirty, hair askew.

"What in the hell did you do to my kitchen?" Hesther demanded, shoving her aside to inspect the damage.

Greta looked forlorn. "The spell didn't work."

Hesther's head whipped around. "You used some kind of concoction in my kitchen?"

"It was a spell," Greta defended. "Now, we'll never get rid of the harpy."

"I got rid of the harpy." Juan launched himself to his feet.

"Who is that?" Greta pointed, but her eyes dropped to Juan's crotch.

Hesther shouldered her way to stand in front of the Cabana boy. "He's mine and who told you that you could concoct your spells in my kitchen? I've told you I don't like that stuff! Look." She clamped her hands on her hips. "I agreed that you and your sisters can come here and hold your meetings, but I didn't say anything about using my home as a laboratory."

"Aren't they your sisters, too?" Gavin spoke up from the floor.

Hesther wrinkled her nose. "Heavens, no! I'm not a witch."

His jaw dropped. "You're not?"

She stared at him. "Why would you think I was a witch?"

He waved a hand in dismissal. "Never mind."

Hesther pointed toward the destruction. "So what are we going to do about my kitchen?"

Claudia came forward and waved her hands, muttering below her breath. In an instant, the smoke disappeared, the soot evaporated and the chrome appliances gleamed as before. "Thank goodness at least one of us was paying attention when you were reading aloud from the Book of Spells, Greta."

"Shhh," Hesther interrupted with a finger against her lips. "Do you hear that?"

All eyes focused on her face.

"I don't hear anything," Greta mumbled."

"That's exactly right." Hesther smirked. "Juan really did take care of the harpy." She angled a look over her shoulder. "So tell them how you did it, Sugar."

With a swagger to his step, he came forward and whispered in Hesther's ear. Her eyes widened for a brief moment and then she laughed out loud.

Claudia exchanged glances with Greta. "What? What did he say?"

Juan, his brown skin glistening with sweat, bowed low. "I promised her a night she would never forget."

Gavin scrambled to his feet. "You promised sex to a harpy? She'll tear you limb from limb!"

"Actually," Juan corrected, "they're quite docile if you know how to tame them."

Gavin gave him a look of disgust and marched toward

the door. "Well, I've had enough of this. I thought I was sleeping with a witch, which by the way, would earn me great points with the wizards, and now, I discover I've only been used and I wouldn't be surprised if that harpy was summoned by this quack crew of witches."

Two of the witches behind Greta grumbled in disagreement, but Greta held up her hand to silence them. "We do not summon harpies, Mr. Wizard." Her eyes narrowed. "Although, had we thought of it, we might have considered it, especially if it meant ridding the town of wizards."

The door slammed shut behind Gavin and Juan began gathering his clothes. Hesther snagged hold of his arm. "Where do you think you're going?"

Juan stroked his knuckles down her cheek. "I fear I must be on my way. My work here is done."

Hesther pursed her lips. "I beg to differ. I can think of many more jobs for you to do."

He winked at her and leaned in to kiss her once more. "Ah, but there are other harpies in other clock towers. The world needs me." He waved a hand as he disintegrated into a cloud of dust, the room fell silent.

Except for the chiming of the clock tower.

Episode 1.2

THE WITCHES OF BROKENOGGIN AND THE DEAD WHO LOVE THEM
By

Gena Showalter

In which the well-endowed Tawdry triplets accidentally raise the dead while dealing with an overzealous peeping John.

Gena Showalter is the author of sexy paranormal romances, including *The Pleasure Slave* and *Heart of the Dragon*. She is also the author of *Awaken Me Darkly*, the first in a darkly seductive alien huntress series. For more information about Gena and her books, visit <ins>www.genashowalter.com</ins>.

The witches always came at midnight.

Gripping his flip phone camera in his hand, John crouched behind the thick marble headstone of Agnes McCloud, the biggest slut he'd ever met. The woman had tried to tell his wife about their affair. Had tried to ruin him. Bitch. She'd done the world a favor the day she'd decided to take a hike around the block and his Cadillac had accidentally (cough, cough) slipped into another lane, jumped the curb, burned rubber, and slammed into her. Anyway…

Overhead, the blood moon drowned him in crimson shadows, and he licked his lips in anticipation of the coming ritual. He was a breast man—God, he loved a nice rack— and the Tawdry triplets had some of the finest boobs in Brokenoggin.

He should be home, sitting at the dinner table across from his wife, chatting about their respective days—and wishing like hell he were dead. Instead of slicing his wrists to escape the constant whine of Hillde's voice, however, he'd come to the cemetery. He knew the triplets would strip to their luscious, lickable, kissable, completely edible skin and dance naked atop the graves, casting their spells and generally causing his slacks to expand. Better than *Playboy*. Every time.

He glanced at his wristwatch and frowned. Six minutes past. Where the hell were they? Didn't they realize he was on a time crunch here? If he wasn't home within the next hour, Hillde would freak and come looking for him and then he'd never be able to work up a good erection, something he hadn't been able to do lately but wanted to real bad. Erections were *the* most important part of a man's life. And he if didn't have another one soon, he'd—

A twig snapped.

Hallelujah! The witches had arrived. His muscles

tightened with eagerness, and his lips lifted in a grin. Oh yeah, baby, let the good times roll. Or rather, let Mr. Givemeattention out of his cage.

John quickly ducked further into the shadows, inching the lens of his flip phone around the tombstone and waiting...

***

"I hereby call this coven to order." Godiva Tawdry removed the band from her hair, letting the long pale strands cascade down her back. She breathed deeply of the night air. "Get naked."

"Yeah, yeah," was her sister, Gladys', reply. Of course, Gladys remained in place, *not* stripping.

"What are you waiting for? Hurry and take off your clothes. I need to get home and feed Romeo." Romeo was her pet wolf. He'd shown up on her doorstep a few weeks ago, sad, alone, and wounded, and had been her constant companion ever since. Already she missed him.

Her other sister, Gerda, anchored her hands on her hips and frowned. She'd been opposed to this meeting from the first, preferring to let the good citizens of Brokenoggin Falls suffer. Godiva even suspected Gerda was the one responsible for unleashing the recent havoc in town. Ever since Marko, the love of her sister's life, had a heart attack in bed, she'd been, well, a witch, capital B.

"We wouldn't be running late," Gerda snapped, "if Tubby over there hadn't made us stop and grab a bag of Doritos, a roll of doughnuts, and an Icy Big Gulp."

Gladys gasped. "How dare you call me Tubby! I have low blood sugar."

"No, actually, you're just a cow."

Another gasp. "Whore!"

"Fat ass!"

"You want a piece of me?" Gladys tossed her broom to the ground. Eyes narrowed, she stepped into her sister's personal space, squaring off nose to nose. "If your greatest wish is to be bitch slapped, color me Genie in a Bottle because I'm about to grant it."

"Girls, please." Godiva knew interrupting the argument would give her sisters yet another reason to call her Goody, Goody but that was okay because she secretly called them Bitch #1 and Bitch #2. "We have spells to cast and your bickering is slowing us down. Now, a lot of weird things have been happening in town. Naked vampires, screaming harpies, deadly ponies."

"Emma Mincemeat getting a man," Gladys added, thankfully calming down.

"That, too. I'm thinking we need to call on the spirits of the dead to guard the city limits and protect everyone inside." As she spoke, Godiva unbuttoned her dress and shimmed it down her voluptuous hips. The buttercup yellow material pooled at her feet. Everyone knew a good spell only worked if the witch casting it was naked.

A chill night breeze wisped around them, and with a sigh, Gerda stripped. Gladys quickly followed suit.

"There," she said, relieved. "Now we can begin. Form a circle and clasp hands."

"I'm not holding onto her." Gerda motioned to Gladys with a tilt of her chin. "I don't know where her skanky hands have been."

Godiva rolled her eyes. Great Goddess, could they never get along? Romeo was probably prowling the house right now, wondering where she was.

"Why couldn't I have been an only child?" Gladys muttered.

Gerda flicked the long length of her snow-white hair over her shoulder. "Because the Great Goddess hates you and wants you to suffer."

Her smart mouth finally pushed Gladys over the edge. "Take that back, you dirty slut. Right now!"

"Make me."

In the next instant, Gladys launched herself at Gerda. The two grappled together on the ground, clawing, screaming and tugging hair, their limbs tangled together.

"Ding, ding," she sighed. "Round one." With another sigh, she plopped onto a tombstone and waited for them to finish...

***

While her husband, John, cavorted with the witches, Hillde used her time alone to invent new ways to torment him. Look at other women, would he? Despise his time with her, would he? Secretly get a vasectomy so she couldn't have children, would he?

Hillde paced her bedroom, steps clipped. She'd replaced John's prescription of Viagra with sugar pills weeks ago, but that wasn't enough. She needed to do more. He needed to suffer more. The bastard was even now spying on the naked witches and their perfect tatas.

What can I do?

Immediately a few ideas drifted through her mind and she smiled an evil, scorned-woman smile.

Twenty minutes later, pepper sauce was blended into his aftershave, Nair was mixed into his shampoo, his tooth brush dripped with toilet water, and his mother's face was glued onto every female face in his *Playboy*. Bastard! He always shaved, showered and jerked off when he returned from his peeping activities. Now all she had to do was await his return...

***

How long had passed since her sisters decided to play Wrestle Mania, Bitch Addition Godiva didn't know, but she was tired of waiting for it to end. Twice she'd thought she heard the tortured howl of a wolf. *Her* wolf. Had Romeo somehow gotten out of her house and now stalked the woods, searching for her?

Another howl erupted through the night.

Her sisters heard this one and stopped for a moment, their ragged breath echoing around them.

"Oh, Goddess." Panting, Gerda shoved her hair out of her face. "We better stop. I think the wolves are out again. Last time they humped my leg for hours, and I'd rather kick your ass later than endure that again."

"Me, too. At least in the old days we'd get dinner first. Now it's just eighty pounds of fur, fangs and bad breath."

"I think it's Romeo," Godiva told them, scanning the forest for a glimpse of him.

"Oh." Gerda.

"Oh." Gladys. "Okay, then."

They jumped back into their fight.

"Girls," Godiva said, exasperated.

They ignored her. Gerda even jerked out a lock of Gladys' hair, and Gladys yelped and pinched her in retaliation.

Godiva was just about to pull her sisters apart when, a few feet away, a *click, click* sounded. Startled, she searched the graveyard until she spotted the source of the noise. A cold sweat broke over her skin when she spied a flip phone camera aimed at her sisters.

"Girls," she whispered frantically. "Someone is taking pictures of you."

Instantly their struggles ceased. Dirt and dried flower petals streaked their skin. Both were sucking in shallow breaths, crouched, their pale hair hanging in their eyes.

"Did you say someone is taking pictures of us?" Gladys' silver eyes narrowed. "Nobody takes secret pictures of me unless I've had time to diet."

"Don't worry. I'll handle this." Scowling, Gerda pushed to her feet, her hands rising into the air, a spell slipping easily from her lips.

A startled scream echoed through the night.

"What did you do?" Gladys bent down and swiped up her broom.

"See for yourself."

The girls closed ranks on the tombstone, circling the intruder and blocking him from escape. They found the flip phone hovering in the air in front of a trembling, horrified man, the phone clamping and snapping its way down his body. Only after it had bitten his favorite appendage (twice) and he screamed like a little girl (twice) did it fall to the ground.

"John Foster," Gladys gasped. "You big pervert. Does Hillde know you're out here? And staring at our breasts, no less?"

"Please don't tell her—your breasts are so big." Eyes widening, he said, "I mean, I don't want her to know—I want to touch your breasts." He shook his head, but his gaze remained glued on Gladys' chest. He licked his lips. "What I mean to say is—double-D fun bags are my favorite."

Gladys smacked him over the head with her broom. "Letch!"

"Bastard!" Godiva grabbed her own broom and popped him dead center in the face.

"Dickweed!" Gerda didn't have her broom in hand, so she raised her arms high in the air and uttered a quick incantation. "You like breasts so much you can have a pair of your own."

His shirt ripped down the middle as a huge pair of breasts grew on his chest. He stared down at them, his mouth gaping open. "What the hell! Get them off, get them—Hey, these are nice." Closing his eyes, he reached up and kneaded his new breasts, a rapturous smile spreading across his face. "Mmm," he muttered.

"Undo the spell!" Gladys scowled. "Undo the spell right now. We'll punish him another way."

"No, this is punishment," he cried, covering the man-boobs protectively. "I swear. Don't take them away. I've got to learn my lesson."

After Gerda did as commanded, and John's chest had shrunk back to its normal size—and he was bawling like a baby—he tried to dart out of their circle, but Godiva quickly muttered an incantation, locking his feet in place.

"Not so fast," she said.

His eyes widened with horror. "What are you going to do to me? I didn't mean any harm. I only wanted a peek at your hoohoos."

Without saying a word, the three sisters tugged at the rest of his clothing, peeling it from his middle-aged body until he wore nothing but a few teardrops. Since he'd gotten a look at their goods, it was only fair they get a look at his.

"We're going to cast our spells around you—" Gerda's gaze darted between his legs, "—*little* John, and you're going to stand there like a good boy and pray the Goddess takes mercy on your soul."

That dried his tears real fast. "You mean you're not going to hurt me, and I get to watch you dance? Naked?" He tried real hard not to grin. "Thank you, Great Goddess. Have mercy. Oh, have mercy. Lots and lots of mercy and breasts and mercy. Amen."

"I swear," Gladys growled, "you're the scum of the earth."

"Ignore him," Godiva said after another wolf howl echoed through the night. "We need to get to work."

"Fine."

"Whatever." Gerda found her broom buried in a mound of dirt, snatched it up, and rejoined the circle.

The three sisters closed their eyes, blocking out John's image and his voice, and in perfect sync began their protection spells. Round and round they danced, their hips undulating, their hair swaying, their brooms raised high in the air. Each one chanted under her breath.

While she danced, Godiva stumbled over the spell's words, unable to push Romeo from her mind. That last howl had sounded pained. Was he hurt? Should she go looking for him? He was one of the biggest, strongest, fiercest wolves she'd ever seen, but he possessed a gentle and loving nature and other beasts of the forest might trample him.

Suddenly Gladys stopped, her breasts jiggling with the abrupt halt.

"What are you doing? Keep moving," John whined. "I'm still praying."

She frowned. "Does it feel like the ground is shaking?"

Godiva stilled, followed quickly by Gerda. In the next instant and seemingly without provocation, Gladys stumbled backward and landed on her butt.

"What's going on?" Godiva gasped.

Dirt began cracking at their feet. Grass began splitting. Flowers tumbled off of tombstones… and then the tombstones themselves tumbled to the ground.

"What's going on?" she asked again, her tone more frenzied.

Gladys popped to her feet, and Gerda paled. "I think—ohmygod—I think the bodies are rising!"

"That can't be." Gladys sucked in a breath, whirling around to scan the surrounding area. "We only called forth their spirits."

"Well, the dirty bastards didn't listen!"

A bony hand shot through the cracked dirt and latched onto John's ankle. Startled, he screamed and would have dropped into a fetal ball and sucked his thumb if his feet hadn't been frozen in place. All over the cemetery bodies rose. Most were completely decayed, but all still wore their worm-eaten burial clothes. As they emerged, they limped, lumbered and trudged toward the triplets. Deadly moans echoed across the distance.

"What should we do?" Gladys gasped, holding out her

broom like a sword. "What the hell should we do?"

In the next instant, Agnes McCloud climbed all the way out of the ground. Seeing her, John started shaking like an epileptic. "Help me," he cried. "Please, help me."

Godiva swatted at the skeleton with her broom. "Shoo." Big chunks of dirt fell out of the dead woman's remaining hair. "Get back in the ground. I command you."

Agnes hadn't yet fully decayed, and it was freaky seeing her half-on, half-off face lift into a grin when she spied John. "John! Oh, my darling Johnnie. I missed you so much."

"We've got to send them back." Gladys' mouth formed a large O as she counted the number of bodies headed toward them. "They're multiplying like rabbits!"

"Demons of the Dark," Godiva shouted, "return to your graves!"

They kept coming.

"Spirits of the Nether World, be gone!"

Still, they kept coming.

Meanwhile, Agnes had leapt on John and was feeding him kisses like she was a buffet of sensual delights and he had been on a year long fast. Except, the man looked like he would rather eat his own vomit than the dead woman's tongue. He kept gagging, but that didn't stop Agnes.

If she'd had time, Godiva would have snapped a picture of the two with the flip phone. As it was, the rest of the dead bodies finally reached them and closed her and her sisters in a circle, moaning and groaning and reaching out to caress them. Having been without human contact for so long, they were probably desperate for it. Or maybe they were simply hungry and she and her sisters looked like a triple stacked Egg MacMuffin.

Gladys shrieked. Godiva swatted at the bony hands with her broom. And Gerda broke into a frenzied run. One of the corpses sprang after her, his laughter ringing through the cemetery like nails over a chalkboard.

"Is that…Marko?" As she defended her and her sister's honor, Godiva watched the tall corpse who wore the same black suit Marko had been buried in chase the flailing Gerda around a tree.

Finally, Marko snagged her, wrapping his arms around her waist, spinning her around and tossing her over his shoulder. Without a pause in his step, he absconded into the nearby forest with her. Her furious shouts echoed from the trees. Then…she giggled. An honest-to-the-Goddess giggle. What the hell were they doing? Having a slap-and-tickle fight? Playing find-the-bone?

Godiva and Gladys continued to fend off their molesters with their brooms, all the while uttering spell after ineffectual spell. Well, not so ineffectual. Each spell conjured something—just not the help they wanted. A harpy. A horny troll. A demon. Each creature materialized at the edge of the forest and stood, watching the proceedings, grinning. One of them even produced a bowl of popcorn and a large soda.

"Two dollars the one with worms in his eyes snags the witch on the left," the demon said.

"You're on," the troll agreed.

Suddenly a fierce growl overshadowed every other noise, and a pack of wolves raced into the graveyard, snapping and snarling.

"Romeo," Godiva cried, her relief nearly a palpable force when she recognized her pet.

His teeth bared in a scowl, Romeo leapt up and latched onto the bony arm reaching for her and snapped it off. The corpse glanced at his armless side, then at the wolf. His armless side, then the wolf. Still holding the bone, Romeo sprinted away.

"Give that back," the corpse shouted.

The rest of the wolf pack chased the skeletons in every

direction. All except Agnes, who was still sucking John's face. Godiva and Gladys dropped to the ground in relief.

"Well, that went well," Gladys said dryly. "I never thought I'd be grateful to the wolves."

A few minutes later, Romeo appeared in front of them. "Come here, boy," Godiva said, reaching out for him. He dropped the arm bone at her feet as if it were the greatest prize in the world and nuzzled her with his nose. She luxuriated in his soft black fur as his tongue flicked out and licked her collarbone. "That's my good boy. Thank you so, so much for saving me."

"Eww." Gladys pushed to her feet with a sigh. "I know I've said your boyfriends were dogs in the past, but hello. This one *is* a dog. Don't let him lick you like that."

"He's my special sweetie." She rubbed her cheeks against his. "My hero."

"At least have him neutered or he'll start to hump you." With barely a breath, Gladys turned on her heel and lumbered out of the graveyard. "I'm outta here," she said over her shoulder.

Romeo growled at Gladys' retreating back then looked up into the sky and howled. As he howled, his body elongated and his fur fell away, leaving bronzed skin in its place. Godiva's mouth went dry, and her heart pounded against her ribs.

"Romeo?" The name emerged on a breathless catch of air.

Pale blue *human* eyes suddenly stared down at her, and she drank in the most beautiful face she'd ever seen. Perfectly chiseled cheekbones, perfectly sloped nose. Full, lush pink lips made for kissing. Her gaze traveled downward, taking in the rest of him. His chest was wide and muscled, like velvet poured over steel. And his dick...? "Oh my god." Hello, Satisfaction.

He grinned wickedly. "No neutering. Please."

His voice was rough and husky, and so sexy she shivered. Gulping, she blinked up at him. "No neutering. Promise."

He licked his way up her neck. "You'll be real glad for that decision in a minute."

***

Later that night, John trudged into his house. He muttered and cursed under his breath. Hillde was sitting on the couch, looking relaxed and at ease while she flipped through a magazine. He'd had to do the Karate moves he'd seen on TV to escape Agnes, then run like hell. Thank *God* her bony legs hadn't allowed her to follow him. If he didn't wash his mouth out with antibacterial soap soon, he'd vomit.

God, he smelled like a rotten corpse.

"I'm taking a long, hot shower," he growled, already moving up the stairs. "Don't interrupt me."

Hillde smiled sweetly. "Take all the time you need, dear."

Episode 1.3

Candy Cox and the Big Bad (Were)Wolf

By

PC Cast

In which Godiva Tawdry casts a spell and shy, unassuming teacher Candy Cox finds the were-lover of her dreams; Janice's cousin Romeo meets Joe, the veterinarian for unscheduled surgery.

PC Cast is the award winning author of the popular Goddess series as well as other "must read" paranormal romances. To read more about PC and her work, or to write to her, go to
http://www.pccast.net.

"Godiva! Wait–wait–wait. Did you just say that you and your sisters called forth the dead last night?" Candice asked, rubbing her forehead where it was beginning to pound.

"Yeah, but you missed the important part. Romeo was...*spectacular,*" Godiva said breathlessly.

"So he actually did more than hump your leg this time?"

"Candy Cox—I swear you haven't been listening."

"You know I hate it when you call me that."

"Fine. *Candice*, you haven't been listening," Godiva said.

Candice kept muttering as if Godiva hadn't spoken. "It's not like I don't get enough of that name crap at school. Why the hell I ever decided to attempt to teach high school morons I'll never know." She cringed inwardly, remembering the countless times some hormone impaired sixteen-year-old boy had made a wise-ass remark about her name. God, she was truly sick and f-ing tired of Brokenoggin High School—Home of the Fighting Fairies.

"You could have kept one of your ex-husband's names," Godiva said helpfully.

"Oh please," Candice scoffed. "I'd rather sound like a porn star than keep any reminders of ex-husstupid number one, two, or three. No. My solution is to change careers. As soon as I finish my internet Masters in Creative Writing I can dump the Fighting Fairies and snag that job as a copy editor for Full Moon Press."

"I could work on a spell that might help shut those boys up whenever they try to speak your name. Maybe something to do with testicles and tiny brains..."

"That's really sweet of you, but you know that magic doesn't work around me, so it probably wouldn't work on my name, either." Candice sighed. It was true. She lived in a town full of witches, warlocks, vampyres, harpies, werewolves, etcetera, etcetera, and her magic was non-magic. It figured. She did magic like she did marriages. Not at all. "Men are such a pain in the ass."

Without losing a beat at her friend's sudden change in subjects, Godiva giggled. "I agree completely, and I know exactly what you need—a werewolf lover."

"Godiva Tawdry! I'm too damn old to roll around the woods with a dog."

"A werewolf is not a dog. And forty-five is not old. Plus, you look at least ten years younger. Why do you think high school boys still get crushes on? You, *Ms. Candy Cox.*"

"Put boobs on a snake and high school boys would chase after it. And don't call me Candy."

Godiva laughed. "True, but that doesn't make you any less attractive. You've got a killer body, Ms. Cox."

"I'm fat."

"You're curvy."

"I'm old."

"You're ripe."

"I've sworn off men," Candice said, exasperated.

"No, I remember exactly what you said. *'Godiva,'* here you raised your fist to the sky like Scarlet O'Hara. *'I will never marry again.'* So you've sworn off marriage, not men. And anyway, a werewolf is only a man part of the time. The rest of the time he really is the most adorably cuddly sweet furry—"

"Fine." She cut Godiva off. "I'll think about it."

"Really?"

"Yes." *No,* she thought. She hurried on before Godiva could press the point. "I've really gotta go. I'm deep in the middle of Homework Hell. I have to turn in my poetry collection to the Internet creative writing professor next week, and I still haven't figured out a theme for the damn thing. I'm totally screwed if I can't get rid of this writer's block."

"Well," Godiva giggled mischievously, "I don't know how it'd work on writer's block, but Romeo sure unclogged me last night."

"You're not helping me."

"I'm just saying—a little werewolf action might fix you right up."

"You're still not helping."

"Sorry. I'll let you get back to your writing. Remember, you said you'd think about a werewolf lover."

"Yeah, I'll think about it right after I think about my poetry theme. Uh, shouldn't you and your sisters be frolicking about the graveyard making sure the dead stay dead?"

"Oh, don't worry about it. I'm sure the spell wore off when the sun rose." Godiva paused, thinking about how her sister, Gerda, had scampered off into the woods with one of the corpses. Yeesh. "Uh, on second thought. Are you going jogging today?"

"Yes."

"Do you think you could take a spin through the graveyard? Between you and the sun, that should make sure the dead are, well, dead. Again."

Candice sighed. "I suppose."

"Thanks! You're a doll! Bye."

Godiva hung up the phone and sat tapping her chin with one long, slender finger. Candy was getting old before her time. Goddess knew she really did need a lover. A young lover. A young werewolf lover. Her fingers itched to swirl up a little love spell, but magic wouldn't work on her friend. Godiva's eyes widened and her full, pink lips tilted up. Magic wouldn't work on Candy, but it would work on a werewolf...

***

She'd never get this damn assignment done. "You'd think after teaching for twenty years I wouldn't have any problem doing homework." Candy grumbled at herself and ran a frustrated hand through her thick hair. "Poetry themes...poetry themes...poetry themes..." Death, time, love, the soul, happiness, sex... "Sex," she muttered, chewing the end of her well-sharpened #2 pencil. "That's one I can't write about. Like I've had sex in..." She clamped her lips shut, refusing to speak aloud the ridiculous amount of time it had been since the last time she'd been laid. As if the last time(s) even counted. Ex-husidiot number three had been, in politically correct terms, the penis impaired. Spoken plainly, he'd had a pathetically small dick, and an incredibly large wallet. Unfortunately, one did not make up for the other. Candy grimaced. Quite frankly, women who said size didn't matter had clearly never been with a man with a small dick. The remembrance alone was enough to turn her stomach.

"Theme!" she said, forcing her thoughts back to the blank notebook page. She wanted to create poetry that would dazzle her professor, replete with complex symbolism, witty phrasing, and possibly even a few clever slant rhymes. She'd come up with exactly—she glanced at the naked page—nothing.

She was screwed (figuratively speaking).

"Okay, so write something...anything... Write what you know..."

What the hell did she know? She knew she was sick of teaching the Fighting Fairies and she knew she would never get married again. Well, she sure as hell didn't want to write about high school, which left...

"What the hell. At least it'll get me writing."

...She drew a deep breath and let her pencil begin moving across the blank page.

Keep your Errol Flynn's, Paul Newman's, Mel Gibson's
all puppets—empty masquerades.

She blinked and reread the first two lines.   Not Shakespeare, but it did have a certain ring to it.   Candy grinned and continued.

Tom, Dick, and Harry, too
the boy next door
I want no more.

Wasn't that the truth.   Her pencil, with a mind of its own, kept moving.

You ask, what now?
Well...

And the self-moving pencil stopped. What now? What now? What now? She jumped as the clock in her study chimed seven times. Seven o'clock already? How long had she been on the phone with Godiva? Now she'd have to hurry to get in her five mile jog, complete with graveyard detour, before the sun set. Crap! She certainly didn't want to be outside alone long after dusk. Weird things had been going on—and it took some doing for anything to be classified as "weird" by a Brokenoggin native. Candy put down her pencil and began pulling on her running shoes.

***

The beat of her shoes against the blacktop road beckoned to him. He'd heard it while he was still deep in the woods and it called him away from the disgruntled and unsatisfied young thing he'd been licking. It was unlike him to leave such a delicious tidbit, but the steady slapping sound seemed to somehow get into his body. It thrummed with his pulse...his heartbeat...it pounded through his loins making them feel hot and heavy. He scented the warm evening breeze. Woman...hot, sweaty, and ripe. And not far ahead of him. He growled deep in his throat as he hurried to catch her.

***

Candy kept her eyes half closed as she sprinted through the graveyard, totally ignoring the creepy shadows that flitted past the edge of her vision. Bleck. She shivered and increased her pace, thinking that the burn in her muscles actually felt good. Godiva had been right about one thing— she did still have a killer body. Sure, she'd like to lose a few pounds, but who wouldn't? Her legs were long and strong, her boobs were full and womanly, and—best of all—she had seriously big hair.

With a burst of speed, she shot out of the graveyard and pounded down the empty blacktop road that would eventually circle around and back to her house, built, log cabin style, at the edge of town. Maybe she could keep up this pace the rest of the way home. Hell, she might even run an extra mile or so!

Which was a lovely thought until the cramp hit her right calf.

"Shit!" She pulled up, hobbling like one of the crones from Macbeth. Breathing a sigh of relief, she realized that the little rise in the road was the bridge that covered Wolf Creek. She could sit on the bank and rub her calf back into working order. So much for sprinting home.

She had just pulled off her shoe and thick athletic sock when she heard the growl. Low and deep, it drifted to her on the breeze, tickling up her spine. She looked nervously around. It sounded too big to be a dog. It was probably a werewolf. Candy rubbed harder at the cramp. She wasn't actually afraid. Werewolves were rarely more than annoying. *Spectacular*...Godiva's breathy moan whispered through her mind. Candy ignored it.

"Did you hurt yourself?"

His voice was deep, with a husky velvet sound that was very much man. She swiveled around in time to see him step from the edge of the pine trees. And her mouth dropped open. He was easily 6'4" and probably 230 pounds. Broad shoulders seemed to stretch on forever, and a wide, scrumptious chest tapered down to a well defined waist. And those legs...even through the relaxed jeans she could see that they were heavily muscled. His face was in shadow, so her entire attention focused on his body and the way he stalked towards her with a strong, feral grace that made her breath catch and her mouth go dry.

Then, like he'd walked into a tree, he stopped.

"Miss Cox?"

"Yes," she said hesitantly, trying to figure out who the hell he was.

"It's me, Jason."

He started towards her again, and she blinked up at him as his face emerged from the shadows. And—good lord—what a face it was! Strong, well-defined cheekbones and a rugged, masculine chin. His hair was thick, with a sexy, mussed curl, and so black it reminded her of a raven's wing. His eyes...oh shit...his eyes were intense Paul Newman blue and were almost as inviting as his beautiful mouth.

"Jason Thinksalot. You know, Janice's uh..." Here he hesitated. "...well, I'm related to Janice. I had you for sophomore English."

She mentally shook herself. He was an ex-student. Did it just figure. Candy frowned, trying to pull her thoughts from the bedroom into the classroom.

"Oh, that's right. Wow. Time flies," she said with

forced levity, feeling suddenly old as hell. "What was that, ten years ago?"

"Twelve," he said. He crouched next to her and nodded at her bare leg. "Did you hurt yourself?"

"Oh, no. It's nothing. Just a cramp." He was so close to her that she could feel the heat of his body and smell him—young and virile and masculine. Holy shit he was sexy!

"I can fix that," he said.

Without waiting for her to respond, he took her foot and propped it in his lap. Then he began to massage her cramping calf. His hands were strong and his touch was incredibly warm.

"Lay back. Relax." His voice had dropped to the deep, throaty tone he'd used when he first come into the clearing. "Let me take care of you."

She stared at him. She should tell him to take her foot out of his crotch and take his hands off her leg. But his touch was doing the most amazing things to her body. His fingers were sending little ripples of shock from her calf up the inside of her thigh and directly to her crotch, filling her with an unexpected rush of heat and wetness.

"Don't fight it. There's no reason to. It's just me," he said. His breath had deepened and his eyes kept traveling from her mouth to her breasts. She realized that her aroused nipples were clearly visible through her damp tee shirt and sheer white sports bra.

What would it hurt? It had been years since a beautiful young man had rubbed anything on her body. Why the hell not? She deserved a good time. After all, she wasn't planning on being a Fighting Fairy much longer. With a sigh, she lay back. His smile was knowing.

"Does that feel good?" he asked.

"Uh huh," she breathed.

His cunning hands moved from her calf to her bare foot.

He began to stroke the arch of her instep.

"You know, I had a huge crush on you in high school," he murmured. "I thought you were the sexiest woman I'd ever seen."

Candy couldn't seem to find her voice.

"You're still the sexiest woman I've ever seen." Slowly, he raised her foot to his lips and kissed the delicate arch his fingers had warmed.

She shivered. "You shouldn't do that," she said, but she didn't pull her foot from his grasp.

"Why not?" His tongue flicked out and touched her foot.

"Because you're my ex-student!" she blurted.

He smiled and scooted forward so that his mouth could move from her foot to her ankle.

"I'm of age. Well of age. I'm twenty-six."

"Oh, God!" She said as his teeth teasingly nipped her bare leg. "I thought you were twenty-seven." As if one year actually made a difference. He was an infant! Practically a teenager.

"I'll be twenty-seven if you want me to be," he said huskily.

"Oh, God!" she gasped (again), and all thoughts of statutory rape and moral turpitude fled from her mind.

"Sssh," he breathed against the sensitive spot behind her knee. "You taught me twelve years ago. Now it's my turn. Let me teach you what I've learned since I left your class."

"You really shouldn't," she said breathlessly, making no move to stop him as his lips grazed her inner thigh.

He continued as if she hadn't spoken. "What I've learned is how to use my tongue and mouth to bring a woman to orgasm before I fill her body with mine and stroke her into another climax and then another."

"So you do this often?" The thought of the possibility that she might be just another in a long line of female conquests began to dissipate her horny haze.

"No," he moaned, his mouth against her skin. "Don't think that. It's you I want to taste—you I want to pleasure. I've fantasized about you for years. You have no idea how much I want you and only you. Let me make my fantasies real."

"But I've sworn off men," she said inanely. Between his husky voice and his clever mouth, she was quickly falling back into a mindless horny haze, and was barely able to form a complete thought.

"That's perfect because I'm not a man," he said, his eyes shining up at her from between her legs. "I'm a werewolf. You can make love to me and still keep your oath."

Her breath caught in surprise. Had she ever known that he was one of Brokenoggin's werewolves? Janice certainly wasn't. Was she? And then, Candy automatically glanced up at the darkening sky, where a full moon would soon be rising above the trees.

"If I remember correctly, *Candy*," his voice caressed her name, "your magic is non-magic. Which means I am unable to shift my shape around you. I am in man form right now, and as long as I'm close to you I'll stay in that form." He nuzzled her thigh. "Let me make love to you, my sweet Candy. Let me be your lover."

I know exactly what you need...a werewolf lover. Godiva's voice whispered through her mind. Maybe her friend was right. And why the hell not? It had been so damn long. A young, virile lover...

With a fierce smile, she made her decision.

"If you can't change form as long as I'm close to you, I guess the right answer is for me to keep you *very* close to me." She pulled the young werewolf to her and let his victorious growl vibrate against her naked skin.

***

Jogging home her pace was filled with newfound energy and her smile never wavered. Godiva had been right. A werewolf lover was *spectacular.* Especially such a young werewolf lover. God, she'd almost forgotten the incredibly sexy strength of a young man's body. And recovery time! Jeesh. The boy/man/wolf had been better than a recharged vibrator. She jumped the steps into her house two at a time. He made her feel twenty again. And the day after tomorrow…they were meeting again the day after tomorrow. He'd wanted to see her again the very next day, but then he had suddenly remembered that he'd promised Janice that every odd day of the week he'd help her with…well, whatever. Candy couldn't remember exactly what job he'd promised to do for the sheriff every other day. She had been too busy staring at his wonderful mouth—there was a whole other world waiting for her in that mouth—and she looked forward to discovering new territory in it every other day. She could hardly wait.

Gulping a glass of water, her eye caught sight of the notebook and pencil sitting on her desk where she'd left them. Candy grinned. Again, Godiva had been right. He'd certainly unblocked her. Eagerly, she sat down and put pencil to the unfinished page, taking up easily where she'd left off.

> *You ask, what now?*
> *Well, love comes with the night,*
> *in the most inexplicable places*
> *leaving the most unexplainable traces.*

Candy giggled.

> *You see…a wolfman is the man for me.*
> *True, hair in the sink is copious*
> *and the house at night tends to be a mess.*

But

The ringing phone jarred her. The caller ID said Tawdry, Godiva. Blushing, Candy answered the phone.

"So," Godiva's voice was smug. "How was your jog?"

Candy's breath came out in a rush. "You know! Did you do it?"

"Do what?"

"Don't play innocent witch with me. How did you manage it? Magic doesn't work on me."

"It might not work on you, but it definitely works on werewolves."

"You made him want me!" she shrieked.

"Certainly not," Godiva sounded offended. "All I did was to cast a lupine drawing spell. If it caught a wolf that didn't find you attractive, he would have never approached you. Think of it like baiting a hook. If the worm—which was you—wasn't juicy and tender and appealing to the fish—or in this case, werewolf—he would never taste the bait."

"Oh," Candy grinned and twirled a thick strand of hair around her finger.

"Details, please."

"Let's just say this worm was well eaten."

They both dissolved into giggles.

"And," Candy said breathlessly, "I'm meeting him again, day after tomorrow. And then every other day after that. He said he can't get enough of me, and, honey, let me tell you. I definitely can't get enough of him!"

"Sounds delicious! Who is he?"

"You mean you don't know?"

"No. I told you—I just baited the hook. I had no idea which wolf would bite."

"Oh, Godiva, it's so deliciously naughty. He's *young*, and," she dropped her voice to a whisper, "he's an ex-student of mine."

"Oh, Goddess! How yummy. Give. Who is he?" Godiva gushed.

"Jason Thinksalot," she said breathlessly.

"Who?"

"Jason Thinksalot. You know, he said he's related to Janice."

"Oh, Goddess."

"What? What's wrong? I know he's young, but it's not like he's still a teenager—which would be totally disgusting—he's twenty-six. Practically twenty-seven."

"Oh, Goddess."

"Godiva Tawdry what is it!" Candy was beginning to feel sick.

"I should have known," Godiva groaned. "But how could I have known? I didn't think it would be *him*."

"Godiva. Tell me."

The witch drew a deep breath and then blurted. "He's a slut."

"What?!"

"He's the most promiscuous werewolf in town—or out of town for that matter. The pack tramp. Truly a dog in all the worst connotations of the word."

"Oh, no…"

"Oh, yes. The every other day thing? That's probably the only way he could work you into his busy schedule."

"And all that stuff he said to me…"

"You mean about making a woman orgasm with his mouth?"

Candy gasped in horror.

"Let me guess—he licked your foot," Godiva said.

"Yes," Candy squeaked.

"That's his move. He does that with all the girls/wolves/whatever."

"I may be sick."

"Hey, don't worry about it," Godiva forced perkiness into her voice. "You had a good time, right?"

"He played me for a fool," Candy said quietly.

"No, he's just—"

Candice cut her off. "He's just not going to get away with it. I said I was too old for this kind of shit, and I am. But not because I'm dried up and unattractive. I'm too old to be lied to and cheated on. So tell me the truth. He's obviously not working with our sheriff tomorrow night. What is he really doing?"

"Uh, if I tell you, what are you going to do?"

"Well, my witchy friend, I can sum that up in one word. Retribution."

***

The full moon was so white against the deep black of the starless sky that it almost looked silver. Sitting at the edge of the clearing, Candice breathed deeply of the warm night air and waited. It wasn't long before she heard them approaching through the trees. They weren't being stealthy—there was no reason for it. They were being young and uninhibited and very, very horny.

Godiva had been right (again). It was easy to tell which of the wolves was Jason. That thick black pelt was as distinctive as his eyes (and his tongue).

She stood up and stepped into the clearing. Keeping the hand that clutched the collar hidden behind her back, she cocked her hip and shook back her hair. With a sexy purr to her voice, she called to him.

"Jason, come here boy!" The big black wolf quit rolling around the ground with the little bitch he'd been licking and cocked his ears at her. Candice ran her hand suggestively over her body. "I have something special for you that I just couldn't wait till tomorrow to give you."

With an enthusiastic woof, he bounded towards her, his all-too-familiar tongue lolling. With one quick movement, she dropped to her knees beside him and slipped the heavy duty choke collar around his throat.

"Arough?" he said, staring up at her in confusion.

"Tonight you're coming with me," she whispered. When the bitches yapped at her, she grinned over her shoulder at them. "Don't worry. I'll give him back to you—but not till I've had my way with him."

He whined and squirmed as she dragged him to her jeep. "Don't bother," she told him. "Remember, my magic is non-magic. You can't change as long as I'm close to you. And I hear that your favorite position is very close to any woman. So get comfortable fur-face."

***

"Thank goodness I caught you before you closed, Joe." Candice smiled as she dragged the whining wolf into the veterinary clinic.

"Is there something wrong with your..." The vet hesitated, narrowing his eyes at the wolf.

"Dog," Candice supplied. "Yes, there is something wrong with my dog. I need you to perform emergency surgery."

"Really? He looks healthy to me." The vet reached down and ruffled the "dog's" dark fur.

Jason whined pitifully.

"You're a big boy, aren't you?" the vet said.

"He certainly thinks he is—which explains the emergency. I need you to..." Candice paused, glanced at Jason, then dropped her voice and whispered into the vet's ear.

"Well, I don't know. It's pretty late. I was just closing," Joe said.

"Surely you can fit him in. Pretty please, Joe?" She fluttered her lashes at him.

Joe smiled and shrugged. "I suppose I could for my favorite teacher. Go Fairies!"

"Go Fairies!" Candice chimed in automatically.

"If you wait here, I'll take him in the back and be done in no time," Joe said.

"Uh, no! I mean, I'll come back with you. If I don't stay close to him he'll change…into something that might surprise you."

"But you won't want to watch!"

"Oh, no, no," she assured him. "I'll stay in the room, but I have a poem I need to finish, so I'll be concentrating on that while you take care of his *problem*."

"Suit yourself, teacher," Joe said. "Bring him back."

Candice settled on a metal folding chair not far from the operating room table, careful to keep her back to the busy veterinarian and his unwilling patient. She picked up her pencil, and smiled as she finished her poem.

But if that wolfman breaks my heart
if he thinks that we should part
I'll wait until the moon is waxing full
that magic time when his change is due,
(my love is quite helpless then, as a puppy…baby…body
in a mortuary)
I'd collar that fur-faced gigolo
and make a timely visit to The Vet.

Ah, well, I'm sure there'll never be a need.
I haven't seen a neutered werewolf…

Candice smiled and glanced up at where Joe obscured her view of the sleeping, spread eagle Jason.

…Yet.

Episode 1.4

CRUNCHING SCIENTIST, HIDDEN DRAGON
By

Sophia Nash

In which Brokenoggin's resident griffin and his wife go to great lengths to conceive, and some visiting archaeologists make an unfortunate discovery about ketchup and A1 sauce.

Winner of Romantic Times' Best Regency of the Year, Sophia Nash still wonders why there are so many, ahem, alarming sensual scenes in her chapter. She has blithely and unsuccessfully tried to blame it on a co-author who Sophia insists cast a C.R.A.F.T. spell. Read more about Sophia and her passionate, award-winning, non-chihuahua infested, historical novels at www.sophianash.com.

"**W**ell, I'll be damned if I'm going to let Vanessa DuMal get her claws in one of them before me." Mavis Gap dropped the edge of her avocado and burnt orange striped curtains back in place and turned to Janice, draped comfortably across a chartreuse loveseat.

"Your pointed ears are glowing, honey."

"Well, I like that. Is that all you gotta say?" Mavis scooped the chihuahua from her native Indian cop friend's lap and paced, a pouty look in full bloom.

"Well, what did you expect? You know how bored I get listening to your Vanessathons. When are you going to learn to just ignore her?"

"The day I win."

"Win what?"

"Whatever." Mavis bent down to kiss the top of Prunella's head, a devious plan emerging.

"Have another Cosmopolitan, honey." Janice patted the seat next to her before giving the cocktail shaker a couple of jigs and draining it into the two V shaped glasses.

"It's not even 7:15 *in the morning*, Janice."

"Think of it as retail therapy."

"Wha? I can't talk to you when you're this far gone." Mavis accepted the glass from her friend and drained it in one swallow.

"It's retail therapy when I had to go out and actually buy this fancy French firewater since you couldn't remember the spell."

"You're changing the subject." Mavis glared at her friend and wondered, not for the first time, if Janice was fifty or one hundred and fifty. It was hard to tell given the amount of Votox Janice had convinced the town vet to inject in her forehead. If she had not been her best friend, Mavis would make fun of the slight droop in one eyebrow. "I have dibs on Dr. Perfectly-Chiseled."

"Does Dr. *Predily-Chisolm* know?"

"He will tonight when he comes for dinner. He and the other two visiting archaeologists end their first day of excavation at five." She looked down at her bosom and rearranged her Miracle bra to extra perky before leafing through the pages of the latest edition of Chihuahua Fancy.

Janice sat up straight and shifted her eyes. "Where'd they say they were digging?"

"Why Corkscrew Falls—where all those old bones are."

Janice's eyes radiated a wolfish color for the merest moment before she downed the cocktail and vamoosed out the door faster than Mavis could say, "Single, white, willing witch. Humans within 1,500 mile radius only. Reply with photo."

***

If there was one thing Vanessa DuMal was sure of, it was that she didn't want to end up like town busybody, Mavis Gap, with her neurotic brood of Chihuahuas and a passion for exotic cocktails. She felt sorry for the woman who lived her life by watching everyone else's. Vanessa shook her head. Did Mavis really think Vanessa hadn't seen her peeking past her curtains whose colors were a scary homage to the dubious design choices of the 70's?

Walking away from Sarah Caldron's Chat & Chew, Vanessa wondered why Mavis was so envious of her, anyway. It was not as if she had any children, the one thing every other witch in town craved. It seemed the woman coveted everything Vanessa possessed. Every time she bought new clothes, not a week would go by before Mavis would be wearing the identical thing—even when the jeans had made her chunky bottom and legs look like, like…Vanessa forced back her mean-spirited thoughts and turned onto Puff Draggy Lane. She knew why she was feeling cattish. Her hormones were on overdrive and Mavis had blatantly propositioned Vanessa's husband Jean-Luc at the annual All Hollow's Eve party at the town hall last week.

The thought of her spouse made Vanessa's stomach churn. Every nerve ending in her body was tingling. Why had she made that outrageous suggestion to the archaeologist at the Chat & Chew? It wasn't like her to flirt. She hadn't looked twice at a male—human, warlock or otherwise— since the day she had laid eyes on the Frenchman of her dreams that warm autumn day in Paris—the day she had realized her lifelong dream of visiting the City of Light. With his wild lion's mane hair, glittering gold eyes, and passion for adventure, the West Bank artist with a slew of fancy French titles had stolen her heart faster than the time it had taken for the paint to dry on the canvas she had purchased from him.

She could still barely believe her luck in having this extraordinary and mysterious man ask her to marry him, and agree to move to middle-of-nowhere America. But he had had no choice given that Vanessa spoke no French and the Parisian financial institutions had shown little interest in employing an investment analyst from Michigan despite her extraordinary knack for picking winning stocks and commodity futures. And so, acting on the spur of the moment, a most beloved French trait, Jean-Luc had packed up his canvases and paints brushes and sailed back with her to America.

Surprisingly, he'd become enraptured by the natural and mysterious elements of Brokenoggin which he featured in all his new paintings. Although why a normal human would like Brokenoggin, she could never understand. Most humans only stuck around because of the various potions and spells secretly disbursed as freely as sedatives on a mental ward.

Selling short May Pork Bellies five years ago had provided the couple with enough cash for them to marry and move into a house that Jean-Luc had quickly filled with his bold, visionary art. But lately, nothing seemed to be going right. They were stuck in a rut of epic proportions. Jean-Luc's art wasn't selling, and Vanessa's depressing hormone charts had long ago replaced their dinner discussions of charting the once exhilarating pre-Silicon Valley financial markets. And lately, many of their friends had stopped including them in gatherings.

Many called Jean-Luc haughty and unapproachable behind her back, forgetting that Vanessa's gift of extraordinary hearing made anyone within a four-block radius subject to her auditory clairvoyance. But she loved Jean-Luc. Always would, despite his bizarre love of Animal Kingdom and Jerry Lewis and his disinterest in daily showers.

There was something about the mysterious glow she sometimes thought she saw lurking in his eyes when he growled and mated with her that made the answering primal urge within her ignite. It was just that lately, she was certain all her childbearing enhancement potions were interfering in their once tempestuous sex life.

And there were times Vanessa was sure he didn't love her as much as she loved him. She sometimes thought the only reason he stayed with her was because of her adeptness at moneymaking ventures. The quarterly visits by her in-laws didn't help Vanessa's self-esteem either. Jean-Luc's father and stepmother Simone could make mincemeat of lesser mortals. Their hawkish features and vague criticism of 'vulgar American ways," cut Vanessa to the quick. When they came, there was no question in her opinion of who came first in Jean-Luc's mind in the familial pecking order. And Vanessa couldn't bear her stepmother-in-law's accusatory stare. Didn't they know that Vanessa wanted to provide them with a grandchild even more than Jean-Luc did? After five years with Jean-Luc, her itch for a child was worse than the time Alice Fairweather mistakenly mixed poison ivy extract in her Preparation H type remedy.

Vanessa just couldn't take it anymore. Her eyelids burned with tears fighting to form as she opened the little gate to her house's cobbled walkway. A few feathers danced in the early morning breeze and Vanessa wondered if the neighbor's cat had finally gotten to the baby eaglets nearby.

"Jean-Luc, this is the only way. For the thousandth time, you should have followed your father's advice and never married Vanessa, anyway. We knew the union could never produce an heir. At least we're grateful it hasn't produced…something canine."

Vanessa stopped dead in her tracks and stared at her red front door. Simone DuMal's voice drowned out Mavis's barking chihuahuas five blocks away. She lost the fight with her welling tears.

"You've gone too far, Simone. I won't do it. Not even for my father. I love Vanessa."

"Love…such a foolish notion Americans put on their greeting cards—" Vanessa could picture Simone's Gallic shrug. "—since when did love have anything to do with producing the next generation's Vicomte de la Gryphon? Vanessa is a nice enough girl. *But what we need is a nester and breeder.* I know the glitter of gold is what got to you. It has been the undoing of most of our kind." There was a pause. "Now, don't make me angry, you know what happens when the mood strikes me and I'm already peckish." Vanessa heard a familiar growl and scratching noise. "It's a *fait accompli.* You're to meet that nice, normal archaeologist lady at eight pm at the house your father and I rent when we come to visit. I told her you were an expert on the history of Brokenoggin and she bought it. I'll make a delicious Foggy Dragon's Breath soup so she'll envision her wildest dream come true—although with your charm and looks you really shouldn't need it—and if you can't get her between the sheets within the blink of a sty, then I'll–I'll, well, we'll all give Vanessa another chance."

"Simone."

"Don't 'Simone' me. This is for the best. And Vanessa would thank us. If you impregnate the archaeologist, we'll cast spells on both Vanessa and the scientist so that they're both convinced it's Vanessa's child after the fact."

"I don't know, Simone. It sounds pretty far-fetched. But…I guess I'm willing to do it, if it will solve our problem. Frankly, I'm sick of the subject."

Vanessa clapped her hands over her ears and ran back toward town. Her cursed extra-sensory hearing. She knew it. Just knew it. Jean-Luc didn't love her. Now, there was nothing stopping her from accepting that offer of a drink tonight. And it would serve them all right if her child looked like the nerdy archaeologist. A new wave of tears erupted. Witches were not known for their willingness to bite off their noses to spite their faces.

***

The table was set, the tarot cards swept under the couch, and the dogs, bless their little hearts, were dead asleep behind the kitchen door after lapping up that mild sleeping draught. Mavis glanced at a chew toy peeping up at her from the harvest-gold shag carpeting and kicked it under the coffee table.

The doorbell rang and Mavis suddenly noticed that the eyes of the lit troll candle were glaring at her. She turned the face away and ran to the door. Opening it, she stared up at the most handsome human she'd ever seen. Wavy chestnut hair, blue-green eyes, full luscious lips. Ah, he looked liked Dr. Kildare, only better.

"Mrs. Gap?" Dr. Predily-Chisolm gallantly swept up her hand and bent to brush his lips upon it. How utterly nineteenth century romantic. There were definitely some things she wished civilization hadn't lost in the name of progress.

Mavis forced back a girlish giggle. "Do come in. I'm soooo glad you could make it. I know how tiring all that digging must be."

He crossed the threshold and Mavis quickly locked the door behind him and turned off the porch light. *Nothing* was going to interrupt her now. "I've prepared a little dinner and—" she licked her lips, "—a lot of *dessert* for after."

"How kind of you, Mrs. Gap."

"*Miss* Gap. But please call me Mavis."

"Alright. Then you must call me John."

"How appropriate," Mavis replied with a giggle she hoped didn't sound like a snort.

He was so cute standing there and looking a bit flustered and disheveled. Mavis rose up on her toes and brushed a fleck of dirt off his cheek.

"Miss—or rather, Mavis, thank you so much for your invitation and for offering to give me a little insight into the history of this town. I really do think we're onto some sort of breakthrough. We're still trying to document the find. Can't tell if it's a woolly mammoth or some sort of ancient dinosaur."

"How fascinating. Tell me more. But first, please, try this little drinky-winky. I've made a batch of piña-coladas and they're divine, if I do say so." She slid a drink into his hand faster than a black widow bites the head off its mate. Potions weren't her forte. She just hoped the aphrodisiac wasn't too potent, but then again, maybe that wouldn't be such a bad thing. She motioned him to sit on the love seat and joined him.

Mavis clinked his glass in salute, forcing him to take a swallow. "Mmmm, Mavis. That's good. What's that unusual taste?"

Must be the dash of ground Mexican fire ant testes. "Paprika."

"Curious," he said taking two gulps in rapid succession. His eyes looked a little glazed. He shook his head in an obvious effort to regain his sense of purpose. "So tell me about Brokenoggin."

"This drear—I mean dear little town? Well, let's see." She really should tell him a little to whet his appetite and ensure his return if the wild sex didn't do the trick. He was simply too handsome to be content with a one night stand. She hunched her shoulders, which forced her cleavage to full frontal attack mode and placed a finger on her Dance with the Devil Red lips. "I understand from a little book I have, written by my ancestor—a grandfather—or rather a great, great, great grandfather. Maybe one or two more greats should be in there." She winked at him. "Anyway, sometime during the seventeenth century, he emigrated here from Plymouth along with a group of other settlers who seemed disenchanted with the whole puritan scene. I think he came with about six or seven other *friends*."

"Really?"

He had the cutest earnest expression on his face. And the hugest bulge in his trousers. Mavis smiled. "Yes. Care for some guacamole and chips?" She dipped a chip and dropped it between his quivering lips before dragging her finger along his willing tongue. "Honey, are you OK? You look a little warm." That was an understatement.

"No, no, I'm fine." He gulped back the rest of the piña-colada and tugged on his tie.

Mavis leaned forward to deftly untie the striped Brooks-Brothers staple. Vanessa would be impressed.

"How were they received?" he asked. A trickle of perspiration slid down his temple.

"What, honey?"

"Your ancestor and his group. How were they received?"

"Oh. Let's see." She touched the tip of her tongue on

her top lip and tried to look thoughtful. Hmmmm, maybe she should let him have another half a piña colada so he'd really let go of his inhibitions. She poured a little more from the Waring blender. "Well, it seems the new settlers were very warmly welcomed because the original town folk were, well, starving."

He tossed back the drink like a man who had just crossed the Sahara. "Starving…" His pupils were dilated, and his voice had taken on a kind of husky vibration. Something was dancing the mambo in his pants. It was an impressive sight—enough to make any girl swoon.

She looked at his transfixed gaze and swooped in for a kiss.

Let the thrashing begin.

She had meant for the experience to culminate in her bedroom. She had spiffed it up for the occasion, pink silk sheets, a pink comforter, ruffles on all the pillows and bows on all the curtains. But it wasn't in the cards. She should have guessed since her tarot cards had forewarned that this was going to be wild, brief, and devastating. *Yummy.*

Dr. Predily-Chisolm was a big boy. And he was adorable, all large clumsy hands between mutterings of 'sorry' every half a minute or so. He didn't seem to know how to unhook her push-up bra or untangle the fishnet stockings around her ankles. But he did know what to do with his, his—well, a nice girl would call it 'his digging *tool*,' she thought with a smirk.

Oh, this felt so nice and normal after all that wild jungle sex with the warlocks in town, when you never knew if they were going to turn into lions or tigers or dragons at the drop of a wand. And this time she was sure she would conceive a real child with magical powers instead of another chihuahua. Not that she didn't love the little darlings. It was just that she was tired of all the pitying looks in town. And boy would it get Vanessa's goat.

Oh my, she might just be reaching the point of having an old-fashioned climax! How novel. Dr. Predily-Chisolm leaned up on his forearms and Mavis gazed at his beautiful abs. She sighed in pleasure and urged him silently with her hips. She was right on the pinnacle and panting.

"I'm so sorry, Mavis. I don't know what's come over me."

"I don't know what you mean, handsome. I'm all yours for the taking."

"I mean, I don't normally do this sort of thing."

"Really? I would've never guessed." If he didn't move again, she thought she would die of anticipation. She bucked against him.

"Wait. What's that noise?" he asked.

Please. Start. Moving. Now. She thought in annoyance. She tried to tug his neck down but he had gone rigid.

"I hear scratching and…and is that barking?"

Oh God. No! And she knew just what they were capable of. Prunella had taught Wisty and George how to balance her on their backs so that she could reach the kitchen doorknob with her paws and wrench it open. No sooner had she envisioned it, when all nine dogs burst through the door and circled them, barking in a laughing sort of way.

The scientist jumped up, pulled up his pants and stood on top of the end table, knocking her precious troll candle to the floor.

Mavis threw the rest of the piña coladas on the small flames now licking the carpet and a purple starburst erupted before it extinguished the fire and left an ashen spot of sodden cinders. The dogs had surrounded the end table like a pack of laughing hyenas and the good doctor was looking mighty uncomfortable.

Mavis was about as frustrated as she had ever been in her life. "Prunella, if you don't herd Wisty, George, Max and the rest back to the kitchen, I'll put you in the pound! And I'll take you for your annual shots *early*!" Mavis snapped a hand to her mouth. He would think she was a raving lunatic talking to her little ones like that. Luckily, he looked too scared to have noticed. "Johnny, darling, no need to cower up there, my little doggies are the sweetest, they'd never hurt a Spanish fly."

Prunella winked and led her brothers and sisters back to the kitchen. The scientist still appeared anxious and only half listening when she helped him down.

"I'm sorry, I don't really like dogs. I'm allergic." His eyes did look a little watery.

"Really? Well, you don't look allergic to me. Let's go back to my bedroom where we won't be disturbed."

"Ummm, thank you, Mavis, but really, I-I think I should be going."

Mavis dropped her gaze to his pants and saw that the dance had ended. Abruptly. Should'a made him drink a full second glass. "But I have ever so much more to tell you about my ancestors, John. And dinner is almost finished cooking."

He looked tempted but embarrassed. "Well, all right, but maybe we should stay in this room. I don't know what came over me, Mavis. And I hope you'll accept my apology. You see, the thing is, well, to be perfectly frank—" He blinked. "I'm gay."

***

Dr. Loindexter's room at Motel 13 gave Mavis Gap's home decorating efforts a run for their money. Vanessa tried not to hyperventilate while she stared at the tilted barrel-shaped lampshade on the nightstand next to the glued-down TV remote. The shiny blue polyester bed covering looked like something right out of Alice's bedroom from The Brady Bunch. As she waited for Dr. Loindexter to emerge from the bathroom, she drew the curtains closed in an effort to ignore the blinking of the neon tavern sign across the street.

Why, oh, why had she let this go so far? She could have said 'no' after their dinner at Transylvania Pizza Kitchen. She could have said 'no' after drinks at Brokenoggin's only tavern. But she hadn't. Every time 'no thank you' had crept onto her tongue, she remembered her stepmother-in-law's voice, '*what we need is a nester and a breeder.*" It made Vanessa so hurt and sick inside. They always assumed it was her problem. Well, had her in-laws ever stopped to think that maybe the problem lay in *Jean-Luc's* prodigious lap? Vanessa had spared Jean-Luc the embarrassment of submitting to an examination by never voicing that thought.

She removed her pale pink Manolo Blahniks that matched her spring tweed suit and Gucci scarf. Jean-Luc had bought the tiny skirt and jacket because he said it made her legs look long and sexy. Oh, she was going to have to stop thinking of Jean-Luc if she was going to do this. She sat on the edge of the bed and straightened her spine.

Reason fought with hurt feelings. Why hadn't he stood up to Simone? He almost always had in the past. Vanessa remembered the secret, and guilty thrill she felt each time he winked at her before maneuvering his unsuspecting stepmother on top of their scratched up trap door. She had thought they were on the same side. Not any more.

The archaeologist emerged from the bathroom, his white Fruit of the Looms pulled high. He had carefully wet and combed his dark hair parted down the middle. He had tiny aureoles and not a single strand of hair on his sunken chest. However, the hair from all the wild beasts in Africa could be found covering his thin legs above his white socks. A lopsided grin stretched from ear to ear. He looked like he was counting his lucky stars.

Vanessa supposed she had chosen him so that she would feel less guilty. It was working. Jean-Luc pumped iron on Mondays, Wednesdays and Saturdays and had some spectacularly sinuous muscles to show for his efforts. This man, and she used the term generously, would probably think a Nautilus machine was a navigational device.

She crooked a finger at him, urging him forward. He eagerly jumped onto the bed and sniffed her. So much for sensual foreplay.

"Vanessa, you're the most beautiful woman I've ever *ever* seen. I still can't belie—"

She leaned forward, held her breath and forced herself to kiss him. It was too bad she forgot to close her eyes. She forced back the bile creeping up her throat.

For all his assumed lack of experience, the scientist sure knew how to undress a woman in less time than she could do it herself. But soon, way too soon, his clammy little hands were exploring every last inch of her body, and she was trying, unsuccessfully, to keep disgust at bay. He kept moaning her name over and over until she thought she would scream. She wished he would just get it over with. Then she would thank him, leave, and get home in time to mix up a post-coital fermentation elixir to optimize the chance of conception.

She dropped her hand to touch him in an effort to urge him to mount. A wilted, placid piece of flesh greeted her hand. What on earth? She had only ever seen Jean-Luc's manhood, something that would spark fear in the eyes of any virgin. *With good reason.*

"Oh, Vanessa. Vanessa, baby. See me, feel me, touch me, heallllll me—"

Oh. My. God. Was he whispering lyrics from the Who's 'Tommy'? "Um, Dr. Loindexter. Are you OK?"

"Oh, yes, Vanessa baby. Just keep touching me. It's been so long. So long since…"

"Yes?"

"Ah, hell…since anyone's hand has touched me other

than my own."

She forced herself to open her eyes and saw a red flush move past his eyebrows to his receding hairline. "I'm sorry Dr. Loindexter." Such an unfortunate surname choice.

"Will you please call me Duncan?" he whined.

"Oh, sorry, Duncan. What can I do?"

He sighed heavily, rolled off of her and covered his face with his forearm. "Nothing. Not a darn thing. You're just too intimidating for me, I guess. No, let me revise that. I *know* you're too intimidating. Hell, I've never gotten past second base with anyone, not even pimply old Betty Sue Bob Michaels. How do you expect someone like me to perform under so much pressure?"

Vanessa's mouth twitched. Poor man. "I'm sorry Duncan. Do you want to try again?" She prayed he would say no. Right now she would give up her first unborn anything if she could just get out of there. If this was not a sign from her friend Lucifer that good witches didn't have to put up with bad sex, then—

But...

Her nature refused to let her leave without doing a kindness toward Dr. Loindexter. She flipped open her Birkin bag, extended her compact wand and flicked it. "*Obliviosus somnus*," she said, wishing she could remember that chapter on organ transformation from her Curses textbook. This would have to do. Her liver wasn't into continuing this ridiculous plan anyway.

Duncan Loindexter slept the sleep of the dead, his jaw slackening in surrender. She was just going to have to figure out another way to have a child. Perhaps Lucifer would be willing to make a deal with her. He always had been more than accommodating in the past.

Vanessa threw her wand back in her bag, snapped into her clothes, and walked away from the preposterously named Dr. Loindexter. She only wished she could experience a little forgetful sleep herself.

***

Jean-Luc DuMal gulped down his stepmother's soup like a fluish Jewish man tolerates his mama's lukewarm Matzo balls. He gazed down the length of the formal dining room table, marked with only a few very faint scratch marks, reminders of some heated family arguments. He wondered about the petite dark brunette archeologist facing him. So very unlike Vanessa, his dear long, tall drink of ambrosia. His wife was the quintessential blonde bombshell of every man's fantasies. How was he going to go through with this? Dr. Heather Lovingood was ordinary in a girl-next-door kind of way. She had huge white straight teeth courtesy of an excellent American orthodontist, a pert nose, and eyeglasses which were just dying to be taken off her face. But she just wasn't his type.

It was also clear, however, that the reverse was not true. Two sips of Simone's soup had made the woman begin to stare at him with a sort of rapt fascination similar to when the conversation at the Ladies Home Wicca coffee-clatch turned to Hugh Jackman. Where was the fun in this? The delicate dance of flirtation was best performed when both parties knew the art of being coy and intriguing with a sprinkle of dry humor, something his wife had in abundance.

When he felt himself harden, despite thoughts of his beloved wife, he began to suspect that Simone had slipped something in his soup too—and it certainly wasn't a potion that made Dr. Lovingood look like Hugh Jackman.

But then, his stepmother had never been known to leave things to chance.

"Mr. DuMal, you were speaking about the new settlers, one of whom was your wife's ancestor, right?

He nodded and pushed away his soup bowl.

"So they were instrumental in helping the original townsfolk survive a particularly harsh winter. A kind of re-creation of Plymouth's first winter with the Indians, right?" she asked.

"Yes, except these newcomers didn't scalp the townsfolk." He smiled at her against his will. Heather was actually fairly cute. *Very cute, really.* "Instead, they brought foodstuffs with them and had some, uh, *original* methods of *stretching* what they had on hand."

"So the inhabitants must have been grateful."

"You would think." He scratched his head. "But you would be incorrect. It seems that once the starving townsfolk's stomachs were full, they began to question the newcomers' methods." He had a sudden, nearly irresistible urge to climb on top of the table and crawl over to this Lovingood babe and lick her. A rumbling from his stomach signaled gastro-intestinal fire burning his ribs and his crotch. He wondered if dear old Simone had found this potion in her Joy of Spooking or in a highly adulterated *Guide Micheline* recipe file.

Annoyance wrestled with desire, and of course, desire won.

"Really?" Heather paused and pulled the rubber band from her hair, allowing the silky dark strands to fall all over her nubile shoulders.

When had she unbuttoned her oxford shirt and pushed it off her shoulders?

The Lovingood ran a hand through her hair and tossed it back with panache. "And how did the newcomers react?" she asked huskily.

OK, no one could blame him. No self-respecting warlock worth his weight in hemlock could resist this potion whatever it was. He felt like he would explode if he didn't have her right here, right now. He got up, trying to casually hold a napkin over his front, and walked the long length of the table to her. She looked up at him with huge brown doe-eyes.

Simone was right. It was for the best. Vanessa would *thank* him if she knew what he was going through to provide a child for them. He would do the Lovingood and make everyone happy by the act. "Miss Lovingood, I have some etchings in my study that might be of particular interest to you. Would you care to see them, my dear?" Not very original, but who needed subtlety with potions like these?

"Ohhhhh, yessss," she said, breathing heavily as they almost raced down the hallway.

It was a miracle their pants were still on by the time they reached the study. "What about your wife, Mr. DuMal?" Heather asked in a moment of clarity.

"Wife?"

His mind turned to mush when the little she-devil did something indescribably delicious with her tongue in his ear. Little did she know she was playing with fire. *Literally.*

He ached for her now with an intensity he had never known. His stepmother sure knew how to cook. And Heather was simmering for him. She was mewling like a cat and arching her back like a rabid raccoon. It was a sight to behold.

He gently nudged her down onto the brown leather sofa and began to unzip his black jeans. The urge to stretch his long length into her was unrelenting. He allowed his pants to drop and anticipated the look of reverence that would light up Lovingood's face.

She giggled.

It was the kind of giggle that felt like a dash of ice cold water. With sickening intuition, he looked down to see the stuff of nightmares. Standing as erect as a tin soldier was a manhood in all its glory. But it wasn't his manhood. It looked...well, it looked like a birthday candle, a child's unlit pink birthday cake candle. Even the revolving pink and white swirls were visible.

Hell...

"Simone," he roared. An involuntary flash of fire came out of his throat.

Heather screamed.

Jean-Luc felt the unmistakable gnawing of shifting in his bones. It was an achy, fiery sensation that reminded him of the sound of fingernails on chalkboard. It actually almost felt good. He hadn't shifted since the day he'd married Vanessa. In fact, for five years he had stoically endured a horrendous case of PGS, pre-griffin syndrome. He didn't need to glance down to see the feathers forming under his skin, his lionish tailbones elongating, and his claws emerging.

Miss Lovingood clearly wasn't going to hang around to see the rest. Moments later, Jean-Luc found himself tripping over his tangled pants in an effort to keep up with her as she raced out the front door. Luckily, it was full dark outside with only a waxing moon to provide any sort of illumination. No one would see them.

The fresh air caused an abrupt halt to his transformation. The fire in his belly calmed and the itch of the pin feathers retreated as they dissolved back under his skin's epidermis. He almost cried out in frustration, the urge to stretch out his wings and fly once more was almost unbearable. He had waited so long for a shift.

If she would only stop that infernal screaming. Miss Lovingood's lungs were only surpassed by her wheels, er, legs. Jean-Luc could barely keep up with her as they raced down Main Street, past the town tavern. Suddenly, the last door of the low-slung Motel 13 opened wide, nearly knocking Jean-Luc off his feet. Out walked Vanessa, with a sphinx-like cool expression on her face, spritzing Chanel No. 718 all over herself.

"Jean-Luc, what are you doing here?" Vanessa asked.

Out of breath, Jean-Luc said not a word—instead he peeked into the motel room. There seemed to be some sort of half man, half primate curled up in a fetal position and passed out cold on one of the beds.

"I could ask you the same question, cherie. But—" he raked a hand through his snarled hair, "—to be honest, if I don't stop that screaming scientist right now, this town might just become prime fodder for a host of National Enquirer reporters. Come on, we'll talk later."

Not for the first time, Jean-Luc blessed his wife's cool head and long slim legs as she surged past him, high heels be damned, up the steep road out of town. About half a mile up, the asphalt turned to gravel and another half mile later, the road skidded into dirt. When he spied a trail of broken branches, he veered into the underbrush toward Corkscrew Falls. Fifteen minutes later, Jean-Luc's sides heaving, he dragged himself up beside his wife. He knew he should have been doing more cardio instead of just pumping weights.

"Where'd she go?" He leaned over in an effort to regain his breath.

Vanessa panted and pointed to the entrance of a cave. Eerily familiar wing-batting and heel pounding noises came from within.

"Father?" he shouted.

Eyebrows raised in question, Vanessa swung around to face him. "Huh? Your father's in there?"

He quickly recanted. "I don't know what I'm saying, Cherie. Look, we've got to get that woman out of there. I have a bad feeling about this. Isn't this the place Janice told all of us to steer clear of?"

"What were you doing with that woman anyway?

"What were you doing in that motel room?"

"Don't change the subject," Vanessa said.

"Look, my love, I'm big enough to forgive you if you'll do the same. You know I love you and no other."

Vanessa looked at him as if she was trying to read his

mind. "Alright—" she pushed her hair over one ear and licked her lips, a movement that always drove him crazy with desire, "—but only if you promise that you'll keep your father and stepmother out of our lives forever."

"Forever is a long time, cherie. How about if I promise to keep them out of our affairs until the next millennium?"

"Deal." Vanessa stuck out her left pinky and he grabbed it with his own. Pulsating warmth spread through his loins and he felt himself harden again. He put his other hand on himself and was relieved to feel a large familiar shape under his jeans this time. Thank God.

A bloodcurdling scream rent the night air and the unmistakable sound of teeth gnawing bone followed. Scientists, it seemed, were crunchy. The slight smell of mustard and ketchup wafted through the air. And if he wasn't mistaken, there was a hint of A1 too.

He grabbed his wife's other hand and pulled her into a fast retreat toward town. "It's too bad she wasn't the fainting type," he said, sadly.

"Well, someone's going to have to concoct a forgetful potion or spell for the other two scientists otherwise we really will learn firsthand about the Enquirer's stellar reporting skills," she said a few moments later. That's what Jean-Luc loved about his wife, ever practical.

"Poor woman. She came for dinner and I was telling her all about the history of this little town. But, I was wondering how I was going to explain the part about your ancestors' mystical leanings and the reason they settled here. She wouldn't have understood the extraordinary primal urges they—and we—have to mate. And the fact that it takes one mystical being and one ordinary human to produce something memorable. A living and breathing…child."

"Oh, Jean-Luc." Vanessa hurled herself into his arms. "Do you think we'll ever have one of our own?"

"Of course we will, cherie. It's only a matter of time—

" he kissed her and held her tight, "—and effort."

"And the right potion," Vanessa added, sensuality dripping from her.

"Well, practice makes perfect," Jean-Luc growled and felt his eyes glow. Practice makes perfect, indeed, he thought as he leaned in to kiss the one witch who made his blood boil.

The unmistakable surge of energy in his emerging wingtips matched the lion spirit invading his lower extremities. There was no stopping this long anticipated shift now. "I've always favored making love to you in the wild. Nothing like the hint of a dangerous, man-eating creature nearby to heighten the mood." Jean-Luc enveloped her with his massive griffin wings and prepared to plunge into her. He prayed he wasn't scaring his dear witchy-wife to death. But he had forgotten her aplomb in the face of change.

"Nothing like being surrounded by soft feathers and the anticipation of first time lion-sex to put me in the mood, my love," she whispered.

"My thoughts exactly, cherie." He growled and thrust into her. Her primal scream of joy melded with a distant werewolf howl, causing a star to burst in a galaxy nearby— surely, the promise of a new life in the making.

2005 was, it seemed, a superb vintage year, after all.

Episode 1.5

HOW TO SEDUCE AN AMNESIAC VAMPIRE
By

Kathryn Caskie

In which the movie "Memento" plays a role in our resident vampyre's love life & Janice, the sheriff, makes excellent use of an indelible laundry marker.

Kathryn Caskie is the award-winning author of three historical romances set in Regency England, a background which uniquely qualifies her as the world's foremost authority on naked amnesiac vampires and middle-aged werewolf law enforcement officers. For more fun and news on Kathryn's latest novels, visit http://www.kathryncaskie.com (during full, harvest, new or eclipsing moons only, please.)

He stood in the blue light of the full moon, his back to the steadily lapping loch. There was no escape. None.

He didn't dare move. Didn't dare take his gaze from the enormous wolf watching him from atop the sandstone outcropping not ten feet up the embankment.

This wasn't good. Why the hell was he out here in the middle of the night anyway? He searched his brain for an answer, but no matter how hard he tried, he couldn't remember a damn thing. Not even his name.

Cautiously, he slid one foot back into the water. He'd just swim out into the loch. It would be safer out there. But then, a rather disturbing thought sprang into his mind. What if he *couldn't* swim? How was he to know? Best not risk it.

The wolf snarled viciously at his sudden movement and crouched low.

He froze in place. Icy water spat at his heels and splashed the backs of his thighs, raising the hair from his chilled damp skin. Lifting the short hairs...*everywhere.*

No. No way.

He risked a half-glance downward and blinked at his own ghostly white skin. *Holy shit.* He was completely naked...and what the hell was *that*—he squinted, trying to make it out—something written on his hand?

There had to be some damned good explanation for all of this. *Had* to be.

The wolf tilted her head back and let out a shrill howl, sending an uncontrollable tremble through his body. He watched, petrified, as she rose up on her muscled legs, prowled a step closer and, with her tongue, lapped the saliva dripping from one of her fangs.

Oh hell.

Okay, risk drowning or be ripped to pieces?

Drowning. Definitely drowning.

But then, the loch behind him began to sputter and pop,

bubbling like a pot set to boil. The sound grew louder and more ferocious over the passing seconds, until it all but muted the roar of the waterfall not five hundred yards away.

His breath came faster, and he couldn't seem to get enough air, as the thrash and splash behind him drew closer and closer still. From the corner of his eye, he saw a massive scaly taloned appendage cut through the roiling water.

Then it was behind *him*.

Something huge. Something that—he sniffed the night air—smelled of rotting meat.

Fuck.

He had to see it. Had to face it like a man.

Lowering his eyes from the she-wolf, he slowly began to turn toward the loch.

He'd only managed a quarter-pivot when a horrific blow slammed his head. Painful shards of light knifed across his vision sending him staggering toward the muddy bank. He fell to his hands and knees, dazed.

"Seth. Get up. Run!"

Dark-winged specks crowded his mind as he lifted and turned his head toward the female voice.

There, on the sandstone outcropping where the wolf had been, was a naked woman.

"Get away from the loch!" She leapt from the jutting rock with amazing agility and raced toward him, her moon-streaked raven hair floating behind her like a silken cape. "Now, Seth, before it's too late!"

***

Janice pulled her rucksack from the crevice in the cave wall, and dug around for her makeup bag and Altoid tin.

First things first.

Seth could wake up at any moment and she didn't want the gorgeous piece of man candy to find her for the first time—this lunar cycle—with residual gray werewolf streaks through her hair and Fido breath.

She glanced at Seth, the beautiful vampyre, who was lying naked before the waterfall curtain that stretched across the mouth of the cave.

How lucky she'd been to stumble upon him when she did. But he was safe now...and better yet, with her.

Janice had to admit she'd never seen such a perfect specimen of a man—mortal or immortal. And in Brokenoggin Falls, where 24-hour hottie spells could be had for a mere hundred bucks, that was really saying something.

Hurriedly, she popped two Altoids into her mouth to remedy her dog breath, then pulled out a pink tube of Maybelline Waterproof Mascara. Angling a hand mirror over her head, she eased the mascara wand from crown to tip, painting over her gray streaks. And, because she was a tad over fifty after all, she used the magic Maybelline wand on a couple gray curlies down under too.

Of course, the streaks were only a temporary thing and, as usual, would disappear once the moon set. But Seth's squeaky-clean memory was temporary as well. The minute he opened his eyes, his amazing blue-ringed eyes, he would remember everything from the incident at the loch onward—at least, until the next full moon wiped his mind clean again.

First impressions were lasting though and therefore Janice wanted to be sure to look her best—or rather, her *youngest* for him.

Of course, this meant making sure he saw her naked...tonight.

Absently, Janice wondered where she might find her shredded uniform this time. It was a pain in the keester to hunt down her clothing after every full moon, but she was a far larger wolf than human, and well, that was probably a good thing. Reports of a wolf running through the woods in a police uniform would no doubt start people talking.

She proudly surveyed her bronze-hued nude form,

pausing on her perfectly pert breasts. There was no question about it, she looked fabulous. Sadly, though, the wolfish effects on her body would be as fleeting as her gray-streaked hair. Janice glanced down at her muscle-cut abdomen, and well-defined arms and legs.

Yup, by tomorrow morning, her boobs would resemble puppy ears, her thighs cottage cheese, her belly a lumpy pillow and her arms—well, they'd have wing flab. She shuddered at the reality of it.

No, if she was going to seduce Seth, it had to be tonight. She'd waited far too long already.

Just then, Seth groaned and scratched at his chest. He was sure to open his eyes at any moment.

No more procrastinating.

Besides, what would it matter if she blew it? She'd only have to live with the humiliation until the next full moon, right? Then she could try again.

A nervous flutter shot through Janice's stomach as she slid open the zipper on her sack and pulled a black Sharpie permanent marker from the leather loop on her ticket pad. She knelt beside Seth, took his hand in hers and studied the words he'd written on his palm.

As the moon waxes, your memory wanes.

Good. Simple block letters. Easy enough to mimic.

Reaching across Seth's hips, Janice accidentally brushed him just *there,* causing him to twitch and quicken. A little anticipatory smile burst upon her lips.

She raised up his other hand and very carefully, pressed the Sharpie to his palm.

Call Janice 555-1805. Trust her.

Looked good. Perfect, actually. Why, she could have had a nice career as a check forger if she hadn't gone into law enforcement.

Okay, now for the *piece de resistance.*

Janice swallowed hard as she reached down between

Seth's legs and took him into her hand. Very carefully, she began to write.

***

His eyelids fluttered, and the first thing he noticed, besides the merciless throbbing pain in his head, was a naked woman kneeling at his side.

He blinked in astonishment. Her golden skin glistened in the light of a flickering lantern as she leaned close and drew a wool blanket over his body.

To his eyes, her female form was absolutely flawless. Her breasts were full and round, her waist small and graspable—what was that? Did she say something?

"Can you hear me? I asked how you were feeling." She pushed her long ebony hair back from her face, forcing him to peer up into her saucy golden brown eyes.

"W-where am I?"

"We're in a cave...behind Brokenoggin Falls. It's okay, Seth. You're safe here."

He was still dizzy and more than a little disoriented, but turned his head toward the roar and splatter of a wall of water a few feet away.

Water.

"In the loch—" He had started to ask her about that scaly...*thing* with the talons, but then it occurred to him that she'd revealed something more important. "You called me...*Seth*."

"I did. And, I'm Janice." She reached out and ran her fingers through his curly damp hair.

"*Seth*." He furrowed his brow. "Are you sure? Why can't I remember my name—anything?"

"Shh, don't worry." She bent, and to his utter surprise, pressed her warm lips to his. "It's the moon. And in Brokenoggin Falls, strange things happen in the light of a full moon." She glanced a little nervously across the cave at a canvas bag near the wall, then turned her attention back to him. "I was worried about you. You really scared me. Never, ever venture so near the loch during a full moon. It's far too dangerous."

Suddenly, he remembered the snarling wolf on the rock...and then the naked woman. Seth pushed himself upright. He stared at Janice. "*You*—the wolf. No, no, no. Can't be." He brought his fingers to his aching head, and found a bandage plastered to his swollen brow. "I hope it's just the bump on my head and I'm not really going mad."

"I promise you, Seth, you're quite sane." Janice remained expressionless for a moment before speaking again. "Here in Brokenoggin, we all have secrets. Unbelievable secrets. But you and I...we keep each other's. We trust each other."

Seth shoved his hand through his hair. This was all coming too fast. "I don't even know you."

"Yes, you do. You know me...intimately. You just don't remember." Janice caught his wrist and turned his palm upright. "See?"

Seth read the words on his hand. *Call Janice 555-1805. Trust her.*

"I know this is hard to grasp. It always is when you lose your memory like this. But I am here for you."

"Then you've got to explain it to me. Everything. How can this be?"

"Seth, we have a lot to talk about—believe me...*a lot*. But for now, you only need to know that you lose your memory each time the full moon rises. Everything you know disappears from your mind and you must start remembering from scratch."

Seth lifted his other hand and saw that there was a message there, too. *As the moon waxes, your memory wanes.*

"All these notes written on my skin..." He cupped his hands and looked up at the dark haired goddess. "I-I don't understand."

Janice trailed her soft fingers soothingly down his arm, quickly pulling them back when he noticed the dirt embedded under her long nails. "It's how you remember, Seth. No matter what happens to you, no matter where you end up, you know what's most important—and how to find me."

He gazed into her glittering eyes, as understanding dawned. He had to admit, his method of note-taking was quite clever. He must be a very intelligent man. "So I remember what's most important," he murmured.

"Yes, my love." She smiled at him.

My love, she said. Just how intimate are we?

It didn't seem to bother Janice in the least that she was naked, for she shifted and sat crossed-legged beside him, her right thigh pressing against his hip.

But he was a man after all and couldn't help but peek into that shadowed area between her legs. When he did, he felt himself stir and harden. He was mortified.

"Seth, I'm a little chilly from the spray off the falls. Do you mind if I share the blanket with you for a bit?"

"Uh..." He started to lift the blanket, but decided to quickly check on his condition, trying to decide the best way to apologize. It wasn't like she wouldn't notice!

But then, he discovered something odd.

He couldn't have.

He'd actually written a message...*down there*! What could have been so damned important, that he felt he *had* to remember—could not forget?

Lifting the blanket a little higher, he allowed the lantern light to illuminate the rapidly expanding inked words.

Janice is the <u>best</u>.

The best, huh? Well now, that *was* good to know. A wicked little grin found its way across his lips.

"Seth? I'm freezing out here."

"Sure, Janice, slip on under. I'll keep you warm. *Real* warm."

Janice gave a long pleasurable sigh as she slid atop his naked body.

Episode 1.6

THE LOCH'S STRESSED DRAGON'S HALF-SISTER

By

Elizabeth Holcombe

In which Rowdy Vanderlight, love-sick centaur and UPS driver, spends solitary moments Googling himself and in the process goes to the post office and finds help for his ailing heart. (New characters by Elizabeth Holcombe)

Elizabeth Holcombe has been nominated and finaled in many awards for her first historical romance, Heaven and the Heather (Jove), which also came out in Russian (and she cannot read Russian!). Elizabeth can be contacted through her website: www.ElizabethHolcombe.com.

Rowdy Vanderlight spent most of his free time, when he wasn't delivering packages for UPS—most of which went to Claudia Choo from QVC—Googling himself. Yet, he couldn't get the image of Claudia's witch sister, Tulah, out of his mind. He wanted to ask her for a date, but Tulah was always out with that cackling, conjuring, moonlight-obsessed coven of hers. In the late night hours, Rowdy had no choice but to find ways to amuse himself after Conan was over and the infomercials took over the airwaves. He discovered Googling. He Googled himself first. But, alas, Googling himself soon grew boring, too. He couldn't shake thoughts of Tulah.

One particularly morose night, while Googling, Rowdy discovered eBay. Never one to shy away from a pursuit that could mildly boost his ego, he switched from Googling and eBayed himself. He was there, too! Someone named "Ticklemypie73" was selling "A Rowdy Ghost Named Vander in a Light Green Brooch". So the three words "Rowdy", "Vander", and "Light" were in an eBay listing. Interesting.

The brooch was an ugly piece, but the bidding was at an astronomical three thousand and fifty-eight dollars.

Rowdy wasn't completely clueless about life outside of Brokenoggin. Mortals loved anything they felt would connect them to the spiritual world. He searched on eBay for such words as haunted, charmed, bewitched, and cursed, among others and found a large amount of crap for auction with huge bids. What fools those mortals be! And how rich he could be! Maybe asking Tulah for a date would be easier if he had financial means. He didn't have looks that was for sure. He was a centaur who wore baggy pants and looked too much like Napoleon Dynamite. Tulah might look past his humble face and huge glasses, and lower half that resembled more Seabiscuit than Secretariat. With wealth,

Tulah might overlook his unfortunate physical attributes.

Brokenoggin had far more than its fair share of haunted, charmed, cursed, and bewitched crap. Yet, he had to be responsible. Nothing that was still haunted, charmed, cursed, or bewitched could leave the town. But stuff that was once involved within the tangents of the metaphysical would be safe and would sell faster than Godiva's delicious sugar maple nipple tips!

Such was it that when no one was looking, Rowdy Vanderlight mild of manner and dependable UPS driver, silently gathered the detritus of Brokenoggin and secretly put them up for auction on eBay.

In seven days after the auctions ended, the money rolled in, causing Rowdy to scratch the bushy dark curls on his head and face another dilemma: mailing the items. He couldn't do UPS. Might not be a good idea. He had never been to the Brokenoggin post office since the new postmistress arrived some weeks ago causing quite a stir among some of the more confident gents in town. Even Joe the veterinarian, who'd gone out and captured some spoiled Wyvern and had it caged in a backroom of his office, looked positively smitten every time he strolled toward the post office, a box under his arm. And when he drove the big brown truck through town, Rowdy never failed to notice Gavin-the-warlock practically floating back down Main Street after leaving the post office.

Rowdy had to go there. His stable-living room combo was covered with boxes that had to be mailed. Monies had been paid to him. People expected to get their haunted crap. He had to go. He had to be indifferent. Should the new postmistress live up to the bawdy talk by Gavin and the other townsmen, Rowdy had to keep his cool and think of Tulah. She was the only woman for him, even if she didn't know it

What a dilemma!

Early the next morning, on his day off, after Rowdy

changed the straw in the bathroom and shoveled out the old into a trash can in back of the house he made his way to the post office. Practically galloped there. He almost literally ran into Gavin who stormed out of the small box of a building.

"She's damn Viagra, I tell ya!" Gavin shouted into Rowdy's face.

Blinking at the wave of steak and onion breath that shunted out of the often naked wizard's mouth, Rowdy asked, "Who?"

Gavin—who, according to some of the town's lady witches, hardly needed help getting a chubby—hooked a thumb in the direction of the post office. "In there." He regarded the boxes Rowdy held with a death grip in his arms. "Forget your truck?"

"Huh?" Rowdy glanced at the boxes.

"Well, good luck," Gavin said, looking woefully across the street at the Wicked Pea Diner. "Stop by sometime. You might need a spell or something I can help you with." He nodded at the diner, with its seizure-inducing flickering neon 'open' sign. "I need steak…"

Gavin thrust his hands into his pants pockets and walked across the street barely avoiding the dozens of marble-sized droppings left by the Chihuahua herd on a pre-dawn run.

The witch-warlock-wizard or whatever he was had no idea the troubles Rowdy had. Sure, he was the only real male spell-caster in a town full of women known for their spells, but he at least had some of his own kind around…

Rowdy drew in a deep breath and clutched his boxes tighter. He used his fingertips to grab the brass handle of the post office's glass door.

Inside, a fluorescent bar light sizzled overhead lending a sickly institutional glow to the small space bisected with a pock-marked wooden counter. Worn mangy velvet ropes hooked to dull brass stanchions made up a U-shaped path to the counter. Stupidly Rowdy complied with the rat maze even though he was the only half-human there. In Brokenoggin Falls, humans were rare and usually ran out of town screaming.

As Rowdy obeyed the velvet ropes he glanced down at the boxes, taking in great sniffs of the air's pungent scent: old paper, glue, and sauerkraut. Sauerkraut?

"May I help you?" The raspy female voice bid him to look up from his parcels.

Oh no. Gavin was right. Viagra for the eyes.

Heat began to rise up from his loins, which were an impressive sight or so he'd been told. He hoped his baggy pants would conceal his inner thoughts about the vixen behind the counter. Rowdy squeezed his eyes shut.

"May I help you?"

He slowly opened his eyes. She was a sexual goddess. If he didn't control himself and soon, he would burst through his khakis.

"Yes," he said stiffly placing the packages on the pock-marked counter. "I'd like to mail these."

Goddess stared at him with glassy, mesmerizing emerald eyes. Her mane of auburn and blonde-streaked hair glistened even in the sparse fluorescent light. One thick lock tippled an arched brow over those gem eyes drawing him in. The heat grew again. She had to be human; she was a civil servant after all.

Goddess broke her stare and looked indifferently at the trio of boxes.

"Anything liquid, perishable, or potentially hazardous?" she asked.

Liquid? One box held a lawn gnome that had been pissed on by a werewolf. The werewolf whiz had dried. Not liquid.

Perishable? Rowdy considered that carefully. Another

box held a dozen of Godiva's maple sugar nipples guaranteed to grow hair-down-there if bushiness was desired. The candy was a favorite among fairies who were generally hairless and not happy to have their privates chilled in the Michigan winter. Rowdy had pocketed these from the windowsill where they cooled, such a cliché, before Godiva had a chance to place a spell on them. Safe for humans, but not really perishable.

Potentially hazardous? The last box contained a white birch root flattened when the Wyvern farted on it. The "dragon" root could be hazardous. The wood still contained the beast's stench. It had sold for quite a lot to a woman in Northern California who dealt in rare herbs. Potentially hazardous? Rowdy had to ponder that one.

"Mr. Vanderlight, do you wish to mail these packages or not?"

"I do, but the question perplexes me." And she knew his name. How?

"Do these packages contain anything liquid?"

"No." Her eyes looked like they had an inner fire. He felt warmth in his impressive loins again.

"Perishable?"

"No." It was growing, pressing into the back of the zipper.

"Potentially hazardous."

He thumped his foot on the floor. Joe'd been right during his last vet checkup. He needed new shoes; something felt loose down there.

"Potentially hazardous?" Her eyes flashed.

"YES!" Rowdy shouted. And he didn't mean anything in the boxes. He scooped up the packages and wrenched around. One of the boxes, the one with the white birch root, shot out from his arms and thudded to the floor.

Rowdy whinnied in frustration, dropped down and scrambled across the cracked grey linoleum floor.

The strong sent of sauerkraut and sudden eclipsing of the fluorescent light caused him to quickly realize that he was not the only one on the public side of the counter.

A puffy pink hand reached down and snatched the package up from the floor. Rowdy looked up from his prone position at the Goddess, whose emerald eyes flashed seductively at him. Her lips, painted in pearly bright pink lipstick, widened into a lovely smile that made Rowdy's large attribute twitch. He quickly looked away willing it to twitch no more.

"Please rise, Mr. Vanderlight." Her voice was as seductive as it was commanding.

Rowdy, clutching his other two packages, did as the beauty bade him. Once to his hooves he kept his gaze to the floor.

"You cannot harm me, Mr. Vanderlight," Goddess said. "Please look at me. I don't bite…hard."

Rowdy belted out a loud neigh that sounded more like the squawk of a demented crow. He looked up at Goddess.

"Look at me, Mr. Vanderlight," she said huskily. "All over."

Rowdy began with her eyes, quickly sliding his gaze to her pink lips, down her neck and her cotton postal uniform of pale blue with darker blue pinstripes with a red, white, and blue patch of an eagle's head. The blouse buttons strained to their limits, tenaciously holding more than generous breasts from bursting forth and sending the eagle soaring from its fleshy outcropping. Rowdy was a breast man and the goddess had given him an eyeful and second helpings to boot with the civil servant before him. Yet, as he dragged his gaze away from her *mammaries stupendi*, he quickly learned why Gavin had recently admitted to be a "booty man". Goddess had booty, hips and booty, and she didn't need a long swishy tail to turn him on!

Other than about Tulah, Rowdy never thought with

exclamation points about a woman. Suppressing such thoughts kept the fire in his loins doused, but the pilot light always burned.

"That's right, Mr. Vanderlight, nothing but you at present is excited."

"I am not," he said.

"Your pants are telling me a different story."

Rowdy looked down at the front of his baggy Dockers. Was that the tip of his impressive appendage sticking out a little over the waistband?

"Who are you?" he asked.

"Potentially hazardous," she replied, or at least that's what Rowdy thought she said.

"I beg your pardon?"

"Portentia Harmonious."

"So you're not a postal worker?"

"When I need to be."

The buzz of the fluorescent lights was the only sound in the silence that followed.

Rowdy still held his packages. Being a practical man and not one to steal from the parties who were expecting his wares, he asked, "So, there's no one here to help me mail my packages?"

Portentia sighed and rolled her eyes. "Those buyers are not human. They are protecting the stupid mortals. Your eBay seller I.D. red-flagged you, Mr. Vanderlight."

"BrokenogginPonyBoy?"

"Duh…Yes. You should know better than to foist your town's unique trinkets on mortals salivating for proof that folk like us exist. A man with your particular attributes shouldn't spend time Googling himself. You have much to share."

"That is none of your business."

"I offer you a solution for your problem with Tulah."

"That certainly is none of your concern."

"It is all of our concern when you nearly unleash mayhem on mortals, Mr. Vanderlight. Come, we're going on a picnic."

"It's morning," he protested. Then curiosity gripped him. "Where?"

"You know the place. I'll drive."

They stepped out of the post office just as Gavin exited the Wicked Pea.

The warlock's mouth dropped open. Rowdy offered him a shrug as Portentia escorted him to her massive black Cadillac SUV.

***

Rowdy looked through the windshield at the police cruiser parked beside the entrance sign to Brokenoggin Falls National Forest.

"Janice is here...somewhere," Rowdy said leaping down from Portentia's SUV.

"I'd like a bright shiny light on top of my SUV like that," she said.

"You want to go into law enforcement now?" Rowdy imagined Portentia pinning down a suspect with those breasts and handcuffing him until he was helpless—

"It would be an appropriate diversion for me," she said hefting a wicker picnic basket from the back seat of her vehicle. "You were thinking it."

Rowdy held up his hands. "OK, look, Miss Harmonious, I need to know right now what you are and why you are here."

"Bluntly put, Mr. Vanderlight, I'm your sex therapist."

"I didn't call for any sex therapist," he protested taking the basket from her. He was still a gentleman after all. "You're wasting your time."

"You are a very silly man. Come along."

Portentia hooked a finger in the direction of a narrow path barely distinguishable from the plain path that led to the dilapidated picnic shelter just a smidgen of a mile from the parking area.

"Don't you want to take that path?" he asked.

"You want me to, but that's not the path you often take, Mr. Vanderlight."

How the hell did she know that?

Portentia walked ahead of him, her booty giving him a show. He was helpless to do anything but follow while carrying that ridiculous picnic basket.

Portentia was leading him to that place beside the lake where the Wyvern dwelled. This was dangerous. He had never brought anyone with him when he visited the open space by the lake. He loved to gallop freely, stretch his legs, and race off his frustration at not having a love of his own.

"Don't look so nervous," Portentia said. "This is for your own good."

"Who sent you?" he demanded, voice beginning to get shrill. "Was it that witch Claudia?"

"No." Portentia continued walking toward a rocky outcropping bordering the northern edge of the lake.

"Godiva?"

"No."

Rather than recite the entire population of Brokenoggin, Rowdy said, "Tell me or I'll stop right here."

"We've arrived." Portentia paused at one particular large and mossy rock. She turned and faced Rowdy with those shining emerald eyes. "Look into my eyes," she ordered. "What do you see?"

Mesmerized, Rowdy stared into Portentia's wide orbs. She was doing something, but he could not look away to see what. She had sucked him into some sparkly emerald field. The feeling overtaking him was warming, giving him confidence as if he was in Louisville beating all of the thoroughbreds and having the attention of all of Kentucky's eligible Southern sweethearts. That was comforting in itself.

Then he felt a cooling sensation, both refreshing and…pungent.

The vixen blinked.

Rowdy snapped out of Portentia's personal Emerald City.

He was naked, in full erection, and smeared with sauerkraut.

She was naked, too, and smeared with sauerkraut.

"I know what you're thinking," she said placing both hands on his shoulders.

She couldn't possibly.

"You're thinking that whipped cream is more traditional. It is for humans, but not for us."

"Traditional?" Rowdy asked. "Us? What exactly is about to occur?"

"This." Portentia took a very firm hold of his erection. She began stroking him with the sauerkraut lubricant. Warmth surged up from his toes, to his knees, along his thighs and to the only source of his pride—which Portentia now possessed.

"Stop," he gasped. "T-Tulah is—"

"Me, my darling," she whispered into his ear.

"Tulah? You?"

Portentia sheathed herself over him while they stood on the lake's edge. The carpet of pine needles provided good traction to this dance with Portentia—or Tulah—leading. She lifted her legs and wrapped them around his waist. Swishing his tail over her ankles, he held her which was no easy task. She was of Rubenesque proportions. Was Tulah that large?

"I've always wanted you," she whispered.

Then the aroma struck his nostrils with a stench like no other. The sauerkraut was cooking on her body. Steam rose from his sex therapist. The sauerkraut bubbled and simmered on his flesh.

"I want to love you, Rowdy. I have loved you, have changed for you. But first I had to temper my fire," Portentia said.

Then this woman lulled her head back as they both reached the achievement to end all achievements. Rowdy whinnied, and Portentia-Tulah laughed.

After the quaking stopped, she wriggled off of him.

Rowdy said the only thing that came to mind.

"I loathe sauerkraut."

"Well, we might try relish or chunky diced tomatoes, but sauerkraut works best."

She stepped away from him and gathered her postal uniform and the biggest pair of panties he had ever seen, her booty sling.

"I have to go now," she said placing her bundle of clothes under her arm. "But I'll meet you here tomorrow."

She turned away, paused, and looked back at him. "Do me a favor."

"Anything," he said breathlessly.

"Tell that veterinarian to release my half-brother from his cage or I'll shapeshift into his worst nightmare—a PETA activist."

"Go?" he asked. Where were his clothes? "But we just got started. I didn't know you were part dragon, Tulah...Portentia...whoever you are. I don't care! I love you!"

"Tomorrow," she said. "I've got to go. I promised my brother I'd pay his lair a call, check on things, bring in the papers and the mail, feed the goldfish." She winked at him. "Tomorrow, Rowdy, and don't forget to bring the sauerkraut. Without it to douse my heat I'll just burst into flame when our satisfaction comes."

Portentia-Tulah stepped into the lake. While holding her clothes she dove, head first, into the dark water.

Earl stood naked covered in congealed sauerkraut in

stunned silence waiting for his true love to surface. She didn't.

"I hate sauerkraut. I'll bring relish."

Just as light dawned in his muddled mind that the woman he had lusted after had given him the best sex he had ever had, a harsh female voice assaulted his reverie.

"Hands up and turn around."

Rowdy did as Janice ordered.

"Rowdy Vanderlight?" she asked. "What in the Sam hell are you doing?"

He could ask her the same question. Her hair was rumpled, her police uniform stained here and there with mud, and her lips were swollen and very pink as if she had been the main contender in a kissing contest. But he was the one who was naked and decorated in sauerkraut, and she was the one with the badge and the gun...and a ride back to town, so he kept his questions to himself.

"It's been a very full morning," he said.

Janice puffed a stray lock of hair away from her right eye. "Tell me about it. Need a ride?"

"Yes, please."

"Clothes?"

"I have no idea."

Janice peeled off her jacket and offered it to him. Rowdy tied it around his waist with the sleeves. "Thanks."

He walked beside her down the narrow path.

"May we make a stop at the market before you take me home?" he asked. "I need to purchase some relish."

Janice just shook her head. "Brokenoggin."

Rowdy smiled. He was glad it was not just a normal day.

"On second thought, Janice," he said handing her the jacket. "I'll just gallop around the lake for a while."

"Naked?"

"Free!" He kicked up his hooves and left her.

"You need a new shoe!" she shouted after him.

Later, Rowdy thought, and he would also speak to Joe about the Wyvern and its cage. For Portentia-Tulah. It was love. Sweet love.

***

Early the next morning, Emma Mincemeat banged on the post office door.

"It's eight-thirty!" she shouted into the glass. "You're supposed to be open!"

Joe walked past her. "A new postmistress is due in," he said.

"A new one? We just got a new person running the post office a few days ago."

"She's gone," Joe said sadly. "Ran off with Rowdy the UPS guy."

"Oh, that's just fine!" Emma shouted at him. "I need a money order for QVC!"

"You sound more stressed than usual, Emma," Joe observed.

"Well, you'd be too if you had twelve kids, Joe."

"I'd kill myself." He stopped and reconsidered his words. "Sorry. They're good kids."

"Most of them," she said while staring into the post office. "Some of them are telling me they're seeing things. Gotta get them to the doctor, check their eyes."

"What sort of things?"

Emma snorted in frustration and turned from the door. She looked Joe in the eyes. "Dead people."

Episode 1.7

FEED YOUR HEAD

or

The *Flaming* Faery Queen *Closeted* at the Bottom
of the Garden ~~Closet~~ *Tool Shed*

By

Patricia Rice

*In which Morgan (aka Morganna or Titania, depending on
her-his mood) is extremely upset because the werewolves'
vet, Joe, has not yet noticed him/her no matter how s/he
dresses (or doesn't dress), and our vampyre Seth has to have
a fang fixed.*

Patricia Rice is the award-winning author of forty romances,
including the slightly abnormal Magic historical series. Check her
latest releases at http://www.patriciarice.com.

With the agility of a trained athlete, Morgan walked backward on the center rafter of the tool shed at the bottom of Alice Fairweather's Wild Herb & Useful Weeds Garden. Artistically swinging her wings, she hummed acid rock from a tape Alice had left moldering in an old tape recorder on a back shelf. No Barbra Streisand for Morgan, uh uh. She was the very model of a modern major general.

Or Fairy Queen, if one must be factual about it. If only she had some fellow faeries to queen it over.

Well, she had half of one. She simply wasn't speaking to him these days.

"White Queen walking backward..." She did a double backflip down to Alice's new leather gardening gloves, neatly avoiding the trap of the birdnetting on the bench beside them.

"I am not shallow," she informed the mouse snacking on the grass seed bag. Morgan insisted on being labeled according to her rightful gender inclinations and not by the usual physical indicators. It wasn't as if anyone could see beyond her hair and wings anyway, and she made such a lovely queen. "He cannot call me shallow. I know all the classics. *All* of them, I tell you. I can boogaloo and slide, and Bette Midler would give the best years of her life for my vibrato."

The mouse didn't reply. The chihuahuas were chattier but they'd discovered a rat pack earlier and had gone yipping off on their own.

Settling into the cushiony couch provided by the glove's palm, Morgan fluttered her wings at the glass witch ball Alice had tactfully provided. "I tried subtle, and he didn't even notice." She examined the shimmering copper tracing on her wings, tastefully intertwined with silver and adorned with genuine turquoise.

Talking to one's self grew old, but she refused to come

out of the tool shed again. If her One True Love would not acknowledge her, she would pine away at home, where no one could see. Perhaps she could develop tuberculosis and perish dramatically. Or was that *Moulin Rouge?*

"If he likes green dragon scale so well, I'll show him scales!" Studying her reflection in the ball, she narrowed her spectacularly long-lashed eyes—one of her best features if she did say so herself—and pictured luminous dragon green.

The copper obligingly developed a rich blue-green patina.

"Makes me look like a garden gnome. Gross." With a flick of her well-manicured fingers, she created a flaming kaleidoscope of red, pink, and orange pulsating through the veins of her wings. "Better. The retro rhinestone Halston, I think." The adorable little pressed khaki mini-skirt and fitted jacket she'd chosen for her southwestern subtle look disappeared with a snap of her fingers, replaced by an iridescent silk and chiffon confection with a slit up the side to reveal the perfection of her silky legs. The rhinestone halter top emphasized the breadth of her shoulders.

"Not bad, not bad at all." She twirled around to catch her reflections in myriad chips of mirror. "No more catering to Jo-Jo, the tasteless wonder. Let him friggin' fag a wyvern and singe his baby blues," she sang in an increasingly operatic scale that would have rivaled Beverly Sills if Sills were a contralto.

Pleased with the result, Morgan added amplification and repeated the scale until the tool shed rang with echoes of *friggin' fag a wyvern.*

"Morgan, it's three in the damned AM. Put a sock in it. That doesn't even make sense," Alice shouted, before slamming the window on the perfect June evening.

"You need a man, Alice, honey," Morgan sang back. "I have the perfect ass I can supply."

Alice didn't reply. She'd probably plugged in her

earphones.

I am not shallow, Morgan repeated to herself, still stinging from Joe's rejection. Morgan knew Shakespeare. *Really* knew him, if you got her drift. Where did people think he came up with those drama queens he wrote about?

She'd been lovely as Titania. Perhaps she should go back to red...

No, the last time she'd tried red hair, a hummingbird tried to sip a hole in her head. She would stay with her gorgeous, gleaming golden tresses, blonde silk that would dance with moonlight, should she choose to come out of her closet.

No way. She was never coming out again. Dancing among the toadstools had lost some of its charisma since she'd moved to Brokenoggin. Perhaps it had been a trifle shortsighted to chuck Oberon and take Puck's suggestion to visit the New World. All she'd wanted was a little freedom to be who she was without all the stuffy expectations of Not So Gay Olde England.

Freedom was just another word for having nothing left to lose.

The damned Chihuahuas kept digging up the toadstools anyway. If it hadn't been for them, she might be with Joe right now, sharing that cozy bed he kept behind the doghouse.

So, she'd given the wa-was ass's heads. It hadn't killed them, had it? She could turn them back anytime she liked. Joe didn't have to be so...so *politically correct* about it. Ass's heads were traditional, weren't they? She could be more helpful with a little guidance. He didn't have to be so nasty about it.

Lost in deliberation over whether she should accessorize with silver or gold, Morgan leaped three feet off her glove at a solid *whump* against the side of the shed.

Could that be Joe, stricken with grief that she'd never

returned? Crawling on hands and knees to beg her back? Ready to admit that she wasn't an air-headed poopsickle who'd erased her brain with polish remover? As if she had any need of polish remover.

She blew on her nails and changed the color from turquoise to orange, then added adorable little red stars and half moons. Being a queen had its moments.

A werewolf howl outside the shed ended that pleasant reverie. So help her, if she'd told Sly (also known among the witches of Brokenoggin as Romeo; *puh-leeze!*) once, she'd told him into eternity that she didn't want him nibbling on the mushrooms! When she got finished with furface—

"You hell-born hound," an irritated—and obviously drunk—male voice shouted from outside the tool shed, "I'll drink your furry arteries dry if you don't get out from under my feet."

Hmmm, male. And she didn't immediately recognize the voice. It seemed somehow muffled. Was this an opportunity to make Joe jealous? Not that she cared if the stubborn dragon-lover had his eyebrows singed.

The werewolf growled a threat the drunken male didn't take seriously enough. Morgan truly didn't like bloodshed.

Flitting out of her tool shed closet into the moonlit night, Morgan tried to warn the stranger, but she could only emit a squeak of awe at the scene unfolding.

Staggering drunkenly through her magic mushrooms, Sheriff Janice's naked vampyre Seth tried to grab Sly by his muscular wolf neck. Morgan could have told him that was a bad move, but the two powerful males weren't paying her any attention as they dodged and weaved in their drunken dance.

She had to admit, Seth was a fabulous specimen of manhood, but blood made her nauseous, and he looked in a drinking mood. His fangs extended further as he finally gripped the wolf. No wonder his voice had been muffled.

She sighed and rolled her eyes as the inevitable occurred. Sly pissed on the vampyre's naked leg.

Slimed, Seth swore a blue streak and flung his prey hard against the tool shed's scarlet wall. A bit of the pink gingerbread Morgan had designed for the roof broke off. Sly yipped as he hit, but landed on all fours and sprang straight at Seth.

"Will the two of you cut that out?" Morgan called, flapping her wings as visibly as she could to catch the moonlight—and their attention. "I won't be able to bake brownies if you crush the damned mushrooms!"

As a pacifying effort, the command failed dismally.

The vampyre kicked the wolf and sent him sailing into the precious little turret Morgan had added to the shed's roof. The copper gnome mounted on the wind vane snapped, and Sly slid off the far side of the roof.

Before she could fly into a rage and kick the big fanged lummox where it hurt, Seth slid in the newly slimed mud, grabbed for the garden rake Alice had left leaning against the shed, and did a slippery little cha-cha before plunging headfirst into the marble birdbath jacuzzi Morgan had just installed in her latest makeover project.

The birdbath flew into the air, flipped over, and crashed down on Morgan's head. Actually, onto all of her. Trapped beneath the china bowl, she bounced off the porcelain like a bug under glass. "I'll stake you to the church tower for this!" she screamed, more shaken than hurt.

On the other side of the bowl, the vampyre groaned.

She thought she heard the disgusting sound of regurgitated stomach contents, but vampyres only drank blood, right? Had he been sucking a wino?

Not her concern. Flying upward at warp speed, she attempted to heave the bowl off of her, with no luck. Just because she had muscles didn't mean she knew how to use them.

"Get me out of here, bloodsucker! This is all your fault. So help me, if you've ripped one rhinestone off this collar, I'll sic the chihuahuas on you. You think werewolves are bad? Just wait until those—"

An unnatural howl of agony rattled her bowl.

Well, that ought to scatter any elves in the vicinity. Gnomes, too. A sick vampyre rated right up there with *fee, fi, fo, fum* as a fumigator.

Deciding on a different tactic, she got down on her silk-clad knees and pried the lid up from the bottom just enough to peek out. She wasn't about to blow her cover if Seth was hunting for blood.

He lay sprawled among the mushrooms, holding a gleaming white fang in one hand and attempting to shove it back in his mouth.

Since he didn't seem too interested in her, Morgan slipped from beneath the bowl and settled on a swaying lavender stalk to study the situation.

The mushroom bed might never recover.

Seth the Vampyre was one hunka, hunka burning masculinity—even with that nasty sawed-off stake in his chest.

And he was never going to get that fang back in without her help.

"Wanta talk about it?" She propped her newly polished fingernails beneath her chin and batted her lashes attractively.

The vampyre only growled and looked at her blankly. Uh oh, full moon amnesia. Morgan flipped a bit of fairy dust in Seth's direction, just enough to rattle his senses back in place.

"If that's you, Morgan, flit your fairy ass out of here." Holding his aching jaw, Seth rose from the muck. He located Morgan with natural instinct and scowled, not showing any gratitude at all for her helpfulness.

"A one-fanged vamp isn't frightening, sweetie." She straightened her newly madeover wings in the moonlight so he might better admire her artistic talent.

Apparently deciding she wasn't worth arguing with, he staggered to his feet and moaned again in pain. "Does this damned town have a dentist?"

"No, and I can't imagine one putting their hand in your mouth if they did," she said, almost with sympathy. He was totally awesome, after all, especially from her vantage point at knee height.

For a very brief moment, she contemplated whether Doc Joe might be equally well hung, but the thought of Doc Joe lit a different bulb. "I bet Jo-Jo knows how to fix fangs. He even brushes that damned wyvern's teeth."

"Jo-Jo?" Seth asked warily, clamping his hand over his mouth and muffling his voice even more than earlier. "The *vet?*" he asked in horror as he realized who she meant.

"Of course. He sticks his hand in fanged mouths all the time. Come on, I'll get him for you."

"I know where the vet is. I don't need your help." Seth started out of the mushroom patch.

"Good luck," she called, standing to show off her athletically trim figure. "It's a full moon tonight, so you won't find him home."

"It's always a full moon around here," Seth grumbled, turning to glare at her, although one eye had started to swell, giving him a malevolent look. "Don't tell me the damned vet is a werewolf too."

"Hardly." Morgan flew to land on Seth's luscious curls and settled in. "Compared to everyone else around here, he's the next best thing to straight. But he doesn't like to be found when he's busy."

"And he's busy at the full moon?" Seth asked suspiciously, turning in the direction of Morgan's hair-pulling. "Sounds like a were to me, and I've had enough of them for one night."

"Oh, and just who do you think takes care of those stupid weres when they go all testosterone crazy like Sly did tonight? Go right there at the church and head toward the graveyard."

"How do you know where to find him? I didn't think you ever came out of the tool shed. You a friend of his?"

"He barely knows I exist," Morgan complained. "He swatted at me as if I were a horsefly. And then I heard him tell Emma all blondes are shallow. He's so cute when he's being dumb."

"You're taking me to a *dumb* vet?" Seth growled. "All blondes aren't shallow, although I suppose a lot of shallow people might be blonde."

"I'm a natural blonde," Morgan insisted. "Except when I'm a natural redhead. And I am not shallow."

"Fey," he suggested generously.

"Fairy fey, and not shallow." Morgan flaunted her wings.

"Anyone who doesn't have anything better to do than paint stars on their fingers isn't exactly Nobel Prize winning material. Here's the graveyard. Where do I go now?"

"To hell would be good," Morgan suggested, disgruntled by his insult. "But I'm hoping maybe Joe will see me if I ride in on a patient. I make such a cute little bow on your curls." She tugged his hair again to steer him toward a barn at the back of the graveyard.

"Why do you like the guy if he ignores you?"

"He's cute."

"That's a shallow reason," Seth pointed out.

"He's kind," Morgan added with a slight growl of irritation. "He's occasionally smart."

"And?" Seth prodded.

"He-takes-care-of-creatures-who-can't-take-care-of-themselves-and-I-want-to-help-him-and-if-I-don't-have-some-company-soon-I-will-die." She spat out the words so fast that they all ran together, then held her breath to see if Seth would laugh. If he did, she would magick him so bad he'd wish he'd lost both fangs.

"All the witches around here make being a Fairy Queen tough, doesn't it?" he asked sympathetically. "With all that estrogen floating around, you'd be better off as a Fairy King."

"I found my king," she said with satisfaction. "There he is, behind the wyvern cage."

"Oh, shit." Seth stopped in his tracks as he saw the baby green dragon. "That thing hates me. He'll fry the damned town if I get any closer."

"Pish posh." Morgan blew a little fairy dust toward Joe's pet. "He'll sleep now. Come along, let's see what my darling can do for you."

"He's not your darling." Back in grumbling mode, Seth walked warily toward the cage. "And he doesn't look like much of a fairy to me."

Indeed, in his white lab coat, with his steel-rimmed spectacles, and that adorable lock of barely-brown hair in his eyes, Doc Joe looked like a scrumptious professor. It was the square jaw and brown eyes that slayed Morgan every time he glanced her away.

"Not everyone can be gorgeous enough to be a queen," she lectured. "But he's fey, all right. How else do you think he can tame a dragon?"

***

Startled when the wyvern fell asleep just as he was about to feed him, Dr. Joe glanced around suspiciously. He didn't fear any of the creatures that walked these woods at night, but he intended to hogtie the next joker who tried to feed chihuahuas to the dragon.

Watching the vampyre cross the graveyard, he relaxed. No joker there. Pity about that stake he carried with him, but it was beyond Joe's capacity to argue with Death.

His glance caught the gleam of a flaming orange-red bow in the vamypre's dark curls, and his gut knotted. *Morganna.*

It was impossible to ignore a flaming fairy queen, but Joe did his quiet best. He knew he wasn't Oberon-handsome or Puck-witty. He didn't have any of those qualities most worshipped by the fey. He couldn't recall a Barbra Streisand song if he was held at gunpoint. The only time he'd managed a dance move was when the harpy tried to claw him in a delicate area. If he was any more boring, he'd be a banker.

If he touched her without permission, Morganna could sizzle his innards into frog legs. No touching allowed.

"Seth?" he asked as the vampyre grew closer. "You need that black eye treated?"

Seth removed his hand from his mouth and held out a gleaming fang. "The eye will heal, but this won't."

Joe shuddered, just a little. He preferred to treat the living. But Brokenoggin had lately become a haven for the dead, it seemed, so he might as well learn to deal with it. He'd thought Seth a decent sort until he'd showed up with Morganna in his hair. Joe was doing his best to ignore that fact, although his insides twitched with jealousy.

"I haven't ordered any books on vampyre anatomy. You'll have to let me look in your mouth. I might not be able to help."

"He's being modest again," Morganna complained, posing with her wings upraised so Joe could see all of her splendid Halston gown.

Joe knew what a Halston gown was. He might be boring, but he was still fey.

He motioned Seth to sit on a stack of crates beside the barn where he stored supplies. Carrying the right feed and medicine for the variety of creatures in this town required a lot of space. He was just glad the living was cheap because creatures didn't often pay well. He had doubts about naked vampyres with memory problems summoning cash either. But he was in this business to help, not become rich.

"Open wide." He waited for Seth to open, then winced at the bloody hole where the fang ought to be. He tried to place a finger in Seth's mouth to test for a fang root, but powerful jaws clamped shut instantly. Joe was lucky he had fast reflexes or he'd be a nine-fingered vet. "You have to keep your mouth open," he admonished.

"I don't think I can," Seth said sheepishly. "It's instinct. I smell the blood and go for it."

"Ooo, lucky Janice," Morganna cooed, batting her eyelashes.

"Why are you here, Morgan?" Joe demanded in annoyance. The last thing he wanted to do was look incompetent in front of his queen.

"To help?" she asked with a big smile. "What do I have to do to win a Nobel Prize?"

"Be a world-class humanitarian, which we all know you're not." Another reason he needed to stay far clear of Morganna. She could turn him into an ass with one angry swish, and he was bound to say something she didn't like.

"Why don't I start small as a vampyre humanitarian."

To Joe's startlement, she dropped fairy dust on Seth's nose. Instantly sleepy, the vampyre tilted from the crate, and Joe had to grab him to hold him up.

"Oops." With what might have been genuine apology, Morganna flitted down to examine Seth's sleeping features. "I should have waited until he was lying down, sorry."

"I can't put my fingers in his mouth while I'm holding him up." Joe shifted his feet to keep from falling over beneath the bigger man's weight. "Get someone to help me lay him out."

"Oh, c'mon, big boy. You and me can do it together."

To Joe's shock, the Fairy Queen darted beneath the vampyre's other shoulder and took some of his weight. A crate slipped as they lowered him toward the ground. Joe winced. Seth would have a sore bum in the morning. Or tomorrow evening, when he woke. But with Morganna's help, the sleeping vampyre sprawled safely on the grass.

"If I'd known you could carry weight like that, I'd have called you to help me with the wyvern." Dusting off his hands, Joe tried to study the vampyre and not the fairy flitting lazily near his ear.

"Now what?" Morganna landed on Joe's shoulder.

It was a trifle difficult to ignore a flaming fairy queen breathing on his neck. She smelled of cherry tarts, his favorite dessert. And there was something…exciting…about the flutter of delicate wings blowing on his ear.

"I have to pry his mouth open, shine a light in there, and poke around to see how the fang attaches. I need three hands, minimum, now that he's out."

"Better three hands than nine fingers," Morganna taunted. "Hold him open and let's see what's in there."

He heard her gagging as he pried the vampyre's mouth open. He was used to the stench of blood, but Morganna wouldn't be. "This won't work. Fetch Janice. She can help me."

"It could take me the rest of the night to find Janice. Am I right, or does Fangtooth there not dissolve at sunrise?"

"I have no idea. I've never asked. Maybe I can put something in his mouth to hold it open while I look. You can hold a flashlight for me."

He could almost feel the burn from her look of scorn.

"Forget your fairy light, Jo-Jo? Forget what you really are, big boy? Is that what this is all about? Pretending to be a regular old run-of-the-mill vet who just happens to pet dragons?"

Yeah, he was doing his damndest to forget that and a lot

of other things, like sex. Damned inconvenient for his sort around here.

"Look at me!" Joe protested, roused to frustration with the nagging gnat. "Do I look like I can dance on toadstools? I have two left feet. I croak like a frog. I *like* white lab coats. I'm happy petting dragons. What do you want me to do, get down on my knees and pretend I can tickle gnomes? And flowers make me sneeze. It doesn't matter who my mother was, I'm no more fey than Seth there."

Morganna swatted his nose with her wings until he sneezed. Dodging her irate assault, Joe attempted to look inside the vampyre's gaping mouth. Seth snored, spattering his spectacles with blood.

"Hold him still," Morganna said with resignation. "If he splatters me just once...I swear, I'll plant him with my toadstools." She darted down to sit on Seth's lip and sent Joe a pathetic look that nearly broke his heart. "I'm really not shallow, am I?"

"*Shallow?* Morganna, you're sitting on a guy's fang wearing Halston and asking me that? Will you just look in there and tell me what you see before he inhales, and I have to cut out his entrails to fish you out?"

She visibly brightened. Fairy lights were clever as well as useful. "You'd do that for me? That's sweet. You'll see, I'll be very handy to have around."

Before he could find a horrified reply, she ducked into Seth's mouth, taking her light with her.

Kneeling on the ground, propping the vampyre's mouth open, Joe could easily see the jagged edge where the fang should be in the light Morganna cast. She was starting to turn green at all the blood, a true sign of devotion if he ever saw one. Green was definitely not her color. "Okay, I can do this. There aren't any nerve endings or muscles involved, just that duct. Get out of there before you get hurt."

"I'll hold the fang while you do whatever you have to

do to glue it back," she insisted.

"Out, Morganna, or so help me—"

Seth yawned.

Without thinking of the consequences of grabbing a fairy, Joe snatched Morganna from the vampyre's mouth before she could be sucked down. His big hand wrapped around her fragile body, and a flutter of excitement shook him as her wings teased his palm. The sparkle of fairy dust spattered his skin like a million fireflies.

He opened up his hand to see Morganna sitting in the center, lazily flapping red-gold wings and smiling seductively up at him. Fairy light glowed in a golden halo that enhanced her hair and played havoc with his mind. He'd never held a queen before.

"Honey, you and me are gonna have a real good time," she purred.

"Do I have a choice?" he asked, feeling the fairy dust already coursing through his blood, exciting lower parts untouched far longer than he wished to remember. The throbbing magic pounded in his head, and the thrill of possession was about to overrule reason.

"Of course you have a choice, big boy." She lay down on his palm, wiggled temptingly, and kicked her Manolos. "That's what faeries do, offer choices. My size or yours?"

Visions of flitting through the flowers with Morganna at his side danced in his head.

Visions of baby wyverns frying them in flames burned up that fantasy.

"Why me, Morgan?" he asked, feeling the magic penetrating, stripping away all the inhibitions he'd used as a shield for so long.

"Because you care," she said honestly. "Because I need someone who cares."

"And you think I don't?"

She looked at him sadly. "I don't think you care about

me, but I care about you. Want me to reverse the spell?"

"I can't help Seth if I'm small," he reminded her, clinging to what remained of his rapidly diminishing practicality. Lust crazed his mind.

"All right.   For now," Morganna whispered softly. "Later, we'll try the tool shed on for size. I have a lovely glove where we can cuddle."

To the shock of Joe's whirling senses, Morganna darted into the air, spun around, and an instant later, stood beside him in white lab coat—with pink satin collar—wings hidden, but whiskers starting to shadow a handsome jaw. Morgan gathered up his thick golden hair in a diamond clasp and winked when Joe stared.

"I hope that fang glue dries quickly," Morgan murmured seductively. "I hate wasting fairy dust."

Joe never quite remembered how he replaced a vampyre's tooth, but he had lots of fine memories of a birdbath Jacuzzi to take home with him the next morning.

Episode 1.8

A SPELL OF C.R.A.F.T.
(Can't Remember A F***ing Thing)

By

Vicki Lewis Thompson

In which Emma, mother of 12 and one of Brokenoggin's few truly human residents, casts a spell and everyone except the amnesiac vampyre Seth gets amnesia.

Vicki Lewis Thompson is the New York Times bestselling author of more than seventy contemporary romances and one wild paranormal story – this one! You can find out more about Vicki and her books at http://www.vickilewisthompson.com and you can email her at VLT_Author@aol.com.

Emma Mincemeat slipped into Spellbound Books at ten in the morning and inhaled the scent of freshly brewed coffee. She would love a cup, would love to sit and munch on a brownie, too, but she didn't dare. She had to make her purchase and leave before somebody spotted her.

One moist brownie…her mouth watered at the thought. She was certain they put something in the mix, some secret ingredient that made her feel wild and uninhibited, but she'd never asked what it was. Better not to know.

The bookstore's owner, Jacob Flyleaf, wouldn't tell her, anyway.   She wasn't like the rest of the population in Brokenoggin Falls. She was *different*. Emma hated that.

But ten years ago, Peter had insisted on investing in real estate here. He'd claimed it would appreciate, but of course, it hadn't. Peter didn't care because he fit in. That thing Peter could do when he was in the mood—changing into a black panther—was valued for some ungodly reason.

All twelve of her children were accepted, too, even little Hortense, who had seemed so ordinary until she'd turned three and started speaking in some language Emma had never heard before, not even in Brooklyn. They all apparently took after Peter's side.

Emma knew of one other person in town who claimed to be normal—Alice Fairweather. But Alice just happened to be over for tea one afternoon when Peter decided to shape-shift as a practical joke. Alice had run screaming from the house and refused to come back, no matter how many times Emma called to explain that Peter wouldn't ever do that during teatime again.

That left Emma feeling more isolated than ever, but today she planned to do something about that. She'd cased Spellbound Books for days to figure out when business was the slowest and Jacob Flyleaf would be alone. Fortunately, Jacob didn't gossip about a customer's purchase. A tongue-knotting curse had struck him mute at the age of thirty.

The book she needed was on the fourth aisle, two-thirds of the way down, second shelf, with a bright yellow spine. That book was her salvation, a chance to feel less like a freak in Brokenoggin Falls, and today it would become hers.

She'd just pulled the book off the shelf when who should come bouncing into the bookstore but Maria Drinkwater.

"Emma!" she called out. "Hi, there!"

Damn it. Emma embraced the book, holding it against her generous bosom in an attempt to hide the cover. "Hello, Maria."

"It's good to see you." Maria's tone was patronizing, as always. She thought a person with no magical powers was beneath her. "What have you got there?"

"A cookbook," Emma said.

"Well, of course you do, with all those children to feed. You probably use a stove and actual groceries to make meals. How quaint."

Emma clenched her jaw. "Yes, isn't it." She was through being insulted by the likes of Maria. By tonight, she'd have engineered a centerfold figure like Maria's and a vasectomy for Peter. He wouldn't consider the surgical kind, but there were other ways, and this book would explain them.

"Well, I'm here for the coffee and brownies." Maria smiled her superior smile. "I'm supposed to meet Juan later, and the brownies have that wonderful aphrodisiac quality. Have you noticed?"

"Um, yes." Emma blamed both her eleventh and twelfth child on those brownies.

"Are you having any, Emma?"

"Not today." Emma edged toward the checkout counter, keeping her book hidden as best she could.

"All righty, then." Maria strolled toward the cozy nook

where the coffee and brownies were served. She kept glancing back to see if Emma would lay the book on the counter so she could get a look at it.

When Maria nestled into a plump easy chair and picked up the plate of brownies, Emma set her book on the counter, which activated an alarm in Jacob's office. He scurried out, took one look at the book and waggled his eyebrows at Emma. Sheesh. You would think she was buying porn.

Instead of responding, she looked bored and drummed her fingers on the counter. Jacob shrugged and scanned the bar code into his computer with his index finger. In seconds, she'd paid for the book and was out the door. *Witchcraft for Dummies* was hers!

***

Late that night she sat alone at the kitchen table mixing the ingredients she'd gathered secretly during the day. Pots of this and kettles of that simmered on the stove. The stench was horrendous, but fortunately the Body Bodacious Potion was nearly done.

Next, she'd brew the Spermatozoa Silencer Charm for Peter. She'd thought of doing that one first, to be safe, but vanity won out. She could hardly wait to get rid of her saggy boobs and her lumpy waistline. Twelve children took a lot out of a person and left some unwanted bits behind. And speaking of behinds, hers would be the envy of every woman in Brokenoggin Falls.

Consulting her book once again, she discovered that she was required to take the potion out into the moonlight and drink it there. Emma crept quietly into the backyard where there was, conveniently, a full moon shining. She wasn't sure, but it seemed as if this place had more full moons than Brooklyn.

If the potion tasted as vile as it smelled, she'd better go over by the well and draw up a bucket of fresh water. She set the vial on the edge of the well while she lowered the bucket into the well.

As she pulled up the dripping bucket, two toads hopped out startling her so much she nearly knocked over the vial. Fortunately, she grabbed it in time. Then she raised it to her lips and pinched her nose to keep the fumes from making her gag.

But before she had taken so much as a sip, Mavis Gap, the nosiest woman in all of Brokenoggin Falls, popped her head over the back fence. Mavis did readings, and it was no wonder they were accurate. She spied on everybody in town.

"Emma!" Mavis didn't bother to keep her voice down, either. "I thought I heard someone out and about back there! What's up?"

"Just felt the need for a drink of fresh water, Mavis." Emma lowered the vial and tried to hide it behind the bucket, but the damned full moon was making secrecy very difficult.

Mavis was another woman Emma loved to hate. She was only thirty, or so she claimed. In this town, people could be three hundred years old and look thirty. In any case, Mavis looked thirty...and gorgeous. It just wasn't fair.

"It appeared to me as if you were about to drink something besides water," Mavis said. "I could use a stiff one, myself." She laughed. "A drink, that is. The other kind is easy enough to get around here, but good liquor is hard to find."

"It's...something for a headache," Emma said. "I don't—"

A third frog leaped from the bucket onto the stone ledge surrounding the well.

Emma yelled as the frog crashed into the vial. She nearly fell in as she made a frantic grab for it and missed. The vial seemed to tumble in slow motion over the side and down into the black depths where it landed with a hollow splash at the bottom.

***

Emma finally got rid of Mavis, but by the time she returned to her kitchen she was too tired and disheartened to start over. She'd tackle the whole thing tomorrow night. After cleaning the kitchen, she crawled into bed beside her sleeping husband, but she didn't cuddle. A hot summer night was not the time to snuggle in with her man, especially because he was presently covered in black fur, which often happened during the full moon.

He did, however, want to cuddle with her, which led to other things. She had to admit that the sex was more exciting when Peter turned himself into a big black cat. If only he would refrain from biting her neck while he was thrusting, she'd enjoy the session even more. Still, all-in-all, she couldn't complain. As for Peter, he went to sleep purring.

***

By about eleven the next morning, Emma decided she was going senile. She ended up at the local witch store but couldn't remember what she needed there. Then she glimpsed a woman in a police uniform wandering the aisles. She looked familiar to Emma, but no name popped into her head.

Come to think of it, Emma wasn't sure what her own name was. Because the woman in the police uniform looked familiar, and because police were supposed to help citizens in trouble, Emma confronted her in the roots and berries aisle.

"Do you know who I am?" Emma asked.

"You look familiar," said the policewoman. "Are you somebody I should know?"

"I was hoping you could tell me my name," Emma said.

"I wish I could." The policewoman shook her head. "But lately I can't even remember my own, let alone other people's."

"But you're an officer of the law. You're supposed to know things."

The woman looked down at her uniform. "I must be a cop, since I'm dressed like this. So why am I in the witch store? There must be a reason. I—oh, *hello, there*." She glanced over Emma's shoulder.

Emma turned to discover a naked man standing behind her, a naked man with fangs, no less. Even more peculiar, he had a stake through his chest. Emma cleared her throat. "Who are you?"

"You don't know, either?" The man looked upset.

The policewoman shouldered her way past Emma and planted herself in front of the man. "I don't know, and I don't care. You're one fine specimen, I can see that much." Her glance dropped to his crotch. "Oh, hey, you respond to compliments. Excellent."

"Ignore that, Janice." The man waved a hand at his erection, which was only slightly smaller than the chunk of wood in his chest. "Listen, something serious is going on here. Everybody's losing their memory. It looks like the town's been put under a spell of C.R.A.F.T."

"Sounds very serious," said the woman who was apparently named Janice. Keeping her attention firmly on his penis, she linked her arm through his. "Let's go back to my place and talk about it, shall we?"

"What kind of spell?" Emma asked.

"C.R.A.F.T." said the man. "Can't Remember A Fucking Thing."

Emma gasped. She never used that word except in the privacy of her bedroom when she was engaged in the act.

"My apologies for the language, Emma," the man said. "But that's what this looks like."

Emma stared at him and struggled to make sense of it all while she tried desperately to avoid staring at his penis the way this Janice person was doing. "You know our names?"

"Yes. I'd already lost my memory, so the spell has the opposite effect on me." He sighed. "I wish it didn't. My memories are coming back and that's what's causing this." He pointed to his erection.

Emma figured she could look at it without being rude now that he was directing her attention there. It was impressive, with veins standing out and everything. "You must have some kind of memories!"

Janice tugged on his arm. "Let's go make some more, honey bun."

The man resisted her tug. "Believe me, I do have potent memories. Apparently I've been a very naughty little vampyre."

"My favorite kind." Janice slid an arm around his waist. "Forget my place. Let's slip into the back room of this fine establishment and do it on the floor."

"And risk me getting killed again? No thanks." The vampyre turned Janice toward the front of the store. "Besides, you're supposed to be investigating a theft of dragon's breath, which is probably why you're here. I'm guessing the C.R.A.F.T. potion got into the town's water supply somehow, so after the first cup or two of coffee, it began to take hold. If I'm right, it was a diluted dose, so it should start wearing off soon."

"I'd like to go home and wait for that to happen," Emma said. "Can you point me in the right direction?"

"Sure." The vampyre walked her to the front of the store and pointed out her house six doors down on the left.

Feeling extremely disoriented, Emma walked home, in the door and back to the kitchen.

A man was sitting there reading a bright yellow book. He glanced up when she came in. "There you are," he said. "Just in time. I haven't had a good roll in the hay since I can remember. Let's go upstairs and have sex all afternoon."

Emma discovered she wanted to do that, too, but she had a vague feeling she had responsibilities. "Are we alone?"

"We are, now. There were twelve kids hanging around, but I sent them all to the movies. The older ones can look out for the younger ones."

That sounded okay to Emma. "Did they...um...drink any water this morning, do you know?"

"Are you kidding? They're kids! They don't drink water. They had Grapalicious Goo-Goo juice. There was a ton of it in the refrigerator." He stood and held out his hand. "Come on. I want you naked and squirming in five minutes."

Although Emma was more than willing because she hadn't had sex in ages, either, another vague thought came to her. "What if I get pregnant?"

"Who cares?" He closed the book with a slap of pages. "It's about time you had a kid, don't you think?"

"Maybe so." She glanced at the book. "What is that book, anyway?"

"Just something I found tucked in the closet upstairs when I was looking for my socks, which I never did find, by the way. It's *Witchcraft for Dummies*. I don't know where it came from."

"Neither do I." Emma stared at the book, trying to think why it would be in the closet.

"One of the pages was turned down, so I read that one. It had two spells on it, one called Bodies Bodacious, and the other one called C.R.A.F.T., which stands for—"

"I know what it stands for," Emma said, blushing.

"Are you shy about such language?" the man asked.

Emma thought about it. The longer she gazed at him, the hotter she became. For some strange reason he reminded her of a panther. She started up the stairs.

"Not when I'm naked and squirming," she said over her shoulder.

Episode 1.9

NIGHT MARES

By

MaryJanice Davidson

At a birthday party for the Disdaine Triplets, the little darlings decide they aren't pleased with the party or the guests and use magic to create their own fun. That night the town and its residents are visited by the infamous Night Mares who wreak mayhem as only giant ponies prancing through houses can.
(Story & characters created by Lynn Warren)

MaryJanice Davidson is the author of the best selling author / creator of the "Undead" series. Find out more about her and her laugh out loud novels via her web site http://www.maryjanicedavidson.net/.

"**O**h, Gawd, this is soooooo boring!" Withering Disdaine cried.

"I didn't think it was possible," her sister Scornful began,

"But this both sucks and blows," her sister Derisive finished.

None of the triplets pointed out that the line had in fact, been stolen from Bart Simpson. The three sisters knew. In fact, they were liars, thieves, cheats, chronic complainers, hypochondriacs, swindlers, whiners, and (is this redundant?) pre-teens.

To put the cherry on top of their sundae of evil, they all planned to be student loan officers when they grew up.

Among other things.

Withering peeked out their bedroom window. Yep, the guests were still out there, milling around like they were waiting for an execution or something. Which, in this town, wasn't exactly out of the question. "Jeez," she said, striving for bored, but instead hitting grudgingly impressed, "looks like the whole town's out there."

"Wrecking the flowers, prob'ly. Mom'll have a fit." Derisive threw herself face down on her bed. "You'd think we'd be happy—we're eleven now." Since she was speaking directly into her pillow, a passer-by would have heard, "Mmm mmm mnnn phhhmm bbbb nnnn mmmmwww," but her sisters understood her perfectly. "Just a few more years until we can jettison our virginity and figure out what all the fuss is about."

"You'd *do* that with a boy?" Scornful gasped. "Urrrgggghhhh!"

Derisive sat up. "Well. In theory. I mean, right now, no way. Urrgggghhhh is right. But maybe someday. Look, how many people live in this town? And they're all boy crazy or girl crazy? They can't *all* be morons."

"Compared to us?"

"Compared to the general population," Derisive allowed. "There's got to be something more to it than those articles we've been reading. We're not old enough to figure it out yet, but when we are, we'll control that, too."

"I don't think *Food and Wine* is our best source for sex ed," Scornful pointed out.

"Well, that's all we could get. They're so damned overprotective of us. Us! We're going to be running this weird little town someday; the least they could do is treat us like adults." Derisive snatched the sky-blue ribbon (which perfectly matched her eyes) out of her butterscotch colored hair and flung it to the carpet, which was pink, and perfectly matched her rosy cheeks. "I mean look. Just *look*. Ribbons in our hair, braids! Jumpers! Pastels! *Knee socks!* We're not five anymore, for the love of Lucifer! We should be in training bras right this minute."

"No we shouldn't," Withering said, looking at her sister's flat chest and grinning.

"Oh, shut the hell up before I hex all your food—how'd you like everything to taste like dog shit?"

"With Mom's cooking, I probably wouldn't notice."

Derisive laughed; she couldn't help it. Meanwhile, Scornful had crept up on one of the twin beds (pastel yellow bedspread, matching yellow bedskirt) and peeked. "They aren't going anywhere," she announced. "They're waiting for 'the darling triplets'—"

"Barf."

"Puke."

"—to come out and do our little triplet song and dance, cut the cake, open presents, blah-blah. Aren't we cute? Haven't we grown? Aren't we just adorable?"

"Aren't we going to hurt someone? Aren't we going to blow something up? Aren't we in touch with our inner juvenile delinquents?"

"Well, let's get rid of 'em. I've got all the Barbie Dreamhouses I need. I want the new Beyoncé CD. I want the Catwoman DVD. I want to be the new LOTF."

"Co-LOTF," her sisters corrected.

"My point is, I do *not* want anything with a Mattel sticker on it. The madness ends here!" she cried, stomping a Mary Jane shod foot.

"We can't just 'get rid of 'em'."

Withering frowned, trying to work that one out. "You mean, we don't have the mystical ability, or we don't have the will, or we don't have the moral elasticity, or you don't want anybody to be seriously hurt, or—"

"The last one," Scornful said. "If we kill anybody else, Mom'll kill *us*. She carved it right into our desks with her fingernails, remember? 'Kill anyone else and I'll kill you'." She sighed fondly. "Tough love. It sucks, but it works."

"So, let's get rid of them without hurting them. You know—chase them away. Then we'll go through our stuff in *our* timeline, keep the good stuff, pitch the rest, have cake for supper, and figure out how to kneecap that annoying LOTF. Then maybe watch Season Two of The Simpsons."

"Season Three," Scornful said.

"Season Four," her sister corrected, and they compromised. Then Derisive added, "Good one, BTW, Withering. And here I thought you were just the pretty one."

"I *am* the pretty one, jerk. So how should we do it? Boils? Nettles? Insects? Girl Scouts?"

"Come on," Derisive said. "Even we're not *that* bad."

"I've got it. It's an outdoor party, poor suckers...let's drive them back to the homes. And then..."

"...when they think they're safe, their nights will be worse than their afternoons!"

"And mom can't nail us for it, because nobody will die," Scornful finished gleefully. "Heck, she can't even trace it back to us—any one of the freaks in this town could have done it, either on purpose or by accident."

"It's good to be us," Derisive chortled. She snatched a (pink) Kleenex out of the (pink) box on her desk, blew her nose into it, crumpled it, and dropped it. Withering leaned over and spat on it. Scornful stomped on it. The three girls held hands but, before they started to chant, Derisive had time for one more complaint. "Guys? How come black magic has to be so damned gross?"

* * *

After fleeing from the little darlings' outdoor birthday party, Claudia Choo bolted the doors and, exhausted from an afternoon of counterspells and running and more spells and trying not to get trampled, fell into a deep, dreamless sleep.

Or so she thought. Moments after her head hit the couch armrest (she wasn't sleeping in the marital bed because of, um, martial difficulties that really were no one's business and besides, where she slept was her business, and where was that fucking Earl, anyway?), a horrific crashing snapped her back awake.

"Oh thank God," she said to the giant black pony currently kicking up its heels in her breakfast nook. "Thanks for coming."

The pony stopped in mid-kick. *Pardon me?*

Is that my power, Claudia wondered, or the animal's? Is it projecting its thoughts into my mind, or did I unconsciously cast a—

The animal stomped to get her attention. *No, seriously. Why are you glad I'm here? Nobody's ever glad to see me, or my herd.*

"Maybe because of all the destruction of property and that sort of thing," she suggested.

We're not getting on your *case for wrecking the planet,* the pony thought at her reproachfully.

"Good one. There's lots of china in the cupboard to your left." Her wedding china, as a matter of fact. She tried not to sniffle. "Smash away."

Thanks. The pony—a striking creature of deepest, unshaded black, crashed about half-heartedly for a minute, then added, *It's not as much fun without people screaming and running and trying to chase me out with brooms or shotguns.*

"Sorry." She brightened. "I could conjure up a shotgun. I'm not so good at brooms, though—I missed that day in school."

No, it won't be the same. You never did answer me.

"Oh. Well, it's a long boring story, and I don't have any alcohol, so I'll give you the short version. My husband and I are—are sort of on the outs. I mean, he doesn't like me. He's wonderful and annoying and handsome and everything a wife could want. But I guess—I guess he doesn't like me anymore."

Why?

"I think it's because I'm barren. I can't give him any children. So when he married me..." She swallowed a sob. "He threw away his chance to be a father. I think he resents it. I think...he hates me."

That's too bad, the pony projected sympathetically. *Here. Maybe the noise will cheer you up.* It kicked over a china hutch and, Claudia had to admit, the resulting crash was satisfying.

"Thanks," she sniffed. "You seem like you take pride in your work."

Yes, that's true.

"Maybe I could be your helper? God knows I can't do anything right around here. Can't even make a baby...can't even cheat on my husband!"

We're full up, the pony said tactfully. *But I'll keep your name on file.*

"Thanks." She rested her forehead on her hands. Hands that had held Earl, stroked him in the dead of night.

Loved him. On memorable occasions, slapped him. *Oh, you bastard. I'd give anything to be free of you.*

What was that?

"Nothing. I wasn't talking to you."

The pony trotted into the living room, shaking dust off its glossy flanks. *Look, you seem like a nice enough person, for a slavering blood-thirsty member of the most rapacious species the planet has ever known.*

"Thanks," she said, cheering up.

So I'm going to help you out. First of all, things aren't as bad as they seem with Earl. It fact, the fix is laughably simple. You just need more information.

"But how can I—"

I'm talking now, if you please. Pay attention. For things to get better, you have to tell your dream to the Vampyre.

"What? I have to tell him what? Dream? You mean, when I go back to sleep I'll dream about Seth?"

Tell Seth about Janice's beast. It's very important: he must know about her beast.

"But what does that have to do with Earl and—"

Remember. People don't always remember. Or they attach no significance to it.

"I'll remember. But what does any of that have to do with—owww!"

Her neck hurt. Her neck hurt because she'd fallen asleep on the piece of shit couch they'd bought on her honeymoon, her neck *always* hurt when she slept on the thing, and she sat up and worked the kinks out, and looked around her spotless house. Kitchen—clean. Hutch—still standing. No pony. No nothing.

A dream.

Episode 1.10

DANCING IN THE STREAK

By

Lynn Warren

*In which our un-frocked warlock gets
his...ummm...comeuppance.*

Lynn Warren has known she wanted to be a writer from the
moment she stopped eating crayons. She is the author of a popular
Vampire Brothers series for Triskelion Publishing as well as the
paranormal series "Immortality Incorporated." Contact Lynn or
join her webloop via her web site at http://www.lynnwarren.net.

It was no secret that there was something not quite right about Brokenoggin Falls. The little hamlet looked like a normal town with paved streets, charming antique lampposts and sidewalks that meandered through the shops around town. The climate always reflected the season, but it never got too cold or too hot, the residents simply wouldn't allow that. Trees that seemed capable of touching the sky grew at an alarming rate along with gorgeous blooms of every shape and color for every season even though weeds never seemed to appear.

Everyone in Brokenoggin knew each other. It was a small place, really, full of charm and old world ideals. People born in Brokenoggin grew up and stayed in town. In fact, no one left. At least, not in anyone's recent memory. And the residents always lived a very long, long time.

And while those things might be considered a wee bit odd, that wasn't the most peculiar thing about Brokenoggin. No, the most peculiar thing about Brokenoggin Falls was the ladies some referred to as witches...

***

Gavin tossed the box down onto the bathroom counter along with his reading glasses. He was going to sue the fucking bastards.

All of them.

In fact, the more the merrier as far as he was concerned. Those evil sons of bitches at the pharmaceutical company didn't know who they were screwing around with, literally. Gavin moved away from the counter to examine himself in the mirror once more.

The full-length mirror concealed nothing and it was a good thing. Gavin wouldn't tolerate an imperfection and if he had one, well, he damn well was going to know about it beforehand.

He looked good. Even if he said so himself. Not many

forty-two year olds, looked as good as he did. He only lied about his age in public. Everyone in the neighborhood believed he was thirty-eight, so why destroy their illusions? Gavin was tall, lean and spent a good deal of time on a weight machine and swimming nude in his pool.

He liked his body. A lot. And he didn't mind showing it off as he did when he took his morning stroll around Brokenoggin, nude. His morning walk was a tradition in the neighborhood. Women kept their underage children inside and went to collect the morning paper themselves. He'd seen sexy girls pulling weeds early in the morning or pulling their trash barrels back into the garage. It made him swell with pride. But he hadn't gone yesterday and there was no way in hell he was walking outside today. Swelling was his problem.

Four hour chubby, my ass.

He'd had a goddamn steel pole for two days now and it wasn't showing any sign of deflating any time soon. Gavin ran his hands through his short, golden brown hair in frustration. He walked back over to the bathroom counter and examined the warning label on the box once more. No, there were no warnings that warlocks shouldn't take the drug. Ha! He had them by the balls.

Meanwhile, what the hell was he supposed to do? Running his hands through his hair again, Gavin glanced at the chaos around his home. His bedroom and bath had spellbooks lying all over the floor. He'd searched high and low for some sort of shrinkage spell. But all the specific spells resulted in permanent damage. He wasn't about to cause any damage to his prize equipment. Reaching for a pair of sweatpants, Gavin made a decision. He'd put some clothes on and go visit the witches. Maybe one of them had a potion or an herbal wrap or something. Because every spell he'd actually tried on his chubby only made it harder. What was worse was how horny he was. Gavin had never experienced such an insatiable desire before. It boggled his mind. No wonder he couldn't cast a decent spell. He needed to quench this desire before he could even begin to think clearly. Right now, he was so damn horny he could fuck every woman in the neighborhood and be ready for a second go round within minutes.

Slipping into a pair of navy sweats, he examined the tent pole protrusion. Oh, wasn't that just sexy? He couldn't go outside like this. No way. Gavin was a proud man. A warlock of esteem and probably the only sexy man in the neighborhood not tied up in knots over the witches of Brokenoggin.

He walked into the kitchen and poured himself a glass of orange juice. From his window, he could see several women milling about in their front yards waiting for something or someone. He drank half a glass of juice in two large swallows. They'd just have to wait. He wasn't going outside like this.

A knock on his front door nearly made Gavin spew juice across his granite countertops. Maybe if he didn't answer, the women would go away. Go back into their homes and put their little fantasies on a shelf somewhere for the next few days. At least for as long as it took him to get rid of the chubby.

The knock came again. This time more insistent and Gavin walked slowly into his living room. What was wrong with these women, anyway? His drapes were drawn, he hadn't been outside in two days. Why didn't they think he wasn't at home?

"Gavin! Gavin? Are you in there?"

He recognized that voice. It was Maria Drinkwater, a nosey little witch who somehow managed to entangle herself in as much gossip and mayhem as she could find around town. He drew the drapes tighter. He took a chance and peeked out of a small crack in the fabric.

"Son of a bitch!" Gavin leaped back as he saw the pale green eyes of Maria trying to peer into his house. "Get away from my house."

"Gavin, we're not going anywhere until you come out." Maria put her hands on her ample hips. "The girls and I have been waiting for two days for you to surface. You can't deprive us, Gavin. It's not nice."

Gavin poked his head through the curtain careful to keep the rest of his body concealed. "What are you talking about?"

Maria crooked her finger at him and pointed across the street where at least fifteen women of all ages and sizes gathered. Turning slowly, Maria pointed farther down the block where even more waited.

Gavin groaned. Some of them were even holding signs. He pressed his face up against the window and squinted to read one of them: *"Where's our hunk?"*

"Oh dear god…"

"So you see you've managed to create quite an event over the years. Now get your British ass out here so we can drool and then get on with our day."

Gavin pulled the drapes shut. "No! Now, go away."

"We're not leaving." Maria's happy little singsong voice was just enough to set his teeth on edge. "You might as well come out."

His lips twisted. His eyes narrowed to slits. "I'm not well," he yelled to Maria while his mind worked over scenarios.

"Gavin, you're gorgeous. You're always well, and *hot*."

His head tilted slightly. Maria'd always had a crush on him. Ever since the first time he'd strolled naked past her door, she'd practically thrown herself at him whenever the occasion arose. Well, now he'd risen to the occasion so to speak and there was no bloody way he'd let her get a look at him like this. The little witch would suck the come and probably the life right out of him.

Pacing in his foyer, Gavin considered his options. He could sit in his house and hide, hoping somehow this massive chubby would vanish on is own. On the other hand, he could bravely stride out his front door and fuck every woman in his path and work it down to a reasonable size.

Obviously, the latter was by far the more pleasurable idea. He wondered what the vivacious and voluptuous Miss Maria Drinkwater would think of such a thing. Would her sensibilities be offended or would she ride him like he was a wild stallion? Part of him wanted to find out. It really did. The other part of him didn't think it was a terribly good idea to mix magicks. Who knew what sort of catastrophe could come flying out at the moment of orgasm. He'd created many a wild storm in his youth while toying with the affections of witches. Gavin shook his head. He didn't need the excess aggravation.

Besides, what made him think it would go down anyway? He'd pleasured himself three times last night trying to get his rod to shrink and no luck. All it'd done was drive him nearly insane. He was so horny now his teeth clenched just to keep a lid on his baser needs. Now, his jaw hurt. His muscles ached and he wanted nothing more than to sink his cock into a tight, wet pussy.

"Gavin? Are you still there?"

"Yes." It was more a hiss than anything else, but he couldn't help it. He could practically smell the magic on her. He raised his head, his eyes lit with a realization that nearly blinded him. No matter what she said, the woman was a witch. She had been known, in the past, to stir the cauldron, so to speak...

"Gavin, are you coming—"

"No, but if you don't get out of here, you will be!" He flipped the locks both magical and mechanical on his front door. With one hand, he yanked the door open and with his other, he caught hold of Maria's wrist. He slammed the door behind her then whirled on the pretty witch. "Did you do this?"

He watched as her eyes turned predatory. She licked her lips as her gaze traveled down from his face, over his chest and settled on his rock hard rod. Gavin sighed; now he knew what women with those big gorgeous tits felt like. She gazed at him as if he was a big, juicy filet that she'd love to sink her teeth into and it made Gavin a bit uncomfortable.

"Stop that."

"Mmmm," Maria's mumble sounded more like a purr.

"*That*. Stop *that*."

She lifted her eyes slowly, blinked and seemed to refocus. "You're kidding, right?"

"No, I'm not." Gavin folded his arms in front of his chest wishing he'd gone and kept those sweatpants on.

"The girls have to see you! My gawd! They will just turn into puddles."

Again with the sexual imagery. Gavin's jaw tightened. Of course, everything right now had sexual connotations as far as he was concerned. "You need to leave."

"What?" Maria's eyes shone with alarm. "Why?" She took a step toward him and Gavin backed up nearly tripping over the ottoman in his living area. "I'm the president, didn't you know? That's why I came."

She just had to say that particular word, didn't she? Another word he didn't want to hear at the moment. "Excuse me?"

"The president of the Naked Wizard Admirer's Association."

Gavin choked. Saliva caught in his throat and turned to ash. He coughed, doubling over and finally hacking his way to the ottoman. This was outrageous! He'd never heard of such a thing. No wonder all these women stared at him.

They were mocking him.

"Oh for heaven's sake, Gavin." Maria pressed a glass of ice water into his hand and knelt beside him. "We're not mocking you. Far from it."

He took a tentative swallow of the water, not wishing to look at her. He didn't believe her. The women of Brokenoggin made a laughing stock of him. "Go away."

"I'm not going anywhere." Maria pushed to her feet, using his arm for support. A tingle of magic ran through his bloodstream and naturally settled in his cock. "Do you have any idea how many women in town want to sleep with you? Outside of old Ms. Dunbar who can't see well enough to tell a man from a bull, I don't know any female within a thirty mile radius that doesn't want to have a fling with you."

Gavin's head lifted, she looked sincere. But you couldn't trust those witches. And the little glimmer of realization that kept tickling around his head all this time finally shone like a beacon. "Does that include you, Maria Drinkwater?"

She smiled. Her pretty lips, full and glossy pink made him long for a taste. Funny, he'd never actually looked at her in that way. Until now. And that made all the sense in the world.

Maria shifted her weight from one hip to the next. "What? Do you think I'm nuts or something? Of course I want you, Gavin. Why do you think I cast—"

Gavin stood slowly. He angled his index finger toward Maria. "*You* cast?" He approached her slowly as the magic tingled through his entire body. Part of him was thinking *Lightning Strike* while the other thought *Fireball*. It trickled over him in a searing heat. "What did you cast, Maria?"

She turned her head away. "Well, you've never noticed me before so I figured I'd help the issue."

"I see."

"Of course, I didn't think it would have such startling

results. I mean, who would've thought I'd get it so hard."

"Maria..." His tone warned, but a weird part of him found himself already intrigued by her behavior.

"I've got some gorgeous lingerie that I just picked up. I think you'll like it." Maria started for his front door. "All you've got to do is walk over to my house and—"

"And what?"

"I'll reverse the spell." She winked. "But first, you and I are going to have some fun." Maria opened his front door and held out her hand. "So I'd advise you to come along and prepare yourself for the best sex you've ever experienced. Unless, of course you want to go through life with that jack hammer."

Gavin raised an eyebrow. "What did you have in mind?"

"Oh, lot's of things..."

What the hell did he have to lose? Only a massive, aching hard-on that showed no signs of retreating on its own. He took her hand and stepped up to the door. Outside, he could hear gasps of pleasure and applause. Gavin looked out and swore one woman even fainted. A small smirk played about his lips before turning into a sexy grin.

He walked outside, his hand in Maria's and reached back to close the door. "I hope you're ready for a wild ride."

She laughed. "Oh, I'm ready. And there are always reinforcements."

Episode 1.11

X MARKS THE G-SPOT

By

Shelly Laurenston

A succubus finds her true love.

Subtle, demure, delicate Shelly Laurenston is a 2005 EPPIE Award
Winner and 2004 CAPA Winner. Her books include the popular
Magnus Pack series as well as the award-winning To Challenge A
Dragon. To find out more about Shelly's books go to
www.shellylaurenston.com.

Mavis brought the binoculars back up. She was bored and uncomfortably hot. Even her sleeveless sundress and sun hat gave her absolutely no respite. Truly, this kind of weather did not give her comfort. In fact, it did the opposite. It made her horny as a tiger in heat. But she couldn't do that anymore. Nope. People would start getting suspicious. Exactly how many husbands could leave one thirty-year-old woman? As it was, six might really be pushing it. She simply couldn't risk seven.

She sighed. All of this celibacy was making her depressed. She didn't like being depressed. It went against her naturally perky nature.

She scanned the streets of her little town, looking to see what people were up to. That's why she'd always loved this house. The top floor porch circled her entire home. On a really good day she could witness all sorts of things from here…and she often did.

At the moment, she could see Officer Thinksalot cruising down Main Street. She snorted. She never could find the energy in her to like that woman. Snotty miss know-it-all as far as she was concerned. And kind of boring. Besides, she never came in for a reading. So she was of no use to Mavis whatsoever.

She swung her sights into her neighbor Emma's backyard. It was a very rare occasion when Emma did anything remotely interesting. And those toads the other night just didn't count.

Oh, who was she kidding? She could care less about Emma, her toads, or the boring town cop. No there was only one thing she really had any interest in at the moment. Only one thing she really wanted to watch that closely…but she shouldn't. She really shouldn't.

Biting her lip and disgusted at her own weakness, she swung her binoculars over to her front yard. That's where she'd left that damn gardener. Goddess, he was gorgeous. Tall, his body one big rippling muscle, he had a shoulder-length mane of black hair and crystal-clear blue eyes. Eyes that stared straight through her. Loose-fitting blue jeans hung low on his lean hips, and his sleeveless blue T-shirt did nothing but bring out those divine eyes. She almost tripped over her own tongue when she opened her front door to him.

And the way he looked at her…like a starving man just offered a slice of prime rib.

Thank you, Maria. Her friend recommended him…although she should have known better. Leave it to Maria to send the hottest man on the planet over to trim her hedges. Maybe it wouldn't be so bad if she weren't so damn horny. But she was…and that would just make it harder to resist him. She had to, though. She had no choice. The town would definitely notice if this one went missing.

She leveled her binoculars at the front of her house. She'd hired him to re-design her front lawn. Maybe plant some new flowers and bushes. Maybe…maybe…*uh-oh.* Her breath caught in her throat. He wasn't there.

Oh, damn!

She whipped her binoculars around to her backyard. And sure enough, Mr. Tall, Dark, and Well-Hung stood in her backyard.

And right by those pesky graves.

***

She slid to a stop in front of him. "Now how did you get back here?" She knew her voice sounded way too high, but trying to pretend she was being light and unconcerned was killing her. "How about some iced tea? Or a soda?"

He stared down at her, those clear blue eyes sizing her up. He didn't seem remotely disturbed by her sudden appearance. In fact, he looked amused. *Very* amused.

"No, thank you." His voice, low and heavy shot her senses into overdrive. Gritting her teeth, she tamped down the Wanton Whore ready to throw the man to the ground, fuck him until his heart stopped, and then bury him with the others. She and the Wanton Whore had been fighting for dominance since she put on her first training bra. And every day it got harder and harder to win.

"You know, I can't afford to have you passing out on me from this heat." Grabbing his wrist, she gently pulled him toward her back patio. His arm, hard as steel, felt wonderful and strong against the tips of her fingers.

He allowed her to pull him to her patio and into the back of her house.

Opening the refrigerator, she perused the contents. "Let's see. Bottled water?"

He nodded as he carefully examined her kitchen. Strange young man. He didn't say much but there seemed to be a whole lot going on inside that handsome head.

Mavis took out a bottle and handed it to him. "You know, I really don't need any help with my backyard. I just let that grow wild. I like it that way."

He opened his water and chuckled. "Is that right?"

She frowned. Was the man laughing at her? "Yes. That's right. So if you'll concentrate on the front…"

"You sure you just didn't want me to find those bodies you've got in your backyard?"

Mavis froze. Afraid to move. Afraid to breathe. After a moment of stunned silence, she forced herself to smile and speak. "Wherever did you get such a ridiculous idea?"

"From the graves I found. Most of them mostly contain bones. But one is still…percolating."

She kept tight control over her emotions, it wasn't easy. It wasn't easy at all.

"There are no bodies in my backyard. You…"

With a shake of his head, he chided, "Don't lie to me, Mavis. Don't ever lie to me."

"How dare you speak to me that way!"

"So you're trying to tell me you *didn't* fuck your husbands to death?"

"That's insane. And insulting!"

"So where are your husbands, Mavis? If not in your backyard."

"You can call me Ms. Gap. And my husbands left me, if you must know."

"All six of them? There were six, right? I counted six graves."

She turned away from him, huffing as if in anger. But it was panic. Pure, unadulterated panic. None of her usual charm was working with this one. And what bothered her most was the fact that he didn't seem too concerned with the multiple graves in her backyard. If she didn't know better, she'd swear he expected to find them.

Mavis shook her head. She should kill him. But to be honest, she didn't know how. And she wasn't entirely comfortable with the whole concept. Was it her fault her mother's demonic genes cursed her to always be alone? She'd only had six lovers in her life and she'd screwed them all to death. She didn't mean to. But once she got going, the succubus buried inside her DNA, made its appearance. So, although technically she may have murdered her husbands, she really didn't. They just couldn't handle her. No man on the planet could.

"I think you need to get out."

She felt him brush his hand or fingers across her bare shoulder. "Don't worry, Mavis. I have no intention of telling anyone. I've been waiting too long for you. But we can't leave those bodies there. That cop will stumble across them eventually."

She stared at him over her shoulder. "What do you mean? You've been waiting too long for me?"

He stroked her shoulder again, but he had one hand shoved in the pocket of his jeans and the other gripped his bottled water. She looked at what touched her and stumbled back, cold fear slamming into her heart.

"Is that a...a tail?"

Casually, he glanced down at the flesh-colored tail whipping lightly around her leg. It should have scared the beejesus out of her. But she was much more concerned with the fact that he actually *had* a tail. A long strip of muscle that angled down into a point. "Yup. I got my mother's eyes...and my dad's tail. Trust me it would have been worse if I got his eyes."

"Who the hell are you?"

He smiled. A beautiful smile that made her pussy clench and her mind scream in panic. "Didn't your precious cards tell you I was coming for you?" He dropped his half-drunk bottle of water on the counter and took a step toward her. "Didn't you see me?"

Mavis stumbled away from him, her back slamming into her stove. Thankfully, she hadn't turned it on; otherwise, she'd have burned her entire backside. And she wasn't sure she would have cared.

"Who are you? *What* are you?"

His grin widened as he stood in front of her, bracing his arms on either side of her. "My name's Cade."

"I know your name!" She looked for a way around him, but he blocked her in. "I just don't know who the hell you are."

"You sure, Mavis? You really have no idea?" The way he looked at her with those eyes. Suddenly they seemed unnaturally blue. Freakish, even.

He leaned down until they were eye to eye. "You don't know me at all?"

"Get...get out."

"Why? What are you afraid of?"

"You have a tail!"

"And you have six dead husbands in the backyard. And

I don't see me running screaming into the night."

She glared at him. "It's daytime. And exactly what is this? Some kind of blackmail? You want money or something?"

"This isn't blackmail." His eyes swept down her body and she knew he was absorbing every detail. "And the last thing I want from you is money."

"Then what…"

She stopped as his lips touched hers. A soft, gentle kiss. No! She couldn't do this. She could overlook the tail, but not his dead body in her kitchen. He was huge. It would take her hours to get rid of him.

She brought her hands up and pushed against his shoulders. With great effort, she pulled her mouth away. "No! I can't."

He smiled, his mouth easing down to her throat. "Why?"

"Because…oh!" He bit her neck. Hard. "Don't." At this moment, she was having a flat-out fist fight with her inner succubus. "I just can't!"

"Afraid you'll kill me?"

She couldn't concentrate enough to come up with a lie. Besides, he seemed to know so much already, why bother? "I *will* kill you…Goddess, stop!" She grabbed his hands with both of hers before they could grab hold of her breasts. "Please, Cade. I don't want to hurt you."

"Do you really think I'm that easy to kill?" He closed his big hands around her smaller ones, his callused fingers rubbing the knuckles of each hand. "Are you?"

"No. But I'm…I'm not…"

"Human?"

"Not completely. No."

"Well…neither am I. Completely."

She let out a little gasp as he nibbled his way down her throat. Three of her husbands hadn't been completely human either. After she fucked the first three to death, she decided to try something not nearly as human. She tried a werewolf, a demon from the fourth level of hell, and a Marine. And none of them could handle her either.

"I'm not just not human, Cade. I'm…I'm a…" She'd never admitted this out loud to anyone, and she really didn't want to admit it to him now. Damn him! Didn't he have some roses to plant or something?

Growling, he stood up. So much taller than her, she felt dwarfed by the man's presence. "I know what you are, Mavis. I know…and you're just what I need, woman. So stop fighting me."

"Don't bark at me!" She snatched her hands back from him and crossed her arms in front of her chest. "I'm trying to protect you!"

He crossed his arms in front of his chest, mimicking her. "I don't need your protection. Not from you. Not from anybody."

"Maybe not. But I can't afford to bury another body in my backyard. And it'll take me forever to drag you out of my house and down to the…oh! Oh!"

She reached back and gripped the stove, her head thrown back.

"You were saying, Love?"

Mavis tried to breathe, but that wasn't working. So focused on where he'd placed those hands, she'd completely forgotten about his tail. That goddamn tail!

It slipped under her sundress and the tip slid past her panties. Now it rubbed her clit. Tiny, tiny circles right around it. She couldn't believe how well he maneuvered that thing.

"Do you want me to stop, Mavis?"

She opened her mouth to say "Yes! Stop!" But he twirled his tail the opposite way and all she could manage was a choked high-pitched sound.

"You know what I hate? I really hate this hat." Snatching the sunhat off her head, he tossed it across the room. The whole time his tail just kept working her. Dragging her closer and closer to orgasm.

"Much better. I don't like you hiding that pretty face when we're in the house. I like seeing it."

He made that sound like a rule. A rule for living in the house...together.

"Who are...oh, God. Oh, oh God!" She grabbed hold of one of the cabinet drawers as his tail kept playing with her.

"And let's get this off you." He grabbed her sundress by the neck and with one mighty pull rendered it in shreds. Then he casually stripped it from her body. She wore no bra, which only left her panties. "You really are beautiful, Mavis."

Cade stepped closer, examining her near-naked body from head to toe. "I didn't think you'd be so beautiful. Although that wouldn't have mattered. What we need from each other goes beyond anything so trivial."

She had no idea what the hell he meant. What they needed from each other?

One of his big fingers circled her nipple and she closed her eyes at the wonderful sensation.

"No. Open your eyes. Look at me. I need to see you come."

And he could do that without her opening her eyes.

He chuckled. "Open your eyes, Love." She gasped as he caught her nipple between thumb and forefinger and squeezed. Hard. Her eyes snapped open. "Don't ignore me, Mavis."

His other hand grabbed her untended breast. "Don't ever ignore me. I don't care what you do to the rest of the idiots in this town. Spy on them. Ignore them. Lie to them. I don't care. But with each other, we'll always be honest.

We're partners in this, Love. Don't forget that."

What in hell was he talking about? In this together? In what together?

He released one breast and she bit back a moan of disappointment as his hand reached up and brushed the dark hair out of her face. "I want you to come for me now, Love. Right. Now."

She screamed as the orgasm tore through her, her body shaking in release. She felt her world tilt and slide away beneath her feet.

***

Mavis opened her eyes and found herself in her bed, a white sheet pulled up to her chin. The windows were open, letting in a slightly cooling breeze and the bright afternoon sunlight.

Really, with a little effort, she could have made herself believe what happened with Cade was nothing more than a dream. A hot, wet nightmare the Wanton Whore dug up hoping to send Mavis out on the hunt for Husband Number Seven. She could have made herself believe all sorts of things if she tried.

But that head between her legs apparently wasn't having it.

Mavis pulled up the sheet and gazed down at the top of Cade's dark head. Her legs began to shake, another orgasm imminent. How did he do that to her? She usually didn't come until the men were in their final death throes. Not the best way to get off, but it wasn't like she had any choice in the matter.

Cade's hands slid under her and gripped her ass tight. She gasped as he lifted her so that his mouth could feast on her comfortably. She reached out blindly and grasped the headboard. Instinctively, she tried to close her legs, but Cade held them wide apart, letting his tongue roam freely over and in her pussy. She tried not to think too hard about the fact that his tongue felt longer than anything she'd ever experienced.

Who the hell was this man? How did he seem to know so much about her? She'd heard about him as soon as he moved into town. Maria practically knocked her door down trying to get to her so she could give her all the details. Yet with all the gossip and "investigation" Mavis had done, she'd yet to find anyone who seemed to have had any kind of relationship with him. And she'd looked. New stud comes to town and a lot of these whores...uh...housewives fell all over themselves being the first to break him in. But from what she could tell, no one had been with Cade. Now she couldn't help but wonder if he'd truly been waiting for her?

An orgasm slashed through her and her entire body clenched hard. Cade held her tight to keep her on the bed and she barely reigned in the Wanton Whore in time. The fact that she'd been able to hold her back this long amazed Mavis. But the difference between Cade and her past husbands was her very real desire not to hurt him.

Cade pushed her body back into the bed and then started licking her all over again. No, no, no. She couldn't do this again. One more time and the Wanton Whore would have her way. And she'd never be able to protect him. Not from that bitch.

She released the headboard and lifted the white sheet, staring at the man who'd turned her whole life upside down in a matter of a few hours.

"Cade...Cade, please stop."

Blue eyes looked up at her. He smiled and dragged himself up her body, kissing her flesh the entire way. Everywhere he touched tingled with lust. He set her blood on fire and she knew she wouldn't be able to hold back who she really was any longer.

"You all right, Love? Feel better?"

She shook her head. "No. I don't feel better...just who the hell are you?"

Gently, he pushed her hair off her face. "I'm Cade. My mother was a Rhode Island blue blood. My father was an incubus. And as entertaining as demons can be for lovers, I wanted something more human...but something I wouldn't kill. A witch I know cast a spell for me. A location spell. To find my true other half. My dark-soul mate. To find you, Mavis. And don't worry about the tail...I can totally retract that in public."

Mavis snorted out a laugh. "Okay."

One hand brushed her cheek. "I'd dreamed you for years before I went to Fanny for the spell. I just never thought I'd find you. And now that I have..."

He didn't need to finish. She saw the desire in his blue eyes. He wanted her. Desperately. "Are you sure, Cade?" She'd only known the man for several hours but it felt like she'd been waiting for him all her life. If she hurt him or worse, she'd never be able to forgive herself.

"Honestly, Love. I think I'm the only man who *can* handle you." He lifted the sheet and, frowning, Mavis glanced down. Her eyes widened at the enormous cock between his legs. Even the demon ex didn't have anything like that.

He grunted. "This is usually where the screaming would start."

Mavis didn't scream. At least not yet. Instead, she reached down and grasped the hard shaft in her hand. It pulsated. Hot and powerful against her palm, her long fingers were unable to close around it. Her pussy wept in excitement. She'd been waiting her whole life for this cock...oh, and the man attached to it, of course.

He sighed as she eased her hand down the entire length of him. She'd seen porno movies at bridal showers where the men weren't this well-endowed. She released the

Wanton Whore who had been impatiently waiting. Released her and didn't look back.

Black talons burst from her hands. Her dark, sassy bob, grew several feet long, streaked with white and blond hair. And she knew her eyes turned completely black, tinged with red. Just the way they always did when she got like this.

"Fuck me, Cade," she grumbled out in that demonic voice her exes really hated, "Fuck me now."

He smiled down into her face, not remotely disturbed by her transformation, and for the first time she saw four fangs. Two on top and two on the bottom, right behind his incisors. He stretched out between her legs, his hot cock right against her pussy. He grabbed her wrists and pinned her arms above her head. His black hair fell across her face, the silky strands heating her to fever pitch.

"Take a deep breathe, Love. The first time is always the roughest."

She did, as he slowly pushed himself inside her. She spread her legs wide, letting all of him sink in. They both gasped in surprise as he went in to the hilt quickly, her body accommodating him immediately...like he was always meant to be there. Her smile as wide as his, Mavis arched into him.

"Do it, Cade. Do it! I want to see if we both survive."

His thrusts started off slow and Mavis' body immediately reacted to them. Her flesh on fire, she shuddered and whimpered beneath him. She wrapped her legs around his waist, urging him on with her body and her cries. Cade sped up, his body slamming into hers, seemingly unable to hold back any longer.

She tried to pull her wrists away so she could bury her talons into his back and tear flesh from his body. But he just chuckled and held her tighter. He controlled her body with ease and she loved it.

He dipped his head and laved one breast. She gasped at the feel of his harsh tongue against her. Then he roughly sucked the nipple into his mouth and she cried out. His free hand grabbed her other breast, twisting and tweaking the nipple until she thought she might explode.

Cade growled against her flesh, his movements becoming stronger, more forceful. And Mavis loved it. She arched again as her orgasm rushed through her. And that's when she felt it. His tail snaked around behind her and the tip slid into her ass.

She exploded, her scream only stopped because he slammed his mouth over hers.

She'd experienced nothing like it before. Even when she'd killed her husbands, she hadn't erupted like this.

Mavis felt the Wanton Whore, finally satisfied and content, go back to the safe place in her body. Her talons retracted, her hair went back to its sassy bob. And even her eyes felt normal once more.

It took Mavis, however, a moment to realize something. Cade wasn't dead. Far from it, in fact. Actually, he was still going strong and there didn't seem to be any signs of him letting up.

"Cade," she panted out as he continued pumping into her. Over and over again.

"What, Love?" His mouth happily returned to her breast, gently worrying the nipple with his teeth.

She shuddered as another orgasm prepared to release itself. "Exactly...ah! How long do you normally keep this up?"

He glanced up at her, blue eyes digging deep into her soul as if afraid she'd bolt. He didn't release her gaze or breast when he spoke.

"Days."

Mavis raised an eyebrow as her toes began to curl from the earth-shattering explosion getting ready to rock her. "Days?"

He nodded slightly, waiting for her response.

"Well…okay…oh. Oh! Do that again, Cade. Oh, yes…yes…that feels really good. Um…but I promised to make my cheesecake for the church bazaar this weekend, so…ooooooooh!"

He shrugged as he went back to sucking her nipples. "That shouldn't be a problem."

She smiled as her orgasm worked its way up her spine. "Okay, then. That'll…that'll work…*Oh, God!*"

Episode 1.11 (b)

(Due to technical difficulties, the chapter numbering is screwed up. No doubt the skeletons are at fault somehow.)

THE TOAD PRINCE

By

Terese Ramin

In which Murphy's Law comes to Brokenoggin Falls and a demonstration of "Be Careful What You Wish For" is brought to bear when a reluctant witch accidentally turns her husband into a toad when he forgets their wedding anniversary.

*"**R**rrrrriiiiiiiibbb-iiiiiittt,"* trilled the Giant Toad (quite literally genus/species *Bufo marinus*, if anyone is keeping track) that sat across the breakfast table from Alice Fairweather. Its slow, low-pitched voice sounding almost exactly like the exhaust of a far-off tractor, the toad spoke again somewhat reproachfully, *"Rrrrriiiiiiiibbb-mmmmeeeeepppp rrrrriiiiiiiibbb-iiiiiittt!"* From behind Alice's husband Greg's black-rimmed Clark-Kent-style glasses-frames, it blinked curiously human hazel-brown eyes and waited for her to do something.

Alice stared back at it aghast. But *I am* NOT *a witch*, was all she could think. *I couldn't have done that. Not just by getting super-upset and calling Greg a giant toad for forgetting our wedding anniversary for the thirteenth year in a row...*

And yet the evidence of her dubious prowess and long-denied heritage put its three-toed left foreleg atop the morning paper—the Thursday new technology section, Greg's favourite—and Greg's hi-tech titanium watch and plain platinum wedding ring *thunked* solidly onto his salsa-and-scrambled-eggs-with-a-side-of-Russian-caviar-and-gourmet-biscuits plate. (It was their *anniversary* for crying out loud!) Alice eyed the further evidence that this particular Bufo marinus (a toad species definitely *not* indigenous to Michigan's Upper Peninsula, nor indeed to anywhere in the United States north of extreme south Texas, Miami, Stock Island, southern Sonora, or the pools and arroyos in the Rio Grande Valley) was, in fact, her husband.

Taken together with the emotional upset over yet another forgotten anniversary, the evidence—glasses, human hazel-brown-eyes, watch and ring—was all too damning and made her feel like crying. She loved Greg to distraction but sometimes he was such a...

She stopped herself from even thinking anything accidentally lethal just in case, just in time, and burst into tears.

"I AM NOT A WITCH," she sobbed loudly, "*I-am-not-a-witch-notawitchnotawitchnotawitch…*"

***

"Trevor Fairweather!" Claudia Choo knocked on her kitchen bay window in an attempt to get the attention of the Golden Retriever digging industriously in her herb and rhubarb bed just below. "Stop it. Stop it this instant!"

Normally a well-behaved canine of immaculate grooming and joyous but exceedingly beautifully-mannered temperament, Trevor suffered occasional bouts of rebelliousness and went, what Claudia had heard his young mistress Amy Fairweather refer to as "rogue."

Instead of desisting, Trevor pointed his impressive golden muzzle directly at Claudia, barked once, and moved over to an exquisite patch of lavender and dragon's breath. He nosed through the expertly tended growth, chose his scent, clamped his teeth around the stem and tore out the largest lavender plant Claudia had.

Then he started to excavate in earnest.

Speechless with fury, Claudia darted for the first available exit and dashed catty-corner across Crestfallen Lane to the Fairweather's. She was damned straight going to give Alice a piece or two of her mind, tell her to come get *"that dog!"* and have her— somehow—replace the prize *rare* English-East-Indian Lavender-*Mint* plant Trevor had just destroyed.

***

"I am not a witch, *notawitchnotawitchnotawitch…*"

The more Alice Fairweather chanted the mantra to herself, the more hysterical she became.

It was a simple statement really, and one that shouldn't need justification or explanation, but every time she said it, her need to justify herself to the universe got worse.

She glanced at the sunlit kitchen table upon which sat the usual, *normal* Fairweather family accoutrements: the breakfast dishes and morning paper, the French press coffeepot, the too-cute-for-words unicorn-creamer and salt & pepper set Amy gave her last Christmas because they were what the nine-year-old thought her mother should have...

An almost imperceptible keening joined the mantra when she glanced at Greg's place.

"—*notawitch-notawitch-notawitch-notawitch...*"

Dear Lord, what had she done? What had she *done*?

Nothing, that's what. She couldn't have because she wasn't a witch, which meant this whole thing had to be...

Greg's own fault.

The keening trickled down to a hysterical giggle. That's right, had to be Greg's fault. He'd been the one to insist they move back to this godforsaken place after all. Said it would pay to live near his biggest and most lucrative clients. *She'd* never wanted him to own an Internet company called Spook-Your-Mama.com in the first place. Or to specialize in items that the magickally enhanced scarfed up like free fresh cookies at a blood drive.

She was also not the one who'd forgotten their thirteenth anniversary, or their fourteenth—which meant he'd forgotten *thirteen times in a row!* Screwing with double-thirteens was just asking for bad luck no matter how *not* superstitious you were or how much you were definitely *not* a witch.

Which she couldn't be. Otherwise, she'd probably like the number thirteen, black cats instead of Golden Retrievers and turning her husband into a *Bufo marinus* whether accidentally or on purpose.

Right?

"*Rrrrriiiiiiibbbbb-bbbbaaaaaaappp?*" the toad trilled in its tractor exhaust voice, sounding for all the world as though it wondered if she was all right.

Alice took in Greg's Clark-Kent-glasses perched askew on its nose, the all-too-human hazel-brown eyes that blinked behind those this-man-is-a-geek-but-a-really-hunkly-one nearsighted-thick lenses and choked, "N-no, I'm n-*not*" and started to sniffle into tears. But just then Claudia burst through the never-locked kitchen door, surprising her out of them.

"Hot damn it, Alice! That dog of Amy's is tearing up my prize lavender and if you don't stop him, I'm going to hex him into—"

She stopped dead in mid-sentence and stride, assessing the situation in the Fairweather kitchen in the blink of an eye.

"Oh, Alice," she said in disgusted sympathy, "what is it with men and anniversaries? The giant toad forgot again, didn't he?"

A tiny bubble of hysterical laughter squeaked out of Alice before she collapsed at the table opposite the Giant Toad, crying as though her heart had broken. Ribitting madly, the toad hopped onto the table and headed toward Alice. Claudia grabbed a potholder and a dishtowel, scooped up the toad and dumped it into the deep ten-gallon soup pot Alice kept on the one end of the counter and used to cook fish stew or chili for the town festivals.

"No you don't," she told the toad, "you've caused enough trouble already." She covered the pot, dropped the towel and hot pad, grabbed up the phone and went to pat Alice's back. "Don't worry, sweetie, it's not your fault. We'll convene the coven klatch and get you back to normal in a flash."

***

"Giant Toads are toxic, aren't they?" Vanessa DuMal

peered closely at the deeply pitted paratoid glands that extended far down the sides of Greg's new body.

Hesther Bellhallow leafed through one of several regional *A Field Guide to Reptiles and Amphibians* she'd thought to bring with her at Claudia's summons. "Highly— to dogs and other animals if they bite it, according to the Peterson's." She climbed Alice's kitchen stepladder to get her own look at the *Bufo marinus*, asking Claudia as she did so, "I'm a medium, not a witch, so why am I here again?"

"In case we need a spirit guide to help us figure out which spell to cast, and because you're part of the coffee klatch," Claudia said for approximately the seventh time.

"So I guess that would mean the second part's true for me, too," Emma Mincemeat suggested apologetically, "but what about the first? I'm only human."

Vanessa tapped the somewhat dog-eared *Witchcraft for Dummies* clutched tight to Emma's bosom, her forefinger tucked firmly inside to mark a possible solution to Alice's problem. "You at least *want* to be a witch," she said, "unlike *some* people who don't even know when they're casting a spell."

Alice snuffled back indignation—and fear. "Maybe *your* ancestors weren't evil arts witches, but *mine* were. I don't want any part of what they did. I can't be tempted. I have Amy to consider. She needs to be raised right. Brokenoggin Falls Community Church is the only—"

"Alice." Harmony Faithful, pastor of Brokenoggin Falls Community Church, who didn't normally attend the coven coffee klatches, slid an arm around her most faithful service attendee and squeezed. "The church is open to everyone. Why Mavis Gap is one of our most active members, and you know she's just recently announced she thinks she's a succubus, so I don't imagine you need to worry if you think you're related to black magick…"

"She needs to worry," Claire Stalwort assured Harmony

in her primmest little girl voice. "We don't take kindly to the black arts in this community."

Gerda Tawdry snorted impolitely behind her hand a word that sounded like "Harpy," and Gladys Tawdry sneezed something behind hers that sounded so much like "Where's Sam?" that Claire immediately withdrew to the far side of the kitchen, a cup of coffee in one hand and a pitcher of warm nutmeg-enhanced milk in the other, and pouted. Then Gladys stuck out her tongue at Gerda and Gerda flipped Gladys the bird and...

"The point is," Godiva Tawdry said firmly, stepping between her sisters before the hair pulling started, "we all have stuff in our pasts we wish we didn't. That's why AnnMarie—"

"I'm here." Mussed and dripping with perspiration, AnnMarie Hathaway blew in through garage breezeway. "I'm sorry I'm late, but I'm a little worried about the skeleton closet. I had the lock fixed at the beginning of the summer, but something's not right. Has anyone put something besides a skeleton in there recently? A Big Bad, maybe?"

Everyone looked around the kitchen at everyone else.

"Well..." AnnMarie chewed her lip. "Probably my imagination then." She didn't look like she thought it was, but as though she knew there was nothing she could do about it even if it wasn't her imagination. At least not here and not now. "Did we get thirteen of us?" She started counting heads. "I brought extra brooms."

Vanessa's jaw dropped. Claudia's mouth worked, trying to form speech but failing. Gladys and Gerda clung together for a change, cackling in perfect accord. The tip of Hesther's tongue showed between her teeth when she bit it to prevent herself from saying something; Maria clapped a hand over her mouth to prevent the same. Harmony, Emma and Claire looked at each other, puzzled, and Alice stared at her in dismay.

"Brooms?" she asked aghast. "I don't even want to be a witch and you brought *brooms!?*"

*Tsk*ing, Godiva simply shook her head. "AnnMarie, AnnMarie, what will we do with you? Brooms? You've just set witchcraft back a thousand years."

"Oh for Goddess's sake, grow up, all of you," AnnMarie snapped. "They're to sweep up the salt when we're done with the circle."

This time she got several winces and some deeply guilty stares from everyone except Vanessa and Claudia, who sent each other, *"Uh-oh, did* you *bring the salt–I didn't bring the salt"* looks.

"We *do* plan to cast a protective circle, right?"

"Uh huh."

"Sure."

"Yep."

"Oh definitely."

"Yes, absolutely."

"Right."

"We're just waiting for Candy Cox to get here with the, er, kosher sea—"

"*Celtic*," Claudia murmured out of the corner of her mouth.

"Er, yes, *Celtic* Sea salt," Vanessa finished, improvising. "Since Alice doesn't like to practice, you know, we thought we'd better use the best and clearest stuff we could find for the first circle cast in her house."

AnnMarie's lips twitched. "There's a five pound bag of Morton's Iodized in the front hall," she said as gravely as she could. "I brought it just in case Alice didn't have enough in the house because she doesn't practice."

Usually the most gracious and seemly of women, Claudia nevertheless stuck out her tongue at AnnMarie. "Witch." It was plain she meant it with a capital 'B'.

AnnMarie grinned.

Candy Cox breezed in at that moment. "Am I the last one?"

Hesther put down the phone. "Hi, Candy. That was Janice. She's trying to get here, but the Disdaine triplets screamed for her and she says she's literally tied up right now."

"Don't you mean a little...?" Godiva began, and stopped. On second thought and where the Disdaine pre-adolescents were concerned, Hesther no doubt meant exactly what she said.

Emma tapped her foot, stuck her left ring finger in the page she'd marked for Alice's situation and began to leaf determinedly through *Witchcraft for Dummies.* "As the mother of twelve," she said furiously, "someone should tell their parents that something *has* to be done about those girls *before* they come into their most powerful years as a charmed trio. But right now we have to un-scream-summons Janice the way you've been promising to all summer, and *do something* to make sure she doesn't have to respond to the bogus any more!"

They didn't even need a second to think about it. "Agreed!" the other eleven women chorused. Even Alice didn't hesitate to join them. She didn't like the way the Disdaines sometimes eyed Amy, and she was also beginning to realize that being in the company of women who'd help each other at the drop of a tear might not be so bad even if they *were* witches...and other things.

Harmony Faithful joined them, too. She wasn't one of them, not really, not in any spiritual or magickal system yet invented, but they'd called her in to help Alice, a member of her congregation, and she was part of their community: their needs were hers. Whatever it was they were about to do here, she had absolute faith in the fact that their intentions were pure and honourable: they meant to help and not harm, not hinder. She could get behind that one hundred percent. There were, after all, more things on heaven and earth and all that...

She would simply have to ignore the fact that she was just a little fuzzy and more than a trifle sceptical about the means.

"But without Janice—" Alice cleared the timidity and teary roughness out of her throat. "Didn't you say, Claudia, that we need thirteen for this because of all the thirteens involved in it?"

Claudia nodded. "Most of the time I wouldn't think about it, but since the number seems so specific we should probably stick with it."

"What about Mavis?"

"No one's seen much of her since Cade..."

"Maria?" Emma interrupted quickly. If anyone even *talked* sex around her she was likely to wind up pregnant again by morning. Peter could *smell* the mere thought of the word on her and responded to it as though it was Viagra and Cialis and oysters all packed into one potent punch.

No one knew where Maria was.

"Morganna's down in the garden tool shed," Alice said, "she'd come."

Vanessa peeked out the kitchen window. "Is that Joe's truck?"

A collective sigh went up.

"Gavin?"

"Eeeeeuuuw! He'd probably come naked."

"Tulah-Portentia?"

"Still pissed because Rowdy hasn't been able to talk Joe into turning her half-brother loose."

"I should say not." Claudia sounded peeved. "Little twerp's a menace, burning up everything in sight and eating whatever he feels like. Why he even tried to dust my Earl..."

Vanessa patted her shoulder and bit her tongue to prevent herself mentioning her own husband's father, Vicomte de la Gryphon, the actual munching scientist culprit. "I hear there's a new gal in town. Dorothea something. Maybe—"

"What about me?" Eight-year-old Amy Fairweather crawled out from under the kitchen table where she'd been hiding and eavesdropping all along. "I'm a powerful witch. It's my daddy. I want to help."

"Oh, Amy!" her mother exclaimed, horrified. "What are you...you're not supposed to be...you should be outside...*how* did you...?" Overcome with questions and admonishments without direction, Alice fish-mouthed into silence. For the space of five heartbeats she stared at her daughter. "No," she said finally, resolutely. "Absolutely not. I forbid it."

"But mo-o-o-o-m!" Amy stamped her foot. "You know I can help. You *know* it! You know we could do it all by ourselves together, just you an' me, but you're too afraid of what might happen and how you'd feel afterwards, but I'm *not* cuz you *wouldn't*. You're the best witch ever-ever-ever, else I can't be and I *am*!"

"Child, what are you talking about?" Vanessa stooped in front of her. If she and Jean-Luc were ever able to conceive, she hoped she'd be able to make more sense out of their offspring than she was making out of Amy right now. "If you have any magicks at all, which is unlikely, you're much too young to have come into them."

"Technically," Claire said slowly, glancing from Alice's dead-set, frightened face to Amy's equally determined, completely unafraid countenance and back. "Technically. I've heard of circumstances..."

"*No!*" Alice shouted.

"*Yes!*" Amy yelled.

"*Rrrrrrrriiiiiiibbbbbbbb-bbbrrrrrreeeeepp-*

oooooowwwrrrr!" the Giant Toad rumbled metallically from the depths of the ten-gallon soup pot.

Mother and daughter stared at each other without giving ground. Everyone else gazed from them to the soup pot then anywhere else in consternation, uncomfortable as they'd ever been in their entire existences.

"You know it's me 'n you with them or nobody." Amy, stubborn: Alice's mother's image to the core.

"I know it's me and them and you visiting Aunt Cecilia for the day if you don't mind your manners now," Alice tossed back, equally stubborn, and firmer than any of the other ladies had ever seen her. Clearly the fruit that was Amy didn't fall far from Alice's oak tree.

Amy stamped a threatening foot. "I'll show them!" She flicked the small fingers of her left hand at the unicorn creamer and the salt-and-pepper shakers, and the ceramic trio came to life and started to dance.

A collective gasp burst from the coven klatch.

"Oh—" started Vanessa.

Alice said nothing, merely sent Amy a chastising stop-showing-off glance then pursed her lips in the direction of the dancing ceramic unicorns. They stopped in a blink and went back to being nothing more than simple decorative accoutrements atop the breakfast table.

"—*shit*," Claudia finished for Vanessa.

They looked at each other, at the rest of the women, at the toad in the pot.

AnnMarie gave voice to their thoughts. "This is—"

At that instant, Trevor fitted his beautiful, furry Golden Retriever body through the doggy door into the kitchen, dashed into the center of the room leaving muddy footprints in his wake, dropped a pair of finger bones on the floor and barked three times. As if on cue, the finger bones unfurled and began to creep across the floor toward AnnMarie who viewed them with fascinated horror.

"No, this is really not good at all," the keeper of the skeleton closet said.

***

The finger bones decided things for Alice. She pointed a brook-no-nonsense finger at Amy. "You're to stay within touching distance of me at all times and don't let go of Trevor's leash."

"Yes, mommy." Amy nodded solemnly.

Alice dropped a green silk cord over her daughter's head, tapped a forefinger against the delicately hand crafted silver amulet of the Green Man with the broken noggin and the waterfall foaming out of his head that now lay over Amy's heart. "And don't take this off ever."

"I won't," Amy promised. Then, "Where's yours?"

"Right here." Alice clipped a silver chain about her neck. An amulet identical to Amy's except for the diamond chips in the falls and the tiny emerald, amethyst, and aquamarine points dangling from the Green Man's beard rested in the hollow of her throat. "Daddy made me one, too. Just in case."

"In case of what?" Candy sounded anxious.

"In case I ever stopped living in denial and started practicing." Alice grimaced. "He thought if he designed something with the falls and the trees in mind, maybe it'd offer some protection for Amy and me from my ancestors."

"Honey," Claudia observed nervously, "I don't think you need to practice, I think what you need is to take control."

"Yeah," Alice said dryly, eyeing her soup pot. "Consider that done. Cast the circle, AnnMarie. Cast it wide."

***

The afternoon waned and evening set in. The salt circle glowed moonlight-bright from the protective power it held, but every single one of the dozens of cast spells failed.

Exhausted, the women looked at each other.

"What haven't we tried?" Claudia.

"Dancing naked under the full moon?" Gladys, poking Gerda, both of them on the verge of giggly hysteria.

Harmony sank to her knees. "Maybe it's me," she offered gloomily. "I'm here for Alice and I'm pretty sure I saw *something* this morning when she and Amy did...whatever they did even if I don't know what, but..." she hesitated. "I can't believe that's really Greg in that pot and maybe a believer's what you really need."

"Nonsense," Emma said briskly. "This isn't like voodoo. My book says so."

"Voodoo!" AnnMarie snapped her fingers and looked hard at the finger bones fidgeting idly away inside their own separate salt circle. Trevor lay with his nose an nth of a degree outside the circle, guarding the bones.

"Maybe," Amy tried for the sixth time in as many hours, "It's like that story daddy—"

This time Janice's arrival interrupted her. Looking somewhat the worse for wear after her afternoon with the Disdaines, she strode through the house, stopping short of the circle. "Haven't you de-toaded the man yet?"

"No, but we've un-screamed *you*," Hesther told her.

Janice's face relaxed into an uncharacteristic smile. "I thought someone screamed when I was on my way over here, but I didn't leap, so...thanks."

"Yeah, thanks." Seth stepped up behind her. Clothed for once, he was merely remarkably handsome instead of godly-gorgeous. "It's a whole lot more convenient when she doesn't leave in the middle of—hey, I know those bones."

AnnMarie started. "You do?"

"Sure." Seth shrugged. "They belong to—"

The full moon rose abruptly, pink and friendly, a harbinger of things not to come.

"Yes?" AnnMarie prompted.

Confused and frightened, Seth looked around wildly. "Where-who-what…?"

Janice turned and took hold of his fly and Alice covered Amy's eyes. "Brokenoggin Falls, Seth, a vampyre. I'm Janice. See? You've got it written on your arm. Let's go and get you undressed, help you remember what else you've forgotten…"

"Get him to remember who the finger bones belong to," AnnMarie called after them, "It's important—"

"That's it," Alice said flatly, putting her foot down. "I've had enough. I appreciate everything you all have tried to do, but we've got too many things going on here to solve one little anniversary problem. Because that's all this is. It's just between Greg and me, and I might need help, and he might be a toad about remembering some things, but most of the time he's my prince and—"

"Mommy." Amy tugged at her arm hard. "That's the thing we haven't tried. Daddy's story, you know the one he always tells me, his favourite one, about the toad prince. He says it's how he found you and you made him the man he is. Remember?"

Brought up short, Alice could only stare down at her daughter, blinking rapidly, mouth agape. "Oh dear God," she breathed at last, teary-voiced. "How could he remember what I'd forgotten?" She dropped to her knees beside the soup pot. "Oh, Greg! You wonderful, glorious, ridiculous toad of a *prince!*"

"Rrrriiiiiiibbbbbbiiiiittttt," the Giant Toad thrummed deeply in its distant-tractor-exhaust voice, *"Rrrrrriiiiiiibbbbbb-wwwwwooooooowwww!"*

"Alice?" Claudia asked.

"What? Oh." Alice offered her a watery laugh and smudged the heel of her hand across her eyes. "I'm sorry, girls. You've all been wonderful, but we can break the circle now. I really do have to do this on my own. Emma, would it be all right if..."

Emma, wife who'd survived countless anniversaries and mother of twelve, caught Alice's drift at once and held out her hand to Amy. "Of course. Amy, how about you come spend the weekend at my house? The quadruplets are dying to show you—" she shuddered delicately, knowing that no eight-year-old worth his or her salt would ever be able to pass up this opportunity no matter how gross "—this new thing they can do with dead people. You can show them that thing you did with the salt-and-pepper shakers..."

Alice turned to Trevor who pushed himself up on his haunches, wagging his tail and waiting for instructions. "Take care of those bones."

"No, wait!" AnnMarie cried.   "There's something wrong with them, I know it. They need to be locked in the skeleton clos—"

But before she could finish or stop him, Trevor pushed his nose deliberately through the salt circle around the bones to break it, scooped them up in his mouth, dashed to the edge of the large circle, pawed it open and was gone.

"You don't know what you've done," AnnMarie told Alice gravely.

Alice made a face. "No," she agreed, "but with my ancestors, if Trevor brought those creeping fingers here and then a vampyre from out of town thought he recognized them before he forgot what he was again..." She offered up a lopsided shrug.   "I'm just thinking the skeleton closet might not be the safest place for them, and maybe that's why they were separated and buried someplace else to begin with."

"On your head," AnnMarie advised her, and Harmony Faithful gasped, took the cross she wore around her neck out of her blouse and automatically countered, "Let the ties between the dead and the living be parted and peace exist between them."

Something calm settled in the air around and within Alice's house and stayed there.

AnnMarie eyed Harmony sharply. "I thought you weren't a witch."

"I'm not." Proudly Harmony drew herself up to her full height and stared AnnMarie squarely in the eye. "I'm a pastor."

"Hunh," AnnMarie said puzzled. "Interesting." She linked elbows with Harmony. "I wonder if there's anything you can do with my closet…"

They wandered off, chatting.

With their departure, Trevor's absconding with the bones, and Emma leaving with Amy, the rest of the group began to drift away, too. Only Vanessa and Claudia lingered, unsure that leaving Alice unsupported was the right thing.

Touched to discover that she did indeed have something in Brokenoggin Falls that she'd always thought she lacked, Alice fingered the gems in the exquisitely crafted Green Man pendant at her throat and smiled.

"Thank you, really. You don't know how much. But it's fine—better than." She glanced again at the soup pot where the toad sat watching her every move through its all-too-Greg-like eyes. "I know exactly what to do now. In fact it was stupid of me to take so long to remember it. So…" She grinned shyly. "Come for coffee tomorrow afternoon, I'll tell you about it?"

Then for the first time in her life, Alice let herself be hugged by her friends.

***

The light pink moon shining down on the rippling upper end of Corkscrew Falls created magical shadows under the spreading branches of the great fox oak where Greg and Alice met, lo those many, *many* full moons ago.

"I can't believe you remembered this," Alice repeated,

setting Greg's warty body down on the huge, craggy, shaped-by-the-falls rock where she'd first seen him. "I didn't even remember—didn't *want* to remember what my parents and grandparents…"

"Rrrriiiibbbb-mmmeeerrrpppp," the toad rumbled gently, *"Rrrrrreeeerrr-mmmaaaapppp."*

Alice nodded. "Yes, I know. They thought they were clever. They thought I'd never do it. But they were the ones who sent me to summer camp. That's where I heard the girls say you never find the prince without kissing a lot of toads so, stupid me, I thought they meant literally. I figured bad taste, warty skin, bufo toxins and all I should get it over with, maybe get to my prince faster. And there you were." She pulled a tall, cone-shaped princess hat with a long, flowing blue gauze scarf-thing trailing off it out of the duffel bag she'd brought with them and put it on, tying its iridescent blue-green-purple-y ribbons beneath her chin. "Right there on this rock."

She perched carefully beside her transmogrified husband, picked him up and brought him to eye level. "It's a good thing princess hats are shaped like dunce caps," she told him apologetically, "because that's what I am—a dunce for not figuring this out earlier."

"Rrrrriiiiibbbbuuurrrppp," the toad disagreed soundly. It inched cautiously forward in her palms, reached out a three-toed forefoot and touched her nose. At the same time, Alice tipped her head and kissed it.

On a breath, her husband's mouth formed under hers, his fingers found her face and tunnelled into her hair, his bare body took shape and fitted next to hers; the rigid length of his cock nudged her gauze covered thigh. Alice gasped and tipped her head back, baring her throat to his tongue and teeth, catching his cock in her hand.

"Oh god, Greg, don't stop, don't stop!"

"I couldn't if I wanted to. The only thing I've eaten all

day is flies and fish eggs. I'm starving."

Alice laughed unsteadily. "I brought sandwiches."

His voice was dark, carnal. "I'm in the mood for something creamier."

He dragged her across his lap, all the while hunting avidly for her breasts with his mouth. The peek-a-boo gauze-and-lace tunic she'd changed into before driving them out here dragged roughly, erotically across her skin and his, teased them both, so that by the time he found an aureole it was puckered tight, the nipple at its crest a hard, thrusting bud bursting for relief. When he rolled it finally between his tongue and the roof of his mouth, tunic and all, Alice pressed into him hard and begged for more.

"Touch me while I suck you, Alice," Greg whispered, "and touch yourself, too. Bring up your cream for me, baby, I need you…aaaahhhhh."

Alice stroked his tip, arched her back and let him watch her run her other hand down her own belly until she tucked the filmy nearly see-through skirt tight over her mons and began to stroke herself, too. The heat from his gaze made it difficult to split her concentration equally, but she did her best to keep her attention focused on him and only on him while she sheathed her hand around him and wet him with his pre-cum, moved the fingers of her other hand rhythmically against her clitoris and lightly inside her own sheath…

When Greg clamped down hard and pulled her nipple deep into his mouth, Alice's focus threatened to shatter. Her breath stuttered, her hands clamped and nearly stalled. Greg tilted his head sideways and looked up at her. Their gazes locked. While his mouth aggressively massaged one aureole, his tongue and teeth the nipple, he teased her other aureole and nipple with the pad of his thumb—slowly, gently, exquisitely manipulated them so that the breast itself had to plump and strain to make sure it felt the pleasure. His other hand simply steadied her, played lightly over her skirt, slowly ruching the fabric higher and higher along her leg and easing his fingers closer to the inside of her thigh.

His cock strained her hand, outgrew its span, spilled a measure more of pre-cum that she used to slicken its generous bulk while her breathing thickened and quickened, and her breasts rose higher, faster, harder into his hand and mouth.

"Please," she whispered darkly, working her inner thighs against his tempting fingers while hers continued to slide her now saturated skirt against her clit. *"Please."*

Driven by the word, he let her breasts slip away, moved to ease the gauzy skirt beneath her hand. When she would have withdrawn it, he clasped her fingers in his and shook his head.

"I need my cream first, wench."

Then he waited for her to grasp his meaning, nod and grin wickedly at him before he pushed her back and spread her legs wide, dipped both their fingers inside her—two of hers and two of his—and urged her to thrust while he manipulated their hands.

It didn't take long to get what they wanted. Her sweet pearly cream spilled over their hands even as her soft moans started to spill into the night.

"That's the spot, right there?" Greg asked, pressing both of their index fingers to the soft little button of flesh inside her that sent Alice's hips bucking high.

"Ye-*es!*" she gasped, shuddering and bucking when another pleasure-spasm sent more thick moisture trickling down her backside. "Come inside me right there, right now, Greg, *yes!*"

Grinning his beautiful, intensely "Greg" smile down at her, her husband scooped their messily dripping joined hands to his lips and said, "Sustenance first," and sucked their fingers clean.

Then while she was still giggling over that bit of nonsense, he flipped one of her knees over one of his shoulders and drove into her hard.

She moaned with pleasure. He did it again; so did she.

And the rest of the night went exactly that way: celebrated precisely the way fourteenth wedding anniversaries are supposed to be celebrated—with good, hot, lusty, loving sex and plenty of it.

And also a few promises to do it again exactly the same way next year.

Only maybe without the forgetting the anniversary part. Or…

Alice came hard and long, simultaneously with Greg, wrapped around him, clutching at the stars.

…Maybe with the forgetting would be okay, too. As long as they celebrated number fifteen together, among their friends in Brokenoggin Falls—

…With perhaps a little mouthwash or a few breath-mints and no bad tasting bufo toxins before the kissing.

Episode 1.12

A DANCE THROUGH THE GARDEN OF GOOD AND EVIL
By

Susan Grant

*Harmony Faithful, pastor of Brokenoggin Falls Community
Church (all faiths welcome), learns that there's more to
Brokenoggin than meets the eye.
(Story and new characters by Susan Grant)*

Bestselling author, RITA winner, and jet pilot Susan Grant loves
writing about what she knows: flying and the delicious interaction
between the sexes. For upcoming releases and more, visit
http://www.susangrant.com.

The Devil scowled at the dirty, sweating demon that had been brought before him in chains. "Kneel before me and prepare to receive your sentence!"

"Aye, Master." The demon crouched and bowed his head. It would not do to act arrogant, not after the torture. At least he still possessed all his important body parts. It could have gone much worse for him. And perhaps it still would. The devil, as always, was in the details.

"Prepare to receive your sentence, Demon." They were all named Demon down here in Hell. The only being with his own name was Lucifer Himself.

"Aye, Master." The demon's hands, bound at the wrist, rested awkwardly at the small of his back as he tried to focus on Lucifer's fiery red eyes, the black goatee, the horns, the pitchfork, and the crimson suit—proof that the whimsies of fashion in Hell had been at a standstill since the birth of time.

Fashion? Why was he thinking of fashion? His concentration simply wasn't what it used to be after the century of torture he'd endured for his crimes. Or had it been two centuries that he'd been paying for his terrible deeds?

Ah, but what was an extra century or two in the grand scheme of things? He'd been on this earth for more than ten thousand years, tasked to bring the worst sort of doubt into the miserable, pitifully abbreviated lives of human beings. For he was a High Demon-Lord, one of the most ancient of them all: the Lord of Self-Doubt and Second Thoughts, the bane of many a human failure, simpering creatures all too eager to listen to the doubts that he could so easily plant in their weak minds. *You can't*, he'd whisper until they believed it. *You won't. Try and you will surely fail.*

Countless men who could have ruled the world had never stepped beyond their front doors because he had made them doubt themselves, made them afraid to take chances, to risk failure. Nor were women any safer from his dark murmurings through the eons. He'd frightened countless wenches, silencing their voices by playing up their fears of sounding too shrill, too stupid, too...different.

Humanity's failures—he'd been the force behind most of them. Until that fateful day he glimpsed true courage and couldn't bring himself to destroy it, giving the Will-To-Go-On to a small, starving band of settlers wandering in the snowy woods of Michigan's Upper Peninsula. He wasn't sure exactly why he'd spared them, why he'd given them the inner strength to push themselves until they reached warmth and shelter, but he had—and it had felt damned good, too. In fact, it had felt so damned good to be good to the damned that he repeated the deed all around the globe, losing himself for years in a virtual frenzy of beneficence, until he was finally caught, red-handed, in the midst of one of those random acts of kindness.

The demon's crimes had been considered so heinous that the Devil Himself had dragged him back to Hell. First, there had been the fruitless, futile explaining, then the torture. Now this, his sentence:

"For your crimes, you are banished—banished from Hell for all time!"

The demon's head jerked up. *Banished?* He'd expected a reduction in rank, the loss of freedom to come and go as he pleased, but banishment? His salary, his benefits—*poof,* gone! Just like that. Heaven's Gates, he'd slaved ten thousand years—for nothing! Done the Devil's deeds only to end up like this: out of date, out of use, and without a transferable retirement plan! *It's your fault. You have no one to blame but yourself.* "Is this to be forevermore?" he almost croaked.

Lucifer chuckled. "Not forevermore, no. For I have made you mortal, as well," he added glibly, cutting short the demon's premature sigh of relief. "Never fear; you won't have many years ahead of you to fret your fate." He waved a clawed hand. "You can thank me anytime."

"Where?" the demon asked instead. "Where will you send me?" Something told him it wasn't mortality itself he needed to fear as much as the locale in which he would suffer it.

"Why, to the very epicenter of your initial act of kindness." He spat out that last word. Literally. The glob of moisture sizzled in one of the many fires burning deep within the bowels of the earth.

"Brokenoggin..." the demon whispered.

Devil's red eyes appeared positively gleeful as his forked tongue darted out to moisten thin, malice-curved lips. "Yes," he hissed with the very faintest of lisps. "The hamlet of Brokenoggin. Such a peculiar little place."

The demon mulled over his options, which were near zero, as far as he could tell. Time was running out to reverse this course. So, he did what he did best: "Are you certain this is the best plan for me, Master? The best punishment?"

The Devil's voice turned deadly. "What do you mean?"

"Let's think this through. What if it doesn't work?" *You can't...you won't. Try and you will surely fail...* "The High Lord of Self-Doubt and Second Thoughts living across the street? Shopping at the local market? Dropping in at the Cub Scout meeting?" The demon forced a weak laugh. "Absurd, is it not?"

The sound of a thousand screams filled the chamber as the Devil roared in incredulous rage. "How dare you!" Goblins and gargoyles somersaulted through the shadows, fleeing the chamber as a rumbling began under the cold stone slab of a floor.

"Your dark magic does not work with me, Demon!"

"No magic intended. I merely suggest that you look at all sides of the equation."

Lucifer roared again. Somewhere far above them, on the surface, the ground also shook. The demon half-wondered how many casualties there would be this time. But that was no longer his job. He'd been fired. He would no longer be tasked with sowing seeds of defeat in the survivors' minds, riddling their psyches with despair.

At that, something close to relief filtered through him. Doing good had taken the fun out of doing evil. He sensed he'd never be 100% good. Yet, nor could he ever return to being 100% bad.

Pulsing like hot coals, Lucifer's eyes glowed brighter, his fangs glinting. A tantrum was coming; the demon could sense it. "I do not doubt, fallen one. I do not err. *I do not have second thoughts!*" Lucifer grew and grew until he towered above the demon, his clothing splitting and hissing as muscled flesh bulged and tore it apart. Horns sprouted from a ridged skull, curling upward, until they, too, were lost in the swirling mist of the chamber.

How many times had the Demon witnessed such showy outbursts during his long existence? In fact, it kindled his own temper, long dormant. It was as if something wrenched open deep inside him. For the first time, emotion, true emotion, filled him: anger, resentment, shame at his past. Just like the humans, he thought. What was happening to him? "I am sorry," he said under his breath. It was the only way to express what boiled up inside him. "I am so very sorry..."

"You don't look sorry," the Devil hissed.

He looked up slowly. "Ah, but I am. I'm very sorry. Sorry for all the centuries of planting doubt, of turning back those beings better than I. In fact, I hereby repent." Take *that,* Big Guy.

"You...re-what?"

"I repent. R-e-p-e-n-t." Wasn't that an Aretha Franklin song? Oh, he was going to suffer mightily for this, but it didn't stop him. "I ask forgiveness for all the deeds I ever did in your name. I truly do." And he truly did. The demon threw back his head. *"Forgive me!"*

"I...do...not...forgive!"

The demon smiled; perhaps it would be his last. "It wasn't of you that I made my plea," he said.

It was the first time in all of history he could ever remember hearing the Great Satan sputter. Then the screaming started up all over again. Two jets of searing red heat shot out from the Devil's eyes and hit the slab where the demon crouched. Rocks exploded, pummeling him. The air was on fire, something that the demon should have been used to—Lucifer's temper was legendary—but this felt different. There was a horrific wrenching, and the demon could no longer see or hear, or even, after a blessed while, feel the pain that wracked him. Bathed in white light, floating...he wondered if this was what it felt like to die. If so, perhaps he would not mind. But he knew, as he spun into oblivion—or, rather, the wilds of Michigan—that Lucifer never would let him get away as easily as that.

***

In a clear, sweet voice, Harmony Faithful concluded her sermon. "Now, go in peace and enjoy this beautiful day that God has given us."

The sound of her six-month-old puppy's tail thumping on the hardwood floor was all that broke the perfect silence.

"Thanks, Bubba." Harmony smiled and glanced up from her eight-page, handwritten sermon that had taken all of ten minutes to read to the twelve rows of empty pews. "It's nice to know someone appreciated the homily today."

Sometimes, she wondered what she possibly could have been thinking, relocating to the remote Upper Peninsula: her, a city girl, thinking she could make church goers out of the people who lived here who, um, weren't anything like any people she'd ever met anywhere else. But after her two tours as an air force chaplain were up, she was ready for another challenge.

Six months ago, this chapel had been a tumbledown farmhouse. With the help of her father and brothers, she'd remodeled the old place. Then they'd returned to Detroit, leaving her to grow her flock. Except that aside from a few curious townspeople, no one had showed up.

"You can do this, girlfriend," she told herself. She'd simply have to drum up a little of the faith in herself that she always tried to drum up in every one else. After all, she was Harmony Faithful, the daughter of Jacob Jethro Faithful, IV, Detroit's most famous, and often infamous, but always ebullient pastor of Elm Avenue Church. "Remember that, Harmony," she said out loud. "It's in your genes. God sent you here because you have a job to do."

Bubba seemed to agree, a long pink puppy tongue draped over one side of his open mouth. Boy, lately she sure was spending a lot of time talking to herself or to the dog. She needed to get out more, meet more of the locals, maybe join in on some of those oddly named "coffee covens" Janice—the town's only law enforcement officer—and the Fairweathers—incredibly, a seemingly *normal* couple—had told her about. Most of the women in town seemed nice, if a little, um, racy. Black lace bra types, Harmony had dubbed them in private. Not meaning any disrespect. Her own sister was a black lace bra type. And not that Harmony had anything against a woman knowing her own charms or being confident about sex. God had never dissed procreation. In fact, He encouraged it—within the context of a committed, monogamous relationship, of course. Something she sure didn't have to worry about, considering her current state of isolation.

Have some faith. Give it time.

Time... Yeah, she had plenty of that lately. She gathered up the sheets of lined paper, crushed them in her fist, and aimed the ball of paper at the wastebasket across from the pulpit. It clipped the rim and spun inside. "Two points!"

She tapped a finger against her chin. "Maybe we can start an after-school basketball team. What do you think of that, Bubba-licious?" The puppy wagged his long black tail.

The idea had worked for her preacher father and some inner-city kids in Detroit. The hoops had brought the kids, and then the mothers, who'd dragged the fathers and the boyfriends, and within the year, there was an entire community with Sunday potlucks and a fifty-two-member choir. Not that she could picture the Disdaine triplets shooting hoops, but it'd be a start. It was all about getting people through the door.

Brokenoggin Community Church. Where all faiths are welcome. That last part she'd painted onto the sign as an afterthought when weeks had gone by and nary a lost soul tromped through the door. Well, save Janice, the town sheriff. She'd drop by sometimes to see how Harmony was settling in, staying for coffee but not the good word. But then Harmony firmly believed everyone was welcome here, for whatever reasons they chose to come. She was taught as a child that a true heart excluded no one, and that the church was the heart of the village. Except in Brokenoggin, that honor was held by the town tavern.

How could she convince the townspeople to congregate here instead? What did she have here that they couldn't find anywhere else? "God, help me figure this out. Give me a sign." *Please*.

The floor rumbled. At first, she thought it was the old furnace kicking on, but it was warm today, too warm for the heat. The earth moved again, and then stopped.

Strange. Everyone knew a fault line ran through Missouri. But Michigan? Just then, a breeze kicked open the front door, carrying in the scent of freshly turned dirt.

Bubba bolted out the door, barking. Something outside was making the puppy bark like crazy. Was that strange pack of nasty little Chihuahuas on the loose again?

Harmony stepped outside. Grabbing the frilly cotton of her skirt, she lifted it higher, her long legs carrying her to the garden she'd planted under an ancient, gnarled apple tree. Birds chirped. The sky was a pure, clear blue. And the sunshine, she could almost taste it. There was another reason she'd come here. Something about this little patch of land drew her. She was so entranced by the outdoors that she swept right past Bubba who was barking at the naked man lying on his side in the shade of the tree.

The naked....

...man?

Harmony froze, the skirt falling out of her hands. There was no naked man.

Oh, yeah? Then how do you explain the after-image that just seared itself onto your retinas?

Heart thumping, Harmony whirled around. He was definitely naked, lying on his side, one thick, muscled thigh thrown forward, the sunshine bouncing off his butt. His skin was tanned, smooth, and his dark hair curled long and loose around his neck. He had the well-hewn body of a NFL running back—powerfully muscled, but without a linebacker's bulk.

She'd asked God to send her a sign. But she never expected anything like this!

Then she blinked. What was she doing, staring? The man was out cold—drunk probably—but still, she should be helping. Her military first-aid training kicked in, and she dove to her knees, her fingers going to his corded neck to feel for a pulse. There...a heartbeat...slow, distant, almost forlorn, as if the man had grown tired of living.

Harmony sat up straight. Gosh, that was a weird thought. Tired of living? And yet when she studied him, his face, she could believe it was true. Well, she'd have to fix that. No man was going to give up the goat on her watch. And especially not while naked and crushing her best zinnias.

Bubba growled, low and deep. "Stop it," Harmony scolded. "I'm a third-degree back belt, baby. If he turns out to be the town serial killer, we'll team up and put him away. Until then, Bubba-boy, you behave."

The puppy obeyed, its brown eyes huge.

Harmony tapped the man on the cheek. "Hello? Are you okay?" He needed a shave and the bristles pricked her skin. But his face was warm, almost as if he was sunburned...or had stood too close to a fire and gotten burned. More likely, he collapsed after a night of carousing. He was going to be pretty embarrassed once he realized he'd left wherever he'd been hanging out without his clothes. "Come on, wake up. I'll brew you a pot of coffee. Lord knows, I make a mean pot of java." He didn't make a sound, not even a snore. She took hold of his solid shoulder and shook hard. "Let's go." Nothing. She tried her air force officer voice. "Time to wake up, soldier! *Now*. Move, move!"

The man cracked open one eye. At first, she thought she saw a red glow, but it seemed to be a trick of the sun. His eyes—or rather the one eye she could see, the other one being buried in the peat—was beautiful, the mellow gold of good scotch, the kind her father would reverently pour out in a glass once each week, late on Sunday night—"Now that God's work is done, Harmony," he'd explain.

"How're we doing?" she asked.

The man groaned and rolled onto his back.

Glory be. Her mouth went dry as she looked him over. For injuries, yes, that was it. Before she administered emergency caffeine, she'd better make sure he wasn't wounded. Anywhere. She gave him a thorough inspection.

After all, it was her citizen's responsibility. There wasn't an ounce of fat on him. Or a single scar. He was as sculpted as a statue of a Roman warrior, except with body hair, the perfect amount, too, short and coarse and dark....

Something drew her eyes back to his face, where she discovered he was watching her with something close to amusement. "You seem very much...whole," she quickly explained.

"Whole. Aye, lass," he murmured in the strangest-sounding accent, almost a Scottish burr. "They kicked me out, but I got to keep all my parts and pieces." He flashed a blinding grin. "You like what you see, then."

She stopped her blush before the heat of it could reach her cheeks. She'd grown up with three brothers. Like heck if she'd let the fact that a man was sprawled naked in her garden in all his very magnificent glory distract her. "No," she lied. "As a matter of fact, I don't like what I see." Was that something wounded that flashed in his eyes? Certainly it was surprise. She let the sin of pride curve her mouth. "I don't care for the sight of a drunk, lying naked in my flower garden on a Sunday morning." She gathered her skirt around her and stood, brushing the dirt off her hands. "But I did pray for someone to show up today, I prayed for a sign, and I suppose I shouldn't complain, because I didn't spell out the specifications."

"I am not drunk." His eyes confirmed that. They were clear, not bloodshot, as they searched around the garden with curiosity and maybe even wonder, as if he were only just now becoming aware of his surroundings.

She thought of his strange reference to keeping his body parts. "Were you in an accident?"

"At first it was, aye, but later it was quite intentional."

Okay. "How did you...end up here?"

"I lived here for a spell, long ago."

"Really? On this farm?"

"No. In Brokenoggin. And now I suppose I'll die here, too." The man let his head fall back onto the dirt with a soft thud.

He looked so beaten, she softened her tone. "Would you like some coffee?"

"Water." His voice was a bit hoarse. "Cold water."

"I hear you on the water." She'd prefer hers in the form of a shower. "Can you walk? Or should I call the paramedics?"

He seemed to test his arms and legs. Long muscles flexed, moving under firm skin, and his tight stomach brought new meaning to six-pack abs. *Harmony...* she warned herself. *Be professional.* "Where are your clothes?" she asked as calmly as she could as he didn't seem to care that he wore none.

"They were taken from me."

"Oh, my, so you were robbed and left here."

"You could say that, aye."

"I'm so sorry. I didn't think we had folks like that in this town."

"They were not from here," was all he said.

"Good. We'll call Janice Thinksalot. She's the sheriff."

"No. No sheriff. 'Tis over now."

"You're awfully forgiving."

The man winced.

"No, that's a good thing."

His gaze softened in a way that squeezed her chest. "I have much yet to learn." And he'd said *that* in a way that half left her breathless.

"First things first." She pulled off her sweater and handed it to him. "Here. Cover yourself, and then you can come inside. I'll find you some clothes. My family was here a while back. They left some things. You can dress and use my phone. I'm Harmony, Harmony Faithful. Who are you?"

"My name..."

"Yes."

He thought on that.

She hid her smile. "I didn't think it was that tough of a question."

"My name is Demon." He appeared almost ashamed.

"Damon. That's my nephew's name. Damon what?"

His dark brows knit together.

Damon sure did seem rattled. But then he'd been robbed, beaten, stripped, and dumped in a pastor's flower bed.

"De–er, Damon...of Brokenoggin," he announced with the strangest mix of pain and pleasure.

Well, she thought, the name was no less strange than any of the others in this town. "Come on. I'll get you fixed up."

Bubba trailed Damon to the door at the back of the chapel where Harmony's living quarters were. The growling had stopped, but Harmony knew the dog would protect her if need be, although Harmony trusted her instincts, which told her Damon held no menace—raw, smoldering male sexuality, yes. But no menace.

Inside she found him some work clothes of her big brother's. When Damon returned to the kitchen after changing into them, she saw she'd guessed right on the size. He sat at her little table, smoothing large hands over the lace cloth. It was as if everything were new to him, everything a wonder. Even her, she realized with an tiny twist of her heart when his gold-brown eyes found hers for a moment before focusing on the glass of water she about spilled in his lap. Sometimes, their eye contact seemed to knock him off balance as much as it did her.

She took a seat as he drank with thirsty gulps. "You feeling better?" she asked after a bit.

"Aye." He winked, pressing the back of his hand to his mouth to dab at the droplets of water left behind in a truly medieval way. "Tended by a beautiful wench."

She lifted a brow. "Wench. Is that a Scottish term for a strong, capable, intelligent woman?"

He laughed, rich and deep. "Aye."

She balanced her chin on her hand. "I don't know what to make of you, Mr. Damon of Brokenoggin."

"Make of me whatever you like, fair maiden."

"Fair maiden. I like that a lot better."

His gaze went soft again. "It fits ye better, too."

She swallowed against the feelings his gentle, sexy tone fired up inside her. "Do you have family you need to call?" she asked quickly. "To let them know you're okay?"

He shook his head. "Nay. I have no one."

"You're not married?" She immediately bit her lip.

His mouth curved. "Nay. Never thought of it. But then my...former job didn't allow for it." His eyes took on a faraway look. When he returned his attention to her face, it was with such bold intensity, such raw consideration, that this time she did blush. "Perhaps, now, that has changed," he murmured.

Harmony got up too quickly, sloshing water out of the pitcher. She grabbed a dish towel and started mopping at the puddle. Damon grabbed her wrist.

Heat and fear spun up her arm to her heart, nearly stopping it. She stared at his big hand and then his face. "I'm a third-degree black belt," she said softly. "And my dog will rip your throat out if you try anything stupid."

He let go instantly. "I did not mean to frighten you."

And she believed him. Gut instinct was her best friend and it hadn't failed her yet. "Listen," she said, sitting back down, "I'm the local pastor here. I'd like to help you in any way I can. But do you think you can be honest with me? How did you really end up in my flower garden, um, butt naked?"

He leaned forward, folding his thick fingers on the table. "The real story?"

Rolling her eyes, she felt her mouth quirk. "No, I want you to lie to me."

"I was the ten-thousand-year-old High Demon-Lord of Self-Doubt and Second Thoughts until I was expelled from Hell by Lucifer Himself after he caught me committing random acts of kindness. Then last night, after several hundred years of torture, I was made mortal and banished to live out my days here, in Brokenoggin, the site of my original 'crime' of beneficence."

Harmony stared at him, and Damon stared back. Gosh, he looked dead serious, too. "I was just kidding about the lying."

"Aye, I know." He drummed his fingers nervously, glanced out the window as if seeking inspiration, before returning his gaze to her. "I will tell you this way: I worked for a corrupt boss. I, too, was corrupt until I learned what it was to be good. I learned that I liked being good over being bad. My boss, he punished me for it, for changing, and then he let me go. And so now I am here, with no job, and no clothes."

Thank you, Lord. *Ask and ye shall receive.*

Harmony smiled as inspiration hit. "Listen, I could use a groundskeeper." She opened her hands so he could see the calluses and paint stains. "In fact, just this morning I was praying for some help with the heavier work around here. The barn needs fixing—I'd like to make it into a social hall, eventually, maybe a school, or even a gym—and I thought if I had some help, it'd leave me more time for recruiting more parishioners. In fact, any parishioners."

"No one comes?"

She shook her head. "If I could figure out a way to lure them here, I would. If I could have something here that they couldn't find anywhere else... In fact, just this morning I asked God to help me figure it out. To give me a sign. And he sends me you: a naked Demon—I mean, Damon." All of a sudden, she began to laugh, laughing so hard that she had to throw her face into her hands. "Oh, my," she gasped. Sniffling, she dabbed at her eyes with her sleeve. "Is this what they call Divine Intervention?"

His sparkling eyes seemed at once impossibly ancient and that of a newborn baby. "Aye, more than you know, fair maiden."

"If I'm the fair maiden then you can be my knight in shining armor. But I can't afford to pay much." She sobered. "I can't really afford to pay you at all." This was crazy. She pushed back from the table. "I'll give you a ride back to town."

"I don't require money. I'll work for...sustenance."

She shivered at the look in his sexy eyes, the way he drew out that last word.

"Food," he clarified. "And a place to lay my bones at night."

Bones...bones...she tried to keep her mind out of the gutter. "Okay, you've got yourself a deal." Why was she whispering? She shook her head and thrust her hand at him. He took it, and she got the most curious feeling that he wanted to lift it to his soft lips. But he shook it and let her go, and she closed her fist under the table so she could secretly hold onto the feel of him.

***

Damon started work that afternoon. The weather was hot and he so easily worked up a sweat. He tossed his shirt on the grass and continued bare-chested. By the end of the week, word had gotten around about the new groundskeeper down at the new church.

"Devastating," Maria confided to the ladies over coffee one morning. "He's built better than any man in this town.

You have to come see."

And so they did. That first Sunday the pews were filled with eager women. The next Sunday the men began trickling in to see where the women were going. With every passing week more townsfolk came, until after a few weeks Harmony had to ask Damon to build her some more pews.

At dusk he came to her kitchen where she'd promised him a special meal. As he sat, showered and dressed in clean clothes, she stood next to him and lit some candles. His hand slid around her waist. She held her breath and met his eyes. They'd never touched, never kissed. It wasn't for the lack of wanting to, either. But, suddenly, she wondered what in the world she was waiting for.

And so she bent down and kissed him.

He didn't let her escape when she was done. Pulling her onto his lap, he pressed his mouth between her breasts and held her tight, as if she somehow anchored him here on Earth. Which made her heart ache when she remembered how lost he seemed when he'd first arrived.

When he lifted his chin to see her, his eyes were dark, very dark. "You have the devil in your eyes tonight, Damon of Brokenoggin," she murmured, imitating his accent.

"Aye, and you've got a bit of the devil in ye, too, I see."

She traced the curve of his mouth. "But I have the feeling that I'm about to find a little piece of heaven in your arms."

Chuckling deeply and with confidence, Damon drew her close for the longest and best kiss of her life, proving just how right-on she was.

***

Belting out her words in a rush of sweet inspiration, Harmony Faithful delivered her sermon to a full house. At the front of the chapel, the door half-open, Damon stood listening, his arms folded over the end of a pitchfork as he leaned against the outside wall. He wasn't yet ready to come inside the chapel during a service, but one day soon, he would. And, just as Harmony hadn't yet come to Damon's bed, she knew that someday soon, she would. Then all would be right with the Fair Maiden and her Dark Knight—or as right as life ever could be in the bizarre little town of Brokenoggin.

No sooner than Harmony conjured the thought than a tremendous screeching filled the tiny chapel, chased by an unseasonably cold breeze. The wind whooshed between the pews, tossing off hats and whipping hair, until it found her, whirling around her like her own personal tornado, scattering the pages of her sermon. One hand fisted in the fabric of her cotton skirt to keep it from flying up, she tried to snatch back her papers from the whirlwind, but it only blew harder, whipping her hair around her face. It was almost as if something—or someone—was tormenting her on purpose. Now, this sort of thing happened all the time in Brokenoggin, only, never on the grounds of the church. What had changed? What had made her fair game?

As Harmony fought to hold down her skirt against the force of the wind that didn't seem to be affecting anyone else, she stumbled away from the lectern, exchanging a glance with Janice, the sheriff, that somehow made her feel better and worse at the same time. Janice's expression was something between annoyed and a little tired as she focused somewhere outside the front door. Harmony followed the woman's gaze. Outside, shadows arced and swooped, but there was no sign of Damon. Her heart dropped.

Harmony joined the crowd exiting the church. Outside, shadows continued to arc and swoop. Harmony squinted in disbelief. They were...flying...monkeys. Yes, just like the winged assistants from the movie The Wizard of Oz!

"Damon!"

At the sound of fear in Harmony's voice, Damon

paused in his battle with the sub-demons, which were still pouring out of a crack in the earth he'd so carefully tilled the week before. Harmony's autumn vegetable seedlings were tossed aside like so much dust as creatures exploded from the ground. That angered him even more.

She was running toward him as the sub-demons tugged on her hair, her skirt, but her concern seemed to be only for him. Heading toward her, he lifted his pitchfork and began whacking the creatures, solid little thuds, leaving as many as he could writhing on the ground. The Sub-demons were dark monsters with little power, but enough of them could kill a man. Could kill a mortal. An unfair fight that, he thought. But who said Lucifer was fair. Damon had thought his sentence of being mortal would have been enough, but it was obvious his former boss wasn't through torturing him yet. He wanted to take from Damon the only woman he'd ever cared for.

"Damon!"

"Stay back, Harmony!" He spun, taking out several of the more brazen of the sub-demons with a sweep of the pitchfork. The creatures lay dazed on the ground. The townspeople ran every which way, complicating his efforts, some screaming, others laughing. He'd seen a lot of scenes during his long years working for the Devil, but none as chaotic as this one taking place on the front lawn of Brokenoggin Community Chapel.

Smacking left and right, he fought his way to Harmony. Just as he reached her, one landed on his shoulder like a parrot. It hunkered down, snuggling against his neck, and with a sinewy hand, caressed his cheek. He grabbed it by the scruff of its neck and threw it aside. Harmony's eyes glowed with disbelief. "Do you know them?"

"Nay." *Nay?* Was he slipping back into the lies that so characterized his past life. "Aye," he amended, taking another swipe with the pitchfork before another could land on him.

"What is it? No or yes?" Harmony ducked as a monkey swooped over her head. "Damon, what are you not telling me?"

"They're...acquaintances of mine," he explained rather weakly.

Harmony gaped at him. "Acquaintances..."

"Well, perhaps co-workers is the better term." He smacked another with his pitchfork. "*Former* co-workers."

One look at Harmony's expression told him that he had a lot of explaining to do. He'd told her—tried, that is—but she hadn't believed him, so she really knew nothing of his being a former High Demon Lord, nothing of what he was. He'd wanted her only to know what he had the potential to become, but alas, that was not to be. His mouth twisted furiously. Thanks to Lucifer.

There was more shrieking, but a human sound this time. Well, semi-human. The Disdaine triplets were on the loose, one of them aiming a weapon of some sort.

"The riot gun," Damon heard Janice shout. "How did they get hold of the riot gun?"

The triplets squealed with laughter as they took shots at the sub-demons. A bullet clanged off his pitchfork. He dove with Harmony to the ground, along with almost everyone else.

"Hit the deck," Harmony shouted at the same time Janice yelled, "Cease fire!"

The creatures squeaked, and suddenly began pouring back toward their hell-hole. Damon's mouth quirked. The sub-demons had encountered something worse than the creatures of hell: they'd met the Disdaine triplets. Damon fancied that he'd like a family of his own someday. But five minutes with the triplets was enough to convince any man to drop all thoughts of procreation.

"Damon," Harmony said in a hiss of a whisper. He

turned his head to find her lips an inch away from his. His body was wrapped around hers as they lay sprawled on the ground, the same body that now reacted rather briskly to that pleasant discovery. He was beginning to quite enjoy the sensations of his very mortal self. There were advantages to being mortal that he'd never realized. But Harmony didn't look pleased at all.

Ah, yes. The sub-demons. "I can explain," he said.

Her lips pursed. "Uh huh."

The last of the sub-demons disappeared down the hell hole. Then, as everyone began to rise to their feet, thinking it was safe, the Disdaine triplets fired off one last shot as they fled their parents. Seth, who had come with Janice, flew backward, clutching his chest.

The sheriff ran to his side, her face revealing her feelings for the man Damon knew was a vampire, even if Harmony did not.

Janice tore open Seth's shirt. "His stake—it's been knocked loose!"

The next thing Damon knew, the town vet was rushing to her side. Physicians, real physicians, were as scarce around these parts as pastors.

Harmony ran to Janice. "Is he...?"

"No." Janice swallowed. "He's not dead." She touched her fingers to the man's broad chest. Not as broad as his chest, Damon thought, but broad nonetheless.

"The stake was shot out," Janice said, almost gasping. "Normally, it would have killed him. But the rubber bullet plugged up the hole." She frowned. "What were those things?"

"I don't know," Harmony muttered. "But Damon does."

Damon tried charming the sheriff with one of his smiles, but her gaze sharpened. "Is there something you want to tell me?"

Before Damon could reply, a clattering noise filled the air.

"AnnMarie's skeletons!" one of the townsmen shouted.

"It's true!" a woman Damon recognized as AnnMarie stated. "It's them. And they're angry. *Run.*" The chaos started all over again. AnnMarie bolted off toward the church with everyone in her trail. Damon and the vet carried Seth to safety.

"AnnMarie has skeletons in her closet?" Harmony asked.

Alice Fairweather glanced at her. "You didn't know that?"

Janice interrupted. "Those...things must have woken them."

Even the Disdaine triplets fled the storm of approaching skeletons. Either that or they were out of ammo.

They got the door closed just in time. Damon could hear several skeletons trying the door, which he, the vet, and the local warlock kept shouldered closed. From outside, an enraged howl rose up like a North Sea wind, cold and bitter. A skeleton clattered against a window, but it was too fragile to shatter the glass. Furious that it could not get to them, it howled and spread its bony hand on the glass. It was missing a finger bone, and looked angrier than everyone else. Something told him it was the ringleader of the skeleton crew.

Then, with a sound so horrible that it reminded Damon of what he'd left behind in hell, the fingerless skeleton flew off. Janice, kneeling by an unconscious Seth, shouted, "No! Someone, try to stop it! It's going to destroy...."

Episode 1.13

THE SKELETONS IN THE CLOSET

Or

Why Remo (Doesn't) Thinksalot Shouldn't Be In Charge Of Installing Locks On Skeleton Closets
By

Annihilation Jones & Leroy

*Due to unforeseen **Technical Difficulties** (superstition and the fact that the skeletons from AnnMarie's closet ate it) there is no episode 13.*

Episode 1.14

A DRAGON'S TALE

or

There's No Such Thing as a Dragon

By

Mary Jo Putney

*In which Claudia Choo deals with an irate dragon-in-law
and discovers her accountant husband's hidden nature.*

New York Times bestselling author Mary Jo Putney has written
somewhere around 30 books – romances, mostly historicals.
Lately, magic, unicorns, and dragons have been sneaking into her
work, which she finds quite delightful. You can find out more
about her and her work at www.maryjoputney.com or
www.mjputney.com

She *winged through the air with steely determination,*
more intent on her mission than the moon-touched forest
below. Where was that blasted town? Ah, that was it ahead,
the lights a bright splash in the northern forest even at this
late hour.

She swooped down when something odd caught her eye.
How interesting, a vampire apparently rising from the dead.
Quite the handsome stud, if one liked humans. Or former
humans. She swooped down on him like a strafing fighter
plane, startling him into falling over backwards. Pleased,
she resumed her journey, serene in the knowledge that there
was nothing abroad in the night more fearsome than she.

All houses looked much the same from the night sky, but
she found her destination easily, using senses other than
sight. She landed and entered through the back door,
opening the lock with her magic, before settling in to wait
the hours until morning. She yawned, glad there was time
for a nap. It wasn't as if her teeth and claws needed
sharpening.

***

After a night of restless dreams, Claudia gave up trying
to rest and swung herself out of bed. Earl, blast him, still
slept the sleep of the innocent, which he most surely wasn't.

She sighed as she studied his taut, golden-skinned body.
How had they come to such a pass? They'd loved each other
when they married, she was sure of it. She'd been crazy for
Earl, with his half-Chinese elegance and tantalizing air of
mystery. He was her dream man, both exciting and reliable.

Reliable had meant a lot to her after a childhood
traveling with a succession of tacky carnivals where her
mother played Madame Zaza, Authentic Gypsy Seer. Her
mother actually was a good seer, though she used witch
wisdom and black hair dye instead of anything remotely

gypsy.

Claudia had left the carney life as soon as she was old enough to go to college. There she studied botany to become a thoroughly modern witch who understood herbs and potions in a scientific way. She'd learned to grow herbs of greater potency, and understanding how species related to each other had allowed her to create new mixtures far beyond anything made with traditional witchcraft. Her internet potion business had made her one of the best known witches in the world.

She'd met Earl when she went to him for tax help. He swept her off her feet, literally—the first time they'd made love had been on top of scattered Schedule Cs. He adored her blond, All-American girl looks as much as she'd loved his Eurasian exoticism.

When he brought her to Brokenoggin Falls and proposed, she'd accepted in a New York minute. She delighted in the town's wild energy and its crazy, charming residents who would accept anyone. Here she could have children and raise them with a normal, stable life. Well, sort of normal.

So they married and moved to Brokenoggin and everything went to hell. How could she ever have believed that life with an accountant would be exciting? The word passionate was not in Earl's vocabulary. It had been her initiative that laid them out among the tax forms. He always treated her like a spun glass angel that had to be handled with care. At first she liked that, but the pedestal soon palled. No wonder she never became pregnant. It took passion to create new life.

She slid out of the bed, thinking that if she had a couple of kids to chase around, she'd be so exhausted that she wouldn't mind his disinterest in sex. Instead, she was bored and hot and horny.

Earl was bored with her, too, or they wouldn't both

have started having crazy flirtations. So far nothing irrevocable had happened, at least on her part. She didn't think Earl had cheated on her, either. Yet. But it was just a matter of time. Maybe she should file for divorce now, before she lost the last remnants of self-control and turned into the town slut. That hunky young landscaper was looking awfully good.....

Resisting an idiotic impulse to caress Earl's bare shoulder, Claudia headed to the bathroom. After a quick shower, she released her long blond hair from its braid and brushed it loose so that it cascaded over the shoulders of her green robe. It was witch hair—unnaturally lush and shiny—and Earl loved it. She suspected that was why he married her.

Maybe she should whack it off and give him her shining locks as part of the divorce settlement? He could own the golden tresses he loved, and she'd be free. With her Hair Blaze potion, she could grow a new crop quick enough. Maybe she'd go to California and turn into a surfer girl. No, at thirty she was too old for that sort of thing....

Yawning, she ambled down the stairs to the kitchen to get the coffee started before she dressed. She adored her kitchen. As soon as she had laid eyes on the warm wood and cool tile, she told Earl this was the house. The kitchen stretched along the back of the structure, looking into the green depths of the Michigan woods. Witches drew their strength from nature, so the kitchen was Claudia's own private cathedral. She had dreamed of teaching her daughters to bake bread and distill potions....

Cutting off the thought, she stepped into her kitchen—and screamed.

Sprawled across the Spanish tile countertop was a...a creature of glittering silver scales and slithering, inhuman motion. A dragon. *"Earl!"*

"Oh, for heavens' sake, child," the dragon hissed.

"Don't carry on so. I'm your mother-in-law."

***

Earl jerked awake when he heard the scream, his blood curdling. *Claudia!*

Before his brain had processed the scream, his body was halfway down the stairs clad only in his sleeping shorts. In this crazy town, anything might turn up at any moment. Though Claudia was an excellent witch, humans were so *fragile*.

He skidded to a stop in the door of the kitchen, horrified. His beautiful Claudia was flattened against the wall, cowering from a menacing beast with smoldering breath and malicious eyes. He stared at the dragon with dismay. "Mother, you *promised*."

The dragon snorted, flame bouncing off the tiled counter. "Yes, and for seven years I've abided by my word and pretended to be human. Seven years, and you have yet to fulfill your part of the bargain and give me a grandchild." Her exhalation of disgust scorched a hickory cabinet opposite her. "If you can't get this useless human female pregnant, it's time you left her and found yourself a dragon bride. A proper scaly maiden who will value the family jewels and give me grandchildren."

"There's no such thing as a dragon," Claudia said, her voice shaking. "I'm hallucinating from the locoweed I used in yesterday's brewing. That happened once before and I hallucinated harpies and animated garden gnomes."

"Uh…that wasn't really a hallucination," Earl pointed out. "Brokenoggin *does* have harpies and live garden gnomes."

"Not a hundred of them dancing like the Radio City Musical Hall Rockettes," Claudia snapped. "After I've had my coffee, this horrible creature will vanish back into the mists."

"You fool of a girl!" The dragon launched herself

across the kitchen, clumsy because she couldn't unfurl her wings properly. "I'm Mei Ling Choo, and I was at your wedding! I never liked you or the marriage, but I didn't think you were so stupid!"

Reflexively Claudia cast a magical damping spell. A burst of green light engulfed the dragon. When it cleared, a petite Chinese woman in neat traditional tunic and trousers sprawled on the Mediterranean floor tiles.

"Mama Mei!" Claudia gasped. "It really *is* you!"

Earl reached his mother before Claudia did and offered a hand up. "Are you all right, Mother?"

With a disdainful sniff, Mei Ling brushed wrinkles from her tunic. "It takes more than a tumble to damage a dragon, boy. Your betrayal of your true nature hurts worse than anything that witch you married can do."

Many women might call their daughters-in-law witches, Earl reflected, but seldom with such accuracy. He punched the button on the electric kettle, then guided his mother to the kitchen table. "I'll make you a nice cup of tea. Then we can discuss this like civilized people."

Claudia stared at him. "You're not denying any of this, Earl. But you're...you're not a dragon." Her voice trailed off. "Are you?"

"I'm only half a dragon, I think." He scowled at his mother. "Mother can't remember who my father was, but she's pretty sure he wasn't a dragon."

"None of your business who your father was," Mei said with no logic but total conviction. "Since you're both being so uncooperative, I'll have that cup of tea and be on my way."

The electrical kettle began to steam, then clicked off. Claudia filled a cup with boiling water to warm it. "What kind of tea, Mama Mei?"

"Earl Grey. Hot." Mei smiled, showing small, sharp teeth. "My favorite. I named my son for the tea—Earl Grey

Choo."

Claudia dumped the warming water, added a teabag, and filled the cup. "I didn't think you hated me," she said in a low voice. "I've always liked you."

"She doesn't hate you," Earl assured his wife. "It's just that being in dragon form tends to…bring out one's aggressive tendencies."

"Which is why you never shape change—you prefer being a wimpy human," his mother said waspishly. "Are you still capable of taking dragon form? If not, you are no son of mine."

She removed her tea bag and drank the scalding contents of the cup in one long gulp. Then she rose to her feet, an unsettling wisp of steam accompanying her words. "Enough. Earl, I order you to resume your dragon form, if you can. Then you must leave this woman and find a proper bride and get her pregnant. I have Spoken. Good-bye." She vanished in a shimmer of magic, leaving silence thick enough to choke an elephant.

Leave Claudia? The mere thought paralyzed him. Sure, they'd been going through a bad patch lately, but they'd find their way back to each other. They had to. Longingly he watched Claudia's luscious figure as she made a pot of coffee with meticulous precision. He liked precision. That's why he'd become a CPA, and it was one of the reasons he fell in love with Claudia. A witch needed to be as precise as an accountant.

Claudia poured herself a cup of coffee as soon as enough had dripped into the pot. After slugging back half the cup, she crossed the kitchen to inspect the cabinet Earl's mother had flamed. Her expression turned grim. "The scorch marks are still there."

She ran her fingertips over the blackened wood, then turned to her husband and said dangerously, "Earl, you have a lot of explaining to do."

***

As Mei vanished from her son's house, she transformed into her dragon shape, glad to stretch her wings properly. The seeds she had sowed would take time to bear fruit, which meant she had a few hours to kill. Maybe she should visit the young wyvern Earl had told her about. The beast sounded as if it needed a good spanking and a lesson in manners. Mei was well qualified to dispense both. And she wouldn't mind getting a look at the chalcedony the little dragon was guarding....

***

Claudia studied her husband's nearly naked body: the smooth, strong muscles, the shining black hair, the entrancing tilt of his dark eyes. She'd always sensed he contained mysteries, but how could she have missed the magic that swirled about him? "Have you been masking your dragon nature the whole time we've been together?"

He glanced away, unable to meet her gaze. "As soon as I saw you, I wanted you. I...I was pretty sure you wouldn't want a half-breed Chinese dragon who doesn't even know who his own father is."

"Well, it's not as if I know who *my* father is. My mother got around." Her calm exploded into anger. "But I *hate* the fact that for all these years, I've been married to a stranger. Was I just another jewel for your dragon horde? A blonde for your collection?"

"No!" Earl exclaimed. Then he paused, an incurably honest accountant. "At least, that was only part of it. I can't deny my nature, and you are a rare and precious beauty worthy of any dragon's collection. But it was you I fell in love with. Your warmth, your kindness to a geeky accountant, your earth magic strength. I...I tried to become what you wanted. Reliable."

So he'd sensed her need for stability from the first, and shaped his image to that. She didn't know whether to be touched or furious. Yes, she'd wanted reliable, but she'd also wanted *exciting*. "You could have been reliable and still told me you were dragon born. Did you think I was some kind of bigot?"

"No!" He bit his lip. She hadn't really appreciated how sharp and white his teeth were. "Maybe it's best if I demonstrate my true nature. If I still can."

He closed his eyes, concentrating hard. A shimmer of magic began to gather around him, blurring his outlines. He was shape shifting, she realized. Or trying to. Snarls and curses sounded from inside the fog of magic, and the dimly seen shape of his body began to change. A—forepaw?— shot out, and then Earl's body switched orientation from vertical to horizontal. "Dammit!" he snarled.

Claudia retreated across the kitchen, fascinated and appalled. Shape changing was obviously not a gentle process. More swearing, this time in a distorted voice and words that sounded like Chinese.

The shape began to enlarge rapidly, and then suddenly the magic dissipated to reveal a magnificent dragon. He was perhaps the size of a large horse and his opalescent scales were colored every shade of indigo and teal, dark at the spine and lightening to silver on his underbelly. His eyes were pure gold and magnificent wings lay furled along his back. "Earl?" she whispered. "Is that really you?"

"Indeed it is," he rumbled in a deep, sexy baritone that made her think of Darth Vader. "Do you see now why I hid myself?"

"But you're beautiful!" Reminding herself that this was Earl, who would never hurt her, she approached and laid a cautious hand on his shining flank. He quivered under her touch. She couldn't help noticing that dragons were—well hung. "A pity I can't turn into a female dragon."

He gave a long, scorching sigh. Her kitchen cabinets were not having a good day. "The fact that you can't is the main reason I've concealed my identity. I...I fear that if I let my inner dragon loose, I might incinerate you when we're making love. That could happen even when I'm in human form. So I've locked down my dragon nature."

"The bottom line is that you're afraid of burning me alive?" she said, startled. "That's no problem now that I've perfected my fire protection potion."

He blinked at her. Who knew that dragons had sexy long eyelashes? "You've created a fire protection potion? I didn't know that!"

She sighed. "We haven't talked much lately."

He looked down bashfully. "Every day I go to your website to see if you've posted any news about your work or new products. It's been a way of keeping in touch, sort of. But I didn't know about this potion."

"I haven't posted anything about it because I haven't figured out how to produce it in commercial quantities," she explained. "But I have enough for personal use. I gave some to everyone who comes in contact with the wyvern. The silly beast can't be trusted not to fry people, but the potion has prevented injuries."

Earl's opalescent eyes widened. "When you work out a method of large-scale production, you'll be rich!"

"Hush your mouth, Earl," she said, annoyed. "I plan to sell it at cost to fire departments. Firefighters deserve all the help they can get."

His eyes glowed even brighter. "That's one of the things I love about you. Your idealism is so...so undragon-like."

Briefly she wondered if her lack of interest in getting rich was part of why Mother Mei didn't like her. Luckily, Earl had enough human in him to appreciate something besides hording jewels—he did pro-bono tax returns for most of the old folks in town.

So her husband was a dragon, a creature of fire and

passion.... The knowledge sent waves of heat through her. She stroked her hand slowly along his sinuous spine. "I have some of the fire protection potion here in the kitchen. Should I drink some?"

"Oh, *please,*" he breathed. "By the time you've taken it, I'll be back to human shape."

Lips parted and heartbeat accelerating, she murmured the spell to unlock her potion cabinet, which was always sealed to prevent anyone from breaking in. It wouldn't do to let the town teenagers get at her frog potion....

Ah, there it was. She took the bottle, unscrewed the cap, and swigged down a large dose. She could feel the cool power as it slid down her throat, then filled every cell of her body with protective light. Yessss....

It would be at least six hours before the effect started to fade—and she knew exactly how she wanted to spend those hours.

More cursing and swearing from across the kitchen, then a thump. She turned to see Earl back in human form, sprawled on the floor. His shorts had gotten lost along the way and....her eyes widened. "Sweetie, is your shape shifting ability something that applies to your human body? Because part of you certainly looks...enhanced!"

"This is what happens when I let my dragon nature loose when I'm in human form." His voice retained some of those sexy Darth Vader vibrations. "That isn't all that changes." Lithely he rose from the floor and stalked across the kitchen, and she could see the fire in his eyes.

A step away he hesitated, sounding like the old Earl. "You're sure that potion works?"

"Guaranteed." Since he was being cautious, she pounced. His mouth and body were dearly familiar, but at the same time new and exciting. *Hot.* She bit his ear, then gasped as he ripped her robe away to reveal her naked body.

From then on, they mated like dragons, flame rolling

through them, raising passion to unimaginable heights. Sex and fire and dragon blood. And dragon endurance and shape shifting magic that made everything fit *just right.*

By the time Claudia regained her senses, the sunshine had shifted from early morning to full day, and then some. She lay gasping, her head pillowed on Earl's shoulder while she luxuriated in the sweet/sharp pain of love bites in numerous places. "A good thing I insisted on tile for the floor, or we might have burned the house down," she murmured. "Oh, Earl, why didn't we do this years ago?"

"You hadn't developed the potion," he said practically. His sated eyes began to glow golden again. "But now that you have..." he nipped her shoulder. "Dragons are very possessive, my jewel. No more flirtations with anyone!"

She smiled with lazy mischief. "You think witches aren't possessive? If you so much as look at another female, you'll lose a few cherished body parts." She rolled onto him, secure in the knowledge that neither of them would ever look at another person again. "Now about that dragon endurance...."

***

Having sorted out the wyvern and acquired some really fine pieces of chalcedony, Mei flew back over her son's house and scanned it with her dragon senses. Ah, so the silly children had worked things out. Claudia might not know it yet, but she was pregnant with twins, a boy and a girl. And dragon nature was a dominant. Cross breeding with a really good witch wouldn't hurt the blood line. If anything, it would strengthen it. Hybrid vigor. Luckily, Chinese dragon magic and Western witch magic were so different that mixing caused no problems.

She smiled toothily. The two of them certainly had plenty *of vigor. Satisfied, she banked and swung west toward her San Francisco home. Her work here was done.*

Now it was time to get to work on Earl's sister, who'd also been fool enough to marry a mere human....

Episode 1.15

LOF-T: ROGG 1

(Lord of the Forest Trolls: Return of the Garden Gnome episode 1)
By

Linda Wisdom

Wherein Sam learns what it's like to be a garden gnome in the Disdaine Triplets' front yard.

Linda Wisdom is the author of more than 70 romance & romantic suspense novels. To learn more about Linda and her work go to http://www.intimatemomentsauthors.com. You can also download her eBooks at http://www.triskelionpublishing.com.
Write to Linda at: PO Box 356, Murrieta, CA 92564

All those beautiful tall leafy trees were better than any house for protection. The lush green canopy overhead filtered out the sunlight while the rich earthy smell of moss caressed his nostrils and the feel of grass beneath his gnarled toes was bliss. The rustling sound of insects serenading the night was better than any music concert. It was all so dark and inviting. No wonder his kind considered it heaven.

Sam knew he was smiling. He didn't just love running through his world. He also loved dreaming about it.

His legs twitched with the anticipation of waking up and running through the forest. How he loved sunny days when he could scramble up trees and scare birds even without going out into the sunlight. Cats had nothing on him for scaring birds. Or eating them. Such a tasty treat for the non-discriminating troll. Then he would jump out of the bushes and scream at the faeries before running through puddles.

Rain? Inside his dream his smile slipped. He didn't smell rain in the air. So why was he getting wet?

His nose worked. What *was* that disgusting smell?

Wait a minute. That wasn't rain coming down on him. He opened his eyes to find a little tan dog's leg way too close to his nose. *That creature was daring to piss on his head!*

Trolls might not have many powers, but they could zap creatures that taunted them. He blinked, concentrating harder than usual it seemed. Surprised he watched the little beast continue its disrespectful business. He *knew* just where to send that current. So why wasn't the dog now a pile of ash? *Where in the Goddess' name was his power?*

Sam looked up at the sky where he'd been told She resided.

"Just tell me what I did!" he screamed. (Even at the

best of times, trolls are excitable. This wasn't the best of times.) Silence. "Okay, whatever I did, I didn't mean it. I had too much ale. I was caught up in the moment. It was just one of those things."

That was his story and he was sticking to it. He didn't know what he'd done, but he didn't see where it was anything unusual for one of his kind. Trolls weren't sweet little angels. They just weren't. He rolled his tongue around inside his mouth and spat out something dark brown. His mouth felt like he'd tasted something disgusting. He swore it tasted like that gross stuff the witches of Brokenoggin thought was so great. He had no idea why they thought chocolate was ambrosia when there were so many tasty mushrooms, along with that oh-so-tasty moss to munch on. Or even a good chewy slug.

He had to figure out where he was and exactly what had happened to him. This wasn't like a hangover from too much Goran ale. But all he could see was domestic blue lawn grass that wasn't very well tended, and flowers that weren't all that special.

He noticed a nearby puddle of water and used that to see why he felt so different. Whatever he expected it wasn't this. Shock sent him rearing back. He was a...a...*Garden Gnome, banished to suburbia!*

If it were possible, he'd have fainted from the shock. He wondered who hated him so much they'd turn him into a gnome. Trying to pick and choose among his enemies, he knew, could turn into a very long drawn out effort in futility—and that was before anyone cited the length of the list. He tended to make more enemies than friends.

Not to mention he could see something bright and glittery hanging off his head. Wait a minute, this didn't feel like his head! If felt...*pointed*! He didn't have a pointed head. Or what looked like disgusting pink paint on him. All right, so now he basically looked like a gnome dork. He decided he should thank the Goddess the thong was on his head and not riding up his ass. That would have been the ultimate humiliation.

I must have royally pissed someone off to end up like this. Time to do some hard thinking so I can get off this ugly lawn. No self-respecting troll should be forced to be near this sorry excuse for a lawn when there's a perfectly good forest nearby.

Sam-the-troll-turned-garden-gnome turned his head to watch a police cruiser roll slowly down the street. He might be a creature of the forest, but he recognized the driver of the vehicle.

"Lookin' hot, babe!" he called out, flashing what he thought was a sexy grin, but which actually looked downright scary to the uninitiated. Namely, anyone who didn't understand a troll's expressions.

The Caprice pulled over to the curb and stopped. Brokenoggin's main, and only, police officer, Janice Thinksalot, climbed out of the patrol car and walked over to him with an animal-like grace he had to admire. The admiration evaporated when he realized she wasn't going to even show the decency to crouch down to his level, thereby forcing him to tip his head all the way back until he had to scramble for balance. She might be one hot mama, if you liked *their kind*, but she was also a cold and rude bitch who didn't respect the lofty trolls.

"What the hell are you doing here?" she asked. She wrinkled her nose in distaste as a nasty smell emitted from the troll-turned-gnome. She stepped back but it didn't make the odor any less offensive. "You smell like Chihuahua piss."

"That's because one of those tiny monsters pissed on me. As for how I got here. Beats me." He kicked up his heels. "But you gotta say I add some class to this ugly place." He waved his hand in the vicinity of the house. He didn't like seeing his once gorgeous mud-colored skin now painted a pastel pink to resemble human skin.

Janice's eyes swung downward then back up. Her lip curled echoing the disgust on her face. "That is so sick."

He looked down at the protuberance poking out of his bright blue shorts. Even his expression of pride couldn't make him look even remotely harmless. He tried to stuff his erection back in his shorts, but it refused to remain hidden. He had an idea it wouldn't be going down anytime soon. He did a hop and a skip across the lawn then spun around.

""I can't help it if I happen to show what I think of a lovely woman." He defended his body's reactions with the same kind of haughty attitude he'd seen the faeries use. "Claire doesn't mind when I'm showing my affection."

"Then Claire has more issues than I knew about. Of course she also has the sad task of being married to you." Janice took a deep breath. "Do us both a favor and get out of here before one of the triplets comes out and gets rid of you in a very painful way," she told him. "You know how much they hate trolls."

He lifted his white-bearded chin. Something else he wasn't happy with. He usually had no more than four hairs sprouting from his pointed chin. "I can't go anywhere."

"Wanna bet?" Janice grabbed his arm and practically pulled him off his feet as she made her way across the lawn.

He yelped a protest at her trollhandling. "Police abuse!" he shouted at the top of his lungs. "We're talking cruel and introll punishment here! Next thing I know she'll try to strip search me even if my clothes are painted on me." He waggled his eyebrows. "Not that I wouldn't mind you checking out all my orifices."

"Shut up you sick and disgusting *thing*!" she ordered between gritted teeth as she dragged him across the lawn with his dug-in heels leaving furrows in the grass. It appeared turning him into a garden gnome added a few, or thirty, pounds to his roly-poly frame. Except when Janice's feet touched the sidewalk a strong force pulled her back to the lawn. She frowned and tried once more but was pulled back again once the troll's toes touched the lawn/sidewalk boundary. She rounded on him with a fury that rivaled his harpy wife. Frankly, he was impressed. Not to mention more than a little turned on. "Dammit, Sam! Stop whatever you're doing! You need to get out of here!"

"I told you!" he shouted. To prove his point, he ran toward Janice as if he had the intention of mowing her down. In the back of his mind, he hoped he could make a run for his beloved forest where he might have a chance of finding someone who could break the spell. His toes barely breached the edge of the lawn when a spark of light snapped at him and he was abruptly thrown backwards. His arms windmilled as he desperately fought for balance. He lost the battle and ended up on his butt. He promptly bounced to his feet. "Talk about lousy taste in grass," he muttered. He didn't care that bits of grass and dirt clung to his shorts since they remind him of home—sort of. But then, considering there was a turquoise-glittery thong hanging off his head, nothing could embarrass him. "There's no cushioning to this grass at all. They need to hire a new gardener. Don't they know a lush lawn makes a dwelling look more homey? It's not like they don't have the money to maintain a nice yard. It would be nice if they planted something that had actual green in it."

Janice shook her head. "Who do you think you are? The new member of *Extreme Home Makeover?* I just want to know why you're here."

Sam snarled. "If I knew how I got here I'd have a better chance of getting outta here, wouldn't I? All I know is, I woke up when one of those little skanky Wa Was pissed me," he said. "It has not been a good day."

The sound of the front door opening and high-pitched

shrieks assaulting Janice's ultra-sensitive ears had the officer stepping back and Sam frantically looking around for a place to hide.

The Disdaine triplets were bitch witches and they hadn't even hit puberty yet. They looked alike, acted alike and created mayhem in tandem. While they were dressed in their mother's choice of cute pastel-colored sundresses, their faces looked as if they'd gotten into their mother's make-up complete with Witchy Woman lip colour smeared red across pouty mouths, Vamp Tramp purple eyeshadow and Demon Glow blush covering rounded cheeks.

"That's nasty!" Scornful Disdaine shouted running up to Sam with a finger outstretched as if a flame would erupt from the tip at any moment. Her yellow ruffled sundress and matching tennis shoes made her look like a little angel. Unless one looked closer and saw the little devil lurking in her eyes.

"That *smells* nasty!" Derisive Disdaine screamed, holding her nose with thumb and forefinger. She glared at Janice. She stamped her sky-blue tennis shoe shod foot. "You're the police and you have to do what we say. Get rid of it!"

"Manners. Manners are good," Janice growled at her as a reminder she was no mere human.

"We don't like gnomes. They're nasty," Withering Disdaine announced with a haughty toss of butterscotch curls. "Especially ugly ones like him." She tried to grab at the thong that danced on his head but a breeze lifted the ends and tossed them in the other direction. She frowned as Sam grinned at her before running off to turn a cartwheel. The thong magickally remained on his head. "Why is his thingie poking out like that?"

"Oh come on, Sam, that is so sick!" Janice yelled.

"And it's not my fault!" He jumped up and down in a typical   troll-tantrum-when-imprisoned-in-a-gnome-body.

"Not my fault, not my fault, not my fault!"

The sisters clasped hands and circled the troll-turned-gnome. "Nasty troll, nasty gnome, make us happy and go home!" they chanted. "Nasty troll, nasty gnome, make us happy and go home!"

"Yeah, like that's gonna happen," Janice muttered. She raised her voice. "You girls want him to leave? Why not drag him out into the street where I can drive over him?"

Three pair of eyes lit up with malevolent glee.

"Hey!" Sam's protests were drowned out by the girls' screams of delight as one took one arm, one took the other and the third pushed from the rear. Sam cursed them every tiny step of the way. His words turned into maniacal laughter when they reached the sidewalk and all four were catapulted backwards.

"My dress!" Scornful screamed, brushing dirt off her backside.

"That hurt!" Withering wailed with ear-splitting sound.

"Bad gnome!" Derisive bounced to her feet and ran over to Sam who was awkwardly scrambling to his feet. "You need to be punished!"

"Like I haven't been punished already by being imprisoned on this ugly lawn." He turned to Janice. "Get me out of here."

"Tell me who sent you here and I'll appeal to them to take off the curse." Janice kept a wary eye on the triplets. They weren't known for their ladylike behavior.

"I don't know who sent me here!" he shrieked, turning his pink skin a bright red. "I don't know, I don't know, I don't know!" He jumped up and down so hard he left holes in the grass.

Janice threw up her hands. "You're on your own." She turned around and walked back to her cruiser.

"No!" Sam ran down the yard but had the smarts to stop short of the edge. "You can't leave me with them!"

"Watch me." Janice's words floated back to him amid the triplet's ear-splitting shrieks of malicious joy as they danced around him.

Sam spent the day learning just what the phrase "*hell on earth*" meant. By the time the sun went down and the triplets were called inside, he was ready to beg the devil himself to take him away.

Nighttime wasn't much better. He spent an hour on his tiptoes looking in one of the Disdaine windows watching the family consume dinner. He didn't think much of the menu and all it did was make him hungry. He discovered the hard way that gnomes didn't have stomachs to process food even if he could have found a toadstool somewhere. He stamped his foot in frustration but it didn't have the scary impression an angry troll could make.

No wonder people made fun of garden gnomes. They were the clowns of the magickal world.

Gnomes also couldn't sleep. Sam listened to the triplets protest bedtime and their whispered chants that were downright scary.

"Little birches," he muttered, settling for making a bed among the flowers ringing a tree set in the center of the yard. What he wouldn't give for a nice large hollow tree trunk. He stiffened as a lean black animal appeared at the end of the street and moved gracefully down the sidewalk. It was too large to be a dog and its eyes gleamed with a fierce hunger not seen among the canine set, and Sam was suddenly grateful he was stone and not skin and bone. He might have ended up a late night snack.

The werewolf loped over to him and sniffed him from the top of the thong to his toes. The way the were kept returning to the thong made Sam wonder just who or what had worn it before it ended up as a colorful accessory.

"Do you happen to know how I got here?" he asked, but only received a growl for his trouble. "Fine, see if I tell you how to get in the house where you can find three tasty treats. *ARGH*!" If he thought Chihuahua piss was bad, he soon learned that werewolf piss was even worse. As for were-shit…well, that was downright indescribable.

By morning, Sam was convinced he'd endured more than any law-evading troll-turned-gnome should endure. The only good thing that happened to him was the sprinklers going off at six a.m. and washing him clean.

Promptly at eight, the triplets were back outside ready to make his life hell again.

Sam wailed like he'd never wailed before, but no one bothered to come to his rescue. Not when it was more fun to stand on the sidewalk and watch a show that was more entertaining than anything found on cable. Emma Mincemeat showed up with her book *Witchcraft for Dummies*, but none of the reversing spells she uttered did the trick. He feared he was doomed to spend eternity as a lawn ornament tormented by the Disdaine triplets.

As his last bid for self-defense, Sam began singing his favorite song. A troll-turned-gnome singing the Lumberjack Song from Monty Python was a sight—and sound—no witch could forget. Especially since singing wasn't one of his few gifts. As he pranced around singing at the top of his lungs, the thong now hung around his neck like an obscene necklace.

The tapping on the sidewalk was a sound he was afraid he would never hear again. The vision approaching him looked like something out of a dream: petite, barely five-foot-one-inches, with cornflower blue eyes, and hair the color of spun gold that hung down her back in spiral curls, she had Faery pink glossed pouty lips that looked ready for a kiss. Her dainty shell-pink dress matched equally dainty high-heeled open-toed sandals that displayed pink-painted toes Sam vividly recalled sucking on more than once. Her large eyes widened in shock as she stood in front of him. He could smell the scent of spring on her skin. His penis wasted no time in popping out in search of a familiar place.

"Euuwww, his thingie is looking at me!" Scornful screamed.

"Oh Sammykins!" The Vision wrung her hands in front of her. "I didn't mean for this to happen."

Sammykins didn't need a real brain to figure out what she meant.

"Claire, you did this to me?" He didn't have to pretend feeling hurt. His beautiful Claire was behind his punishment?

Her lower lip trembled. "You were mean to me," she said in her little girl whispery voice. "You made me cry."

"We were having an argument! No one says anything nice during a fight! And I didn't say anything mean to you until you called me a gross mushroom eating trog," he reminded her. He stood up as tall as he could. "I am not a *trog*."

A teardrop hovered on the curve of her cheek before slowly making its way downward. "And I am not…" she sniffed, unable to continue in front of what looked like a gathering crowd of fifty witches, a few interested weres, a naked vampyre—to name only a few of the Brokenoggin residents lining the sidewalk. The smell of popcorn filled the air as they settled down to watch the show.

Sam wiggled his fingers. If Claire was behind his change, then it was only fair she share his humiliation.

"Not a…?" he prompted.

"This isn't nice, Sammykins," she whispered. "I don't want to say it."

"Not a-a-a-a…?" he drew out the last word.

Her tiny chin trembled. "You said I was flat."

Men's gazes immediately zeroed in on her double-D breasts.

"Man, that is one Wonder Bra," John loudly announced.

Claire glared at him. "I am not flat!" Her whispery voice suddenly rose in pitch. "I am not flat!"

"Whereas *I* have perfect pitch," Sam announced to one and all with a dramatic sweep of the arm—except the gesture lost its sense of drama since his arm was merely a tiny pink painted extension with even tinier fingers. He began singing his favorite ditty, the Lumberjack Song from Monty Python complete with his favorite gestures. What he didn't realize was that while he thought his singing voice was magnificent, it sounded more like a wood chipper in serious need of a grease job.

"I *hate that song*!" Claire screeched loud enough to crack more than a few windows. "HATE IT! *HATE* IT!" She reared back and looked down at the grinning and singing Sam with bulging eyes. She was no longer the pretty and dainty little darling she'd been two seconds ago.

Her porcelain skin shimmered into a brownish color and her body suddenly elongated, bones popping as her arms lengthened to papery wings. Her perfect doll features receded with her mouth turning into an ugly *V* and razor sharp teeth glistened white in the afternoon sun. She flapped her wings until she hovered a foot above the grass, her stick-like legs kicking thin air. As Sam kept singing, she lifted her head and screamed a shrill sound that might have shattered more than a few eardrums if it wasn't for most of the residents being protected by magick, and the fact that those who weren't knew who to go to, to have new ones conjured up.

The screeching harpy flew higher, her large wings flapping heavily. With one last scream that shattered most of the windows in a five-mile area, she flew off.

"Flat!" Sam shouted after her, his tiny arms waving. "Your scream is flat!"

"Good going, dog hydrant," Janice said from the sidelines. "After the way you just humiliated her, she's not going to allow the curse to be lifted anytime soon now."

Sam froze. As the police officer's words sunk in, he realized the mistake he'd just made was the biggest he'd ever made in his life.

"I'm sorry, sweetheart!" he shouted after the diminishing figure in the air. "I didn't mean it! You have a beautiful voice. And I'll only sing in the shower!" When she didn't turn back, he shrugged. "She'll be back. You'll see." He settled down in the grass. "She never holds a grudge. It's not in her."

A little after midnight when the black were stopped by to piss on him again, Sam knew there wasn't a chance in his lifetime that Claire would be back to take the curse away. He wrinkled his nose at the pungent smell on his clothes. He sat down to wait for the sprinklers to come on.

"Good thing I never said what I think of her mother."

Episode 1.16

PIECES OF DESTINY

By

Michelle Rowen

Wherein teenaged Destiny Hopewell attempts to leave
Brokenoggin and comes radically unglued in the process.
(Story and new characters by Michelle Rowen)

Michelle Rowen is a self-confessed Reality TV addict and *Buffy*
the Vampire Slayer fanatic from the Toronto area. Her first novel,
BITTEN & SMITTEN, will be published in January 2006. Visit
her website at http://www.michellerowen.com.

"**O**nly a matter of time," Destiny Hopewell said into her tiny, pink cellphone. "And I'm finally getting the hell out of this town. For good."

"Yeah, yeah," her friend said. "You've been saying that for eighteen years."

"You won't be hearing it much longer. I've got a date with Tad tonight."

"Tad, the hotty college guy you've been emailing for, like, forever?"

"That's the Tad."

"Hey Des, that's great. Just don't get your hopes up, okay?"

Destiny stopped walking. The warm, summer evening air felt like it was closing in on her. "What did you just say?" she snapped.

There was a pause. "Uh…"

"Look, Pru, I don't care if you want to stay in this town of freaks for the rest of your life. I don't. I want to go somewhere normal where I don't bump into naked vampires or where garden gnomes don't try to look up my skirt as I pass them. Don't even get me started on those trailer trash witches who have it in for me. I can't take it anymore. There's a whole world out there that I want to see, and when I get out of here, I'm not looking back."

"What about your parents?"

Destiny rolled her eyes. "When did you become the voice of reason? My parents are a huge part of why I want out of here. Look, I have to get home and get changed, okay?"

"That's cool. I have to get ready myself."

"Why? What are you doing tonight?"

"I'm babysitting the Disdaine triplets."

"You're kidding."

"They're paying me amazing money, too. You babysat

for them before, didn't you?"

Destiny reached down and tenderly rubbed her knee as she thought back to her babysitting stint with the Disdaine triplets. They hadn't been happy with their assigned bedtime and hidden her kneecap for a few hours. She'd dragged herself around the garden looking for it while the brats stayed up watching TV and eating candy. When she finally found the kneecap, she had to fight with a talking squirrel over it for a half an hour. Talking squirrels were hard to reason with.

Ever since, she'd been walking with a bit of a limp that became more pronounced when she wore fashionable footwear.

Should she warn Pru? Not that it would be a surprise for anyone living in town that the triplets were evil incarnate. But still...

Nah. Let her figure it out for herself.

"I'm sure it will go fine," she said. "Nothing to worry about. Anyhow, I'll tell you all about my wonderful date tomorrow."

There was a long sigh on the other end of the line. "Have fun, okay?"

Destiny hung up. Oh, she was going to have fun, all right. Nothing was going to go wrong tonight. It wasn't every day an outsider came into town who wasn't a total freakazoid. Like that naked vampire guy. What was his name? Seth...Stephen... something like that. Granted, he was a major hotty. But *way* weird.

He'd fit in just fine in Brokenoggin Falls.

But Destiny didn't. Never had. And she never wanted to.

She pulled her notepad out of her purse, and flipped forward to her to-do list.

FRIDAY – D-DAY

1. Shift at Brokenoggin Burger – 2:30 – 7:30 pm
2. Date with Tad – 8:00 pm
3. Make Tad fall madly in love with me – 8:15 pm
4. Have Tad propose marriage – 10:00ish pm
** ***Note to self:*** *Remember to scrape windshield of Toyota to remove remnants of suicidal fairy. ***Buy Windex. ****

Tad Anderson was the answer to all her problems. He'd take her out tonight and she'd make him fall madly and passionately in love with her. He'd see her plight, her pain, her naturally large breasts, and want to rescue her. They'd drive off into the sunset together in his Porsche—in her mind he drove a red Porsche—and bye-bye Brokenoggin.

Forever.

The thought made her very happy. But nothing could go wrong tonight.

Nothing.

She had precisely, she looked at her watch, less than a half hour to get gorgeous, and wash the french fry smell off herself from working a six hour shift. No time to waste.

As soon as Tad took her away from town, she'd never work for minimum wage again. She was going to be a model. Or maybe an actress. She had the looks, after all. Just another thing this lame ass town had kept her from achieving.

She picked up her pace, but at the end of the block two familiar figures stepped into her path. She stopped. Great, just what she needed. The two trailer trash witches she'd been talking about a minute ago. Sabrina and Tabitha Wartly. Tabitha had been in her computer class at Brokenoggin High and had made her life practically unbearable.

She sure was one ugly bee-yotch.

"Well, looky here," Tabitha sneered at her. "Destiny

Hopeless, walking home from the greasepit."

"I'm not walking home from your face," Destiny said. "And that's the only greasepit I can see."

"Ha ha, that's so funny I forgot to laugh."

Sabrina didn't say anything, but even in the near darkness, Destiny could see her eyes were red and puffy from crying. They finally matched the rest of her face.

Destiny tucked her notebook back in her bag and crossed her arms. "What do you want? I'm in kind of a hurry here."

Tabitha glared at her. "Like the hurry you were in to steal my sister's boyfriend?"

Destiny stared at her blankly for a moment trying to figure out if she'd just gone insane. Sabrina's boyfriend was a troll. Literally. She started to laugh.

"Yeah, I so stole your boyfriend," she said. "Not."

"He told me he's in love with you," Sabrina sputtered. "I saw the love letter he wrote you." She stomped her foot. "You *stole* him from me!"

"Look, loser-girl. I didn't steal your boyfriend. If he has a fixation with me because I'm the only girl he's met who isn't covered in ugly warts, it's not my fault."

Sabrina's bottom lip wobbled. "My mom calls them *beauty* warts."

"Riiight. Look, I'm going home now. I have an important date with a *normal* guy. Do you know what normal means? No, I didn't think so."

She started walking but could hear the girls whispering behind her back. Then one of them laughed. Destiny turned around to look. They were holding hands and had their eyes closed while they chanted something through their giggles.

Oh shit. Maybe I shouldn't have said anything about the warts, Destiny thought. It was obviously a sensitive issue.

"What are you doing?" she demanded.

"Important date, huh?" Tabitha grinned. Her two good teeth glinted in the moonlight. "Wouldn't want it to come apart at the seams, would you?"

Destiny stared at her. "What are you talking about?"

Sabrina snickered. "Just try to keep it together…Destiny. Geez, don't fall apart on us, okay? Wouldn't want anything bad to happen to you since you've always been so nice to us."

Destiny felt tense. The girls had done something— some spell. That much was obvious. But she didn't feel any different. Shit. She'd been stupid to tease the two of them. Apart it was okay. Together they were…well, evil.

But before she could ask what they'd done to her, the sisters waved at her and laughed. Then they turned around and ran away.

***

Tad arrived right on time, and Destiny raced down the stairs at the sound of the doorbell. Didn't want her father answering the door. Or her mother for that matter. If she could help it, he wouldn't meet her folks at all.

Ever.

She took a deep breath and opened the door.

Tad stood there looking as hot if not hotter than the photo he'd emailed her. Six feet tall, blond hair, high cheekbones, full lips. He even had a damn dimple in his chin. She could have sworn she heard a chorus of angels singing, but noticed that the next door neighbors were having a karaoke party. Two furry people she didn't recognize were outside howling at the moon in the key of G.

She grabbed Tad's sleeve to pull him inside so he wouldn't witness the weirdness.

She worried he was going to be disappointed in her since the picture she'd sent him was from a distance. A prom photo. It was a good picture of her, but she'd tried to cut out her prom date, a wizard by the name of Willard who'd brought her an enchanted corsage. They'd had to leave the dance early after the corsage ate a good chunk of the front part of her dress.

"Wow," Destiny said. "You look amazing."

"Thanks."   Tad   smiled—a   bright,   handsome, completely normal in every way smile. "You know, it's weird. I could have sworn I saw a naked guy with a piece of wood sticking out of his chest on the other side of town."

"Really? That's weird."

Change of subject, she told herself. Pronto.

"Ready to go?" She grabbed her jacket and made for the door just as she heard a very familiar voice behind her.

"Not quite yet, young lady. Don't I get to meet the young man?"

Destiny tensed. "Dad, I thought you were in your workshop. I didn't want to disturb you."

Her father came towards the door. Destiny tried to block the view but it was too late. Tad had already gotten an eyeful. Well, a mini eyeful, anyhow.

Destiny's father stood barely four feet tall. He wasn't officially a "little person," though, since he was perfectly proportioned to his height. His nose came to a curving point as did his ears, and he wore green and red striped stockings underneath a red sweater and green shorts. His shoes were handmade, and jingled as he walked.

Destiny's father was an elf. A Christmas elf, that is. Twenty years ago, he'd escaped from the North Pole. "Damn slave labor it was," he always told her. "That Claus is a tyrant!"   He'd heard about a small town called Brokenoggin Falls that welcomed unusual people, and packed up his best candy canes and toy-making tools, and then stole a reindeer for his getaway.

He hadn't been in Brokenoggin for much more than a year when he ran over a dog with his car (an Austin Mini, of course), a big, black, shaggy dog that he took to the vet and then helped nurse back to health. But it turned out it wasn't a dog at all. It was a wolf.

A werewolf.

Her mom.

Nine months later, out popped Destiny.

She decided not to share this little walk down memory lane with Tad. He wouldn't understand. She wasn't even sure *she* understood most of the time.

"Look here," her father said with a great smile on his diminutive face. "I've made a gift for your friend."

Tad stepped forward to accept the small, carved wooden sailboat.

"*Da-ad*," Destiny whined. "Don't embarrass me."

"Embarrass you?" he exclaimed. "I wouldn't dream of it."

Yeah, right.

"Okay, we're like, *leaving*." Destiny grabbed Tad's very firm and nicely muscular arm and tried to steer him outside.

"This is *amazing*," Tad said to her father as he inspected the boat. "Where did you learn to do this?"

Destiny's father gave a little bow. "Thank you, my boy. I was well taught from the time I was a child by none other than—"

"Leaving," Destiny cut him off before he said too much. "Now?"

"Give your poppa a kiss first."

Kill me, Destiny thought. *Just kill me now and put me out of my misery.* But she forced a smile, leaned way, way over, and air-kissed her father's cheek.

***

Perfect date.

It was going to be perfect.

Stamped it, no erasies.

Turned out Tad didn't drive a Porsche after all. It was a

Mercedes. Destiny decided she could live with that. He hadn't seemed mortified by meeting her odd father. Thank God, her mother was out that night at a laser hair removal seminar.

And her brother?

She thought she'd seen him earlier out of the corner of her eye. But it had just been her imagination. Luckily, too. He was extremely overprotective of his sister and was guaranteed to hate Tad on sight.

They sat in his car in the parking lot of Brokenoggin Burger. The thought of eating the greasy food made Destiny's stomach turn over, but she forced back the cheeseburger and fries with a smile. She glanced at the clock on the dashboard. Eight-thirty. According to her schedule, Tad should have fallen madly in love with her fifteen minutes ago. She wasn't positive, but she didn't think it had happened yet.

It was okay. Fifteen minutes off schedule was nothing to worry about.

She bit down on another fry and felt something strange in her mouth. She frowned, and turned her head to the side so she could fish out whatever it was. Hard, small, white...

A tooth.

Holy shit, she'd just lost a damn tooth on a Brokenoggin fry.

But the fried potato wasn't that hard. The tooth had just...slid out...all by itself.

She eyed Tad. He wasn't paying attention while he fiddled with the car radio to find some "mood music." She took the tooth and tried to slide it back into place. She expected to feel pain, but there was nothing. There. All fixed.

He finally found a decent station, and leaned back in his seat clearly proud of himself. The music cut through the uncomfortable silence in the car. Destiny had been trying to think of something incredibly witty and intelligent to say. But since Destiny was neither witty nor terribly intelligent, she was coming up blank.

"You're so beautiful," Tad finally said.

A dribble of ketchup landed on Destiny's shirt and she grabbed for a napkin. "Oh? Um...thanks."

"You know, I was hoping to meet a girl like you."

"Really?"

"Everybody thinks I'm weird, see? Because I'm sort of mature for my age. My friends, my folks, they all tell me that I should just have fun. But I really want to do is settle down with a nice girl. Get married. Have a couple of kids. Like, right away. I don't want to wait until I'm too old to care about those things anymore."

She nodded sagely. This was perfect. Everything was going according to her plan.

He reached over and tucked a strand of her freshly highlighted auburn hair behind her ear. "I just figure, when you know what you want, you just gotta go for it."

"I totally and absolutely agree."

"You're special, Destiny. I knew that from the first moment you uploaded your picture."

How romantic was that? Destiny sighed with happiness.

He leaned towards her and she closed her eyes, waiting for the kiss. Hoping that she didn't have anything stuck between her teeth.

She waited.

And waited some more.

Then she opened her eyes.

Tad was chewing on a french fry. "The guy at the drive through was kind of weird, huh?"

She cleared her throat and tried to compose herself. "Yeah, that's Cy. I guess he is a little strange, isn't he?"

"Something was up with his eye. What was that? Kind

of freaky if you ask me."

Cy was a Cyclops. So there was nothing wrong with his eye other than the fact that he only had one of them right in the middle of his forehead. Nice guy, though. Always let her leave early. Plus, for a guy with only one eye, he had a very nice body. It was a trade-off.

She didn't think it was all that nice for Tad to pick on him and was about to say something, but her nose started to itch. She absently rubbed at it and after a moment, it came clean off her face and fell into her lap. Horrified, she immediately ducked under the dash to try to reattach it.

"Destiny?" Tad asked. "You okay down there?"

"Yeah, fine. I just dropped something."

"Should I turn on the light?"

"No! No lights!"

Destiny gently turned the nose in the right direction and pressed it to her face. She touched it, waiting to feel blood, waiting to feel pain, but there was nothing. She took her hand away and the nose stayed exactly where it was supposed to be.

She was just about to start freaking out over what the hell was happening to her when she remembered something the Wartly sisters had said earlier.

"Just try to keep it together...Destiny. Geez, don't fall apart on us, okay? Wouldn't want anything bad to happen to you since you've always been so nice to us."

A spell.

That's what this was. A spell by those ugly bitches meant to ruin her date. Really funny.

Not.

She'd show them. Nothing they could do would stop her from making Tad fall completely in love with her. After the night was over...then, and only then, would she think about her revenge.

Just because she didn't have any magickal powers

didn't mean she didn't have ways of paying them back big-time.

"Let's go somewhere else," Tad suggested.

"Out of town?" she suggested hopefully.

"Nah, there's got to be somewhere," he lowered his voice and grinned at her, "*private* where we can get to know each other better?"

Since the entire town of Brokenoggin was surrounded by a thick thatch of evergreens, there were plenty of private places Destiny could think of. She directed him to a little nook where she'd made out a couple of months ago with Johnny Franklin. At least until the full moon came out and he bolted from the car and into the woods.

Wonder what ever happened to him after that? she thought. *Were-chipmunks were so unpredictable.*

"Damn it!" Tad swerved the car, snapping her out of the memory. "Almost hit that stupid dog. Where do all these little dogs come from anyhow?"

She just shrugged.

"This town is messed up," Tad said. "How can you live here without turning into a freak, yourself?"

It was on the tip of her tongue to tell him it wasn't that bad. And that it was okay for her to say those things about Brokenoggin, but not for him—a total stranger to the town. But she bit her tongue.

Which then fell out of her mouth.

"Shit!" she yelled, but since her tongue was gone it sounded more like, "Shhhd!"

She undid her seatbelt and scrambled to the floor to look for the elusive appendage. She thought it had bounced over on the driver's side of the car so she crawled in that direction and grabbed onto Tad's knee for support.

"Oh yeah, baby," Tad said. "That's what I'm talking about. But can you at least wait until I pull over?"

There it was, under the brake pedal. She grabbed the

tongue but it slipped away from her.

"Shhhhddd!"

She finally got her hand on it and shoved it back in her mouth. It was covered with dirt that tasted disgusting, but it reattached itself right away.

Then she tried to get back into her seat, but Tad now had her hand pressed firmly against his lap.

Just like a guy, she thought. Didn't matter if they were human or not. Only one thing on their minds.

If Destiny had been in a laughing mood any more she'd think it was funny.

"Let me up," she said.

"Now you want up." He looked down at her. "But you just got down there."

She pushed herself up with one hand and tried to wrench the other away from him. It popped clean off of her body and Tad was left holding her entire arm without the rest of her attached to it.

Great, just great.

He looked at her, as she calmly put her seatbelt back on, and then at the warm limb now lying in his lap. His eyes widened.

"Don't freak out," she told him. "I can explain."

He started to scream. Then he swerved off the road and slammed into a tree.

So much for the perfect date, Destiny thought as she dragged herself out of the car.

"Tad, you okay?" she asked. Tad was still screaming. She saw her arm shoot out the window as if Tad had thrown it as far away from himself as he could manage.

She frowned. Talk about rude.

She walked over to it and picked it up gingerly. Then pressed it back into place. She helped Tad out of the ruined Mercedes. His wallet fell out of his now ripped leather jacket.

"Don't touch me." He shuffled away from her.

"Okay, okay. Look, just relax."

"Just relax?

"Yeah, it's just a spell. I'm not normally like this."

"What do you mean, it was a spell?"

She sighed. "Look, Brokenoggin is a little different, okay? That's why I want to get the hell out of here as soon as possible."

"Bunch of freaks." Tad looked around nervously. "I'd heard that about this town."

Her frown deepened. "*Freaks* is a little harsh, I'd say. Unusual occurrences, sure. Witches, werewolves...maybe an elf or two."

He nodded. "Freaks."

"Look. They're not freaks. You don't even know them to make that kind of judgment."

Why was she defending Brokenoggin now? This was not part of the master plan. She just didn't like somebody else insulting her hometown. Ironic? Perhaps a tad.

"I'd heard it was different here. I just didn't realize how different." He eyed her. "So what are you, anyhow? A werewolf?"

"No way. I'm human. One hundred percent. That's why I want to go live somewhere else."

"Good luck with that."

She grabbed his arm and he flinched. "No, listen to me. I like you. You're great. You're perfect, in fact. That's why I wanted to go out with you. I figured you and me...maybe we could do something together."

"I was thinking the same thing."

She took in a deep breath and let it out slowly. She could salvage this. It wasn't too late.

She smiled at him, and he smiled back. She leaned over and picked up his wallet.

"So were you serious about wanting to get married right

away?" she asked.

He nodded. "Very serious."

A photo was peeking out of the top of his wallet. She pulled it out to take a look at it. It was of a pretty blonde girl.

"Who's this, your sister?"

He laughed, and grabbed the wallet away from her. "No. That's my fiancée."

Destiny blinked. "Your *what*?"

"My fiancée. Did your ears just fall off, too?"

She reached up to check them just in case he was right. No, they were exactly where they were supposed to be.

"You have a fiancée?" she repeated in disbelief.

He shrugged. "Kind of helpful to have one when you're planning on getting married, right?" He paused, and looked at her strangely. "Shit, Destiny, your eyeball just fell out. That is messed up."

She leaned over and picked it up, absently popping it back into its socket.

"If you're going to get married, then why are we out on a date?"

He studied her for a minute, then started to laugh. "Oh no, you didn't think..." He pointed at the car then back at her. "...you thought I was going to ask you to marry me?"

Destiny wasn't laughing. She didn't think she'd ever laugh again.

"Look," he continued when he caught his breath, "this doesn't have to end this way. We can still have fun tonight. I know you want to."

She narrowed her eyes. "You know I want to what?"

He grinned. "My girlfriend doesn't want to put out until the honeymoon. That's why I came here."

Destiny waited. "You came here because..."

"Because Brokenoggin girls are easy," Tad said. "It's a well known fact. Now come over here, baby, and I'm going to rock your world."

She kicked him in the groin. Lost her entire foot in the process but it was worth it. She hopped back towards the car to grab her cellphone so she could call her dad to come pick her up.

Maybe Brokenoggin wasn't so bad. If Tad represented the men she would find outside the town, then maybe she didn't want to leave after all.

She wondered what Willard the wizard had been up to since prom. Maybe she should give him a call.

"Hey," Tad yelled from where he was writhing in pain on the ground. "Is this your dog? Get it the hell away from me, will you?"

There was a chihuahua standing three feet away from his prone form. It growled viciously at him.

"That," Destiny said, holding a hand over the speaker of the cellphone while she balanced precariously on one foot, "is my brother ChiChi. And he is *sooo* going to *kick your ass*."

Episode 1.17

SUZI STILETTO: RECOVERING DEMON SLAYER

By

Alesia Holliday

Suzi Stiletto, former demon slayer, winds up selling lingerie in Brokenoggin Falls and, much to her dismay, finds herself at the epicenter of magical dysfunction without her slayer's license…
(Story and characters by Alesia Holliday)

Alesia Holliday is a recovering trial lawyer and the award-winning author of very funny books. She also writes for teens under her pen name, Jax Abbott. Please visit her on the web at www.alesiaholliday.com for more info, and read her online journal to see that life really does imitate art.

"You're through, Stiletto," the chief roared at her. *"You broke Union rules five months in a row. You're out. You're done!"*

The assistant chief, Herman Milquetoast, smirked at her. He'd wanted her out for ten years. Guess the little prick was finally going to get his wish. She took a menacing step toward him and had the satisfaction of watching him flinch back.

Then she turned back to the man who'd been like a father to her since somebody had dropped her off at Slayer Academy when she was only six, 'Take care of this freak' scrawled on a note pinned to her dress. He couldn't just throw her out. She had nowhere else to go.

"But, Chief," she held up her hands, dropped them again. "If I'm not a Slayer, I'm nothing."

For a moment, she though she saw tears glimmer in his eyes, and she had hope.

He looked at her and sighed. "Then you're nothing."

Then he walked away, never looking back, stepping over the bodies of the seven Lawyer Demons she'd slain that night.

***

Six months later

"We're totally screwed."

Suzi's grip on the steering wheel of her used neon-green VW bug tightened until she was sure she'd leave fingerprints in the plastic. "I don't want to hear it. We need to make rent and the car payment, plus buy you some more of those eucalyptus leaves you insist on eating," she said, shooting a glance of sheer disgust at her so-called best friend in the passenger seat.

"I don't care," Jimmy whined in that screechy voice of his. "There are more important things than money.

Suzi slammed on the brakes so hard the car fishtailed,

finally shuddering to a stop. The headlights illuminated an ancient sign creaking off a rusted pole. She peered at the writing, trying to make it out. "Is that Latin?"

Jimmy was struggling to jump back up on the seat from where he'd fallen on the floor. "I wouldn't know Latin from Pig Latin, remember? I was monolingual even before you got me changed."

She sighed and clenched her eyes shut for a moment, struggling for patience.

She lost.

"Look, you little insect. I told you five times to stay home that night. Lawyer Demons are the worst—their powers are unstable and they always want to closing argument me to death. Thank God Shakespeare started the Slayer Academy when he did. *Let's kill all the lawyers.* Brilliant. And people thought he was a writer." She snorted. "Anyway, you're the one who stowed away in the back of the Jeep."

"Yeah, and saved your fine ass from the big ugly one," Jimmy squeaked back at her. "You promised no more insect cracks, too. Don't make me tell your mother on you."

Suzi looked at her best friend, transformed by a random blast of a Death Affidavit Ray into a cricket. The irony smacked her in the face, as it always did. Her foul-mouthed, trouble-causing, total instigator of a best friend was now, quite literally, Jimmy Cricket.

"I'm sorry. Look, this traveling lingerie and sex toys sales job was the best I could do when they kicked me out of the Union. Overuse of powers, my ass. Anyway, suck it up. The woman who invited me, what was her name—Hillde Foster or something? She said the town definitely needs more sexy lingerie, whatever that means."

Suzi glanced up at the road sign again, then felt her mouth fall open. Hard. "Um, that sign was in Latin not two minutes ago. I swear it was."

Jimmy, who'd probably been preparing one of his zingy comebacks to *bug* her, twitched his little antennae in the direction of the sign. "Well, it's not now. Plain as day: *Welcome to Brokenoggin Falls*. Brokenoggin—what is that? Ojibwa? Algonquin? Anyway, I don't like it. This town was clearly marked in the Slayer Handbook as OFF LIMITS."

Suzi clenched her jaw, then threw the Bug into gear. "Well, I'm not a Slayer anymore, am I? We have nighties and nipple clamps to sell. Let's get going, already."

***

"It's just like a Tupperware party, but no, nobody is allowed to practice burping anything—or anybody!" The same line she'd said a hundred times in the past half-year rolled off her lips as three grown women rolled off the couch. Literally. They were the something triplets and they were a pain in the ass. They'd bickered so much, she'd finally started pushing the hostess's champagne at them, hoping they'd get sloshed and shut up. Now they kept trying to take their clothes off.

Hillde had been right, though. There had to be forty…women…at the party.

Except they weren't all human.

Not many were, in fact. Suzi's Slayer instincts had kicked so far into overload the minute she'd stepped out of the car, it was a wonder she hadn't flashed into a killing frenzy and slain the potted palm tree in the foyer. Or the weird guy who kept lurking at the doorway, trying to catch somebody undressed, probably, given the six cameras dangling from his neck.

"Okay, okay, now to the very best part of our evening—the modeling show! Who will go first? How about you?" She held up a red corset and panties and smiled at the pastor, stepping a bit closer to the woman to confirm what she'd smelled earlier.

Yep. She smells like demon. She's not the demon, but she's been rubbing naked flesh with one really recently. Must be some interesting church.

"Um, sounds good. I'm…trying to break away from being 'white lace girl'," the woman answered, turning a little pink and taking the scarlet silk set from Suzi, then backing away.

Probably wondering why I'm sniffing at her, like a freak, Suzi thought, trying to feel guilty. *I need to chill. But Holy Freaking Gates of Hell, I sense so many vampires, demons, and witches in this town, I can hardly breathe.*

As the women swarmed around the couches where she'd set out her samples, Suzi wandered over to the table where snacks and drinks were displayed with fresh flowers, pepper sauce, and…*hair removal cream?* She leaned down and whispered to Jimmy, who was hiding behind the cheese ball. "Do you smell it? Demons, demons, everywhere, and not a stake in sight."

Jimmy's tiny green body quivered. "No, no, no. I don't care if a demon steps right up and smacks you with one of your own sample dildos. You're sanctioned. If you slay now, you're on automatic death sentence. No kidding around, Suzi. I can't lose you."

She softened, staring down at what was left of her friend. "Aw, you say the nicest things."

Jimmy hopped on top of the cheese ball. "At least until you find a way to change me back. Hey, did you see the tits on those Tawdry triplets? Butter me up and call me a triple-decker, baby."

Suzi choked on her cracker. "Right. Sentimental to the last."

Just then, one of the guests touched her arm. "Excuse me, honey. I have a serious saggy boob issue, after having twelve kids. Do you have anything even more wondrous than a WonderBra? We're talking Miracle Bra, here."

Suzi put her plate down and turned to her new client. "I happen to have just the thing. It uses titanium underwire. And I think *you're* the miracle, if you don't mind my saying so, with twelve kids. How do you *do* it?"

As they threaded their way through forty half-drunken women—*does* THAT *woman smell like Dragons mating? No way are there dragons this far north!*—all laughing hysterically and in various stages of undress, Suzi noticed a sheriff lurking in the doorway. She stiffened and nodded toward the woman. "Is there trouble?"

Miracle Mommy glanced over, then shook her head and laughed. "Nah, that's just Janice. I don't think she's had sex since way before I got my first stretch mark. She's probably looking for a little action, if you know what I mean."

"Well, I've got BOBs, no problem," Suzi responded absently, looking for that latest shipment of bras that out-of-work NASA engineers had designed.

"Bob? Bob who?"

"Battery-Operated Boyfriends. We even sell batteries, so you can go right home and let 'em rip. Here we go—are you about a 44D?"

***

Never piss off a Gypsy King.
Don't Rile a Romanian.
Life Sucks, Then You Die.

He'd had seven thousand years to think up a damn motto, and this was the best he could come up with? Don't Rile a Romanian? Shit, he deserved to be cursed, to never know happiness. He was a freaking loser. Ever since he'd defiled the virgin Antonia (and let's face it, if Antonia was a virgin, he'd been an aqueduct), and suffered her father's wrath, Lucius had been doomed to absorb the Anguish, Vitriol, and Suffering of mankind for all time. Which, with jerkoffs like Satan in action, pretty much sucked.

Yeah, he'd picked up some colloquialisms in the past

few years, too.

Doomed Never to Enjoy. Never to Appreciate. Never to Love.

Never to Laugh.

It had to be a helluva curse, too. 'Cause if there was ever a bunch of screwballs destined to crack him up, it was the residents of Brokenoggin, located straight up, a hundred and fifty feet of rock and dirt over the stupid, dank, smelly cave he called home sweet prison.

But he'd been hatching a plot for the past seventy or eighty years. Just one night. That's all he wanted. One night to see the sky again—the sun would sear him with agony without the benefit of death, agonizing or otherwise—so he'd planned just one night of freedom. Seeing people again would give him the courage to endure another seven thousand years of solitude and isolation.

Or maybe he'd squash a few of the suckers, just for fun.

Either way, he was gonna do it. He *was*. Soon. Just as soon as . . .

What is that sound? Laughter? Peals of laughter? There must be dozens of women laughing to create a resonance in the very rock that binds me—maybe half a hundred. Laughing and laughing and laughing...

He hadn't heard laughter since the night of the curse, and that was more of the *Mwah Ha Ha* variety. Prick Gypsy King.

Laughter—Tonight's the night, then. Now.

Stretching up from the hunched position he'd taken in a corner about three hundred years previously, give or take, Lucius stretched for the rock ceiling.

Then he began to smash through it.

***

The rumbling started off low and quiet, but Suzi's Slayer senses were so jazzed, she picked up on it first thing. She was trying to find a Merry Widow that wasn't just flame-retardant but actually fireproof for one of the guests, when the first vibrations started. Now the framed photos on the hearth were rattling around, but the drunken party guests were too busy shrieking with laughter and dancing around the room with the dildo assortment to notice.

Jimmy did, though. He hopped up on her leg, and she picked him up and put him on her shoulder. "Hey, Suzi, what the hell is that? Earthquake? This freaks me out."

It freaked her out, too, but she wasn't going to admit it. Not with her damn Slayer gear locked up at Union headquarters. "What's the matter, Jimmy? Spidey sense going haywire?"

"I'm a cricket, not a spider, you overgrown freak of nature. And, yeah, something is seriously wrong here—"

Before she had a chance to make a smart-assed comment about insects that said *I told you so*, the earthquake rumbled out of control. The guests finally noticed when a giant painting smashed to the floor. Everybody started shrieking and trying to pull their clothes back on, except for the sheriff, who was pretty calm—*like most sheriffs, no surprise there*—and the triplets, who howled even louder and ripped their remaining clothes off. Jimmy hopped off her shoulder in the general direction of the couch.

Suzi didn't have time to worry about any of them, though, because the floor in front of her started to buckle. She slammed her arms out and shoved everybody in reach back and away from the huge hole that was opening in the floor. This was going to be the mother of all sinkholes. *Holy crap!*

"That's my new coffeetable!" her hostess screamed, not seeming to get that the whole house might go at any minute.

"Everybody down!" Suzi shouted. "Try to stand in a doorway or under a table, until the shaking stops!"

But the shaking wasn't stopping. At least not the shaking in her knees. Because the biggest hulk of a butt-ugly demon she'd ever seen shoved first his fist, then his head, then his entire rock and mud-encrusted body up out of the hole in the floor.

"We're screwed," Jimmy squeaked.

"Shut up, Jimmy," she said, scanning the room frantically for something—anything—that she could use to beat the foul fiend. Nothing sharp and stake-y—except the heel of her new Jimmy Choo. *Dammit!*

"Begone!" she said, Firmly and Dramatically, like it said on page one of the Slayer Handbook. (She'd never made it past chapter three: *Succubi and the Men Who Love Them*). "Get thou Demon Self back to Hades where thou art more...welcometh!" She grabbed the first thing to hand, cursing the lack of her Slayer bag.

Okay, two vibrators in the shape of a cross is not quite Union protocol, but who's gonna report me?

The Demon cowered in front of her, clearly in awe of her fury and righteousness. The sounds it made were truly hideous: the rending of flesh and the gnashing of teeth, and the...*laughter?*

Okay, that totally pissed her off. Did even the freaking *demons* know about her getting dumped by the Slayers' Union?

She marched closer to the demon, fearless in her fury. "Departeth, thou Foul Fiend from Hell! Get thee back to the depths of slimebucketness from whence thee came!"

The demon fell over with a resounding crash onto its side. She'd killed it with only her words! The power of that last Mucous Demon she'd slain must have stayed with her—it could kill with mere words, too. (Well, that and copious quantities of green phlegm, which made her want to hurl just thinking about it, but with a name like Mucous Demon, what did she expect?)

The foul fiend gasped its final breaths. Rattled its final death rattle.

Laughed at her again.

Shit! This is totally not going my way.

Jimmy piped up from where he'd been hiding on the couch, behind the leather bustier. (He'd had a thing for leather when he'd been a human, too. Go figure.) "Suzi! You know you're not allowed to do any unsanctioned slaying. The Union Decree was very clear."

The demon howled even louder, then it started to talk. Suzi backed away, wishing for holy water or at least her crossbow; something to hold firm between herself, the partygoers who crouched trembling on the floor behind her, and the evil monster. She tried to understand its words, hoping she would recognize enough of its fiendish incantation to effect some sort of blocking spell with the remains of the powers of the Succubus Sorceress she'd slain in January.

"Oooniast Inga VayVairs Eeen," rumbled the demon.

What? Oooniast, oooniast, what was that? Ancient Atlantaen? One of the Sixty-Six Demon Dialects she hadn't studied as well as the others? Not that she was much of a book-learner, in fact.

Oh, holy transformation. The demon started glowing: first, the faintest golden glow played over it—*skin? Scales? Ugly rock-like protrusions?*—then a nimbus of pearlescent light covered it from head to–to whatever the heck was attached to its legs. This was not a guy you'd take home to mother, to loosely quote from a song about another Super Freak.

She backed away even more, holding her cross of vibrators out in front of her, but suddenly a massive sonic boom of a blast thundered through the house, and the demon disappeared in a burst of light, just before everything else in the room disappeared in a burst of black.

***

Suzi woke up to find herself cradled in the massively-muscled arms of the most astonishingly beautiful man she'd ever seen. She stared into his pale silver eyes for a long moment, captivated by their shifting shimmer, before allowing her gaze to drift over his sculpted cheekbones, classical Roman nose, perfectly kissable lips, and firm jaw. Then she had to stare at his eyes again, just to check that they really were silver, and it wasn't just a delusion caused by her temporary blackout and ensuing concussion.

Nope. Definitely silver. Which went well, you know, with the wickedly black waves of hair that hung down to his shoulders.

His naked shoulders.

Oh, crap. She stole a glance down.

His naked shoulders were on top of his very naked and majorly muscled chest and the naked arms she'd noticed earlier. She squirmed a little, trying to stand up, and his arms tightened around her.

Oh, holy hard-on, Suzi. Either he was very, very happy to see her, or she was sitting on the world's largest roll of quarters.

In his very naked lap.

"But where the hell is the demon?"

Silver eyes smiled fondly down at her. "You're the funniest thing I've ever seen, little Slayer."

She jerked in surprise. "How did you know I'm a Slayer? Er, *was* a Slayer? And let me up," she said, pushing ineffectually against his chest. "You...wait! *'Funniest thing I've ever seen?'* Oooniast Inga VayVairs Eeen? *You're* the demon?"

He smiled again. "Not any more. Experiencing laughter after seven thousand years broke the damn curse. Now I am your Eternal Love Slave, little Slayer."

Suzi sighed and watched as Jimmy fainted dead to the floor, little cricket legs pointed straight up at the ceiling. "I'm totally screwed."

Episode 1.18

LOF-T: RROGG 2

(Lord of the Forest Trolls – Repentance [& Revenge] of the Garden Gnome episode 2)

By

Judi McCoy

In which it is learned exactly who threw Sam into the sunlight and turned him into a garden gnome – and why – and revenge is exacted on the Disdaine triplets.

Judi McCoy writes...a different kind of romance. If you like your paranormals with a little bit of whimsy and humor, visit her website at http://www.judimccoy.com.

Sam was worried. Ever since he'd last seen Claire, things had grown fuzzy, murky even, in his mind and his body. He'd been finding it very difficult to move and, if one pardoned the pun, harder and harder to get an erection. Stranger still, last night he'd actually slept for the first time since he'd found himself in this miserable condition.

It was as if the sight of his wife, coupled with the knowledge that he'd hurt her, had caused some kind of off-kilter reaction in the spell. Never in a million years, had he thought she'd turn postal on him and resort to spousal abuse, but there was no doubt in his mind that's what had happened.

Weird thing was she'd taken his derisive comment totally out of context. When he'd said she was *flat*, he'd meant she was off key when she screamed her incredibly frightening—though he loved to hear it—harpy's song. Poor Claire must have thought he'd meant she was flat in the boobs, which to her was a huge insult, and she'd cast the retaliating spell.

After hearing her side of it, Sam realized Claire had every right to do what she'd done. He'd been unkind, and his baby doll wife didn't deserve his nasty or cutting remarks.

Today had been a long day filled with little motion on his part, and a lot of pain in his stocky limbs. Now that it was evening, and he felt like the trunk of a dead tree, he was afraid to nod off for fear he might never wake up in the morning. If that happened, he wouldn't be able to talk to Claire and explain that a guy was a guy. He was sorry he'd caused her grief. He now realized he hurt her whenever he spoke to other women or let his joystick get out of control.

But she had to understand that he was a horny bastard and proud of it. Women turned him on, but he would never be unfaithful to his lamby-pie. Ever.

If only he had another chance...

Thunder rumbled in the distance, pulling Sam from his thoughts. Great. Just what he didn't need. Another night of standing in the drenching rain on the Disdaine triplets fucking front lawn, smack in the middle of town. Since being held prisoner here, he'd been soaked, spit at, and peed on, not necessarily in that order, at least a dozen times a day.

Him! The man who was once in charge of the entire forest that surrounded this pitiful community. To think that those nasty triplets had laughed at him while they told him how they planned to take over *his* territory. When he caught those miserable creatures, he was going to turn them into toadstools. Or gnats. Or maybe three blind mice. Then he could feed them to a cat. That would certainly fix their dirty little wagons once and for all.

More thunder had him raising his eyes, the only part of his body he was able to move easily. How could it be flood weather when he could see stars in the remarkably clear sky? Then again, this was Brokenoggin Falls, a place where the curious happened on a daily basis. And the citizens liked it that way.

He glanced around the lawn and sighed. There were a few other gnomes spaced apart on the grass, but Sam felt certain he was the only one that had a heartbeat. Still, he felt sorry for them, mainly because the kids in town sometimes used the garden gnomes as skateboarding cones or goal posts. Sam had yet to see his exact form, but imagined he appeared very much like the rest of them: short and stocky with flowing white hair and a beard to match. Not to mention ugly.

Only with him, the rhinestone-studded thong he'd been forced to wear as a crown was now somewhere down around his neck. And the humiliation continued...

Besides being the Disdaine triplets titillation du jour, people passing by pointed and laughed. Teenagers spit on him. And the dogs, werewolves, and other assorted townsfolk used him for their own personal port-o-potty. He'd enjoyed egging them on, until he'd seen Claire and started experiencing this strange freeze-form existence.

It was enough to make a once powerful and commanding troll cry.

The thunder grew to a deafening roar. He heard screaming, then watched helplessly as a few of the partygoers who'd been living it up in the Disdaine's garden came running frantically from the back yard.

Then he saw the reason why.

With hooves flashing in the darkness, wild horses thudded from the far end of the estate. And leading the charge were those miserable spoiled brats, the banes of his existence, the boils on his ass: the Disdaine triplets.

Riding bareback on the lead beasts, the spawns of Satan were screaming at the top of their nasty little lungs, shouting with glee as they trampled, ripped apart, and generally destroyed whatever they plowed over.

Sam winced when he saw a few of the plaster gnomes smashed to smithereens. In an instant, he was knocked flat, certain he'd be ground to powder. He held his breath, closed his eyes and waited…

***

Sam awoke to morning sunshine and a headache the size of Lake Michigan. Lying on his side, he couldn't move a muscle, and there in front of his nose sat the top of his once pointed head. He'd been spared the powder crushing, but he'd definitely been flattened. He was probably the only person in Brokenoggin with a truly *broken noggin.*

He wriggled, trying to make his muscles work, but nothing happened. He was well and truly stoned. His only hope was that someone, maybe Janice Drinksalot, the town constable, or Earl Choo, the mayor, would be along to survey the damage that had certainly spilled into the town center. Instead, the pack of roaming Chihuahuas that had recently arrived in the area descended and used him as a pissing post.

Again.

Footsteps in the distance told him a savior might be at hand. Rolling his eyes upward, he saw a woman ambling toward the square, reading a yellow book as if she had no idea of the destruction. Sam could only see her legs and the top of her head, bent in concentration as she strode slowly in his direction.

When the woman reached the square, she raised her head and glanced at the trampled lawn. Emma Mincemeat, one of the few normal—if there was such a thing—residents of Brokenoggin Falls, frowned as she stopped and sat on the only bench that hadn't been decimated under the Disdaine triplets vengeful romp.

Sam remembered that Emma, a nice woman who had migrated here from Brooklyn with her husband and twelve—count 'em *twelve*—children, always wanted to fit in when she was, in actuality, one of the village misfits.

"Hey, Emma, it's me," thought Sam, throwing her a silent plea. Maybe she would stand him up, dust him off, and glue back the top of his head in order that he regain a shred of his former dignity.

She raised the book up and the title became clear. Emma was reading *Witchcraft for Dummies*. He imagined it probably was her latest, and surely her most worthless, attempt to 'fit in'.

Just then, Emma set the tome down and took a second survey of the lawn. Raising a brow, she ran her gaze over a gnome broken in four or five pieces. Her eyes darted to another and its decapitated body. Heaving a sigh, she finally looked at Sam.

"Oh, you poor thing," she said aloud. Walking over, she stood him on his tiny flat feet.

To Sam's mortification, his erection sprang to life. Immediately, he reminded the miscreant body part that it was getting the hots over a mother of twelve, for Goddess's sake. That was all it took to make the offending member calm down and allow him to enjoy the moment.

Emma swiped a tear from her eye. "Someday, those rotten triplets will get their comeuppance. At least, I hope so. In the meantime, not one of my children is going to be allowed near them and their crazy, misguided, and altogether evil ideas. Ladies of the Forest Trolls, indeed."

She *tsked* again. And then she did the unthinkable. She picked him up and carried him to the bench like a baby, where she cradled him in her arms.

Wonder of wonders, though his body was frozen stiff, the force field that had kept him on the lawn was gone.

Sam felt Emma's heart beat against his shoulder as she brushed the dirt and grass from his wizened face.

"Poor Sam," she whispered. "Someone should do something to help you." She ran a hand over his flat head. "It's not so bad, really."

Then, with a twinkle in her eye, Emma sat him beside her on the bench and again perused her book. Smiling, she picked it up and began to thumb through the pages.

"Bring boils...bring frogs...bring warts..." she muttered. "Bring hail...bring a hurricane...bring rain..." She turned the page. "Bring to life," she said with a grin. Then she gave Sam a forlorn smile. "Do I dare?"

Sam worked to give his eyes an encouraging expression, but feared the attempt was lost on Emma. Then he realized the enormity of the situation and changed the look to one of denial. She wasn't a witch. She was a no-talent mortal. She was reading a book written *for dummies* for Goddess's sake.

No telling what might happen to him if her spell or incantation failed. He wasn't ready to be her experiment!

Besides, once Sam realized Claire had put the spell on him, he assumed she'd be the only one who could set him free. But getting help from Emma? The one Brokenoggin citizen with the least amount of magical ability…?

That was stretching it by a mile.

Emma closed the book and stood. Then she tucked it under her left arm and hoisted Sam under her right. Turning, she headed in the direction from whence she'd come, mumbling under her breath as she walked.

***

Emma arrived at the clock tower and knocked as politely as she could with a book tucked under one arm and a two-foot garden gnome wedged under the other. She had never made a house call to any of the citizens of Brokenoggin, but Sam's predicament was too serious to ignore.

Besides, she was married with twelve children. It wasn't right for her, a happily married woman, to allow a rift to continue between a husband and his wife—at least, not if she could be of some help.

She'd seen the anger and pain in Sam's eyes and the despair and plea for forgiveness in Claire's the day the two had last met, and knew they were both sorry for the things they'd said. Sam and Claire just didn't know how to put things back the way they were—no, better than the way they were—and begin again.

"Who's there?" came a timid, breathy voice from behind the heavy oak door.

"It's Emma Mincemeat. I have something for you."

"I don't want to see anyone."

"Please," Emma said in answer. "I promise it's something you need."

When she heard a chain scrape the door, then the drawing of a bolt, Emma turned so the side with the book faced the tower.

"This had better be important," said Claire, peering through the narrow opening. "Because I'm really not up to entertaining visitors."

"May I come in?" asked Emma, who prided herself on being polite, even under duress.

Claire narrowed her baby blue eyes. "Is this a trick?"

Emma crossed mental fingers. "Not really. But I do have something you need to see."

Shrugging, Claire stepped back and opened the door.

Emma slipped inside and leaned on the door, slamming it shut. Then she turned fully. With a hand to her mouth, Claire gasped.

"No...please take him back. I can't bear to see my Sammykins in that horrid condition." She held her hands to her lovely face. "What have I done? Oh, what have I done?"

Emma's heart swelled with pride. Her suspicions were correct. Claire did love her husband. Now if only Claire could reverse the spell, all would be well. She marched through the hall with Claire wailing from behind. When she reached the kitchen, she set her book on the table, then did the same with Sam.

Claire's eyes grew round as dinner plates. "His head! What happened to Sam's head?" Walking around the table, she eyed him from the top of his flat crown to his gnarly toes. "Why does he look like as if he's made of plaster? And how did you manage to remove him from the Disdaine's front lawn?"

"I don't know why he's stiff as a board, but I suspect it has something to do with being able to bring him through that force field. I can tell you this. Last evening, the triplets rode the night mares and wreaked havoc through the entire town. I suspect Sam got caught in the upheaval and had his head trampled. You're lucky he wasn't smashed to pieces or decapitated."

"What have I done?" cried Claire, pulling Sam to her chest. When she held him to her ample bosom, his erection sprang to life. Giggling through her tears, she stepped back and threw him a sappy look. "Oh, Sam, you naughty troll, will you ever change?"

"Surely whatever you've done can be undone," said Emma, pleased to see that Claire was showing her husband a little sympathy. "Something tells me he's had time to think about all this and he'll have that nasty projectile under better control, once we free him from the spell."

Claire's beautiful face grew red. Her eyes leaked tears as she shook her head. "I can't."

"You can't?"

"I mean I don't know how. I didn't do it on purpose in the first place. He just made me so angry that I wished he would suffer. He was always poking fun at the garden gnomes, so I imagined one of them in my head and the next thing I knew—" she snuffled a watery sob "—he looked like this."

Emma sat down with a plop and opened her book to the page she'd turned down. It was time to find out whether or not she'd gotten her money's worth. "I found a spell..." she began.

"You did? Truly?" Claire rushed to read over Emma's shoulder. "I'm not a witch and neither are you. Perhaps we should call on Claudia or Gerda—"

"Don't be stupid. The last time they got together at Maria's to cast a spell they blew up her kitchen. This is merely an incantation, no ingredients or dynamite. I say we try it ourselves."

Claire worried her lower lip. She'd missed her Sammykins these past few months, missed him so terribly she couldn't even go to the triplets' house to look at him. The one time she had, they'd argued in front of strangers, which had humiliated her further. She wanted her husband back, but only if he promised to behave.

"I have conditions," she stated.

"I'm sure you do," said Emma. "So talk to him, tell him what you want."

"But how do I know he'll listen? I mean, can he hear me?"

"He got a woody, didn't he?"

Claire frowned. "But he does that whenever he sees a woman, any woman. That's part of the problem."

"So look him in the eye. Last time I checked, that's where I saw a spark of life."

Folding her arms, Claire gave her husband a thorough examination, and couldn't help thinking how much he resembled a piece of garden statuary. His face was set in a scowl and his arms stuck out rigidly at his sides. The only part of him that appeared different was his flat-as-the-bottom-of-an-iron head.

Then she gazed into his eyes and saw a tiny drop of water creep from the corner of the socket and onto his rounded cheek. Her heart lurched in her chest. "Are you still alive in there, Sam?"

He blinked, but she could tell it took quite a bit of effort.

"Emma," she said, still staring at Sam. "I think he's fading fast. If we don't do something…"

"I agree. So finish what you have to say while I go over this spell again."

Claire focused on her husband's eyes. It was too painful to look at him fully. "Sam, I want you to promise me there will be no more poking fun at my chest."

Sam's eyes moved up and down.

"I'll take that as a yes," said Claire. "And there will be no more erections for any woman, except me."

Again, his eyes went up and down.

"And no more fighting. I hate it when we fight. We

don't have to agree, but I want to talk over our differences in a rational manner. You cannot continue to sing that stupid lumberjack song to annoy me, or shout out slurs in front of strangers."

This time, his eyes moved more rapidly in agreement.

A feeling of hope fluttered in her chest. "I've come to realize that I, too, need to make a few promises in order for this marriage to work. For one thing, I'm going to try to control my temper, and be less…harpish."

She sighed. "And I promise to work on expanding my bustline. Since you seem to find my boobs deficient, perhaps Emma can find a spell that will make them bigger."

"First things first," muttered Emma, still perusing the book.

Claire grinned when Sam's eyes moved 'yes, yes, yes' in a frantic motion.

Bending forward, she kissed him full on his grim lips. "I'm so sorry, my darling. But we'll make it right." She turned to Emma. "I'm ready whenever you are."

***

"Ah, this is the life," said Sam sometime later. He gazed at his beloved, who was smiling as she sat across from him on their picnic blanket under an oak tree in the woods. "Naked, with the woman I love, and fully sated. It can't get any better than this."

He and Claire had thanked Emma and raced here, to the forest, as soon as the spell had been lifted. Then they'd made love, ate, and made love again. He grinned when his wife gazed down at her bountiful breasts.

"You're sure they're not too small?" she asked in a breathy little voice. "Because I'm willing to let Greta or Claudia experiment, if it will make you happy."

Sam reached out and ran a finger over one budded nipple, happy to see it pucker at his touch. Claire shivered and he smiled. "I don't want anyone, especially those idiot witches, doing anything to your perfect body. If they do, they'll die."

"What are you planning to do to the Disdaine triplets?" she asked, snuggling closer.

"What would you like me to do?"

"Something righteous, but nothing cruel," Claire answered. "They are only children."

"Hah! Children of the devil. I'm planning to speak to their parents. If they don't discipline those girls, the town will do it for them, and I'll lead the charge."

"Those rampaging Chihuahuas have made a mess of the city's streets. How about a week of picking up dog droppings?"

"Make it a year." Sam's smile grew wide. "And they have to do it with their bare hands—no pooper-scooper."

"Sounds like a plan."

"I say we take it to the next Brokenoggin town council meeting, first."

"Can I go with you to the meeting?"

"Of course, you can. I promised you we would never be apart again, remember."

"Oh, Sammykins," said Claire, squirming when he cupped her breast and bent forward to suckle the tip. "You do such wonderful things to me. I love you so."

Sam's penis grew to its full length, prodding Claire's belly as it begged for attention.

She reached between them and caressed the rigid digit with both hands. "Maybe we should leave? Someone might find us, and I'd be so embarrassed if they did."

He used a knee to part her legs and slid into her, sheathing himself fully in her moist, silky heat. "Let them see us," he said, kissing her. "I don't care."

Settling himself atop her, Sam pumped his hips, slowly at first, then with abandon. Claire arched beneath him and met every thrust. When her cries of pleasure turned to her harpy wail, she didn't change into her other self. Instead, she gazed up at him and drew him to her lips where their tongues tangled in a duel as old as time.

He drove her to the brink of exquisite madness, and she did the same to him.

And Sam finally realized the secret to taming a harpy.

Episode 1.19

DOROTHEA'S WIZARD

By

Jennifer St. Giles

In which Dorothea and the Great OZZ meet and ... er...
seriously consummate their relationship.
(Story and characters by Jennifer St. Giles)

Award winning author, Jennifer St. Giles writes Gothic Historicals
for Berkley Sensations and Contemporary Paranormals for Pocket
Books. Go to www.jenniferstgiles to electrify your life with the
magic of unforgettable love and hot stories.

"**W**ell, Yodo, this isn't Kansas *or* New York." Sheltering her toy poodle from the drizzling mist with the edge of her cherry-red jacket, Dorothea Davenport tentatively followed the ebony brick road leading to Dr. O. Zexton Zinclair's residence.

She hadn't considered rain as a factor when she'd concocted her plan to meet the author of *Pleasure Potions*. A flat tire on her rented Jaguar, courtesy of a well placed nail, and one dead cell phone for show would hopefully gain her entrée into the recluse's home and make use of her nearby, bodyguard driven limo unnecessary. But she hadn't realized that the town of Brokenoggin would resemble an adult *Jumanji* either: dogs as large as wolves running loose, women wearing hopeful expressions and Victoria's Secrets best but least lining the streets, and a fanged man parading around naked while the sheriff sat in her cruiser ogling rather than arresting. This place wasn't just over the top, it was stratospheric. And none of it compared to the unfolding scene before her.

Droplets of water dewed her skin and dampened the silk of her dress, giving her an eerie chill that stood at odds with the increasing, sultry heat of the surrounding air. She'd noted the change in temperature the moment she'd passed through the gargoyle studded gate, but at first attributed it to nervous exertion. Now she wasn't so sure. The further she intruded, the stranger her surroundings became, and the warmer the air turned, reminding her more of a tropical beach than a late afternoon in Michigan. Even stranger still were the ghostly tendrils of Spanish moss hanging from the twisted branches and the tangy scent of sea flavoring the breeze. Her heartbeat doubled to the click of her red heeled boots and her cherry-slick mouth went dry as the dark, spire-ridden mansion rose from the shadow of the gnarled trees.

Yodo yipped in protest and she brushed a comforting

hand through his dark curly fur. "It's okay boy. If there had been anything unsavory about Dr. Zinclair, I'm sure Dr. Susan wouldn't have mentioned meeting him or the successes he achieved in his clinic before dropping off the face of the earth." But then Dr. Susan claimed Dorothea's anorgasmia was a self imposed response to her material rich emotionally bankrupt life, like a patient with hysterical blindness or amnesia. Deep inside, Dorothea supposedly didn't believe herself worth loving and couldn't accept a man's love. The sexual dysfunction had cost her a marriage and two other relationships, and she wasn't going to give her heart again until she conquered her problem, no matter what. And she was determined to find the answer before her thirtieth birthday, which, according to the ruby studs on her watch, gave her twelve hours to get the elixir the AMA—not the FDA—had banned and make her day.

Clutching Yodo and her red leather bag closer, Dorothea quickened her pace. The blending of stone and iron in the mansion bred a monolith filled with forbidding shadows and hidden threats, but none were as dark as the one clouding her life. The faint strands of a sexy instrumental tune thrummed in the air, informing her that someone was home. Drawing a bolstering breath, she marched up the steps and rang the doorbell, nearly jumping from her skin when the theme music to "Jaws" surrounded her.

She swung in a circle, catching herself looking for an approaching menace of yawning teeth before stopping and then sighing with self-disgust. Undeterred, she rang the bell persistently, and followed each echoing sound bite with a firm rap on the lion-faced brass knocker. "See, Yodo, how's that for courage."

Sweat now beaded her brow, adding to the dampness of the humid rain. The temperature near the house was like that of a steam sauna, forcing her to slip off her jacket or grow faint from the heat, but even the droplets of rain hitting her bare shoulders and sliding beneath the halter-top of her dress provided little relief. After five attempts to rouse someone from the mansion, she decided to follow the music and walk around to the back. Grass and fecund earth gave way to diamond bright sand that immediately swallowed her heels as the sight before her boggled her mind. A vast, misty playground of turquoise pools, lush vegetation, and waterfalls stretched for acres.

"Beware, beware, beware." The squawking warning came from a large green and gold parrot perched on a nearby cushioned lounge chair big enough to pass for a bed. Yodo yipped and squirmed to be let down. Realizing that any forward motion would only occur bootless, Dorothea set Yodo down and sat on the damp sand. She unzipped her boots as she kept one eye on Yodo who sniffed a circle around the turning parrot. They seemed to be sizing each other up, more curious than antagonistic, so she decided to let Yodo walk. She stuffed her jacket and boots in her bag and left her red fishnet thigh highs on to keep some semblance of formality. If she wasn't careful, she could easily find herself naked and comfortable in this kind of heat.

The music played softly over some sort of surround stereo system, providing her little help in locating what she hoped would be Dr. Zinclair. As she moved down the beach, the rain turned to mist then stopped. It wasn't until she reached the edge of a steamy pool with Yodo close behind that she saw him. A naked and sun-bronzed him. He stood beneath the spill of a soft waterfall less than ten feet to her left with his back to her, a scarred back. The whitened skin of lash strokes crisscrossed his back and whipped across her heart. Dear God, what had happened to him? Who'd carried out such a barbaric punishment upon him and why? She clenched her fist as the urge to soothe long healed pain coursed through her, making her almost forget why she'd come to him. His muscular arms held onto a bar over his head, and as she watched, he pulled his lean body slowly up, lowered himself, and then repeated the motion several more times while rivulets of water poured through his dark hair and down his tanned body.

She stepped silently back, planning to return to the man's porch and wait, but couldn't quite stop watching his powerful, fluid movements. He was pure sensual magic in action.

"What in the hell do you want?" he asked, suddenly dropping from the bar and turning to face her. His snarling deep voice had more fear impact than the "Jaws" theme and the dark countenance of his sharp brow, determined nose, and square jaw were just as threatening. For the first time she wondered if maybe her desperation to know a moment's pleasure was going to cost more that she was willing to pay.

Really?, she asked herself. Could she resign herself to an anorgasmic fate or would she rather die trying to change it?

"I need help. My name is Dorothea and this is Yodo. My car has a flat." She spoke the lie lamely.

"Right. Dorothy and Toto. And I'm the Tin Man. You're in the wrong place, lady. Get lost. Go back to Kansas." He turned his back on her and grabbed the bar he'd been exercising on.

"I'm called Thea. My cell phone is dead!" she shouted, feeling the bite of tears sting her eyes. Had she really thought it would be so easy? *Can I use your phone? And by the way, aren't you the man who wrote that book? I have this friend who really needs help. Surely, you could sell me a bottle of Nymph.* Desperation had a way of making any action sound good. Yodo buried closer to her ankle, trying to comfort her.

"Do us both a favor, lady. Drop the pretense and just

leave. I don't have what you're looking for."

"Are you Dr. Zinclair?"

"Not any more. Get lost."

Dorothea exploded. "I want an orgasm before I turn thirty tomorrow. You had a clinic. You helped women like me. Dr. Susan praised your success rate. All I want is to buy a bottle of Nymph and I'll leave."

He laughed, turning to face her again. "Do you really want the drug? Are you willing to take it regardless of its side effects?"

"Yes," she whispered, her heart hammering. "Yes," she said louder. "I can't live this way anymore."

His humor died. This time he stepped into the pool and strode toward her, unashamedly naked. Not that he had any reason to hide anything. His assets rivaled her trust fund and appeared ready make any deposit he wanted. She had to fight to keep her gaze somewhat aimed at his face. A feat that grew less difficult as she met his intense gaze. Long ebony lashes framed sea-green irises, creating a mesmerizing study of light and dark.

He stopped when his arousal brushed her silken covered stomach, making her gasp at the shock of sensual heat lightning that pierced through her. It was unlike anything she'd ever experienced. Her purse slid from her grip and landed on the ground. She considered backing up, but didn't. Yodo yipped then sounded like he jumped into her purse for a nap, something he often did when she went shopping. The tangy scent of salty air gave way to the doctor's heady cologne, something that urged her to breathe deep and relish the flavor.

"Since we're being so truthful here," he said, his deep voice vibrating sensually. "There is no Nymph. It was nothing more than a concoction of brandy and peach liquor."

Dorothea shook her head, refusing to accept his answer, or back away from him. "No. You cured women, made them whole, normal. How?"

Instead of answering, he smiled, slowly, sending another fissure of heat right to an unfamiliar, almost clenching core inside of her. Grabbing her hips, he pulled her tightly against his erection, pressing hotly to her damp silk. Then he ran his hands up to brush the sides of her breasts, stopping where the cut of her halter covered her soft skin.

Dorothea gasped as her hips automatically pressed to him.

"How?" He lifted a dark brow. "Usually counseling worked, but on rare occasions when it didn't, my touch did. I made love to them, Dorothea. I'm the drug." To prove his point, he slid his thumbs beneath her top and flicked them over her nipples. She gasped as the tips hardened beneath the assaulting tingle of heat his touch gave her, a tingle that lingered long after he'd moved his hands back to her hips and stood looking at her, waiting for her reaction.

"Cure me," she whispered, finally. Every ounce of her agonized desperation echoed in her voice. She'd come this far, and at this point in her life she was ready to try anything she hadn't before, even sex with a charismatic stranger.

His grip on her hips tightened, but he didn't move. He just stared at her and she saw both indecision and a shadow of pain flicker in his eyes. "What if I choose not to? Do you think that I don't pay a price? Besides the toll on my own body and soul to be used for sex, there's no guarantee that tomorrow you won't wake up in the same condition."

Shamefully, tears filled her eyes and she took a deep breath, edging back from him. "You're right. I'm sorry." She'd given no thought to him, only herself.

He released her hips and she averted her gaze to stare out over the water and falls, as she desperately tried to come to grips with her situation. "How is all this possible?"

"Brokenoggin's hot springs, a lot of ingenuity, and a

little magic." He said the last in a wry sort of tone that had her glancing back at him for a moment.

He was looking at her as if puzzled, but her pain at having to walk away into anorgasmia was too great to try and figure out what he found so odd. "I'm sorry to have disturbed you, Dr. Zinclair."

"Ozz," he said. "I go by my initials."

She laughed sadly. "So you're the wizard?"

"That's right."

She reached for the handle of her bag where Yodo napped. "And Dorothea is going home."

He caught her hand. "That's it? You're willing to walk away from your heart's desire after coming here?"

"I've no right to assuage my pain by inflicting it on others. Besides, from the looks of your back, you've suffered enough. What happened?"

"A curse I'm powerless to avoid," he said, softly, running his finger across her palm and then up her arm. "Take your dress off, Dorothy. I'll take you to OZZ."

She gasped from the pleasure and the tenderness in his touch. "Thea," she said. "Dorothea." She meant to ask him what he meant by a curse, but forgot as his hands splayed over her bare skin.

"Dorothea," he whispered in her ear. Spreading fire with his touch, he slid his hands to the nape of her neck and pulled the tie of her halter loose. The damp silk fell away, exposing her breasts. Her nipples tightened, this time just from the intensity of his gaze as he looked at her. He moved behind her and a shiver followed the path her zipper took down her spine. When she stepped from the puddle of her red dress, she wore only her thigh high fishnet stockings and a matching thong. Dressing as sexy as possible and becoming comfortable with her own body were at least two positive results from the years she'd spent in therapy. She went to slide down a stocking.

"Leave them," he said gruffly. "Come with me." Taking her hand, he led her into the water that seemed to cool and warm at the same time as it swirled around her legs and lapped at the flesh between. Reaching the cropping of rocks and waterfall she'd first seen him under, he patted a large flat rock that was about hip high to him. "Climb up here and sit on the edge facing me."

She gave him a questioning look, yet did as he asked, surprised to feel that the rock wasn't rock, but some softy spongy foam. Once settled, she met his gaze. The "now what?" on the edge of her tongue disappeared as he slid between her legs and kissed her, his tongue gaining entry into her mouth as his arousal pressed intimately against her lace covered sex. The moment she shut her eyes, the fireworks and heat disappeared as a familiar numbness and a killing anxiety raced through her. She froze.

"Open your eyes, Dorothea. Don't close them again. To get to where you want to go, you have to fill yourself with me. The sight of me pleasuring you and you pleasuring me, the feel of me touching you and you touching me, the taste of me on your tongue and the taste of you on mine, the smell of me in your soul and the scent of you burned into mine. I'm the drug you need to drink, eat, and, inhale."

He kissed her again and she kept her eyes open, at first fixed on the mesmerizing passion in his gaze then watching his hands palm her breasts, kneading them to aching points that his mouth covered and sucked. She filled her hands with the silk of his hair, the slick feel of his water-beaded skin, and the supple heat of his flexing muscles as he slid off her thong.

Running his tongue down her stomach, he hooked his thumbs into the edge of her thigh highs, but instead of pulling her stockings down, he used the leverage to lift and spread her legs, opening her sex to the searing heat of his mouth. She shuddered as pleasure rippled through her. On fire, her hips arched to him, forcing her back to her elbows. Her eyes fell shut and suddenly the pleasure stopped. She remembered her condoms were back on the beach in her purse and a thousand other thoughts intruded.

"Watch me, Dorothea," he demanded. She opened her eyes and he slid her knees over his shoulders, lifting her hips high, giving her no choice but to see his mouth devouring her. When he reached up and plucked her nipples, a coiling tension began to build inside of her and spread, catching her pulse and her breath, rushing them forward, leaving her gasping and writhing and more on edge than she'd ever been before.

"Please," she cried, reaching for him. "I need..."

He lowered her back to the padded rock. "This," he said, snapping his fingers and a half dozen foil packets appeared in his hand.

She sat up and stared at him, taking a condom from him. "How did you do that?"

"Magic," he said.

She glanced around to see where he could have a box stashed, but he slid his finger up her thigh and along the groove of her sex to flick at the swollen spot that throbbed to feel more. He was beautiful in a dark, rough, majestic way. Intense eyes, shadowed jaw, determined brow and nose, jutting, demanding erection. He was so purely masculine that he made her feel utterly female.

Breaking open the condom, she ran her hand down the rippled muscles of his stomach, feeling his abs clench beneath her fingers. But before she put it on him, she met his gaze, lifting her mouth to his and kissing him softly, thankfully, tenderly. Pressing him back, she slid her hands over his shoulders and the flat disks of his breasts, enjoying the dark silky hair smattering his chest and tapering down his stomach. The ridges of scars on his back, gave her pause, and she pressed her hand against them. "I'm sorry for your pain."

He groaned as she cupped his heated sex in her hand. She bent, pressing her lips to his sensitive tip and swirled her tongue softly around him. She could feel his racing pulse throb in his shaft beneath her fingertips and she took the satiny, hard heat of him into her mouth, tasting him, wanting and needing to pleasure him, to excite and comfort him all at the same time.

He pulled her up, kissing her deeply, more searchingly than before, as if he were now trying to connect with her soul. Then he eased the condom from her fingers and covered himself. Sliding her hips to the edge of the foam rock, he opened her with his fingers and drove inside, filling her completely. She tensed, suddenly afraid that what she wanted to happen, wouldn't.

"Don't close your eyes, Dorothea. Lie down and watch the pleasure. Yours and mine." He pushed her back and hooked her knees behind his hips. Moving slowly, he eased almost, but not quite out of her and pressed slowly in, again and again as he flicked his finger over the tender hot spot of her sex. The coil of tension inside her curled tighter and tighter, sending her heart racing and stealing her breath.

His gaze met and held hers. "Come with me. Ride with me. Let yourself go, free your body, mind and soul to feel nothing but the hot pleasure burning through us both. Pleasure that is going to wipe everything from your mind." His deep voice vibrated through her as if he entered her mind, taking away every thought but her need and feel of him. He captured her and nothing mattered but what she felt with him. Her hips met the thrust of his faster and faster as a whirlwind of passion spun her around and around. Her toes curled, her muscles clenched and…and…

"Now," he demanded, thrusting deeper than ever before.

"O, O, O," she cried, her body shuddered with the

orgasm that erupted through her.

"More," he said thrusting again, driving another fissure of pleasure into her heart. Moving his other hand to her breast, he pulled gently on her nipple and sent her sky-rocketing higher.

"Oh God," she screamed as white hot pleasure seared her soul.

His body shuddered forcefully against hers and he fell forward, bracing his weight at her sides and resting his head against her chest. She wrapped her arms around him, pulling him closer, though he was closer to her than anyone had ever been. Then his body tensed, jerked, and he exhaled forcefully as if in great pain. In fact, Dorothea could feel the pain ripping though him into her. "Oh God," she whispered. "What just happened? I feel your pain. Did I hurt you?"

He lifted his head, surprise and deep pain in his eyes. His arms trembled at her sides. "What do you mean, you feel my pain?"

"You're hurt. I feel a burning pain inside me almost as great as the pleasure."

He rose up and pulled himself from her body, leaving her bereft, taking both the pleasure and the pain. "You must go now." He braced an arm against the rock as if needing help to stand. The color had washed from his face.

She sat up, and on shaky knees, eased into the soothing pool of water, turning to him with her hands on her hips. "No. Not until you tell me the truth. Not until I know how I hurt you. I'm not blind and something has."

He stared at her for a long moment, then reached out and brushed a shaky finger down her cheek. "You are different." He smiled sadly. "I can never experience pleasure without pain. The greater the pleasure, the greater the pain. My pleasure with you was greater than ever before."

Dorothea shook her head, not wanting to believe him.

"How? Why?"

He snapped his fingers and a soft robe appeared in his hand. "I'm a wizard and it is a curse from the realm of magic. It has nothing to do with you or what you did."

She took the robe and tossed it on the rock, amazed and still unsure if she believed in magic, but she wasn't going to be distracted from his pain. Then it hit her, and emotion deep and strong, gripped her, squeezing into her heart. "You knew this before, yet you still...made love to me." Then she saw a slight discoloration in the water behind him. "Turn around."

"Dorothea, it doesn't matter. You got what you came here for, now just go."

"No. Never." Pulling on his arm, she slid around to see his back. A fresh, deep laceration crossed from shoulder to shoulder. She gasped, tears filling her eyes. "How long has this been happening to you?"

"All of my life."

Moving to face him, she cupped his rough cheeks in her hands and pressed a soft kiss to his lips. "Is there a way to break the curse?"

He wrapped his arms around her, pulling her tight. "Not that I have found. I've learned to live alone and minimize my pleasure."

"I live alone and had no pleasure," she said, pressing closer to him then plunged headlong into the emotion filling her. Her whole life seemed to zero in to this moment. "Can I be your pleasure and share your pain?"

"Why? Because there is magic in my touch?"

"No, because there is magic in what I feel for you after just so short a time. I've had everything in life except for real love. If there is a chance that love can grow from this, I can't walk away no matter how great the pain."

Groaning and leaning down, he kissed her deeply, as if searching through to her soul. Careful not to hurt him more, she wrapped her arms around his waist, responding with her heart. Heat, pleasure, and his arousal grew between them.

She pulled back. "You'll hurt yourself."

He smiled. "I'll heal. Right now, I want you more than anything else."

"Then let me make love to you." She patted the foam rock. Climb up here."

He lifted a questioning brow, but did as she asked. She grabbed a condom, slid it lovingly on his erection. Then climbing up, she straddled him, guiding him inside her, and the magic began again, taking her to an even greater peak as bits of her heart again followed OZZ to heaven, whipping intense pleasure through them both. The pain hit in the last throes of her climax. She gasped and tensed, crying at its strength. He tried to push her away, but she clung to him. "No. I'll share your pain."

He groaned pulling her closer to him, as tears filled his eyes. "God help me, but I cannot deny you. I need you."

Suddenly, the world around them spun in a dizzying circle, catching them up in a whirlwind, tearing them apart. He reached for her, but the second their fingers touched, he disappeared. "No!" she shouted to the whirling wind, feeling as if she were being ripped apart. "No! I love him! He's my heart's desire. You can't take him!"

She landed on the beach next to her bag, where Yodo yipped at her. She was clothed again, dress, jacket, boots on—even her thong, which had been floating in the pool the last time she saw it. "Ozz!" she called, immediately searching for him. He stood under the waterfall, naked. His back to her. A back with no scars. "Can you hear me? What happened?"

He turned, smiling, stepping from the shower of water. "I think you broke the curse."

"How?"

"Brokenoggin is a magical place but—"

She clicked her heels and laughed. "There's no place like Brokenoggin."

"You didn't let me finish." He walked toward her and didn't stop until his erection brushed the silk of her dress. "But you've proven love is stronger than magic."

She grabbed his hips pressing harder against his hot arousal. "Are you sure the curse is broken?"

"Let's go inside and find out." He swung her up into his arms and she wrapped her arms around his neck.

"By the way," she said, as he strode across the sand. "What is your name?"

"The truth?"

"Yes."

"My mother, being a naughty witch from Brokenoggin had a wicked sense of humor. Like you, she was anorgasmic until she encountered my father. She named me after that encounter. Later in life I added the T-O-N to Zex and Zinclair."

Dorothea gasped. "She didn't."

"She did."

"Orgasmic Zex?"

He reached the huge, cushioned lounge chair and dropped her on it. "I'd thought you'd never ask." He stripped her in seconds and in minutes proved himself worthy of his name. This time no pain followed the pleasure. Dorothea had found her wizard and her home.

Episode 1.20

(Or 1.21, depending upon whether or not the skeletons have been
caught & the episode numbers sorted)

SOULLESS FROM SEATTLE

(aka *The Big Bad*)

By

Fiona MacLeod & Terese Ramin

*Wherein Annihilation Jones returns from the skeleton closet,
Seth's brother Simon arrives from Seattle and Janice's beast
arises from the depths. The first vampyre heart transplant
occurs during the apocalypse.*

(Written by Terese Ramin with extra characters, background
and general "Oh let's try this coz it'll be fun!" kibitzing by
Fiona MacLeod)

Fiona MacLeod is the author of Silent Fire, also available from
www.triskelionpublishing.com. In her other persona, she is the
director of the annual Writers Weekend retreat held in Bellevue,
WA. You can find her at www.writersweekend.com or write to
her at: writerfi@yahoo.com.

Seth stretched in the late August moonlight and scratched around the Duct-tape-and-Goop patch on his itchy chest. With his other hand, he reached around to scratch the identically patched opposing area in the middle of his back.

The edges of Janice's blunt nails slipped gently under his on his back. "Here, let me," she murmured huskily. Briskly, she rubbed the area all around his wound while he continued to massage his chest. "Must finally be healing if it's this uncomfortable."

Seth shook his head, without looking at her. "I think the hole's getting bigger and the riot bullet's slipping." Janice's fingers stilled. Her forehead dropped to his shoulder in silent protest. He rested his cheek against her hair. "I'm sorry, but I can feel it, Janice. A little jab in the right place and..."

Her "*no*" slipped out before she could stop it. She wasn't a panicky person, or at least not one good at showing it, but he'd come for her, done for her, been there for her in ways no one ever had in her two and a half plus centuries, and...

It had only been a summer, but she loved him.

"What can I do, Seth? Ask anything—*take* anything, my soul, my heart, my blood..."

"I don't *drink* blood, Janice," he reminded her patiently. "I don't remember *why*—exactly—but we've established that. It's disgusting. See, I wrote that right here..." He showed her the bright red laundry marker caps on his left forearm where he couldn't possibly miss it that read: **NO MATTER HOW FAR MY FANGS EXTEND, I DO <u>NOT</u> DRINK BLOOD. YUCK!**

Her slow, wry smile kissed his arm. "Not to drink, idiot, in a transfusion. It's shifter blood, *were* blood, *ancient tribal* blood. The regeneration factors are strong. Joe can do it for us. Maybe..."

She stopped. Grabbed his arm and swung him about. "Wait," she said in a voice that Seth knew meant she was excited. Used by anyone else no one ever would have guessed they'd changed expressions. "You said you don't remember *exactly*. Does that mean you remember *sort of*?"

"Ah…" Seth cocked his head and took stock of the muddle his brain had become ever since his arrival in the unconsecrated section of Brokenoggin Falls Community Cemetery after Nihil staked him with the Womanized two-by-two… "Holy shit," he swore.

He tugged on the much-washed Levi's 505 button-flies Janice had given him so he wouldn't have to wander around town naked and embarrassed by the huge and constant hard-on any thought or visual of her seemed to produce and caught her hand. "Come on."

"Wha– Where…?"

Janice hung back, trying to catch up and pull on her own clothes as he tugged her along. Seth might not have remembered telling her that since he'd found her in Brokenoggin's cemetery he wanted to make love to her for the next century, but his body certainly did.

"The Falls." He halted long enough for her to put on a bra and T-shirt, tug her pants over her hips and grab her boots.

"Huh?"

Bewildered she splayed a hand across his abdomen to steady herself. He responded the way he always did: instantly, by drawing her into the deepest, most drugging kiss she thought she'd ever die and go to heaven from, and falling into it with her.

This time, though, when her boots hit the floor, startling them both, he called them back from heaven.

Resting his forehead on hers, he scraped his thumbs across her cheeks. "Later," he promised. Then he picked up her boots, reached for her hand, and pulled her out the door.

"Which falls, and what's at them?"

Seth opened the driver's door of Janice's personal vehicle—an old military jeep—and ushered her in. "The high end of Brokenoggin Falls—the place where Corkscrew Falls Rapids begins—where not even the griffins or wyverns go."

Realization hit Janice like a freight train. She swallowed hard. Seth nodded.

"I know," he said simply. "Your beast, the secret, who you are, why I came here, where I came from, what happened that night, who the finger bones belong to, the only thing that will save me...I remember everything."

For a minute, Janice gazed at the night shadows, carefully thinking nothing. Then she turned over the ignition and the jeep roared to life.

"Get in and let's go," she said.

***

Nihil and the few skeletons that weren't recaptured, laid to rest, or revealed and forgiven in the currently destroyed version of episode thirteen watched from the rocky hillside nearby as Janice's jeep pull out of her isolated, wooded driveway onto the highway.

"Hunh," Nihil ventured. "Looks like I'm not the only one got my memory back."

Unable to speak, the skeletons rattled their bones together and flapped their jaws in a gruesome semblance of laughter. The one missing the finger bones Trevor Fairweather had dug up then re-hidden gesticulated wildly at the moving jeep, itself, then Nihil, clearly making a statement of things they needed to get cracking and do. The barrel-chested vampire waved off the skeleton impatiently.

"All right, all right. Hold your pelvis together, Leroy, climb aboard, we're goin'."

Thus invited, the skeletons clambered onto Nihil's back and shoulders. The vamp took a few warm-up steps downhill after Janice's jeep then started to run.

Fast.

***

Simon Drake, chief of the Naga—Seattle magick's deadly police force—and next in line for the throne of the Principality of the Mists (as long as he found himself a soul within the next few months) stepped out of his rental car in front of the Chat & Chew. Leaning this way and that, he tried to stretch the cricks out of his back. Irritated when the simple isometrics didn't work, he straightened. What the hell use was being undead if he still got stiff from traveling? It was a damn long way from Seattle to Brokenoggin Falls, with no direct flights, and way too many connections—Dallas, Denver, Minneapolis, Marquette...and then he'd gotten stuck in this damned compact Honda when he'd wanted a full size Town Car or something even bigger.

A Hummer would have done.

He glanced around Brokenoggin's marginally deserted streets under the bright light of the melon-colored full moon. Something about the place creeped him big time. After working Seattle's iniquitous Underground nothing should do that.

Especially nothing as innocent as this innocuous little hamlet.

Suddenly three werewolves and a were-panther still on its way to full change burst out the door of the Spiked Pig Saloon across the street and ran off howling into the forest behind the parking lot. From out of nowhere, a pack of yapping Chihuahuas dashed excitedly after the weres, tumbling over each other in their haste to keep up with the larger beasts. Down the middle of the road behind *them* galloped a panicked flight of Night Mares, whinnying in fear. And after them came a pissed-off Centaur wearing a pink tutu, ballet slippers, a ruffle-covered jock and a daisy chain harness, and bearing three snickering, identical-looking eleven-year-old girls on his back.

Simon was just about ready to recant his thoughts about the "innocent, innocuous little hamlet" when three identical-appearing adult women witches with substantial bosoms and a naked witch man spilled out of the Chat & Chew. Two of the women immediately started arguing and fell to the parking lot gravel wrestling and pulling each other's hair. The third stamped her foot, chastised them, hauled them apart and got them moving again while the male witch observed it all in a state of semi-arousal. Then all four went off into the woods to—if Simon heard correctly—*"dance naked and anoint the early harvest moon with fertility spells and couplings."*

A hairless, guilty-looking man with a cell phone camera at the ready skulked from shadow to shadow after them, the fly of his khaki Dockers looking heavily—and embarrassingly—damp.

Okay, yes. Simon grimaced. He, Simon Drake, soulless vampire, bound by oath to protect if not serve magick's powerful—and oftentimes cruel—aristocracy truly thought he'd seen everything. But apparently, Brokenoggin Falls had a thing or two to teach him.

So maybe Seth wasn't out of his mind when he'd talked the wild crazy about all the legends surrounding this place. Maybe this *was* the only place a vamp like Seth could find his *twainnoctu*—soul mule, the person born to carry a vampire's soul until he found and mated with her.

If Nihil hadn't killed him yet.

Growling at the thought, Simon strode to the door of the Chat & Chew and stepped inside. He'd find his brother, by damn, if he had to destroy every last resident of Brokenoggin Falls to do it.

***

The forest night was alive with shadow and sound the way forest nights always are: a rash of insects sounded off here, a chorus of frogs there; the sough and sway of the tall cedars and pines wove erratic patterns across clear patches of ground, teasing the imagination to strange thoughts.

Ahead, upper Brokenoggin Falls gurgled and rushed, shaping hill and stone, carving its path into the lower, grander falls and the loch below. Though he'd never been here before, Seth stepped surely along the treacherous trail that led to the upper falls, tugging the even more sure-footed Janice along in his wake.

At the edge of the forest, they paused.

"Look." Seth pointed at the melon moon. "The moon's full again and I haven't lost my memory."

Janice smiled tremulously. "That's good." She didn't sound sure. At least when he lost his memory with each full moon she had a chance to shift and start over in her best skin with him instead of having him remember what she looked like by the end of the moon cycle: a little more dumpy, somewhat older, a lot less fresh…

"Hey." Grinning slyly, he slid a hand up under her T-shirt to cup a breast that would be a great deal perkier after she shifted. "I like the puppy ears. They speak to your wisdom, intelligence and longevity, and those are all things I want in my mate."

"Ummm…" Janice squirmed uncomfortably, though her body was certainly behind the erotic things his fingers were doing to her flesh. Then, stunned, "Mate?"

Seth pulled off her shirt and bent to nip her ear with his fangs. "Of course. You carried both our souls for close to three centuries, who did you think you were if not my beloved, my mate?"

"Uh," Janice mumbled panting, "Just Janice. Tribal scourge, pariah, cursed were-thing, keeper of the beast, town cop and jailer, and virgin for all time."

"Hmmm," Seth murmured, dropping to his knees to plant pinprick fang bites down her belly while he stripped her out of her pants. "Hardly." He tongued and nibbled the sensitive skin of her inner thighs, knowing exactly how to drive her mad. "You're the mother of my unborn children, and the only creature in the world that can help me get back my heart now that you've given me my soul."

"Seeeeetthhhhh...*whaa-aaat?*" On the verge of losing all sense of what he was talking about and giving herself up to the pleasure of simply having him, Janice yelped. "Children?" Pleasure forgotten, she shoved his mouth away from her mons. "What the hell are you talking about? I'm menopausal."

"Paus*al*," Seth said earnestly, scrambling after her, "but not yet fully paus*ed*."

Janice wrinkled her eyebrows and fish-mouthed him. "Are you nuts?" she managed finally. "I'm two hundred and sixty-something years old. I look fifty...ish. I don't care how hot you are or how much I feel for you, I can't have your children. I can't have anybody's children. I wouldn't know what to do with 'em. I'd be a disastrous mother. I don't have enough *imagination* to raise kids. Why every time I see the Disdaine girls all I want to do is turn into the big bad wolf and *eat* them. And Emma's kids? Hell no! And they're good kids even if they do see dead people. Even Amy Fairweather and Destiny and Chi-chi Hopewell aren't up my alley. So what the *devil* would I do with vampyre-ancient-tribal-were-beast mixes, Seth? Tell me that."

When he stopped laughing long enough, Seth chased her down where she'd stalked off to when he started laughing—the upper falls lowest whirlpool—took her hands and again knelt before her.

"Janice, Janice..." A chuckle threatened him. Heroically, he swallowed it back. "You wouldn't have to do anything with our kids except bear them. Then you can go straight back to work and I'll stay home with them."

Janice regarded him suspiciously. "I'm sorry. That doesn't fit with this all-alpha-all-the-time vampyre image you've been showing me all summer in between bouts of amnesia—not that I mind it from the alpha thing from the lover standpoint, you understand. It's just that I'm not sure I can accept your word about the other from the "I'm-an-alpha-bitch-wolf-and-the-only-cop-in-town"   standpoint. And I really can't let people fuck with me because as a cop they tend to try to lie to me a lot so I've got a few trust issues—if you catch my drift."

Seth's lips twitched. "All right. Let's just say that I'm a whole lot of alpha with gamma rising, and that's why I seriously don't fit into the whole Seattle Underground scene, which is only part of the reason I left it. The main reason was you, just like I told you that first night—"

"Sethanimus Drake once of the Daimonos aristocracy, now condemned for treasonous behavior," a hard, heavy voice roared out of the night.

Whipping around fast, Seth shoved Janice behind him. "Annihilation Jones," he called back, voice thunder-deep and storm-savage. "I thought you were dead."

"After you, noodle fangs," the thinks-fast-with-his-weapons-but-not-with-his-brains vampiric hitman said.

The sound of running feet and rattling bones surged across the damp earth toward Janice and Seth. With an oath, Seth shoved Janice hard away from him and turned to meet the onslaught.

"Now would be an excellent time to trust me with your other beast," he suggested, "the one you haven't turned loose for almost three centuries. Because it looks like I could use a little help."

Then he leaped forward to engage the Naga's annihilator and his vicious Brokenoggin allies: the leftover skeletons from AnnMarie's closet.

***

The Forest Trolls were having a party.

It wasn't every day that the last full moon of August arrived full and melon-ripe, heralding September and Labor Day on the immediate horizon, which meant, like death and taxes, the certain return of the Brokenoggin Falls school year. School meant Strictly Enforced Bed Times, and Strictly Enforced Bed Times meant no more Disdaine triplets to wreak havoc upon them at all hours until All Hallows—unless some witch threw in a Sabbat they'd forgotten about, and the Disdaine parents let the triplets attend *that* in between times.

Forest Trolls preferred to forget things that weren't in their best interests to remember. Life made a better—and longer—rock-*out!* that way.

"Come, my little harpy pelican," Sam Stalwort, Lord of the Forest Trolls, beseeched his wife Claire. "Let down your taloned birdy feet, release your wings and screech for me. You know how I love it when you screech your harpy song when we join…"

A short distance away in a far less private glade other FTs danced and cavorted more openly with each other and the lesser forest elves and pixies who'd come to join them, uninvited. The taller, aristocratic Elves would never be caught dead, unconscious or drunk near a gathering of trolls—Forest or otherwise. Faeries, on the other hand…

Morgan-Titania-Morganna flitted lightly among the revelers, pausing now and again to dip up a drop of troll ale—dreadful stuff, unless one added a drop of faery nectar to it, then it totally *rocked.* She'd done her hair up in a rather violent shade of neon chartreuse and was a little nervous about showing it to her lover, Joe. He seemed to stand in awe of everything she did, no matter how potentially disastrous or unsuited to her complexion, but she worried nevertheless. She was his Queen, and it had still taken so long to get his attention…

Of course, that was because he was so shy to begin with, the big, darling, macho fey.

Going into the half-swoon she feigned every time she thought of their first kiss, and then their first time together back in her madeover tool shed closet at the bottom of the Fairweather's garden, Morganna didn't pay attention to where she was flying. Consequently, she flew straight into the chin of a larger-than-life vam*pýre* who clapped his hand around her and brought her up to eye level.

It could probably go without saying that the vam*pýre* didn't look happy to see her.

"What are *you* doing here?" Simon Drake asked.

Morganna posed in the middle of his palm, arms akimbo, and drew herself up to her full height. "I might ask you the same thing, vamPYRE. *I'm* the Faery Queen and I belong here. You're not Seth, so *you* don't."

"You're not the queen," Simon said rudely, "you're a guy."

Morganna fluffed her hair and dangled her queenly ring hand in front of him, suggesting he might want to kiss it. "I beg to differ. Ask anyone who the fey Queen is hereabouts and they'll tell you, it's me." She stomped to the edge of Simon's palm and shook her fist in his nose. "And call me a *guy* again and I'll stick my chartreuse stilettos so far up your snout you won't be able to sneeze for a week."

Simon's lips compressed either clamping back an ill-advised grin or a frown. "I see," he managed at last. "And that would certainly be unfortunate." He swallowed a few times as though digesting something difficult. Then, finally as light dawned, "Did you just mention Seth? A vampire?"

As was usual for most places outside of Brokenoggin Falls, Simon did *not* emphasize the second syllable in vampire but put slightly more emphasis on the first, less combustible syllable.

Morganna changed her hair color to hot Titania red and

switched her clothes to battle black leather and tall boots. "Maybe." Fists on her straight hips, she stuck out her square chin belligerently. "Who's askin'?"

"His oldest brother, Simon Drake." Simon tipped his head. "I haven't seen him for three months, but I finally tracked him here. If he still...exists...I've come to bring him home." He hesitated while the unaccustomed words stuck for a moment in his soulless craw. "Or at least save his worthless hide."

***

The battle along the edge of upper Brokenoggin Falls raged up and down, back and forth, in and out. From forest to grassy glade to rocky whirlpool to slippery streambed, Seth and Nihil fought hand to hand and foot to face, fist to chin and jaw—grappling, bobbing, weaving, dancing and wrestling.

Stripped naked, Janice fought the skeletons three-on-one, first in human form, then in wolf. She chomped their bones in her great, wolfish jaws, shattered femurs and ulnas, radiuses and thighs—destroyed cervical spines and ripped apart rib cages. But the skeletons found a way to piece themselves together and keep coming.

Especially the one with the missing finger bones.

It warred savagely, used its sharp, bony digits to try to score her pelt and tear it away. She bit and slashed at it, but it did not give ground, parried every move, wearing her down.

Devoid of flesh and muscle, it had less weight to carry and memory weighed little, adrenaline born of the thirst for revenge counted for much. Janice was disadvantaged by her desire to survive, her thirst for life. Her adrenaline surge was half concentrated on Seth and her desire to make sure Nihil didn't destroy him.

The skeleton knew that.

With the few teeth left in its jaw it bit down into her

wolf shoulder and hung on even when she yelped and shook its skull free of the rest of its bones.

"Your beast, Janice." Seth's deep voice, faint and fading. "Loose your beast. It's now or never. Use it to save us both."

Tortured by doubt and in pain from her wounds, Janice tried to see where Seth was, how he fared. She saw him give Nihil a swift roundhouse kick to the side of the head and then snap back and reach stiff-fingered for the other vamp's chest. At the same time, Nihil came back from the kick and aimed a powerful punch straight at the Goop-and-Duct-tape patch in the center of Seth's chest.

"No!" Janice howled.

She lurched sideways, away from the skeleton fray, and lunged madly across the slick ground toward the vampyres. There was a sickening, sucking *spluurrtch* of sound and Seth's hand drew back from Nihil's chest full of something pulsing and reddish. At the same time Nihil's fist connected solidly with Seth's chest, sent the rubber riot bullet bouncing out of his back and into the upper falls with a *sploonk-plop*.

For a moment time paused long enough for everyone to register shocked surprise, then the vampyres fell backwards away from each other, Seth holding Nihil's heart aloft, while Janice started to scream and change…

***

The minute the…whatever it was started to scream, Simon whipped around, his heart cold with dread. The Seattle Underground was full of tormented pieces of magick, but none of them sounded like that.

"What's that?"

Morganna blanched and went from her Titania red and battle black leather straight back to the alarming neon chartreuse hair and shocking lime and purple dance outfit she'd been trying out before Simon showed up. "I'm not sure." She flittered about Simon's palm making sure her strappy chartreuse "do-me" pumps were strapped on securely. "But whatever it is, it sounds like it'll need a vet in the very near future, so I'd better get mine."

So saying she *fouffed* her hair, dashed to the edge of Simon's hand and flew off at speed.

Open-mouthed, Simon stared after her until she was almost out of sight—at which point he thought to ask, "Wait! Where...?"

"The falls," Morganna shouted without looking back— or at least that's what Simon thought she said. "Get some trolls and meet me at the fa*aaalllss*..."

"Trolls?"

Feeling deeply out of his depth, Simon looked around at the drunken, troll-ish revelers. Then he gazed in the direction from whence the horrible screams came. Sized up the situation and weighed the possible abilities of drunken Forest Trolls against whatever the bellowing wounded thing might be against his brother's existence and what he knew of Annihilation Jones' capabilities.

And turned and loped off toward the screaming beast alone.

***

There was, Simon realized almost at once, something wholly magnificent about the monster and the way she—it could only be a she—protected and defended his brother's inert body on the treacherous shoreline beside the stepping-down falls.

Part wolf, part dragon, part demon—or so she seemed—she fought with fury and fire, crushing bones to powder under her feet, crunching them between her jaws or swallowing the pieces whole. The skeletons—Simon could see they were skeletons, and that equally stunned and frightened him because Seattle, for all its savagery, was still more civilized than this—fought bitterly. They re-formed with whatever pieces were left, battled to get around her, to reach Nihil and the bloody, dripping piece of him clutched aloft in Seth's unmoving hand until, nearly exhausted, she captured the last metatarsal, gleefully chewed it up and swallowed it.

Then she turned her wrath on Nihil's body.

A wrench of her huge, clawed paws tore off the hitman vamp's head; a gulp and it was gone. Simon watched in fascination while she destroyed what was left of Annihilation Jones's body—devouring certain bits and burying others deep at a distance from each other. A small pile she even set aside and coated in her apparently acidy wolf-dragon-demon venom; it disintegrated into a residue of damp reddish-brown chalk that she ground into the bank beside the falls with the pads of her feet.

Finished at last, she swung her head around to look at Seth. Her grief was palpable.

That's when Simon finally realized he hadn't made a move to help his brother.

It's also when he knew what his brother held clenched in his hand: Nihil's heart. He could still smell the blood pulsing through it.

It was alive.

That meant whatever was wrong with Seth, there was still time to save him.

Galvanized by the thought, Simon started forward. The great creature heard him. Her head swung in his direction and she positioned herself defensively over and around Seth and despite the glittering tears in her eyes, she growled.

"Whoa, baby." Simon went still. "I don't want to hurt him. He's my little brother. I'm here to help. Just let me help."

Clearly not in the mood to believe anyone she didn't recognize, the monster took two steps forward, thrust her muzzle at Simon and pulled her lips back in a deeper, more menacing, more *convincing* growl.

"Oh dear Goddess and her seven sisters," someone behind Simon swore softly. "What the holy Sam Hill is that and where did we get *it* from?"

"You ask me," Morganna said brightly, buzzing up beside Simon to size up the situation and flitting away again, "That's the beast Janice's been hiding all these centuries. Or maybe…"

She fluttered to the ground in front of Simon and took a few mincing steps forward. "Janice, honey, is that you? You're looking awfully snarly tonight, you don't mind my sayin'. Did you and—oh my sweet Jimmy Choos, Seth!" With a *come-on* flick of her hand behind her, she darted forward, straight under the beast's massive muzzle to light on Seth's shoulder and peer closely into his face. "Dear Goddess, Janice, no wonder you're upset. Why the boy's on his last legs! Joe, *Joe!* Get up here my beautiful, darling lover and *do* something this instant!"

She shoved at the dragon-wolf-demon's foreleg. "I know you're worried, dear, but you're going to have to move and let the veterinarian in to have a look at him. Come on—" she hopped down and patted the ground beside Seth's head. "You sit right here and hold his head in your paws. Ooooh, and look at those tears!" She flew up, pulled off her hat—a cunning little number if she said so herself, just right for searching out Janice-beasts and misplaced vampyres— and collected a single diamond tear. "If I know my folklore, this'll be the perfect thing to help heal a transplanted vampyre heart…"

* * *

"…And that, children, is how daddy got to be the first vampyre to ever have a heart transplant in the history of the known universe as well as Brokenoggin Falls."

"*Kewl!*" Karen Thinksalot sighed.

"Awesome," her brothers Michael and Leroy agreed.

"But what about the finger bones?" the youngest Thinksalot, Andrew asked.

"And Uncle Simon?" his five minutes older twin sister Delores put in.

"Well," said their father, who'd been better than his word about the staying home with them part, and even happier when Janice shyly asked if she could stay home with them sometimes, too, "Remember how your mother first found out about her beast and everybody got scared and made her hide it?"

All the young Thinksalots nodded. They'd heard the story before, of course, but it tended to get better with age and telling.

"The finger bones belonged to the first man who tried to slay her. She bit them clean off in battle. Her family never forgave her for it because that man was an important tribal chief who wanted to marry her. But she knew she was made for me and couldn't possibly marry anyone else, so she fought for her honor and virtue like a demon—"

"Until she turned into one," Karen finished excitedly. "I can hardly wait until that happens to me."

"Well…" Seth cleared his throat as Janice walked into the room and made a gagging face at him. "I think you'll find if you ever reach that point, darling, that you'll wish it happened any other time than when it does."

"No I won't," Karen said firmly.

Janice shuddered theatrically, then announced, "Bedtime." She reached for a twin.

"But Uncle Simon—"

"Is in Seattle and has his own story for another time."

"And then there's the part about daddy becoming a Thinksalot instead of you becoming a Drake…"

"Because I'm Indian and our group is matriarchal which means the men marry into my tribe instead of the other way around," Janice said patiently. "You would think I'm explaining this to a television audience the way you like this story repeated."

"We just like to keep the facts straight," Michael told her.

"So we know what we're doing when some bride claims us," Leroy agreed.

"God save us," their mother said, and put them to bed.

Then the Thinksalot parents went out in their isolated backyard and played in the light of the Brokenoggin Falls blue moon and briefly contemplated what interesting things puberty might have in store for them in a few years when they found out exactly what kind of creatures their vampyre/ancient-tribal-werewolf-dragon-demon beast might have created.

And then they got right down to the bare facts of things and did what two preternatural beastly creatures that loved and couldn't get enough of each other did on a regular basis...

...They fucked each other's brains out.

APPENDIX I:

Bonus Footage & Additional Material

Everybody Loves Dragons

Intro by

Terey daly Ramin, editor

When we got down to putting the chapters for this work together, a basic problem came to light: several of the authors volunteered to write dragon chapters.

Possibly this is because, when romance and fantasy are combined, the dragon is a natural creature to add to the mix. Knights slew dragons to win fair ladies, dragons themselves have always been somewhat fond of princesses (it's that golden-haired, maidenly quality that fits right in with their fondness for treasure hoarding, I suspect—either that or the gold chastity belts and all the jewels princesses are reported to wear), and so romance novelists and dragons are a natural fit. For that reason—and possibly because they were the best established actual romantic *couple* in the original story outline—we wound up with too many stories and episodes based on the characters of Earl and Claudia Choo.

Normally I'm not the family pack rat, my husband is. I'm easily the "when in doubt, leave it out" girl. But these episodes were terrific stories in their own right, so though the individual authors were marvelous about redoing the chapters, I hated to discard the originals. Thus, the "bonus DVD-style-outtakes-footage" materials package plan hatched.

So here they are, exclusive to the print edition of *Bewitched, Bothered & BeVampyred*: the original versions of episodes 1.4 by Sophia Nash and 1.6 by Elizabeth Holcombe. Enjoy!

Terey daly Ramin

18 June 2005

"Flaming, Hot, and Bothered"

By

Sophia Nash

"**W**ell, I'll be damned if I'm going to let Claudia Choo get her claws in one of them before me." Mavis Gap dropped the edge of her avocado and burnt orange striped curtains back in place and turned to Janice, draped comfortably across a chartreuse loveseat.

"Your pointed ears are glowing, honey."

"Well, I like that. Is that all you gotta say?" Mavis scooped the chihuahua from her native Indian cop friend's lap and paced, a pouty look in full bloom.

"Well, what did you expect? You know how bored I get listening to your Claudiathons. When are you going to learn to just ignore her?"

"The day I win."

"Win what?"

"Whatever." Mavis bent down to kiss the top of Prunella's head, a devious plan emerging.

"Have another Cosmopolitan, honey." Janice patted the seat next to her before giving the cocktail shaker a couple of jigs and draining it into the two V shaped glasses.

"It's not even 7:15 *in the morning*, Janice."

"Think of it as retail therapy."

"Wha? I can't talk to you when you're this far gone." Mavis accepted the glass from her friend and drained it in one swallow.

"It's retail therapy when I had to go out and actually buy this fancy French firewater since you couldn't remember the spell."

"You're changing the subject." Mavis glared at her friend and wondered, not for the first time, if Janice was fifty or one hundred and fifty. It was hard to tell given the amount of Votox Janice had convinced the town vet to inject in her forehead. If she had not been her best friend Mavis would make fun of the slight droop in one eyebrow. "I have dibs on Dr. Perfectly-Chiseled."

"Does Dr. *Predily-Chisolm* know?"

"He will tonight when he comes for dinner. He and the other two visiting archaeologists end their first day of excavation at five." She looked down at her bosom and rearranged her Miracle bra to extra perky before leafing through the pages of the latest edition of Chihuahua Fancy.

Janice sat up straight and shifted her eyes. "Where'd they say they were digging?"

"Why Corkscrew Falls—where all those old bones are."

Janice's eyes radiated a wolfish golden moon color for the merest moment before she downed the cocktail and vamoosed out the door faster than Mavis could say, "Single, white, willing witch. Humans within 1,500 mile radius only. Reply with photo."

***

If there was one thing Claudia Choo was sure of, it was that she didn't want to end up like town busy-body, Mavis Gap, with her neurotic brood of chihuahuas and a passion for exotic cocktails. She felt sorry for the woman who lived her life by watching everyone else's. Claudia shook her head. Did Mavis really think Claudia hadn't seen her peeking past her curtains whose colors were a scary homage to the dubious design choices of the 70's?

Walking away from Sarah Caldron's Chat & Chew, Claudia wondered why Mavis was so envious of her, anyway. It was not as if she had any children, the one thing they both craved. It seemed the woman coveted everything

Claudia possessed. Every time she bought new clothes, not a week would go by before Mavis would be wearing the identical thing—even when the jeans had made her chunky legs and bottom look like, like... Claudia forced back her evil thoughts and turned onto Puff Draggy Lane. She knew why she was feeling cattish. Mavis had blatantly propositioned her husband Earl at Chi Chi Chong's dinner party last week.

The thought of her devoted spouse made Claudia's stomach churn. Every nerve ending in her body was tingling. Why had she made that outrageous suggestion to the archaeologist at the Chat & Chew? It wasn't like her to flirt. She hadn't looked twice at a male—human, warlock or otherwise—since the day she had first laid eyes on her darling Earl. Maybe others did call him a nerd behind her back, forgetting that Claudia's gift of extraordinary hearing made anyone within a four block radius subject to her auditory clairvoyance. But she loved Earl. Always would. Plastic pocket protectors and all.

There was something about the mysterious glow she sometimes thought she saw lurking in his eyes when he tried to mate with her that made the answering primal urge within her ignite.

But there were times Claudia was sure he didn't love her as much as she loved him. And then there were the days that her mother-in-law popped in. If Mei Choo's hints about infertility were not depressing enough, some days the lady seemed to come before Claudia in Earl's eyes. And Claudia couldn't bear her mother-in-law's accusatory stare. Didn't she know that Claudia wanted to provide her with a grandchild even more than Earl did?

Claudia just couldn't take it anymore. Her eyelids burned with tears fighting to form as she opened the little gate to her house's cobbled walkway. After seven years with Earl, her itch for a child was worse than the time Alice

Fairweather mistakenly mixed poison ivy extract in her Preparation H type remedy.

"Earl, honey, this is the only way. For the thousandth time, you should never have married Claudia, anyway. We knew the union could never produce a child. At least I am grateful it hasn't produced…something canine."

Claudia stopped dead in her tracks and stared at her red front door. Her mother-in-law's voice drowned out Mavis's barking chihuahuas five blocks away. She lost the fight with her welling tears.

"You've gone too far, Mom. I won't do it. Not even for you. I love Claudia."

"Love, Shmlove. That has nothing to do with it. Claudia is a nice enough girl. But what we need is a *breeder*. Now, don't make me angry, you know what happens when the mood strikes me and I'm already smoking." Claudia heard a familiar coughing, gagging noise. "It's a *fait accompli*. You're to meet that nice, normal archaeologist lady at eight pm at my house. I told her you were an expert on the history of Brokenoggin and she bought it. I'll make a delicious Anti-fog Dragon's Breath soup so she'll sce the real you and if you can't get her between the sheets within the blink of a sty, then I'll, I'll, well, I'll give Claudia another chance."

"Mom."

"Don't 'Mom' me. This is for the best. And Claudia would thank me. If you impregnate the archaeologist, we'll cast spells on both Claudia and the scientist so that they're both convinced it's Claudia's child after the fact."

"I don't know, Mom. It sounds pretty far-fetched. But…I guess I'm willing to do it, if it will solve our problem. I'm sick of the subject."

Claudia clapped her hands over her ears and ran back toward town. Her cursed extra-sensory hearing. She knew it. Just knew it. Earl didn't love her. Now, there was nothing stopping her from accepting that offer of a drink tonight. She would just have to try not to think about how much that nerdy archaeologist reminded her of Earl.

***

The table was set, the tarot cards swept under the couch, and the dogs, bless their little hearts, dead asleep behind the kitchen door after lapping up that mild sleeping draught. Mavis glanced at a chew toy peeping up at her from the harvest-gold shag carpeting and kicked it under the coffee table.

The doorbell rang and Mavis suddenly noticed that the eyes of the lit troll candle were glaring at her. She turned the face away and ran to the door. Opening it, she stared up at the most handsome human she'd ever seen. Wavy chestnut hair, blue-green eyes, full luscious lips. Ah, he looked liked Dr. Kildare, only better.

"Mrs. Gap?" Dr. Predily-Chisolm gallantly swept up her hand and bent to brush his lips upon it. How utterly nineteenth century romantic. There were definitely some things she wished civilization hadn't lost in the name of progress.

Mavis forced back a girlish giggle. "Do come in. I'm soooo glad you could make it. I know how tiring all that digging must be."

He crossed the threshold and Mavis quickly locked the door behind him and turned off the porch light. *Nothing* was going to interrupt her now. "I've prepared a little dinner and—" She licked her lips. "—a lot of *dessert* for after."

"How kind of you, Mrs. Gap."

"*Miss* Gap. But please call me Mavis."

"Alright. Then you must call me John."

"How appropriate," Mavis replied with a giggle she hoped didn't sound like a snort.

He was so cute standing there and looking a bit flustered and disheveled. Mavis rose up on her toes and brushed a fleck of dirt off his cheek.

"Miss—or rather, Mavis, thank you so much for your invitation and for offering to give me a little insight into the history of this town. I really do think we're onto some sort of breakthrough. We're still trying to document the find. Can't tell if it's a woolly mammoth or some sort of ancient dinosaur."

"How fascinating. Tell me more. But first, please, try this little drinky-winky. I've made a batch of piña-coladas and they're divine, if I do say so." She slid a drink into his hand faster than a black widow bites the head off its mate. Potions weren't her forte. She just hoped the aphrodisiac wasn't too potent, but then again, maybe that wouldn't be such a bad thing. She motioned him to sit on the love seat and joined him.

Mavis clinked his glass in salute, forcing him to take a swallow. "Mmmm, Mavis. That's good. What's that unusual taste?"

Must be the dash of ground Mexican fire ant testes. "Paprika."

"Curious," he said taking two gulps in rapid succession. His eyes looked a little glazed. He shook his head in an obvious effort to regain his sense of purpose. "So tell me about Brokenoggin."

"This drear—I mean dear little town? Well, let's see." She really should tell him a little to whet his appetite and ensure his return if the wild sex didn't do the trick. He was simply too handsome to be content with a one night stand. She hunched her shoulders which forced her cleavage to full frontal attack mode and placed a finger on her Dance with the Devil Red lips. "I understand from a little book I have, written by my ancestor—a grandfather—or rather a great, great, great grandfather. Maybe one or two more greats should be in there." She winked at him. "Anyway, sometime during the seventeenth century, he emigrated here from Plymouth along with a group of other settlers who seemed disenchanted with the whole puritan scene. I think he came with about six or seven other *friends*."

"Really?"

He had the cutest earnest expression on his face. And the hugest bulge in his trousers. Mavis smiled. "Yes. Care for some guacamole and chips?" She dipped a chip and dropped it between his quivering lips before dragging her finger along his willing tongue. "Honey, are you OK? You look a little warm." That was an understatement.

"No, no, I'm fine." He gulped back the rest of the piña-colada and tugged on his tie.

Mavis leaned forward to deftly untie the striped Brooks-Brothers staple. Claudia would be impressed.

"How were they received?" he asked. A trickle of perspiration slid down his temple.

"What, honey?"

"Your ancestor and his group. How were they received?"

"Oh. Let's see." She touched the tip of her tongue on her top lip and tried to look thoughtful. Hmmmm, maybe she should let him have another half a piña colada so he'd really let go of his inhibitions. She poured a little more from the Waring blender. "Well, it seems the new settlers were very warmly welcomed because the original town folk were, well, starving."

He tossed back the drink like a man who had just crossed the Sahara. "Starving…" His pupils were dilated, and his voice had taken on a kind of husky vibration. Something was dancing the mambo in his pants. It was an impressive sight—enough to make any girl swoon.

She looked at his transfixed gaze and swooped in for a kiss.

Let the thrashing begin.

She had meant for the experience to culminate in her

bedroom. She had spiffed it up for the occasion, pink silk sheets, a pink comforter, ruffles on all the pillows and bows on all the curtains. But it wasn't in the cards. She should have guessed since her tarot cards had forewarned that this was going to be wild, brief, and devastating. *Yummy.*

Dr. Predily-Chisolm was a big boy. And he was adorable, all large clumsy hands between mutterings of 'sorry' every half a minute or so. He didn't seem to know how to unhook her push-up bra or untangle the fishnet stockings around her ankles. But he did know what to do with his, his—well, a nice girl would call it 'his digging *tool*,' she thought with a smirk.

Oh, this felt so nice and normal after all that wild jungle sex with the warlocks in town, when you never knew if they were going to turn into lions or tigers or dragons at the drop of a wand. And this time she was sure she would conceive a real child with magical powers instead of another chihuahua. Not that she didn't love the little darlings. It was just that she was tired of all the pitying looks in town. And boy would it get Claudia's goat.

Oh my, she might just be reaching the point of having an old-fashioned climax! How novel. Dr. Predily-Chisolm leaned up on his forearms and Mavis gazed at his beautiful abs. She sighed in pleasure and urged him silently with her hips. She was right on the pinnacle and panting.

"I'm so sorry, Mavis. I don't know what's come over me."

"I don't know what you mean, handsome. I'm all yours for the taking."

"I mean, I don't normally do this sort of thing."

"Really? I would've never guessed." If he didn't move again, she thought she would die of anticipation. She bucked against him.

"Wait. What's that noise?" he asked.

Please. Start. Moving. Now. She thought in

annoyance. She tried to tug his neck down but he had gone rigid.

"I hear scratching and...and is that barking?"

Oh God. No! And she knew just what they were capable of. Prunella had taught Wisty and George how to balance her on their backs so that she could reach the kitchen doorknob with her paws and wrench it open. No sooner had she envisioned it, when all nine dogs burst through the door and circled them, barking in a laughing sort of way.

The scientist jumped up, pulled up his pants and stood on top of the end table, knocking her precious troll candle to the floor.

Mavis threw the rest of the piña coladas on the small flames now licking the carpet and a purple starburst erupted before it extinguished the fire and left an ashen spot of sodden cinders. The dogs had surrounded the end table like a pack of laughing hyenas and the good doctor was looking mighty uncomfortable.

Mavis was about as frustrated as she had ever been in her life. "Prunella, if you don't herd Wisty, George, Max and the rest back to the kitchen, I'll put you in the pound! And I'll take you for your annual shots *early*!" Mavis snapped a hand to her mouth. He would think she was a raving lunatic talking to her little ones like that. Luckily, he looked too scared to have noticed. "Johnny, darling, no need to cower up there, my little doggies are the sweetest, they'd never hurt a Spanish fly."

Prunella winked and led her brothers and sisters back to the kitchen. The scientist still appeared anxious and only half listening when she helped him down.

"I'm sorry, I don't really like dogs. I'm allergic." His eyes did look a little watery.

"Really? Well, you don't look allergic to me. Let's go back to my bedroom where we won't be disturbed."

"Ummm, thank you, Mavis, but really, I-I think I should

be going."

Mavis dropped her gaze to his pants and saw that the dance had ended. Abruptly. Should'a made him drink a full second glass. "But I have ever so much more to tell you about my ancestors, John. And dinner is almost finished cooking."

He looked tempted but embarrassed. "Well, all right, but maybe we should stay in this room. I don't know what came over me, Mavis. And I hope you'll accept my apology. You see, the thing is, well, to be perfectly frank—" He blinked. "I'm gay."

***

Dr. Loindexter's room at Motel 13 gave Mavis Gap's home decorating efforts a run for their money. Claudia tried not to hyperventilate while she stared at the tilted barrel-shaped lampshade on the nightstand next to the glued-down TV remote. The shiny blue polyester bed covering looked like something right out of Alice's bedroom from The Brady Bunch. As she waited for Dr. Loindexter to emerge from the bathroom, she drew the curtains closed in an effort to ignore the blinking of the neon tavern sign across the street.

Why, oh, why had she let this go so far? She could have said 'no' after their dinner at Transylvania Pizza Kitchen. She could have said no after drinks at Brokenoggin's only tavern. But she hadn't. Every time 'no thank you' had crept onto her tongue, she remembered her mother-in-law's voice, '*what we need is a breeder.*" It made Claudia so hurt and sick inside. They always assumed it was her problem. Well, had her mother-in-law ever stopped to think that maybe the problem lay in *Earl's* prodigious lap? Claudia had spared Earl the embarrassment of submitting to an examination by never voicing that thought.

She removed her pale pink Manolo Blahniks that matched her spring tweed suit and Gucci scarf. Earl had bought the tiny skirt and jacket because he had said it made her legs look long and sexy. Oh, she was going to have to stop thinking of Earl if she was going to do this. She sat on the edge of the bed and straightened her spine.

Reason fought with hurt feelings. Why hadn't he stood up to his mother? He almost always had in the past. Claudia remembered the secret, and guilty thrill she felt each time he had winked at her before maneuvering his unsuspecting mother on top of their fire-singed trap door. She had thought they were on the same side. Not any more.

The archaeologist emerged from the bathroom, his white Fruit of the Looms pulled high. He had carefully wet and combed his dark hair parted down the middle. He had tiny aureoles and not a single strand of hair on his sunken chest. However, the hair from all the wild beasts in Africa could be found covering his thin legs above his white socks. A lopsided grin stretched from ear to ear. He looked like he was counting his lucky stars.

Claudia supposed she had chosen him not only for the reason that his face reminded her slightly of Earl, but also so that she would feel less guilty. It was working. At least Earl pumped iron on Mondays and Thursdays and he had something to show for his efforts. This man, and she used the term generously, would probably think a Nautilus machine was a navigational device.

She crooked a finger at him, urging him forward. He eagerly jumped onto the bed and sniffed her. So much for sensual foreplay.

"Claudia, you're the most beautiful woman I've ever…ever seen. I still can't belie—"

She leaned forward, held her breath and forced herself to kiss him. It was too bad she had forgotten to close her eyes. She forced back the bile creeping up her throat.

For all his assumed lack of experience, the scientist sure knew how to undress a woman in less time than she could do it herself. But soon, way too soon, his clammy little hands were exploring every last inch of her body, and she was trying, unsuccessfully, to keep disgust at bay. He kept moaning her name over and over until she thought she would scream. She wished he would just get it over with. Then she would thank him, leave, and get home in time to mix up a post-coital fermentation elixir to optimize the chance of conception.

She dropped her hand to touch him in an effort to urge him to mount. A wilted, placid piece of flesh greeted her hand. What on earth? She had only ever seen Earl's manhood, something that would spark fear in the eyes of any virgin. *With good reason.*

"Oh, Claudia. C Claudia, baby. See me, feel me, touch me, heallllll me—"

Oh. My. God. Was he whispering lyrics from The Who's 'Tommy'? "Um, Dr. Loindexter. Are you OK?"

"Oh, yes, Claudia baby. Just keep touching me. It's been so long. So long since…"

"Yes?"

"Ah, hell…since anyone's hand has touched me other than my own."

She forced herself to open her eyes and saw a red flush move past his eyebrows to his receding hairline. "I'm sorry Dr. Loindexter."

"Will you please call me Duncan?" he whined.

"Oh, sorry, Duncan. What can I do?"

He sighed heavily, rolled off of her and covered his face with his forearm. "Nothing. Not a darn thing. You're just too intimidating for me, I guess. No, let me revise that. I *know* you're too intimidating. Hell, I've never gotten past second base with anyone, not even pimply old Betty Sue Bob Michaels. How do you expect someone like me to perform under so much pressure?"

Claudia's mouth twitched. She tamed the hysterical giggle in her throat. Poor man. "I'm sorry Duncan. Do you want to try again?" She prayed he would say no. Right now she would give up her first unborn anything if she could just get out of there. If this was not been a sign from her friend Lucifer that good witches didn't have to put up with bad sex, then—

But...

Her nature refused to let her leave without doing a kindness toward Dr. Loindexter. She flipped open her Birkin bag, extended her compact wand and flicked it. "Obliviosus somnus," she said, wishing she could remember that chapter on organ transformation from her Curses textbook. This would have to do. Her liver wasn't into continuing this ridiculous plan anyway.

Duncan Loindexter slept the sleep of the dead, his jaw slackening in surrender. She was just going to have to figure out another way to have a child. Perhaps Lucifer would be willing to make a deal with her. He always had been more than accommodating in the past.

Claudia threw her wand back in her bag, snapped into her clothes, and walked away from the preposterously named Dr. Loindexter. She only wished she could experience a little forgetful sleep herself.

***

Earl Choo gulped down his mother's soup like a fluish Jewish man tolerates his mama's lukewarm Matzo balls. He gazed down the length of Mom's formal dining room table, marked with only a few very faint scorch marks, reminders of some heated family arguments. He wondered about the petite dark brunette archeologist facing him. So very unlike Claudia, his dear long, tall drink of ambrosia. His wife was the quintessential blonde bombshell of every man's fantasies. How was he going to go through with this? Dr. Heather Lovingood, was pretty in an all-American-girl-next-door kind of way. She had huge white straight teeth, a pert nose, and eyeglasses which were just dying to be taken off her face. But she just wasn't his type.

It was also clear, however, that the reverse was not true. Two sips of Mom's soup which was supposed to transform him into a Hugh Jackman look-alike, in Heather's eyes only, made the woman begin to stare at him with a sort of rapt fascination on her face. That worshipful gaze was a novel feeling, truth be told. It had been many years since any woman, with the exception of Claudia, had looked at him with any interest whatsoever.

He had almost forgotten the delicate dance of flirtation. But when he felt himself harden, despite thoughts of his beloved wife, he began to suspect that Mom had slipped something in his soup too—and it certainly wasn't a potion that made Dr. Lovingood look like Hugh Jackman.

Mom had never been known to leave things to chance.

"Mr. Choo, you were speaking about the new settlers, one of whom was your ancestor, right?

He nodded and pushed away his soup bowl.

"So they were instrumental in helping the original townsfolk survive a particularly harsh winter. A kind of re-creation of Plymouth's first winter with the Indians, right?" she asked.

"Yes, except my ancestors didn't scalp the townsfolk." He smiled at her against his will. Heather was actually pretty cute. *Very cute, really.* "Instead, they brought foodstuffs with them and had some, uh, *original* methods of *stretching* what they had on hand."

"So the inhabitants must have been grateful."

"You would think." He scratched his head. "But you would be incorrect. It seems that once the starving townsfolk's stomachs were full, they began to question the newcomers' methods." He had a sudden, nearly irresistible urge to climb on top of the table and crawl over to this Lovingood babe and lick her. A rumbling from his stomach signaled gastro-intestinal fire burning his ribs and his crotch.

He wondered if dear old Mom had found this potion in her Chinese Dragon Witchbook or the Joy of Spooking. Annoyance wrestled with desire, and of course, desire won.

"Really?" She paused and pulled the rubber band from her hair, allowing the silky dark strands to fall all over her nubile shoulders.

When had she unbuttoned her oxford shirt and pushed it off her shoulders?

Lovingood ran a hand through her hair and tossed it back with panache. "And how did the newcomers react?" she asked huskily.

OK, no one could blame him. No self-respecting warlock worth his weight in hemlock could resist this potion whatever it was. He felt like he would explode if he didn't have her right here, right now. He got up, trying to casually hold a napkin over his front, and walked the long length of the table to her. She looked up at him with huge brown doe-eyes.

Mom, was right. It was for the best. Claudia would *thank* him if she knew what he was going though to ensure an heir for them. He would do the Lovingood and make three women happy by the act—Lovingood, Claudia, and Mom. "Miss Lovingood, I have some etchings in my study drawn by my ancestors, of course. They might be of particular interest to you. Would you care to see them, my dear?"

"Ohhhhh, yessss," she said, breathing heavily as they almost raced down the hallway.

It was a miracle their pants were still on by the time they reached the study. "What about your wife, Mr. Choo?" Heather asked in a moment of clarity.

"Wife?"

His black framed glasses fogged when the little she-devil did something indescribably delicious with her tongue in his ear. Little did she know she was playing with fire.

Literally.

He ached for her now with an intensity he had never known. Mom sure knew how to cook. And Heather was simmering for him. She was mewling like a cat and arching her back like a rabid raccoon. It was a sight to behold.

He gently nudged her down onto the brown leather sofa and began to unzip his chinos. The urge to stretch his long length into her was unrelenting. He allowed his pants to drop and anticipated the look of reverence that would light up Lovingood's face.

She giggled.

It was the kind of giggle that felt like a dash of ice cold water. With sickening intuition, he looked down to see the stuff of nightmares. Standing as erect as a tin soldier was a manhood in all its glory. But it wasn't his manhood. It looked...well, it looked like a birthday candle, a child's unlit pink birthday cake candle. Even the revolving pink and white swirls were visible.

Hell. . .

"Mom," he roared. An involuntary flash of fire came out of his throat.

Heather screamed.

Earl felt the unmistakable gnawing of shifting in his bones. It was an achy, fiery sensation that reminded him of the sound of fingernails on chalkboard. It actually almost felt good. He hadn't shifted since the day he had married Claudia. In fact, for seven years he had stoically endured a horrendous case of PDS, pre-dragon syndrome. He didn't need to glance down to see scales forming under his skin, and his tailbones elongating.

Miss Lovingood clearly wasn't going to hang around to see the rest. Moments later, Earl found himself tripping over his tangled pants in an effort to keep up with her as she raced out the front door. Luckily, it was full dark outside with only a waxing moon to provide any sort of illumination. No one would see them.

The fresh air caused an abrupt halt to his transformation. The fire in his belly calmed and the itch of the scales retreated as they dissolved back under his skin's epidermis. He almost cried out in frustration. He had waited so long for a shift.

If she would only stop that infernal screaming. Miss Lovingood's lungs were only surpassed by her wheels, er, legs. Earl could barely keep up with her as they raced down Main Street, past the town tavern. Suddenly, the last door of the low-slung Motel 13 opened wide, nearly knocking Earl off his feet. Out walked Claudia, with a sphinx-like cool expression on her face, spritzing Chanel No. 718 all over herself.

"Earl, what are you doing here?" Claudia asked.

Out of breath, Earl said not a word, instead he peeked into the motel room. There seemed to be some sort of half man, half primate curled up in a fetal position and passed out cold on one of the beds.

"I could ask you the same question, darling. But—" he raked a hand through his hair "to be honest, if I don't stop that screaming scientist right now, this town might just become prime fodder for a host of National Enquirer reporters. Come on, we'll talk later."

Not for the first time, Earl blessed his wife's cool head and long slim legs as she surged past him, high heels be damned, up the steep road out of town. About half a mile up, the asphalt turned to gravel and another half mile later, the road skidded into dirt. When he spied a trail of broken branches, he veered into the underbrush toward Corkscrew Falls. Fifteen minutes later, Earl's sides heaving, he dragged himself up beside his wife. He knew he should have been doing more cardio instead of just pumping weights.

"Where'd she go?" He leaned over in an effort to regain his breath.

Claudia panted and pointed to the entrance of a cave. Eerily familiar snuffling and heel pounding noises came from within.

"Mom?" he shouted.

Eyebrows raised in question, Claudia swung around to face him. "Huh? Your mother's in there?"

He quickly recanted. "I don't know what I'm saying, darling. Look, we've got to get that woman out of there. I have a bad feeling about this. Isn't this the place Janice told all of us to steer clear of?"

"What were you doing with that woman anyway?

"What were you doing in that motel room?"

"Don't change the subject," Claudia said.

"Look, sweetheart, I'm big enough to forgive you if you'll do the same. You know I love you and no other."

Claudia looked at him as if she was trying to read his mind. "Alright—" she pushed her hair over one ear and licked her lips, a movement that always drove him crazy with desire "—but only if you promise that you'll keep your mother out of our lives forever."

"Forever is a long time, darling. How about if I promise to keep her out of our affairs until the next millennium?"

"Deal." Claudia stuck out her left pinky and he grabbed it with his own. Pulsating warmth spread through his loins and he felt himself harden again. He put his other hand on himself and was relieved to feel a large familiar shape under his chinos this time. Thank God.

A bloodcurdling scream rent the night air and the unmistakable sound of teeth gnawing bone followed. Scientists, it seemed, were crunchy. The slight smell of mustard and ketchup wafted through the air. And if he wasn't mistaken, there was a hint of A1 too.

He grabbed his wife's other hand and pulled her into a fast retreat toward town. "It's too bad she wasn't the fainting type," he said, sadly.

"Well, someone's going to have to concoct a forgetful potion or spell for the other two scientists otherwise we really will learn firsthand about the Enquirer's stellar reporting skills," she said a few moments later. That's what Earl loved about his wife, ever practical.

"Poor woman. She came for dinner and I was telling her all about the history of our little town. But, I was wondering how I was going to explain the part about our ancestors' mystical leanings and the reason they settled here. She wouldn't have understood the extraordinary primal urges they—and we—have to mate. And the fact that it takes one mystical being and one ordinary human to produce something memorable. A living and breathing…child."

"Oh, Earl." Claudia hurled herself into his arms. "Do you think we'll ever have one of our own?"

"Of course we will, darling. It's only a matter of time—" he kissed her and held her tight "—and effort."

"And the right potion," Claudia added, sensuality dripping from her.

"Well, practice makes perfect," Earl growled and felt his eyes glow. Practice makes perfect, indeed, he thought as he leaned in to kiss the one witch who made his blood boil.

"I've always favored making love to you in the wild. Nothing like the hint of a dangerous, man-eating creature nearby to heighten the mood," Claudia whispered into his ear.

"My thoughts exactly, darling."

The Loch's Stressed Dragon's Half-Sister

By

Elizabeth Holcombe

In which Earl Choo spends solitary moments Googling himself and in the process goes to the post office and finds help for his sexual problem.

Earl Choo had spent most of his free time, when he wasn't cooking the books, Googling himself. When Claudia was out with that group of cackling, conjuring, moonlight-obsessed friends of hers he had no choice but to find ways to amuse himself after Conan was over and the infomercials took over the airwaves. But, alas, Googling himself soon grew boring too.

Oh, he could stroll to the lake and have a one-sided chat with that spoiled brat Wyvern about his overbearing mother and her displeasure about his marrying Claudia. Wyvern didn't even pretend to be listening to him anymore. Earl caught the beast more than once picking its teeth with a yellowed talon while staring disinterestedly up at the pointy fir tree tops. So the lake for out for a while until Wyvern stopped being so self-absorbed. Earl was the one with the real problems.

Then one particularly morose night, while Googling, he discovered Ebay. Never one to shy away from an pursuit that could mildly boost his ego, something he rarely got at home lately, he switched from Googling and Ebayed himself. He was there too! Someone named "Ticklemypie73" was selling "The Earl of Wymouth's

Haunted Choo Dog Tung Dynasty Brooch". So the two words "Earl" and "Choo" were in an Ebay listing. Interesting.

The brooch was an ugly piece, but the bidding was at an astronomical three thousand and fifty-eight dollars.

Earl wasn't completely clueless about life outside of Brokenoggin'. Mortals loved anything that they felt would connect them to the spiritual world. He searched on Ebay such words as haunted, charmed, bewitched, cursed, among others and found a large amount of crap for auction with huge bids. What fools those mortals be! And how rich he could be! Maybe Claudia would appreciate him having financial means if he could have the "means" in bed she so desired and he so wanted to give her.

Brokenoggin had far more than its fair share of haunted, charmed, cursed, and bewitched crap. Yet, he had to be responsible. Nothing that was still haunted, charmed, cursed, or bewitched could leave the town. But stuff that was once involved within the tangents of the metaphysical would be safe and would sell faster than Godiva's delicious sugar maple nipple tips!

Such was it that when no one was looking, Earl Choo respected citizen and mild of manner, silently gathered the detritus of Brokenoggin and secretly put them up for auction on Ebay.

In seven days after the auctions ended, the money rolled in and causing Earl to scratch the bushy dark curls on his head and face another dilemma: mailing the items. He had never been to the Brokenoggin post office since the new postmistress arrived some weeks ago causing quite a stir among some of the more randy gents in town. Joe the veterinarian, the only person Earl would ever trust to harness the Wyvern, looked positively smitten every time he strolled toward the post office, a box under his arm. He never failed to notice Joe practically floating back down Main Street after leaving the post office.

Earl had to go there. His desk was covered with boxes that had to be mailed. Monies had been paid to him. People expected to get their haunted crap. He had to go. He had to be indifferent. Should the new postmistress live up to the bawdy talk by Joe and the other townsmen, Earl had to keep from turning the post office and a five block radius into ashes.

What a dilemma!

Early the next morning, after Claudia has given him a dry kiss good-bye and another of those looks that told him she was not happy with his performance in the sack last night, Earl made his way to the post office. He almost literally ran into Joe who stormed out of the small box of a building.

"She's damn Viagra, I tell ya!" Joe shouted into Earl's face.

Blinking at the wave of steak and onion breath that shunted out of the veterinarian's mouth, Earl asked, "Who?"

Joe hooked a thumb in the direction of the post office. "In there." He regarded the boxes Earl held with a death grip in his arms. Wife been shopping again?"

"Huh?" Earl glanced at the boxes emblazoned with QVC. He had recycled them from the trash. "Yes. Claudia has a thing for cubic zirconias." An obsession actually. She and her coven thought the human-made diamond must have some charm powers given the fact that QVC sold enough to fill an abyss. Half of those orders, Earl figured, had to be delivered to Brokenoggin's 45666 zip code. He knew the charms those faux diamonds possessed. They lured money out of women's purses.

"Well, at least you're married," Joe said looking woefully across the street at the Wicked Pea Diner. "You'll have no troubles at all." He nodded at the diner, with it's seizure-inducing flickering neon "open" sign. "I need steak..."

Joe thrust his hands into his pants pockets and walked across the street barely avoiding the dozens of marble-sized droppings left by the Chihuahua herd on a pre-dawn run.

The vet had no idea the troubles Earl had. Wyvern certainly did, but Wyvern was too involved with himself to care lately. The spoiled dragon was too concerned with when that naked vampire and the undead's woman, Janice, who had recently invaded his lakeside lair. Earl made a mental note to ask Joe about a big cage for that dragon the next time the vet awoke from his steak and onions-induced coma at the Wicked Pea.

Earl drew in a deep breath and clutched his boxes tighter. He used his finger tips to grab the brass handle of the post office's glass door.

Inside a fluorescent bar light sizzled overhead giving a sickly institutional glow to the small space bisected with a pock-marked wooden counter. Worn mangy velvet ropes hooked to dull brass stanchions made up a U-shaped path to the counter. Stupidly Earl complied with the rat maze even though he was the only person there. As he obeyed the velvet ropes he glanced down at the boxes, taking in great sniffs of air's pungent scent of old paper, glue, and sauerkraut. Sauerkraut?

"May I help you?" The raspy female voice bid him to look up from his parcels.

Oh no. Joe was right. Viagra for the eyes.

Heat began to rise up from his toes. It always began with his toes. Earl squeezed his eyes shut and tried to think of his mother, Mia, and overbearing perfectionist who could zap any sensual thoughts from his mind by a simple conjuring of her image. He had thought of his mother every time Claudia rolled over on top of him and began her seduction. He loved his wife. He didn't want to burn her up, literally. So he had to think of Mother.

"May I help you?"

Earl slowly opened his eyes. She was a sexual goddess. If he didn't control himself and soon, he would turn the entire town and surrounding forest to cinders.

Mother. Mother. Nagging. Hateful. Mother... There. OK. The heat in his toes that had crept to his knees dissipated. If it had made it up between his legs, his male torch would be ignited and all would be lost.

"Yes," he said stiffly placing the packages on the pock-marked counter. "I'd like to mail these."

Goddess stared at him with glassy, mesmerizing emerald eyes. Her mane of auburn and blonde-streaked hair glistened even in the sparse fluorescent light. One thick lock tippled an arched brow over those gem eyes drawing him in. The heat grew again. She would surely perish if he didn't stop looking at her. She had to be human, she was a civil servant, and like his witch wife, she wouldn't survive his sexual inferno.

Goddess broke her stare and looked indifferently at the trio of boxes.

"Anything liquid, perishable, or potentially hazardous?" she asked.

Liquid? One box held a lawn gnome that had been pissed on by a werewolf. The werewolf whiz had dried. Not liquid.

Perishable? Another box held a dozen of Godiva's maple sugar nipples guaranteed to grow hair-down-there if bushiness was desired. The candy was a favorite among fairies who were generally hairless and not happy to have their privates chilled in the Michigan winter. Earl had pocketed these before Godiva had a chance to place a spell on them. Safe for humans and not really perishable.

Potentially hazardous? The last box contained a white birch root flattened when the Wyvern farted on it. The "dragon" root could be hazardous. The wood still contained the beast's stench. It had sold for quite a lot to a woman in Northern California who dealt in rare herbs. Potentially hazardous? Earl had to ponder that one.

"Mr. Choo, do you wish to mail these packages or not?"

"I do, but the question perplexes me."

"Do these packages contain anything liquid?"

"No." Her eyes looked like they had an inner fire. He felt warmth in his toes again.

"Perishable?"

"No." Now his knees were very warm.

"Potentially hazardous."

The heat snaked up his thighs toward his growing torch.

"Potentially hazardous?" Her eyes flashed.

"YES!" Earl shouted. And he didn't mean anything in the boxes. He scooped up the packages and wrenched around. One of the boxes, the one with the white birch root, shot out from his arms and thudded to the floor.

Earl dropped to his knees and scrambled across the cracked grey linoleum floor.

The strong sent of sauerkraut and sudden eclipsing of the fluorescent light caused Earl to quickly realize that he was not the only one on the public side of the counter.

A puffy pink hand reached down and snatched the package up from the floor. Earl looked up from his prone position at the Goddess, her emerald eyes flashing seductively at him. Her lips painted in pearly bright pink lipstick widened into a lovely smile that made Earl's torch twitch. He quickly looked away willing his torch to twitch no more.

"Please rise, Mr. Choo." Her voice was as seductive as it was commanding.

Earl, clutching his other two packages, did as the beauty bade him. Once to his feet he kept his gaze to the floor.

"You cannot harm me, Mr. Choo," Goddess said. "Please look at me. I don't bite...hard."

Earl belted out a quick laugh that sounded more like the squawk of a demented crow. He looked up at Goddess.

"Look at me, Mr. Choo," she said huskily. "All over."

Earl began with her eyes, quickly sliding his gaze to her pink lips, down her neck and down to her cotton postal uniform of pale blue with darker blue pinstripes with a red, white, and blue patch of an eagle's head. The buttons of the blouse strained to their limits tenaciously holding back more than generous breasts from bursting forth sending the eagle soaring from its fleshy outcropping. Earl was a breast man and the goddess had given him an eyeful and second helpings to boot with the civil servant before him. Yet, as he dragged his gaze away from her *mammaries stupendi*, he quickly learned why Joe had recently admitted to be a "booty man". Goddess had booty, hips and booty!

He should be a bonfire now. Earl never thought with exclamation about a woman. Suppressing such thoughts kept the fire doused, but the pilot light always burned.

"That's right, Mr. Choo, nothing but you at present is on fire."

"I am not aflame," he said.

"Not on the outside, but your pants are telling me a different story."

Earl looked down at the front of his Dockers. The torch was at twelve o'clock, and he was cool.

"H-how?" he asked. And more importantly, "Who are you?"

"Potentially hazardous," she replied, or at least that's what Earl though she said.

"I beg your pardon?"

"Portentia Harmonious."

"So you're not a postal worker?"

"When I need to be."

The buzz of the fluorescent lights was the only sound in the silence that followed.

Earl still held his packages. Being a practical man and not one to steal the parties who were expecting his wares, he asked, "So, there's no one here to help me mail my packages?"

Portentia sighed and rolled her eyes. "Those buyers are not human. They are protecting the stupid mortals. Your Ebay seller id red-flagged you Mr. Choo."

"BrokenogginPyro?"

"Duh...Yes. You should know better than to foist your town's unique trinkets on mortals salivating for proof that folk like us exist. A man with your particular attributes shouldn't spend time Googling himself."

"That is none of your concern."

"I offer you a solution for your problems satisfying Claudia in the bedroom."

"That certainly is none of your concern."

"It is all of our concern when you nearly unleash mayhem on mortals, Mr. Choo. Come, we're going on a picnic."

"It's morning," he protested. Then curiosity gripped him. "Where?"

"You know the place. I'll drive."

They stepped out of the post office just as Joe exited the Wicked Pea.

The vet's mouth dropped open. Earl offered him a shrug as Portentia escorted him to her massive black Cadillac SUV.

***

Earl looked through the windshield at the police cruiser parked beside the entrance sign to Brokenoggin Falls National Forest.

"Janice is here...somewhere," Earl said jumping down from Portentia's SUV.

"I'd like a bright shiny light on top of my SUV like that," she said.

"You want to go into law enforcement now?" Earl imagined Portentia pinning down a suspect with those breasts and handcuffing him until he was helpless—

"It would be an appropriate diversion for me," she said hefting a wicker picnic basket from the back seat of her vehicle. "You were thinking it."

Earl held up his hands. "OK, look, Miss Harmonious, I need to know right now what you're and why you are here."

"Bluntly put, Mr. Choo, I'm your sex therapist."

"I didn't call for any sex therapist," he protested taking the basket from her hand. He was still a gentleman after all. "You're wasting your time."

"You are a very silly man. Come along."

Portentia hooked a finger in the direction of a narrow path barely distinguishable from the plain path that led to the dilapidated picnic shelter just a smidgen of a mile from the parking area.

"Don't you want to take that path?" he asked.

"You want me to, but that's not the path you often take, Mr. Choo."

How the hell did she know that?

Portentia walked ahead of him, her booty giving him a show. He was helpless to do anything but follow why carrying that ridiculous picnic basket.

Portentia was leading him to that place beside the lake where the Wyvern dwelled. This was dangerous. He had never brought anyone with him when he visited Wyvern.

"Don't look so nervous," Portentia said. "This is for your own good."

"Who sent you?" he demanded, voice beginning to get shrill. "Was it Claudia?"

"No." Portentia continued walking toward a rocky outcropping bordering the northern edge of the lake.

"Godiva?"

"No."

Rather than recite the entire population of Brokenoggin', Earl said, "Tell me or I'll stop right here."

"We've arrived." Portentia paused at one particular large and mossy rock. She turned and faced Earl with those shining emerald eyes. "Look into my eyes," she ordered. "What do you see?"

Mesmerized, Earl stared into Portentia's wide orbs. She was doing something, but he couldn't look away to see what. She had sucked him into some sparkly emerald field. The feeling overtaking him was warming but not in a potentially volcanic way where he could lay waste to the entire forest like Mount St. Helens. That was comforting in itself. Then he felt a cooling sensation, both refreshing and...pungent.

She blinked.

Earl snapped out of Portentia's personal Emerald City.

He was naked, in full erection, and smeared with sauerkraut.

She was naked too and also smeared with sauerkraut.

"I know what you're thinking," she said placing both hands on his shoulders.

She couldn't possibly.

"You're thinking that whipped cream is more traditional. It is for humans, but not for us. It's a precaution against any mishaps."

"Mishaps?" Earl asked. "What exactly is about to occur?"

"This." Portentia took a very firm hold of his torch. She began stroking him with the sauerkraut lubricant. Warmth did not grow, it surged up from his toes, to his knees, along his thighs and to his torch which Portentia possessed.

"Stop," he gasped. "F-fire."

"It's doused, my darling," she whispered into his ear.

"Doused...how?"

Portentia sheathed herself over him while they stood on

the lake's edge. The carpet of pine needles provided good traction to this dance with Portentia leading. She lifted her legs and wrapped them around his waist. He held her which was no easy task. She was of Rubenesque proportions.

"Doused," she whispered.

"Doused?"

Then the aroma struck his nostrils with a stench like no other. The sauerkraut was cooking on his body. Steam rose from his arms wrapped around his sex therapist. The sauerkraut bubbled and simmered on his flesh.

"Now you see that you can love your wife," Portentia said. "It just requires a little creativity and conductant for you. It douses your external fire."

Then his therapist wriggled from his hold and his torch.

"B-but I'm not finished," he said.

"Save yourself for Claudia," she said.

"She despises sauerkraut."

"Well, you might try relish or chunky diced tomatoes, but sauerkraut works best."

Portentia stepped away from him and gathered her postal uniform and the biggest pair of panties he had ever seen, her booty sling.

"I have to go now," she said placing her bundle of clothes under her arm.

"Go?" he asked. Where were his clothes? "I need a ride back to town."

"Can't help you," she said. "I've got to go. I promised my brother I'd pay him a call after I helped you with your particular problem."

"Brother?"

"Half-brother actually. He says you're a bit of a bother, always talking about your own problems and never listening to his."

"Half-brother? Who?" And where in the hell were his clothes?

"And if I hear that you and that veterinarian, Joe, are even thinking of getting a cage, I'll be back and castrate the two of you myself."

Portentia stepped into the lake. While holding her clothes, she dove head first into the dark water.

Earl stood naked covered in congealed sauerkraut in stunned silence waiting for Portentia to surface. She didn't.

"Half-brother?" he asked himself.

Just as light dawned in his muddled mind that the Wyvern and Portentia were somehow related, a harsh female voice assaulted his reverie.

"Hands up and turn around."

Earl did as Janice ordered.

"Earl Choo?" she asked. "What in the Sam hell are you doing?"

He could ask her the same question. Her hair was rumpled, her police uniform was stained here and there with mud, and her lips were swollen and very pink as if she had been the main contender in a kissing contest. But he was the one who was naked and decorated in sauerkraut, and she was the one with the badge and the gun...and a ride back to town, so he kept his questions to himself.

"It's been a very full morning," he said.

Janice puffed a stray lock of hair away from her right eye. "Tell me about it. Need a ride?"

"Yes, please."

"Clothes?"

"I have no idea."

Janice peeled off her jacket and offered it to him. Earl tied it around his waist with the sleeves. "Thanks."

He walked beside her down the narrow path.

"May we make a stop at the market before you take me home?" he asked. "I need to purchase some sauerkraut."

Janice just shook her head. "Brokenoggin."

"Well, just home then." Earl tied the sleeves tighter

around his waist and didn't look back when he heard lapping water. Or was that laughing water?

Brokenoggin. Just a normal day.

***

"I have a craving for knockwurst," Claudia said later that night.

Earl lay back on the bed. "And mustard," he said.

"I've never been this hungry after making love to you," she said breathlessly. "Or this satisfied. Thank you, oh...thank you, my kinky man. Have you been doing some sort of internet research? Whipped cream is so conventional. I can't imagine you thinking of sauerkraut on your own."

"So you like it," Earl asked.

"Every luscious bit." Claudia kissed him.

Earl closed his eyes. He would take tomorrow morning off and pay Wyvern a visit. No whining. No woeful dirges about his overbearing mother. Just thanks. Thank you very much.

"Thank you. Thank you very much," Earl said.

"Ooh, do your Elvis voice again," Claudia purred. "You sexy thang."

Gladly. Earl grinned. The night was still quite young.

***

Early the next morning, Emma Mincemeat banged on the post office door.

"It's eight-thirty!" she shouted into the glass. "You're supposed to be open!"

Joe walked past her. "A new postmistress is due in," he said.

"A new one? We just got a new person running the post office a few days ago."

"She's gone," Joe said sullenly.

"Oh, that's just fine!" Emma shouted at him. "I need a money order for QVC!"

"You sound more stressed than usual, Emma," Joe

observed.

"Well, you'd be too if you had twelve kids, Joe."

"I'd kill myself."   He stopped and reconsidered his words. "Sorry. They're good kids."

"Most of them," she said while staring into the post office. "Some of them are telling me they're seeing things. Gotta get them to the doctor, check their eyes."

"What sort of things?"

Emma snorted in frustration and turned to look Joe in the eyes. "Dead people."

Coming in October 2006

Bewitched, Bothered &
Be Vampyred
(Season 2)
Fangs for the Memories

To benefit breast cancer research

With your favorite authors from Season 1 and a host of
new best selling authors, too!

Triskelion Publishing
www.triskelionpublishing.com

All about women, all about extraordinary.

Don't miss

Hex & the Single (Weird) Were-Monster
(or How Janice Got That Way)

By
Terese Ramin

The novella prequel to **Bewitched, Bothered &
BeVampyred** that introduces Janice Thinksalot and the
true historical background of Brokenoggin Falls.
Included in the **SEX ON THE BEACH** anthology.

**On sale now at
<u>www.triskelionpublishing.com</u>**

And watch for

By
**MaryJanice Davidson
Susan Grant
Gena Showalter
PC Cast**

An anthology of novellas expanded from their episodes in
Bewitched, Bothered & BeVampyred season 1.

Coming from Berkley, Summer 2006